Acclaim for *In*

"*In The Name Of Help* is one of the most important stories of our time. It could have happened to anyone."

—*Barbara Ayash, International Woman of the Year, International Freedom Medal Winner*

"*In The Name Of Help* portrays the horrors that we face when our emotional moorings drift loose and the consequences that arise from our misplaced faith in 'professionals' who could very well be suffering from a greater spiritual sickness than we are. It is also a tale of genuine love and the redeeming value of loyalty and true friendship."

—*Matthew J. Pallamary, Author of Land Without Evil, San Diego, California*

"[This] book has touched me in ways I never dreamed possible. There are workable, drugless, abuse free, legal alternatives for people in need. Psychiatry is not part of the cure, it is the problem. Thanks Diane."

—*Sheldon Bauer, Clearwater, Florida*

"Diane Klein's novel *In The Name Of Help*, dramatically illustrates that psychiatry and psychology are too important to be left in the hands of professionals."

—*Gerald Angelo Cirrincione, Host of the radio program TOWARD 3000, San Diego, California*

"In the tradition of the novels of Charles Dickens, Harriet Beecher Stowe, Charlotte Bronte and many others, Diane Klein's novel depicts a social condition that must be changed, and must be made clear to a much larger number of people in order to bring about a demand for change."

—*Karin Koski, Portland, Oregon*

"Klein details with well-researched authenticity how profit and political gain motives, force Cathryn to remain for many years drugged and incarcerated in psychiatric institutions, the kind of horror Kate Millett described in her much earlier book, *The Loony-Bin Trip.*

"Fortunately for the Cathryn of this novel, she has friends who use the law and their own considerable wits and courage to finally secure a release for Cathryn from this terrifying life of bondage and suppression …." —*Douglas Eby, Beverly Hills, California*

"This first novel by Ms. Klein is more than an interesting story. It is a chockful-of-truth wake-up call for all of us for whom it is not yet too late." —*Bill Anthony, Los Angeles.*

"A wake-up call to a 'Free Country'. If you think you live in a free country where you are free to do as you please as long as you hurt no one, read this book! Diane Klein does a superb job of demonstrating psychiatry's role in the prostitution of our justice system. By the end of the book, you can be sure that there is hope, there is help and *you* can do something about it." —*Gary Baren*

"*Don't* read this novel if you are easily scared. Because by the time you've finished it, you will know that someone *could* be about to knock on your door, to haul you away to a shortened life of misery and horror in the name of help." —*Rich Byrd, Clearwater, FL*

In the Name of Help

In the Name of Help

a novel exposing psychiatric abuse

by

Diane Klein

Laguna Coast Books
Laguna Hills, California

Cover and book design by Pete Masterson
Aeonix Publishing Group, www.aeonix.com

Grateful acknowledgement is made to the L. Ron Hubbard Library for permission to reproduce a selection from the copyrighted works of L. Ron Hubbard.

Publisher's Cataloging-in-Publication
(Provided by Quality Books, Inc.)

Klein, Diane, 1943-
    In the name of help : a novel exposing
psychiatric abuse / by Diane Klein.
        p. cm.
        LCCN: 00-100722
        ISBN: 0-9678552-0-9

        1. Abused wives--Illinois--Chicago--Fiction.
    2. Psychiatrists--Malpractice--Fiction.
    3. Mentally ill--Abuse of--Fiction.   4. Chicago
    (Ill.)-Fiction.   I. Tktle.

    PS3561.L3442516 2000   813'.6
                    QBI00-231

00   01   02   10   9   8   7   6   5   4   3   2   1

Published by Laguna Coast Books
Post Office Box 2086, Laguna Hills, California 92654-2086
877-717-BOOK (2665)   www. lagunacoast.com

Author Photograph © 2000 by Tony Franza

Printed in the United States of America

My gratitude and love —

To RON for helping me to become myself.

To Paul, Michelle and Kristy, my extraordinary son and daughters who have always loved me unconditionally and who have never lost their faith in me through the most trying times.

To each of my true friends who were sincerely supportive and encouraging throughout a venture that, to me, was an aspiration of astronomical proportions.

And finally to my David, for giving my heartfelt project a chance to live the way I intended it to from the very beginning.

Without real help from these people, the dream would never have become a reality.

Author's Note

I S IT POSSIBLE THAT A STRANGER could step into another person's life and take it over completely? Could a stranger gain the legal right to dictate where another person will live and what medical treatment he will be given? Could they then cause that person to be lost for years, or even a lifetime, in an abyss of mental hospitals and board and care facilities?

Could this really happen in spite of the fact that the person continuously states, even to the judge himself, that he does not want this stranger to make decisions for him? Could this stranger still be given the legal authority to decide where the person is housed, when he is sedated, and if he is to be institutionalized?

Could a judge allow these actions without ever asking for all the facts? Could such disingenuous and destructive practices actually happen and be implemented all in the name of help? And, could this happen to someone you know and love?

Fiction, you say? Drama? Not possible. In a civilized society this could never happen.

Look again.

Only by confronting something as it actually is, can we learn how to take responsibility and then become able to do something about it.

DK

help - **1.** to make things easier or better for (a person); aid assist; specifically, a) to give (one in need or trouble) something necessary, as relief, succor, money, etc...; b) to do part of the work of; ease or share the labor of...; c) to aid in getting (up, down, in, etc. or to, into, out of, etc.)... **2.** to make it easier for (something) to exist, happen, develop, improve, etc.; specifically, a) to make more effective, larger, more intense, etc.; aid the growth of; promote; b) to cause improvement in; remedy; alleviate; relieve...

betrayal - **1.** a) the act of helping the enemy of (one's country, cause, etc.); being a traitor to; b) the act of delivering or exposing to an enemy traitorously **2.** the act of breaking faith with; failing to meet the hopes of **3.** act of leading astray; deceiving; specifically, seducing and then deserting **4.** revealing unknowingly or against one's wishes...

Webster's New World Dictionary
Third College Edition

S ome people cannot help. They can only injure and destroy. And if in the name of help they only injure and destroy, then know them carefully, for they are criminals.

—*L. Ron Hubbard*

Prologue

Evanston, Illinois, early 1970s...

THE THREE OF THEM SAT CLOSE to the sturdy old brick building around a white metal table, sipping coffee from mugs and bursting into loud, heartfelt laughter from time to time. They were only a few blocks from the beautiful, sprawling campus of Northwestern University at their favorite meeting place. It was an old, long-time established coffee house on the main street of Evanston, Illinois, just north of Chicago.

The sun shone brilliantly, casting deep shadows below the swaying trees, while a pleasant breeze drifted off of Lake Michigan and rustled through the leaves of the branches over their heads. The lucent sky, an intense, bright blue, was dotted with chunky puffs of white, billowing clouds. It was one of those splendid and rare days that the Chicago area boasts of in early summer, just before the inevitable blazing heat and humidity begin. And, it was just after seemingly endless months of bone-chilling winter temperatures and raw, wicked winds tearing furiously off of the twenty-two thousand, four hundred square miles of the huge lake that is the city's entire eastern border.

This particular afternoon, birds sang in the outstretched branches of the old elm trees over their heads, multitudes of budding new leaves sprang forth along the already full limbs, patches of deep emerald green grass glistened between the curb and the sidewalk, and the traffic moved lazily along the streets of the little college town.

Diane Klein

Linda Dawson, almost eighteen, was the typical Northwestern coed, a paradigm, the classic coed, if there were such a thing. She had shiny, straight, honey-blond hair, neatly cut to just above her shoulders, dark, liquid brown eyes, a small, straight nose, full soft sensuous lips, and a remarkably bright, warm smile. Linda could have easily posed for college promotional literature standing comfortably in front of the imposing stonework of Alice Barrington Hall, smiling broadly, eyes sparkling, textbooks in hand, bidding welcome to prospective undergraduates, and inviting them to join her at the beautiful, highly respected, affluent and rather Waspish campus community that was Northwestern University in the early seventies.

She was wearing a pale yellow T-shirt, white shorts and tennis shoes. Her complexion, smooth with an olive cast, was unusual for a blond, and, now, in the very beginning of summer, her arms and legs were already very tan. She was sitting next to her cousin, Cathryn Silberg, a strikingly beautiful young woman with coloring that contrasted sharply with Linda's. Cathryn's hair was a dark, shiny, chestnut color, her skin was very fair and her eyes were deep violet with grayish specks.

Linda's attention was focused wholly on the good looking young man across the table, who at the moment was enthusiastically entertaining them. Completely absorbed, Linda listened intently to the story that he was telling. Her deep brown eyes were involuntarily riveted on Nick Martin's face, while the rest of the scene around her tended to flutter away as he spoke. She was distracted from his face, his eyes, his mouth, only by his gesturing hands, as he told his story, embellishing the original incident, and thoroughly enjoying the attention from both Linda and Cathryn. After a few minutes, they all burst out in uncontrollable laughter, so hard that tears came to their eyes. Nick's own dark green eyes were sparkling with mischievous delight at the effect he had on the two girls.

"You *are* crazy," Linda exclaimed, incredulous. "I can't believe you did that!" Nick was telling them how he had posed as a frantic but innocent law student two days ago, and how he had unmercifully charmed the young, attractive receptionist of an adversarial law firm during lunch time when everyone else was out of the office. He persuaded her to let him look at a document that technically he was not supposed to see, at least not until after he followed the accepted procedure of submitting formal requests and then responses to the responses that would come from those requests.

Nick looked at Cathryn for support, and with the most humble, hurt expression he could conjure up, replied, "Your cousin doesn't trust my words." He touched his right hand, fingers spread, palm to his heart. "I'm an attorney," he pleaded. "How can she even begin to disbelieve me?" Nick grinned. "Anyway, time was of the essence," and he laughed out loud, amused by his own intrepidity.

His obvious enjoyment of his antics caused Linda and Cathryn to roll their eyes heavenward and giggle out loud again. As they leaned towards each other now, their eyes moist with joy and wide with amazement, Nick smiled at them from across the table and crossed his arms over his chest, leaning back in the chair.

"You are such an incredible brat!" Cathryn declared, holding one hand on her abdomen and wiping the corners of her eyes with the back of her other hand.

Nick, still grinning, looked thoughtfully at the two cousins and then slowly shook his head with a half-hearted effort to sound very serious. "Must be the last of a dying breed. Both pretty, both virgins; not too many left on our college campuses these days," he teased in an affected intellectual tone.

"Shut up, Nick," Cathryn flung the words at him. "Just shut up!" Nick laughed again, threw his head back insouciantly, and leaned the chair precariously away from the table onto its back legs.

Linda dipped her chin down, unable to meet Nick's eyes with her own, color rising in her cheeks. No one else could make her feel so shy or so self-conscious. Not that both she and Cathryn hadn't gotten themselves heatedly tangled up with someone more than once, but they still clung to a fast fading, old-fashioned notion that they needed to wait until marriage for real honest-to-God sex.

As for Nicolas Alan Martin? He certainly wasn't a virgin. But Nick, in his own way was one of another apparently diminishing types. He happened to be a genuinely caring, good guy, with some values and ideals that seemed to be disintegrating rapidly in the radically changing society of the seventies. "I really believe in fidelity in a relationship," he had told them. "I believe in family and I feel a lot of respect and love for both my parents. I even believe that there's something more to personal worth than physical belongings," he smiled wryly.

Funny he hooked up with someone like Carrie, Cathryn thought.

"There's such a thing as personal integrity, treating people the way I want to be treated," he continued. No, Nick was definitely not the average, beer drinking, carousing, college jock. He stood out, a little different, almost always smiling, sincere, and extraordinarily full of life and good humor.

Nick leaned even further away from the table. He was handsome in a rugged way, with features that contributed to a sensuous mien that easily attracted women. "He really listens to you when you're saying something," Cathryn had once told Linda, trying to explain what she found wonderful in her friend. *And,* Linda thought, *his deep green eyes crinkle when he laughs, he has a strong chin with the slightest cleft, a nose that's not too small, not too big, and a very soft mouth.*

When he was serious about something, there was a fierce intensity about him, but at the same time, warmth and a gentleness. When he spoke enthusiastically, gesturing with both hands, his dark brown hair fell forward onto his forehead, and he would shake his head back or distractedly push it out of his way with an firm hand.

Nick Martin is the kind of man women say is hard to find, Linda thought.

౩

He and Cathryn and Linda would never have fit into the sought after Greek fraternity-sorority cliques on campus. They never felt comfortable with that lifestyle. They formed a separate little group, and, within it, they developed a close and caring feeling for one another. Nick and Linda were both at Northwestern on scholarships. They lived at home and this tended to set them apart from the majority of the more affluent undergraduates.

Cathryn, though financially able to live on campus, never felt as if she belonged there. Cathryn never really felt as if she belonged anywhere. She had her secrets; undisclosed uncertainties and insecurities. Living closely with a group of giggling, social young women, would never work for her. But with her two friends she found some sense of belonging and acceptance that gave her a strength and comfort that she didn't find anywhere else.

Over two years, they fell into a routine of meeting and sounding each other out whenever there was an important decision to be made. They discussed their romances, careers, troubles and dreams with one another. In fact, Nick, Cathryn and Linda shared nearly all of their most intimate feelings in their casual meetings. Nearly all, that is.

But now each of them was on the brink of significant changes, more portentous than they realized.

⏳

Nick had just begun practicing law, and he was going to marry Carrie Lindsay Clark, another Northwestern student.

Cathryn had just received her Bachelor of Arts degree, majoring in English with a minor in French. "I'm not so sure how useful my choices are going to be," she joked.

Cathryn was planning to get married soon, too, to Edward William Kent. They planned to move across the country to the Napa Valley in northern California, where she was going to be a wife and school teacher, and try to fit in graduate school.

Linda was going to work in the editing department of Harcourt, Brace and Jovanovitch during the summer, and then she would start her third year at Northwestern in the fall. She would be, for the first time in a long while, without her two closest friends.

Linda's changes, though less significant than those facing

Cathryn and Nick, were causing her more trepidation, and she felt a tremulous nagging fear that she didn't really understand. She sat with them now, her thumbnail nervously tracing the lines in the textured table top, looking up first at her cousin's lovely profile and then over at Nick, whose smiling eyes had become serious and thoughtful. Linda's heart felt as if it were thumping too quickly, her cheeks were flushed and her stomach felt taut and uneasy. She pressed one arm against her abdomen.

The thought of day-to-day life without Nick and Cathryn close by made her uncomfortable. She wasn't involved in any relationships and she wasn't engaged or in love with anyone. No one except her friend across the table with his sparkling green eyes. And that couldn't possibly count.

کب

Just by sitting across from him, with his tall, athletic body, his dark green eyes, his warm smile, Linda could hardly think of anything else. His sense of adventure and his ideas made her adore him, it was as simple as that. In fact, it was joyful for Linda just to be near him.

She thought back to a Friday night last September when he had called and talked her and Cathryn into meeting him in the parking lot off of Sheridan Road near the University. It was late and all he would tell them was, "I have a great idea, sort of a picnic!" Linda was easier to persuade than her cousin.

"Are you crazy?" Cathryn demanded. "It's ten o'clock at night."

"Yes, undoubtedly I am crazy. Hurry, okay?" Nick answered.

It was almost eleven o'clock by the time Nick, secretive and grinning, ushered the two of them into his battered little Volkswagen. Carrie was at a country club dinner with her parents. That was not Nick's kind of evening if it could be avoided, and this time he had managed to beg off. Edward had called Cathryn just before dinner and told her that he needed to be at a business meeting, that he would talk to her tomorrow. Cathryn was disappointed and so she was grateful to get Nick's call, glad to be distracted for awhile.

Linda had been curled up in pajamas on the couch with a novel, successfully putting her homework off until Saturday morning when the phone rang. She was elated to hear Nick's voice. Happily she pulled on jeans and a sweatshirt, told her mother that she was going to meet Nick and Cathryn and hurried out of the house. Her mother called out after her, "Linda, not too long, it's already late."

"I won't be, Mom. Don't worry."

Lois stood at the front door shaking her head, a small smile on her lips. *Now what's Nick up to?* she wondered without too much concern. The girls would be okay if they were with Nick.

"Okay, what's going on?" Cathryn asked him, her violet eyes narrowing suspiciously, her head tilted a little to one side.

Nick grinned as he drove north on Sheridan Road with Linda in the front seat and Cathryn leaning towards them from the back seat. He was humming, pleased with his own idea, happy to have them both to share it with him.

"What are you up to this time?" Cathryn demanded again, determined to get some sort of an answer out of him.

"You'll see. You'll love this," was all Nick would tell her.

Linda giggled a little. Nick's enthusiasm and excitement flowed over her, captivating her with his mystery. Her face was radiant as she watched the curving road in front of them, loving the adventure, like a child eager for any happy surprise.

Anyway, she thought to herself, *nothing Nick comes up with can disappoint me.*

He took them along the beautiful, winding, tree-lined North Shore road, driving slowly until they reached the northeast part of the sleepy little town of Wilmette. Finally, they came to a long, narrow driveway that was bordered on both sides by huge, majestic pine trees. Nick turned the wheel and headed the little car up the drive. They couldn't see where the driveway led from the road, but Nick knew exactly where he was going. He was still humming and still grinning.

Although the early fall weather had gotten very cold several times with the temperature dipping down into the thirties as another harsh Chicago winter approached, this night was exquisite. It was a little chilly, but with a clean crispness to the air. Linda looked up at the tall pines. The leaves on the maple and elm trees along the main road were clearly visible in the bright starlight. In the past weeks, they had turned to breath-taking shades of gold, red, yellow, orange and bronze. The moon was full and bright, throwing beams of light that reflected off the splendid old trees and glistened in the drops of moisture that formed in the leaves from the cool, damp air.

Linda was quiet, mesmerized by row upon row of tall pine trees, when she suddenly looked out through the windshield and made a soft, little gasping sound.

"What?" Cathryn whispered, looking through the windshield in the same direction. Then she saw, too, and drew her breath in and held it for a moment. "Wow...." she breathed quietly.

Nick stopped the car. The quiet was sudden and peaceful. They rolled the windows down and sat very still for a moment, listening. There were new sounds of the wind rustling through the trees, and small, crunching noises from some tiny animal that scurried along the ground close by. In the distance, off to the north, someone was burning logs in a fireplace and the pungent smell of the blazing wood drifted to them on the breeze. Linda breathed deeply as she looked upward, her lips parted and her eyes wide.

Just in front of them, rising in majestic and elegant splendor toward the star-filled sky, stood the nine-sided Bahai Temple, the House of Worship, in magnificent whiteness against the dark sky, with each of its sides decorated spectacularly with symbolic designs that were clearly visible in the brilliant moonlight.

After a few silent minutes, Nick got out of the car, motioned to the girls to do the same and he went around and opened the hood. He took a small cooler out, set it on the ground, handed a blanket to Cathryn and some packages to Linda.

"Follow me, please, ladies," he said.

Linda and Cathryn giggled happily as they followed him up

the path, lifting their faces to the awesome sight in front of them. Nick glanced back, saw their expressions and smiled. When he found the spot he wanted, just past the thick expanse of pine trees in a clearing thirty yards or so in front of the magnificent structure, he took the blanket from Cathryn and spread the big, old worn fabric out next to the path leading up to the temple. He motioned to the girls to sit down. The grass and leaves beneath the blanket crunched under them.

Although they had grown up in Chicago, neither Cathryn nor Linda had ever seen the temple before that night. Nick began telling them a little about the background of the Bahai faith and they listened, fascinated, their faces serious and their lips parted a little as they looked beyond him at the beautiful building in the serene night.

"The religion teaches about the oneness of mankind, the harmony of science and religion, a world order that would assure peace, justice and international cooperation," he said, with awe and some sadness in his voice.

"It's too bad none of the religions of the world bring about the peace and harmony they advocate. They have good ideas, but no way of getting us there," Linda remarked.

"Yeah, I agree." Nick said. "I wonder what it would feel like to live in a world that isn't filled with insanity or disease or crime or war. And what exactly would it take to make that happen?"

Cathryn shook her head, frowning at them. "People are the way they are," she said. "Some of them are good and some of them are not so good. Some are purely rotten. No religion is going to change that. It's just the way it is."

Linda and Nick were startled by her cynicism. They glanced at her and then at one another.

She sounds more and more like Edward and less like herself, Linda thought.

Cathryn saw them exchange looks, saw their expressions but she just shrugged. She realized that that was something that Edward had said to her, but she didn't care.

Edward's the most perceptive and intelligent person I've ever known, she thought to herself.

But the beauty of the night and the enchantment cast by the temple, so splendid, bright white outlined against a midnight sky, won out. Nick and Linda were quiet. They passed over Cathryn's comment and when Nick spoke again it was about the indisputable magnificence of the structure architecturally, not spiritually.

༄

They had their picnic. Nick took some wine out of the cooler and they shared it, drinking from the bottle as he hadn't thought about glasses. There were Cokes which they never got around to drinking, a box of crackers, a small salami that Nick sliced for them with his little silver pocket knife, a hunk of cheddar cheese and a bag of cookies. They nibbled intermittently, gazing up at the building, and they discussed the meaning of life, the insanity of war, the struggles of mankind and the importance of friendship. After a little while, silly from the wine, they toasted one another and their futures.

Any feeling of uneasiness about what was to come was still only a tiny seed of disquietude that Linda could feel in her gut whenever they talked about the future, but she could not yet identify it.

The two girls pulled their heavy sweatshirts closely around their bodies and turned on their backs on the blanket. Linda, looking up at the stars, felt very tiny, a little overwhelmed, even frightened. Nick was lying on his back between the two girls and when he felt Linda shiver, he put his arms through theirs. She felt better then, somehow connected and less alone.

༄

Nick was fervently dedicated to learning the legal system. When he finished law school, ranking high in his class, he was pursued by a number of respected Chicago firms.

He finally accepted an offer with Smithson, Ellingsworth and Naples, a legal firm whose reputation was well known and unblemished. That was important to Nick as he entered a field that was beginning to draw quite a lot of criticism for its dwindling ethics, integrity and sense of responsibility.

The principal partners of Smithson were enthusiastic about Nick joining their organization. They were impressed with his academic accomplishments and his intensity, but they also found themselves attracted to his refreshing straightforwardness and his lack of pretentiousness.

Nick Martin has the makings of a brilliant young attorney with a bright and lucrative future as part of the firm, one told another, as they smiled and puffed on pipes after a lunch in their private dining room.

ॐ

It was a spectacular beginning of a promising career for the boy who had grown up in a small farming community near St. Catharines, not far from Toronto. He had come to the States with his parents, in the middle of high school, feeling more than a bit lost for a while. His father was desperate for opportunity south of the Canadian border, hoping to be able to better support his small family.

Nick had made some firm decisions as a Canadian living amongst Americans. He was determined to be successful in school and to make things go right in life. Having lived through the uncertainty and upheaval that his parents experienced when they lost their small property, Nick became determined to find a profession that would never allow for the fear he had seen in his father's eyes.

With exceptionally high SAT scores, he won a full scholarship to Northwestern, a prestigious university that his parents never could have afforded. While remaining dedicated to having as much fun as he could cram into a day, Nick managed to achieve the excellent grades he needed throughout his undergraduate studies. He had the advantage of being genuinely inquisitive, of really wanting to know, of enjoying the pleasure that comes from learning something that one can use and apply in one's life. When Nick began law school, he was driven by an intense desire to really understand the law. He wanted to know how mankind had developed its systems of codes and penalties. Nick sensed that they were supposed to promote a civilized and peaceful society which would flourish and prosper.

But he wondered, *Why does it seem as though society is going in the opposite direction?*

Nick believed that he would find the answers to his questions in the laws and the dramatic history of their development. When he passed the bar, he could have accepted positions with successful law firms across the country, but he chose to stay in the Midwest near his friends and family.

Nick's compelling good looks and warm personality attracted women from the time he was a young teenager, and his residual bit of a Canadian accent added to the interesting package that was Nicolas Martin.

Cathryn once told him bluntly, "Your only saving grace is that you aren't a jerk about girls falling all over you!" And Nick just grinned, with the tiniest, intriguing bit of embarrassed flush on his cheeks.

Nick was committed to his relationship with Carrie. They had been together for over two years and they planned to be married the following year. This pleased Carrie's parents, especially now that Nick was practicing law and earning an excellent income. These were vital considerations to Carrie and her North Shore parents.

꒰꒱

Carrie Lindsay Clark, a pretty girl with long, thick, blond hair and blue eyes, had drawers and closets filled with cashmere sweaters and matching skirts, and few ambitions other than to follow in her mother's footsteps.

"The things that are important, Carrie," her mother told her many times, "are correctly managing a beautiful home, doing charitable works well, and raising well-behaved children who will eventually go to Ivy League schools." It was understood that if they were boys, they would one day earn huge sums of money in businesses similar to those of their fathers. If they were girls, they would have terrific fashion sense, and if truly fortunate, they would attract special men like Nick and live happily ever after. Life was not at all a complicated affair to Carrie Lindsay Clark who had never lived one moment that was difficult, challenging or uninfluenced by great wealth.

ↄ

Now, the three friends were meeting once again. It was Nick who had left work early to meet with Cathryn and Linda for coffee this particular afternoon. It was ostensibly to catch up on news but it was really one last opportunity to grab some precious minutes together before Cathryn and Edward left town.

Linda looked at them now, her stomach tightening at the thought of the long distance calls and letters that would have to replace warm hugs and supportive communication. Simple caring gestures that were part of every one of her days.

Though no one put it into words, Nick sensed that the real reason they were together now was an anxious attempt to hang on to some of the innocence and joy of the lives they had been living as students.

Students, with very limited responsibilities, he thought, rubbing his brow. *They're supposed to be learning how to handle the circumstances of life and they'll never really learn how until they just have to do it. Sometimes I feel as if I'm looking at them — laughing, arguing, defending, performing for each other — all from a distance.*

Cathryn reached for her coffee cup and Nick reached across the small table and gently put his hand over her wrist. They looked at one another, but no one said anything for a long moment.

On this sunny and bright afternoon they were each feeling a vague uneasiness, some premonition about the future. It was a distant, unreal piece of time that loomed before them with so many possibilities, but also with uncertainties. It was intangible and vague in comparison to their structured, insulated and protected pasts.

Linda saw something serious in Nick's expression that was not there before. The time for them to begin to take responsibility for their own lives, to confront the *real* world, was getting closer.

Even now, sipping their coffee and joking as they usually did, there was a heavy overtone to their conversation. There were long silent pauses as they looked from one to the other, staring, trying to capture and hold the moments. They were hanging onto one another hard, one last time.

꒳

Cathryn sat back in her chair and looked from one to the other of her two friends.

Linda's like a younger sister and a best friend at the same time. And Nick's a rare man we both found we could trust with our lofty aspirations and dreams as well as our silliest problems. Nick's never judgmental or harsh and no one could be a better listener, Cathryn thought.

Linda's bright smile faded, but her attention was still focused across the table on Nick. She respected his relationship with Carrie completely, but no matter how hard she tried or how much she berated herself for her foolish feelings about him, she couldn't do anything about the quickening of her heartbeat or the flush in her cheeks whenever she was around him.

One day, she told herself, *I'll meet someone like him, my own Nick — only that someone will look at me the way I'm always trying not to look at Nick.*

Cathryn saw Linda's reactions to Nick, she knew Linda's feelings about him. They teased each other unmercifully, but both of the girls adored and respected Nick. From the beginning, Nick had treated Linda as if she were his little sister. He would do anything to help or protect either of them, but his affection was brotherly. Linda accepted this intellectually, but on some emotional, involuntary level, she remained infatuated, glowing in his presence, as she did with no one else.

꒳

The girls liked Carrie well enough, but away from Nick, to one another, they questioned the match of their personalities. Nick was usually vibrant and enthusiastic in his approach to every aspect of his life. But he always seemed to become somewhat subdued when he was with Carrie, who could best be depicted as merely content. Nick could raise the emotional tone level in a room just by stepping into it and smiling. Carrie was affable but complacent. Nick wholeheartedly believed that a person could change things and improve conditions; Carrie truly believed that everything was fine just as it was.

Ↄ

Now, Linda watched Nick and listened to his story-telling with gentle affection in her eyes, an uneasiness in her chest and a knot in her stomach. Her uncomplicated and secure world felt as if it were beginning to erupt volcanically, and she struggled to hide those feelings from both Cathryn and Nick.

Nick is one of the most special men I've ever met and Carrie is one of the luckiest women, she thought to herself with a small sigh.

Linda turned in the chair to look at her cousin. Cathryn turned towards her and her clear violet eyes met Linda's eyes for a moment and they both smiled.

Linda winced a little, thinking, *Cathryn understands me better than anyone else on earth. My God, what's going to happen now, without everyone I've been depending on?*

Cathryn watched the others, and she, too, was wondering about the directions that the three of them were about to follow.

Ↄ

She was going to marry Edward. She had made her decision about him and that was all there was to that. In a few weeks she would be Mrs. Edward Kent and they would move to Napa, California, not far from Edward's parents. Her eyes glowed with excitement at the prospect of living in the beautiful, rolling, vineyard country she had seen glorious pictures of, but then they began to cloud over with a quiet anxiousness as she considered leaving everyone and everything that was familiar to her. Edward, on the other hand, could not wait. He couldn't have been happier about what he called their *fresh start.* He was more than a little eager to have Cathryn to himself, entirely to himself.

The lukewarm, hesitant, questioning reaction of her family and friends to her decision to marry him had not been what Cathryn had hoped for. She stubbornly pushed aside what she believed to be their doubts and not her own.

I have none, she told herself more than once.

Edward clearly had her entranced, as he had since the first day she saw him.

          ↬

When Edward first saw Cathryn Margaret Silberg on the campus of Northwestern, the beautiful, young woman unexpectedly and abruptly grabbed his attention. He was immediately captivated, though no one would have been able to tell from his reactions. His expression remained impassive, his features immobile like chiseled stone.

Cathryn wore a soft powder blue cashmere sweater and a matching skirt that day. Her thick, shining, chestnut hair was pulled back away from her face into a low, wavy ponytail that accentuated her high cheekbones and lovely eyes. She looked as if she had just stepped off the cover of a fashion magazine. Even in an atmosphere where she was surrounded by dozens of fresh, young, pretty coeds, Cathryn's unusual, exotic beauty turned heads.

She was having lunch with some girlfriends between classes. Edward sat alone in a booth near the window in the little restaurant, sipping coffee from a mug, while his eyes discreetly took in everything about her as she talked and laughed with two other girls at the counter.

After a minute or two, Cathryn felt his eyes on her, and as she turned on the stool, she came face to face with a handsome man, but his expression was very cold. He didn't smile at all and she felt a chill along her arms, but at the same time, her cheeks grew warm and flushed. The man was smoking a pipe and he looked down as he tapped the ashes out in the ashtray alongside a handsome leather briefcase that lay on the table.

He looked up again and this time it was Cathryn who was staring. She smiled shyly, just a little, but the man continued gazing directly into her eyes. It was clear that whatever he was going to allow between the two of them just then, would be done without talking, without even a change of expression.

Cathryn, embarrassed, turned back towards her friends.

"Who is that?" Sandy whispered.

"I've never seen him before," Barbara, the other girl replied. "God, he's good-looking, but those serious dark eyes! He hasn't taken them off Cathryn for a second," she muttered, shielding her mouth and words with her hand.

"Do you know him, Cathryn?" Sandy whispered.

"I've never seen him or anyone like him before," murmured Cathryn, still feeling the chill over her arms and the heat in her cheeks. "Let's get out of here. I've got another class and a ton of reading to do tonight."

"Me, too," Sandy groaned, as they gathered their notebooks and briefcases together and walked towards the door.

჻

Edward sat there for a long time after they left. He watched through the window as Cathryn nervously rushed away with the other girls.

Now there's something worth looking at, he thought. *What a magnificent looking woman, like a young, unbroken thoroughbred,* he mused.

Normally Edward had little time for women. He found them too silly, too time-consuming. Having finished college a year ago, he now had very great ambitions.

I'm going to have money and power. More important than anything else, I will be the one in control, he promised himself.

Edward Kent had no time to be making the rounds with airy-headed little things that fell into his arms and bed too easily. There was too much work to do to get what he wanted and he found that there was no challenge in the usual games with women. Ordinarily when he saw someone he wanted, he simply told her what to do: *Sit down. Come here. Wear blue, I like it.* Edward had no doubts or reservations that his wishes would be followed. After all, that's how his entire life had been.

Why should anything be different now when I'm more deter-

mined than ever? His mouth curved into a small smile, but his eyes were without emotion.

Edward had been raised by two rather arrogant and self-satisfying people, parents who were older than most of his friends' mothers and fathers. Maxwell and Helen Kent had come to the U.S. during the forties, and though they had been poor refugees from Germany, they did well financially in their new country. They never found it necessary to be terribly concerned about who they needed to shove about in order to secure their small successes. Nor had either his mother or father felt compelled to explain or justify either their deeds or the repercussions. They carefully taught their only son to follow in their footsteps and this suited Edward. He was fascinated with the concept of power and the ability to control others. It was what he wanted more than anything else in the world.

Edward William Kent, tall and dark complected, was unquestionably handsome, but in an almost sinister way. He was emotionally cold and he always had been. As a small boy he watched his father carefully, and he learned that an arrogant, almost disdainful attitude would protect him from potential attacks from others. He didn't value or cultivate friendships, only connections, and the acquaintances that he did have were quickly made aware of how Edward operated. If they crossed him in any way, if they failed to live up to his expectations, they did not remain in his small circle or benefit from the few political and financial associations his family had established in their community.

Edward was ruthless in school, in business and in his personal relations. He expected a great deal and gave very little in return. What kept some people associating with him regardless, was an always present, if unspoken promise of future benefits, the kind that come from being connected to someone who is entirely determined to attain and wield power and influence.

Now this unusually attractive young woman had seized his attention. He enjoyed the look of strength, vibrancy, and vulnerability that there was about Cathryn.

But, he thought, *how interesting it would be to teach her about real strength.*

His dark eyes narrowed as he watched her walk away. Edward drew on his pipe and leaned back against the booth.

Edward knew the campus well and he found ways to be in places where Cathryn would go, locations where she felt comfortable and safe, where they could accidentally walk past one another. He didn't speak to her for a long time, but more than once she knew that he was there and that he was looking at her. And each time she felt inexplicably excited and nervous, her cheeks flushed and the palms of her hands moist.

Late one afternoon, Cathryn was in the drug store at the corner of Church Street and Main. She nervously dropped a magazine just as she was walking up to the cashier, fully aware that Edward was in the store somewhere behind her. She leaned down to pick it up and his hand brushed against hers.

"I've got it," he said firmly, his gaze enveloping her, taking her breath away. He slowly put the magazine and a five dollar bill on the counter, took his change, turned and handed the magazine to her. Then, without smiling, his eyes staring directly into hers, he said softly, "Come and have a cup of coffee with me. It's time I introduced myself. I'm Edward Kent," and he gently took her hand in his.

"I'm Cathr…." she murmured softly.

"Yes, I know who you are," he said quietly.

That was the beginning.

Weeks later, when they were finally alone together, Edward manipulated and orchestrated their romance specifically for the effect that he wanted to have on her. At first he didn't touch her at all, except to place a strong hand on her shoulder as he guided her into a room, or later when they sat next to one another on his couch, a dim lamp glowing on the low coffee table before them, he brushed her cheek very softly back and forth with his fingers.

He gazed intently into her eyes and told her, "I knew, from the first time I saw you, that you belonged to me and that we would be together forever." She looked back at him with wonder in her eyes. This man wasn't in awe of her like some of the others had been. He was so self-assured, so confident. He sounded and looked absolutely serious and Cathryn felt caught up in his strength, and carried along by his plans.

When he gently held her chin with his hand and leaned towards her, she was aching to feel his lips on hers.

"Not yet, beautiful," he said softly, "not just yet."

Cathryn felt as if she could hardly breathe. The longing that he was awakening in her was something that she did not expect. She didn't know quite how to deal with the flood of emotion she felt towards this unusual and strange man. But she was fascinated and one thing was certain. She wanted more.

జ

One Saturday afternoon he took her out for lunch and a drive. When they went back to his apartment, Edward turned on the stereo and very nearly drove Cathryn crazy, very slowly caressing her back, her arms, the curve of her hips, the firm swell of her breasts and then he was kissing her, softly at first, then more deeply and passionately. But he didn't try to take any of her clothes off as his large hands kept moving over her body and she trembled involuntarily.

When her breath was coming so hard and fast that she thought she would burst and her body was leaning towards him, yearning for his touch, he reached under her skirt and moving her underpants aside, he pressed his fingers searchingly inside of her. She could feel him touching her hot wetness. Her back arched towards him and she was filled with a longing that she had never known before.

"Please, Edward, please, yes," she breathed.

Then, abruptly, he stopped, and while he was watching her face, he straightened her clothes and then his own. Cathryn was still trembling, her face a picture of passion and confusion. Edward smiled knowingly at her and gently stroked her hair as he pulled her back into his arms, calmly pressing his lips against her cheek.

"Not yet," he whispered, "not yet."

⟡

Perhaps Cathryn would have reacted differently, if not for Dr. Krauss. At the same time that Edward was arousing, frustrating and confusing her, Dr. Aaron Krauss was instructing, comforting, touching and scaring the hell out of Cathryn. Just a little bit more and he would push her completely into Edward's eager, controlling and dangerous arms.

⟡

"Hey, don't you guys ever let anyone else have that table?" Cathryn was startled back to the present by two blond girls with two tall, muscular boys in football sweaters, walking past the little cafe. They waved, but went on with their conversation, still intent on one another.

A half hour later, though, Cathryn looked at her watch and a frown crossed her face and she caught her lower lip between her teeth. "Jesus, it's already 4:30," she said. "I've got to get downtown and meet Edward and my mom and dad." She got up from the table and then leaned down and hugged Linda. Linda's arm went around her cousin's shoulders. She could smell Cathryn's familiar perfume.

Why do I keep feeling so sad? Linda asked herself, keeping her arm tightly around her friend for another moment.

"Gotta go. You two behave. I'll see you soon, hmm?" Cathryn looked down warmly at Linda, grabbed her books, went around the table and pressed her cheek against Nick's and said, "God, I don't know what I'll do without you two. Can't you come and live in my house in California?" she smiled weakly.

Cathryn started to walk away down the sidewalk, but then she stopped and turned towards them. They were both quietly watching her. Cathryn felt a weird, anxious feeling in her abdomen that she couldn't shake off, as if there were something that she should know or do or say, but she couldn't figure out what it was. She lifted her fingers to her lips and blew a kiss back to her friends at the table and then she quickly walked away, west on Church Street away from the campus, with the sunlight gleaming in her wavy hair.

~

Cathryn had tears in her eyes. She realized that she wasn't at all sure when she would see the two of them again. Edward wanted to leave for California as soon as possible and he wanted to be married by a justice of the peace, somewhere along the way, with just the two of them at their wedding. At first Cathryn was startled by his idea and she protested feebly, but Edward was adamant. He flatly refused to consider the kind of wedding that Cathryn's mother and father wanted so much to give their only daughter. After a while, as she had from the beginning, Cathryn acquiesced to Edward's wishes and then she began to hear herself sounding like him in her explanations to her parents.

"It just doesn't make sense to put so much time, energy and money into a few hours, for a party for people we hardly know and who we probably won't see again for years, if ever," she declared to her mother, as Anna stood in the kitchen making a pot of coffee.

The attractive, pleasant older woman turned, and looking at her daughter with gentle caring in her eyes, she paused, considering what Cathryn had said. For a moment they were both quiet, looking at one another. During that moment, they each had their own mental picture of Cathryn, resplendent in a magnificent white gown, her dazzling smile, the quintessential bride, and then, a bit grudgingly, they allowed the images to fade away.

Anna sighed, resignedly, and hugged her daughter to her for a long time before the two women made their way dilatorily into the living room with the fresh coffee.

Edward and Cathryn's father Joseph sat stiffly facing one another on two couches, separated not only by a long, low glass coffee table, but also by totally opposing points of view on just about everything, except the importance of Cathryn in their lives.

❧

At the cafe, Linda felt a burning sensation in her chest and the smile faded from her face again.

She thought, *My days will be different without Cathryn, without Nick's teasing, without our meetings, our phone calls.*

Her lovely, young face clouded over and her smooth forehead creased with lines of concern as she tried to hold back tears.

Nick felt it, too. He came around the table, sat in the chair that Cathryn had just left empty, put his arm around Linda's shoulders and pulled her close to him. "Hey, kid, it's gonna be fine. She's going to be a very, very happy lady and we're going to go and visit her and drink terrific wine, okay?"

Linda looked up at him, still trying not to cry, hating how easily tears came to her dark eyes. She leaned towards Nick, wanting his reassurance and wanting to get comfort from the picture of the future that he described. But they knew Edward and they didn't feel very hopeful. They didn't like him, and they both loved Cathryn very much.

Just at that moment Carrie came hurrying across the street, carrying packages from Carson's, the department store at the corner, her blond hair blowing around her face in the breeze. Nick stood up and pulled a chair out for her, leaning over as Carrie touched her cheek to his.

"Hi, guys," she said, breathlessly. "Can't sit. Nick, we're supposed to be at Mom's in an hour and I need to make a couple more stops. Can you put these in your car and meet me there?" She paused, finally seeing the looks on their faces. "Where's Cathryn? What's wrong?"

There was a pause before Nick answered, "She went to meet Edward and her parents."

"So, what's wrong?" Carrie repeated.

Nick and Linda looked at each other and back at Carrie. Nick shrugged. Linda didn't say anything.

Linda thought, *There's no point in talking about it, it's some-*

thing that's just going to happen. Anyway, I really don't know exactly what's wrong; just some weird feeling, a not very good feeling. Linda sighed deeply.

Carrie looked at her and shrugged, turning towards Nick again. Nick took her packages from her. She really didn't want any more explanation. Carrie clearly had more shopping on her mind. "I've gotta go. I'll see you there?" Nick nodded yes, and Carrie was off across the street. "Bye, Linda," she threw back over her shoulder not waiting for an answer, and she disappeared into one of the little shops that lined Church Street. Nick sat down again.

Linda pushed her hair back away from her face, looked over at Nick, and trying to sound happier than she felt, said, "I've still got an English Lit report to do. I'm going to the Library. Some of us aren't through with this stuff yet, Mr. Lawyer." She stood up and gave Nick a quick hug, letting herself feel the warm, smoothness of his cheek for just a second, and then Linda started to walk away from the table. He caught her hand and stopped her for a moment. Without saying anything he smiled up at her, but his eyes were sad.

Something's changing too fast and I don't like it, Linda thought.

"Okay little girl," Nick said, softly, loosening his grip on her hand. "See you."

Then Linda, with her books in her arms, walked a few steps away down the sidewalk, east on Church Street towards the campus and the huge, ivy-covered building that was the Deering Library. As Cathryn had done a short time ago, she turned back towards Nick and waved, forcing herself to smile. The uncomfortable feeling that burned in her chest was getting worse and now she felt it spreading through her stomach as if her intestines were knotting and twisting.

I have to get out of here, get busy, shake off all this, this not right feeling, Linda told herself.

Nick watched her walk away down the street for a minute, and then he got up from their table feeling strangely alone and terribly sad. He picked up Carrie's packages and walked across the tree-lined street towards his car. He went south, crossing Church Street.

As he put the key in the car door, he thought, *The three of us just went off in three completely different directions, on the same street, exactly what we're about to do with our lives.*

Nick, too, was feeling an uncomfortable sensation in his chest and stomach, some uneasiness about something he didn't know or something he should be doing.

What, though? he asked himself.

One

Twenty-five years later, Southern California...

CATHRYN MARGARET SILBERG KENT was at one time an extraordinarily beautiful woman. She wasn't one of those women whose appearance comes together with smart clothes and clever make-up. Fortunately or unfortunately, nature had given Cathryn an absolutely natural and soft beauty, beauty that attracted the admiring attention of both men and women from the very beginning.

Cathryn had been an adorable child who never went through a clumsy or awkward stage and who seemed to be exempt from even an ordinary blemish on her adolescent skin. As she passed from one stage to the next, she became more beautiful.

Looking at herself in a mirror, Cathryn never saw it.

My eyes and nose are okay, she thought, critically turning her face one way and then the other. Always feeling uncomfortable with herself and somehow inadequate, she stared at her reflection, and she only saw a person that no one else ever saw and that person was not attractive. Cathryn saw only her flaws, the imperfections that were not evident to anyone else.

The framed pictures displayed in her father's spacious study documented her changes. On his huge mahogany desk there was a photograph of Cathryn when she was a pretty and happy baby sitting on her father's lap. The lips of her tiny mouth were almost heart-shaped and her big, violet eyes were liquid and sparkling with life, as she looked up into her father's adoring face.

Next to the mahogany-shuttered window, there was a close-up taken of a charming, smiling toddler, her shiny, wavy hair flowing behind her in the breeze as she stood on her tiptoes and reached up to help her mother hang clothes on a line.

Over the low bookcase that ran the length of one entire wall, amidst photographs of his wife and sons, there was a photograph of a lovely little girl with beautiful almond-shaped eyes and perfectly arched eyebrows. The picture was taken at the edge of a football field as Cathryn gazed up worshipfully at her favorite brother, Steve. Always the hero quarterback of the game, dressed in his dirt-smudged uniform, he knelt, his arm around his young sister.

Still another shot of Cathryn hung on the rich, tan grass cloth covered wall, showing wooden benches at a high school pep rally. She was on the right side of the picture, a strikingly attractive teenager with arms raised upward in exhilaration. Her smile was wide and dazzling, her long hair pulled back off her face into a thick, shining ponytail. Her already stunning figure was not at all obscured by the jeans and sweater she wore. Her radiance was so bright that the rest of the crowd within the perimeter of the picture seemed dim and a little hazy, though right there beside her.

There was another large photograph in a chrome frame on the wall opposite her father's desk. It was taken in Cathryn's last year of college and it captured an image of her as a remarkably beautiful young woman, who despite the gentle, sweet expression on her face, scintillated such an exotic sensuality, that even in a photograph, it was almost overpowering, like an expensive, heady perfume.

ॐ

Cathryn even had pretty feet and above them her legs had been long and shapely from the time she was ten years old. Her slim hips curved into a slender waist. She had perfect breasts, firm and full, incredibly clear skin and a lovely face that was framed with shiny waves of golden, chestnut hair. Her almond-shaped warm eyes changed from sparkling bits of violet, to dark gray when she was angry, and her high cheekbones bore an ever-present natural blush. Her complexion was fair and clear, like fine china. Her lashes were dark, long and curved and even her hands were flawless, with long fingers and strong, tapered nails.

‿ᗡ

That was a long time ago. That was Cathryn before she got caught up in a web of insane circumstances that never should have happened. That was before Edward.

‿ᗡ

Clothes were easy for Cathryn. She could wear anything from clinging, strapless gowns, to T-shirts and cut-off jeans. There was clearly a strong familial resemblance between Cathryn and Linda, something about their smiles was very similar. But Linda's hair was much lighter, and her eyes and skin-coloring much darker than her cousin's. Linda was unquestionably attractive, but Cathryn... Cathryn was breathtakingly beautiful and everywhere the two of them went together, the attention from men was enormous and disconcerting.

"I feel like they don't even see my face," she complained to Linda. "Are they all so obsessed with boobs and asses that they don't know there's a person inside?"

"Some do," Linda said laughing, but with her own degree of discomfort showing in her eyes as she grew thoughtful. "Maybe we'll find one of them one day."

They both laughed, but Cathryn still felt the same vague nervousness in her stomach that she felt before. It had something to do with the men who stared at her breasts when she was walking down Michigan Avenue earlier that day, but this time it was taking a long time for it to go away.

She couldn't explain exactly what it was or where it came from, not to Linda, not even to herself. But, her thoughts drifted back to one morning in elementary school when her mother had helped her dress while she was still groggy with sleep. She wore a navy and peach plaid, wool skirt and a full slip, over which Anna had buttoned a soft, peach cardigan. Cathryn walked into the warm room where the children had their lockers and unconsciously unbuttoned the sweater, thinking distractedly that she had a blouse on underneath it. She didn't realize that she was in her slip and skirt, until she stood before the teacher's desk a moment later and Mrs. Kinsley kindly, quietly advised her of her mistake.

Cathryn rushed back to get her sweater and probably no one but the teacher ever noticed. But Cathryn never forgot the startled, sick feeling that had invaded the pit of her stomach when she realized that she was standing in front of a roomful of boys and girls, clad only in her underwear and skirt.

That self-conscious, sick feeling of having done something wrong, then drawing some kind of sexual interest, stayed stuck within her mind and sometimes something happened that would cause her to feel that disturbing feeling again.

Cathryn felt that same sickening, nauseated discomfort ooze into her gut when she thought about her Uncle Craig. Married to her father's sister Carol, Craig was a boisterous crude man, who always wanted to play with her and her brothers when they were younger, on his visits to their home with Aunt Carol.

Cathryn didn't like him, she felt uncomfortable with him. Craig was a pharmacist, but he always looked unkempt. He was rarely clean shaven and he often had dirt under his fingernails. When Cathryn got close to him, his clothes and skin smelled like stale tobacco.

One Saturday afternoon, Craig was wrestling with her brothers, Steve and Martin, when Cathryn walked into the family room looking for a doll. Craig reached out and grabbed her hand, pulled her down onto the floor with the boys and he began tickling her. He laughed loudly at her surprise and obvious discomfort, but he wouldn't let her go when she protested and struggled to get out of his reach. Steve and Martin, bored with this and eager to be outside, ran from the room leaving Cathryn still trying to get away from Craig's thoughtless game.

She tried to remember exactly what had happened, but the memory clouded over until she got that same nauseated, horribly embarrassed, wrongly sexual feeling. Then her recollection of the incident faded and became unreachable.

He must have touched me, she thought, appalled, years later, trying to look back at herself as a child of six years of age from a distance, as if that little girl were another person entirely.

Maybe he touched me, maybe he actually put his hand on my nonexistent chest or between my legs. Cathryn's stomach tightened, bile rising in her throat. *What a horrible creep he was,* she thought.

In the far recesses of her mind, there was also a troubling question about what that little girl had done to provoke that to happen. Whether she had done anything or not, Cathryn buried the question before it could even form itself into a complete thought. Totally unable to confront her own question, she could never come up with any answers to it.

Craig died when Cathryn was eleven and she remembered that although she knew she was supposed to feel badly about his death, something like relief changed places with the self-conscious, embarrassed sickening feeling deep in the pit of her stomach whenever she heard his name.

Cathryn, though truly physically beautiful, was also very troubled.

↭

That same woman, now forty-two years old, was almost unrecognizable.

Cathryn sat shivering and hugging her body on the bare wood floor of her bedroom. An early photograph of her with Edward sat on the dresser just over her head, and in that picture she looked up at him, smiling happily. She wore a short-sleeved, pale yellow silk shirt and her face glowed radiantly with life and love and hope. Her delicate chin was lifted slightly, her lips moist and soft. The expression on her face was one of complete trust and devotion as she gazed up at him.

At the same moment, the photographer had caught Edward looking straight into the camera with an expression of impatience and irritation. Edward, a tall man, six foot four, stood almost a foot above the pretty woman next to him. His features, dark and strong, but lacking in emotion or warmth, caused him to appear formidable, even foreboding, rather than handsome or appealing. He held his chin up slightly in a firm and resolute manner, despite the glow of radiant beauty from the woman at his side. There was no hint of amusement or pleasure or love on his face.

Edward and Cathryn were a strange combination. Early on, people close to Cathryn tried to point this out to her in one stumbling attempt after another, but Cathryn stubbornly refused to listen to them. Even Linda and Nick concurred with her family at first. Her mother and father questioned her more when she began spending time with Edward than they ever had in her lifetime before.

Steve boldly demanded of his sister, "What can you possibly want with such a self-centered bastard?"

The tears that sprang to her eyes, rather than Cathryn's spitting anger, made Steve back up a bit, but Cathryn would not discuss it.

Edward is not cold, she told herself. Her heart beat faster as she thought of his hands, his strong, teasing fingers and his hot lips touching her body.

For a while, less severe criticism with seemingly endless questions went on and on. Cathryn simply would not have this and her eyes would grow dark and stormy.

"This is my life, not yours! I know what I want. I know what I'm doing," she declared harshly to her startled mother when Anna merely asked if she and Edward were going out again that weekend. "Why can't anyone just see how happy he makes me," she cried, her voice breaking into sobs. Her mother stood at the doorway to Cathryn's room, feeling puzzled and helpless, twisting a dish towel in her hands and pressing her lips together so that she wouldn't begin to cry as well.

Cathryn never spoke to me like this before, never, Anna lamented sorrowfully.

Joseph, Anna and Cathryn's friends retreated, thinking that

something would change. *She'll get to know Edward better. She'll see him as he is,* her father thought.

After some time the feeble protests stopped entirely. Whatever the reasons, Cathryn was hopelessly committed to Edward, and she called it love.

৴৶

Time passed and her attachment to Edward grew stronger instead of weakening. Cathryn's family and her closest friends resigned themselves to the fact that Cathryn had completely and adamantly made a choice and it was most certainly Edward. They admitted that Cathryn seemed happy. Though Edward was not by any stretch of the imagination, the effusive, warm and loving human being they envisioned for her, he did have something that had completely captivated their lovely Cathryn. Not one person who knew Cathryn and Edward could begin to guess exactly what that might be.

However, they did realize begrudgingly that Edward had somehow persuaded Cathryn to devote her life to him, along with anything else she might have to offer.

৴৶

The room Cathryn sat in now was dreary and dim. The king-size bed was unmade, and dirty clothes and towels lay in piles on the floor by the windows. There was a thick layer of dust on the furniture. On the floor, the dust mixed with dog hair was so heavy that it was easy to see where someone had scuffed paths through it as they moved about the bedroom. Just a bit of gray light came in through the two bedroom windows between the slats of blinds that were closed almost all the way. Outside an overcast morning gave way to a steady sprinkle of rain. Thick, dismal dark clouds hung ominously over normally sun-drenched southern California.

It was almost impossible to tell that the lovely young woman in the photograph on the dresser was the same bedraggled woman who sat alone on the bare floor. She was barefoot, wearing only a pair of filthy tan sweatpants and a torn, faded pink T-shirt, that was stretched too tightly across her pudgy middle. She was a bloated thirty pounds heavier than she was in the picture and her lined skin had a grayish cast to it. Her eyes were dark gray without the slightest flicker of light in them. The blush was long gone from her cheeks.

Cathryn rocked mechanically back and forth as she sat on the floor in front of the dark wooden dresser, facing the doorway, waiting. She wasn't looking at anything in particular but her body was turned towards the hallway as if she expected something to appear there. She stopped rocking and leaned forward a little, staring into the space three or four feet in front of her where there was nothing. Dark, puffy spots blotched the skin under her eyes and extended to where her cheekbones were obscured with soft, grayish flesh. Her once lovely, shiny hair was unevenly cut. It lay close around her face in thick, matted tangles, looking as if it had gone unwashed for days.

ॐ

At the same moment, just sixty miles away, Linda sat in front of her computer in the little office she worked from in her North County home. The room, next to her small kitchen, in spite of the grayness of the day, was open, airy and light, deeply in contrast to Linda's mood. She was unhappy. The expression on her face was serious, contemplative. She stared at the screen, her forehead creased with a frown. Linda felt troubled, but she wasn't certain what it was that was nagging at her so hard.

This isn't like me, she thought, annoyed with herself.

That was true. Linda was normally an unstoppable optimist. While those around her were busily listing their problems, Linda was usually seeking out solutions. She was unshakable in her belief that such a way always existed, only waiting to be discovered, no matter what the situation.

She began a little mental checklist, hoping that she could get some flicker of awareness about where the discomfort, the concern, the tightening of her stomach was coming from on this quiet, pleasant, if gray day, with nothing extraordinary looming on her horizon.

"The kids are doing fine. Mom's okay," she mumbled out loud

to herself. "The bills are there, but getting better. I'll get them handled," she promised herself. "Work's good. I love what I'm doing, I love where I live."

Haven't met the man of my dreams yet, her thoughts continued, *but at least I'm not involved with anyone who isn't, either,* she declared silently.

Cathryn and Nick, a voice that wasn't quite a voice, but just the flutter of a thought, said in her head.

Linda felt a chill along her arms. She got up and made a pot of coffee.

Cathryn, Cathryn, Cathryn ... she heard, no, felt.

I haven't talked to her in years ... I'm losing it, Linda thought.

For two days now, she had had this crazy, uneasy, nervous feeling with absolutely nothing going on around her to warrant it.

Cathryn keeps popping into my head, she mused sipping the steaming hot coffee. *I feel like an alarm went off. I didn't hear it but I can feel it.*

ॐ

Linda wore a faded red and blue flannel shirt tucked into worn jeans. She was barefoot, she didn't like to wear shoes in her house. Her hair, still a shiny, honey-blond, was even lighter than when she had lived in Chicago. Her skin was tan, a warm, bronze color even at this time of year. She often sat out on her deck off the living room, spreading her papers out on a table in front of her, working in the sunshine for hours at a time. She looked years younger than her age.

Pensively, Linda turned and looked out the sliding glass doors to her right. Though the other buildings of the condominium complex were visible beyond the trees, she saw only the rich green leaves of the macadamia nut trees that lined the oval park and walkways. Somehow, an aesthetically-minded landscape architect had persuaded the developer to build his complex around this small, but lovely park, in spite of the objections that were raised. Less park area meant more units that could be squeezed into this very valuable land just three blocks from the Pacific ocean and the magnificent sunsets that adorned it.

Aesthetics over financial gain in southern California? Linda thought, smiling wryly. Through some miracle, the park had survived.

As she looked out into the peacefulness of the place, Linda thought, *You would have to be able to look out your windows and glass doors and see beautiful trees on one side and a piece of the ocean on the other to make up for living so close to so many other people.*

It was near enough to the ocean so that she could smell the moist, clean air when the sliding glass doors were open as they were now. She breathed deeply and relaxed a little. The complex was quiet and this helped her work.

I love it here more than anywhere else I've ever lived, she thought.

She took a sip of the coffee sitting beside her on the computer desk, then she sighed and rested her chin on her hands, her elbows on the desk in front of her. It was so long since she had heard anything from Cathryn, or Nick either, for that matter. Their lives had gone in completely different directions after college.

Back then we would never have believed that we would ever have become so separated, Linda thought sadly.

౨

Not too long after Cathryn's move across the country and her marriage, Nick and Carrie were married. They moved into a huge, beautiful two story brick home in Winnetka, north of the city, where they were close to Carrie's parents' estate.

They might as well have lived in three different countries for all the times that Nick and Linda managed to see each other after Cathryn left the Midwest. Nick's lifestyle changed drastically and abruptly, both with the demands of the law firm and those of his new wife. Time to see Linda all but disappeared.

Then Linda finished college and made her own attempt at marriage. She met Dan Clinten at the gym where she went to work out in the early mornings.

Dan, a decent, hard-working young man, was a successful young architect, and he was attracted to Linda immediately. Steady and conservative himself, he was fascinated by her energy and enthusiasm. Linda liked him, too, as soon as they met, but it was fairly obvious that they were already going in different directions. Unfortunately, they were both so eager to have someone in their lives that they refused to see the great disparity in their goals and purposes in life that would eventually rock their marriage.

Dan, so accepting of the status-quo, continuously argued with Linda when she disagreed with what she saw happening in the schools, in government and in the field of mental health. Dan kidded her and said that she was born late, beyond her time.

"You're a sixties radical," he told her. Though he teased, her strong views made him uneasy. Dan didn't want to make any waves. He was content at his office and in front of the television while Linda wanted with all her heart and soul to change any poor conditions that she saw around her. The popular quest for money and possessions as a way of life was ludicrous to her. She had never seen it make anyone around her happy, unless they had been happy to begin with. At the same time, business and accumulating wealth were Dan's entire focus and way of life.

Looking back, Linda thought, *we made no sense at all. Ah, hindsight's a wonderful thing,* she smiled grimly. *It was my fault. I should've seen it coming.*

Somewhere in her heart she always knew that she had picked Dan out as a likely choice, a suitable husband, when she thought it was time to get married. *More a fifties thing, than seventies,* she grimaced. *I was stuck in the appeal of "Father Knows Best."* She shook her head ruefully and took another sip of coffee.

She remembered sitting in Dan's favorite German restaurant the night, that he gave her an engagement ring. It was a beautiful but very cold night and snow had begun to fall outside the window. A huge fire blazed in the big stone fireplace just fifteen feet from their cozy booth. The smells of beer and ale, cooked meats and spices drifted through the huge dining room. The restaurant was known for its wonderfully seasoned heavy German dinners, and the huge Lazy Susans filled with mounds of cottage cheese, chopped liver, pickled beets and homemade apple sauce, that were promptly placed on each table as customers were seated.

Dan scooped up another forkful of wiener schnitzel and sauerkraut and put it in his mouth. Linda was pushing her vegetables around on her plate and staring at Dan's gentle face.

"What?" he asked her, tilting his head to the side and reaching across the table for her hand. "What're you thinking so hard about? Nice ring, hmm?" he smiled at her, admiring his gift on her finger. She remembered struggling with her own thoughts.

Do I tell him that I'm trying to figure out if I really love him, or if I just like him a lot? And, now, just an hour after we've decided to get married. What am I doing? Do I say that my parents think he's wonderful and so do my friends, that I think he'll make someone a terrific husband, but I'm just not positive that that someone is me? Don't think so.

Instead, Linda smiled back at him, looked down at his hand holding hers, said nothing and the moment passed.

After that dinner, Linda looked out the window at the blanket of new snow that was covering everything in sight. The otherwise barren branches overhead were topped with it like cake frosting. Even the cars that had just arrived were tucked under a fluffy, thick layer of the white stuff. The new snow was beautifully untouched and it glistened in the bright moonlight. Enchanted with how it looked, and a little uncomfortable from the heavy meal, Linda had asked spontaneously, "Dan, let's walk outside in the snow for a few minutes, okay?" Her face began to glow with enthusiasm now at the prospect of tramping through the fresh, soft, snowfall, like a carefree child.

"You're kidding. It must be ten degrees above zero out there," Dan dismissed the idea. He picked up his glass of ale and finished it off. "Let's go home," he said, reaching for her coat and helping her into it.

In the next few days, they were caught up in excitement and planning, the momentum that developed from their decision. Both families met and within a few weeks their wedding date was set. Linda convinced herself that she was doing the right thing. Dan was, after all, a very suitable person for her to marry.

Suitable? she thought ironically, as she remembered those times.

What has that got to do with anything? What was I doing in those days? Christ! She put the coffee down and walked out onto the deck and into the little bit of sunshine that was breaking through the heavy clouds overhead.

A woman was walking towards the pool along the pathway down below her. Something about her walk was so familiar. *Cathryn?* Her heart lurched within her chest. It couldn't be. Just then the woman scooped up a little kitten and turned back towards Linda. She was a complete stranger. Linda had never seen her before.

I am losing my mind, she thought. *Why do I keep thinking about her?*

Two

Cathryn, Cathryn...?

IN THE FIRST YEARS OF THEIR MARRIAGE, Linda and Dan got along fairly well, especially when Linda was home taking care of their two small babies. But Dan, solidly conservative and conventional, more lacking in confidence with any sign of independence from Linda, began to find it difficult to trust her out of his sight. There was nothing that Linda could do to convince him that his suspicions and fears were irrational and that, to her, marriage meant fidelity. "You should know that about me," she shouted back at him one night, waking Julia and Michael with their loud voices.

Dan wasn't able to stop himself, he became increasingly jealous and overbearing. "Where *were* you?" he demanded one afternoon, when he came home from work early and Linda wasn't in the house.

She was barely out of the garage when he started shouting at her. Julia was hungry and irritable, Michael had fallen asleep in the car and Linda wanted to get him into his crib. Dan followed her up the stairs, insisting on an answer.

"Dan, please! Let me put the baby in bed first, for God's sake. Where the hell do you think I was with two little kids? At my boyfriend's house? Christ, Dan! Stop this! I went to see Elaine. It's five minutes from here!"

Dan was only comfortable when Linda was at home, being

what he considered a dutiful wife and mother. Linda, though she enjoyed that role so much of the time, began feeling suffocated by her husband's inability to understand that she might want to work, or study another course, or even take horseback riding lessons.

"If the kids are fine and the house is clean and dinner's ready when you get home, why not?" she demanded of him.

"Because I don't like it!" he shouted at her. "It's not what I want!"

When it was too obvious that they couldn't resolve their conflicts over Linda's struggles to expand, to grow up really, Dan insisted that they see a psychologist. After several weekly meetings with a group, doing some sort of role playing with an empty chair, Linda felt as if she were sinking. The group games were absurd to her. Dan thought that they were helpful. Their discussions with Dr. Marriage Counselor, with a too-tight belt around his ample middle and his equally over-flowing opinions, made her more and more certain that she would not survive within the confines of their relationship. She refused to continue with the meetings and eventually she asked Dan for a divorce. Their marriage disintegrated after eight years and two children.

When it happened, Linda wasn't frightened or uncertain. She felt like a baby chick must, as it struggles and pecks its way out of a shell, into an immense and unknown world, feeling that anything waiting out there must be better than being forever trapped inside.

She was twenty-nine years old, the mother of two young children when the divorce was final. But, Linda, faced with being on her own for the first time, really, after having gone from the comfort of her parents' home, to the insularity of school and her friends, and then to the stifling protection of her marriage to Dan, was, at last, truly on her own. And, she was excited about the prospect. She found a young girl from Wisconsin to move in with her to watch Julia and Michael, and Linda went back to her job at Harcourt Publishing.

ↄ

At first, it was amazement and wonder, rather than uncertainty or fear, that Linda felt about the whole new world of possibilities and choices that had opened up for her.

I can go anywhere I want and I can do anything, she thought dreamily, as she watched little Julia pulling Michael across the driveway in a tiny green wagon. Her eyes were bright and little laugh lines crinkled at the corners.

ᴄᴏ

An executive from the West Coast branch of Harcourt, Tim Perkins, stopped at her desk when she was working late one evening. "Nice job on this report, Linda, very nice," he said, handing the paperwork to her. Then he looked at his watch and asked, "Linda, would you have lunch with me tomorrow? I've got some things I want to talk over with you," he said. Linda agreed, a little warily.

She had just finished the final stages of her divorce from Dan and was still feeling a little off balance facing the world as a single woman after eight years of marriage. Some of her friends were already calling to introduce her to someone or to persuade her to venture out into the world of the lonely, eager, and, too often, desperate singles. Worse still, two of the husbands in her neighborhood, whom she had known as Dan's wife, seemed to have radar concerning her new status — or maybe it was hard to miss that Dan's prized little Mercedes was no longer in the driveway, even if they hadn't actually seen him moving his things out of the house. At any rate, they were coming around to see if she was doing all right in the house alone, with just a little too much interest.

I'm not ready for this, Linda thought to herself, politely answering their questions, then closing the front door as fast as she could. As she leaned back against it, tears ran slowly down her cheeks. *A whole new game,* she thought. *And a whole bunch of unfamiliar rules.*

"What's the matter, Mommy?" Julia asked, startling her. "Why are you crying?"

"It's okay, honey. I'm okay, see?" Linda said, bending down

and hugging the little girl close to her. She wiped at her cheeks with her shirt sleeve, looking tenderly at Julia's innocent face to be certain that the concern was erased.

※

Some little warning light flickered in her mind about the lunch invitation. She found herself bracing up for what Tim might want to talk to her about. He was a strong, but pleasant man, nice-looking, in his late forties, very efficient at his job, respected by Harcourt's staff, and he wore a plain, gold wedding band on his ring finger.

※

Linda was ten minutes early, but Tim was already seated comfortably. He was sipping a glass of Merlot when Linda came up to the table. He got up, smiling and held her chair for her.

"Would you like something to drink?" he asked.

"No, Tim, thanks, just some coffee."

Tim spoke to the waitress and then he pushed the menus to one side. He leaned towards Linda and said, "Look Linda, I don't have a lot of time to accomplish everything that I need to do this trip. Let me tell you exactly why I wanted to meet with you and then we'll think about lunch. Okay?" Tim didn't wait for Linda to answer. "I want to relocate you. I like your work and I like the way you do it. I've never seen anyone as hard-working and diligent on the job in this branch. I could really use someone like you in my department in San Diego. Have you ever thought about living in southern California?" he smiled a broad, warm smile, and waited for her to digest his proposal.

"Wow," she breathed softly, relieved that this was his reason for the lunch, and a little embarrassed that she had thought it was something else. She felt surprised and pleased at the same time. "No, not before this minute, I never did," she said slowly. Then Linda paused for a moment, looked straight at Tim, and with her eyes bright with excitement, said, "But I am now!"

Tim laughed. "Well, good. Let me tell you some of the details." And, for the next hour and a half, he described what he had in mind, while they had lunch and laughed, discussing her love of editing and writing and Tim's love of having capable people working with him.

Though the thought of living in California had never occurred to Linda before, after Tim offered her the job in San Diego County, she found it drawing her like some magnetic force. In a matter of days, Tim handled the logistics involved between the two branch offices, and arranged for an apartment for her, temporarily, in Solana Beach. Then he took off for home, leaving Linda to wrap up all of her personal affairs. It was the beginning of spring and Linda wanted to drive her own car out west so that she could see some of the country that she had only seen in pictures, and so she could spend time alone with Julia and Michael. Tim agreed to this with a good-natured warning, "As long as you're at work bright and early on the twentieth. We're going to have plenty to do."

Dan was astounded by Linda's impulsive decision to move out of the state. He snarled and complained for a little while. In reality, though, he was not enjoying the role of a visiting Sunday father. Besides he was already involved with Miriam, a dark-haired, serious bank teller, who had vowed to him, "Should we ever marry, Dan, you and our home will always take precedence over my career or anything else."

॰ঌ৴

Not stopping to think that perhaps it was a bit courageous of an adventure for a woman with two young children, Linda tearfully hugged her mother for a long time, got into her car, and moved her small family across the country. Their trip took twelve days. Linda loved driving steadily, stopping early for dinner and getting a good night's sleep in cozy motels. She was up at daybreak and on the road, finding wonderful breakfasts in delightful little cafes. They were enchanted watching the country change as they traveled, poking around this little town or that historic monument, with Linda taking photos of Julia and Michael everywhere they stopped.

Their journey went from Chicago to St. Louis, through Springfield, Tulsa, Oklahoma City, Amarillo, Albuquerque, Tucson, Yuma,

El Centro, the Imperial Valley and finally into San Diego. They traveled first through small farm towns in southern Illinois and across corn and grain fields in Missouri. They saw Hereford and Shorthorn pastures and huge wheat and cotton fields in Oklahoma, acres of wheat and the richest oil and gas fields of the U.S. in the Panhandle Plains of Texas. Then into Albuquerque where they stopped long enough to take a ride on the world's longest aerial tramway to the top of Sandia Peak, the highest point west of the Rocky Mountains.

Julia stood at the front of the cable car, wide-eyed, with her little hands pressed against the window of the tram for the thrilling fifteen minute ride up almost three miles. Michael's eyes were wide with wonder on the trip down when they passed two big-horn sheep staring back at them with nonchalant regard. Linda was very happy.

The evening that they drove into San Diego County, coming down out of the Cleveland National Forest, heading towards the Pacific Ocean on Interstate 8, Linda was nervous. She was shaken by the traffic zooming past her while she was still getting used to roads that went not only up and down, but banked to the right and then to the left. She was so used to the table-top flatness of the Midwest and the predictability of Chicago streets which go directly, invariably, north and south or east and west.

But then she saw hundreds of welcoming lights of San Diego just below her, with the Harbor in the distance, and she said softly to the two sleeping children in the back seat, "We're home, guys, we're really here."

During the following years, every time Linda returned to San Diego County from one of her trips, she would get the same feeling. *Home ... I'm really home.*

❧

Linda immediately fell in love with the rolling hills, the abundance of citrus and avocado groves and the incredible explosion of vibrantly colored flowers that bloomed everywhere in the spring, even in the desert and along the sides of the freeways. San Diego was a magic place to Linda where she could be on the beach in the bright afternoon sunshine and then build a blazing fire in her fireplace against the evening chill, and she was continuously amazed and enchanted by the climate.

She slept well at night and in the early mornings or evenings, she walked for hours along the powerful Pacific coastline. Her olive skin took on a warmer bronze tone and her honey blond hair bleached out even lighter. She felt as if she were coming alive after the artificial heating and air-conditioning that she had lived in for three quarters of every year in the challenging cold winters and oppressively hot summers of Chicago.

Her son and daughter took to the beaches and their life in the small coastal town as if they had always lived there. All three of them were enchanted by the surfers who waited in the ocean patiently for their waves, and by the hang gliders over Torrey Pines. They were delighted by the colorful hot air balloons drifting up towards the bits of puffy clouds over Del Mar. Linda took them to Julian in the fall to pick apples, and up to Palomar Mountain to play in the snow.

When Linda drove between Escondido and Fallbrook, where the encroachment of the developers hadn't yet reached, she looked up into the hills and she imagined long absent Indian tribes sitting on their ponies at the crests of the hills.

I feel as though I must have lived here before in some long ago time, maybe in a civilization that wasn't quite as complicated. Certainly one that was less destructive and maybe more sensible, she wrote in her journal.

Yes, she knew that she could live happily in this place, close to the calming beaches, and where the hills laden with avocado groves gently rolled up towards the sky, where those Indians she could almost see had once treasured and cared for the land and its products, until *civilization* came with its changes, some good, others greedy and evil.

꒰

Linda did well working for Tim. He appreciated her abilities and was fair with her, becoming an important friend as well as her mentor. Her relationship with Tim made the job exciting, rather than tolerable. At his side, she became cognizant of the actual workings of the publishing industry and valuing her viewpoint, Tim kept her from being relegated to the mundane clerical duties that, despite changes in recent years, many of the female employees still handled.

"Linda, look at this copy and tell me what you think," Tim said, dropping a file on the corner of her desk as he left the deserted office at seven o'clock one night. "No rush, tomorrow's fine. I'll see you in the morning." He called back over his shoulder, "Now, go home!"

Linda put the folder in her briefcase, straightened up the paperwork on her desk and turned off her computer. It was getting late and she had promised the kids, and her baby-sitter, dinner from Carl's Jr. She smiled down at the two little beaming faces that looked up at her from the photograph on her desk, Julia with her missing front teeth and sparkling eyes, her arm protectively around Michael, with his perpetual look of mischief framed by fine, shiny hair that fell almost to his eyebrows.

༄

"Well?" Tim asked the next morning.

"It's awful," Linda answered simply. "I read the whole project folder until after twelve last night and then I read it again because I thought maybe I missed something. I couldn't even figure out why you were bothering with it. Why are you?"

"Conflict of executive opinion," Tim answered, rolling his eyes upward. "And you have just reinforced my own one hundred percent. I agree. It's crap. But, to some, it has the appearance of being a big money maker and that causes principles and intelligence to go out the window sometimes," Tim said, sounding weary. "You know, Linda, it's really helped me to have you around here. Some days, I think I'm nuts. And then I get your refreshingly honest and candid viewpoint, and I know it's just that we both are," Tim laughed, his face brightening. The sound was heartfelt and contagious and Linda laughed with him.

They continued working together so comfortably that Tim's news later that year made Linda feel as if the floor had dropped out from under her.

∽

Tim called Linda into his office one afternoon, eleven months after she had come to San Diego. She was smiling, busily involved in the reports he needed the next morning.

"Linda, I'm leaving Harcourt," he said.

"You're joking," Linda answered, the smile instantly gone from her face. When she saw Tim's expression, she knew immediately that he was not. "Tim, why?" she asked in a small voice.

"Without getting into the specifics, which don't matter anyway, it could have been a hundred different situations," Tim explained, "of politics and mechanisms of corporate structure."

This was something that, working for Tim, Linda had never paid any attention to.

"It's something I need to do," he explained, "and something that's best for me in the long run. Unfortunately, I have to move back to the East Coast, to New York. I'll always have a job for you, Linda, wherever I am." He told her, "If you would consider such a move after falling in love with California." Tim looked at her now and waited.

Linda turned and looked out the window of his office. She could see the ocean. It was January, yet the sky was blue with wisps of white clouds. The sun shone brilliantly, reflecting a lovely, nacreous shimmer off the water.

In her eyes, Tim thought, *I can see the considerations, one by one, as she looks at them, weighing each one.* He watched the familiar way she had of scrunching her eyebrows together as she contemplated, deep in thought, troubled. The way she had of studying her fingernails, as she did now.

"Linda," he said kindly, "you have so much talent. You can do anything you want. And anywhere. Follow your heart, kiddo. I've rarely met someone with as much heart as you have. Leaving you here is going to be harder than leaving this damn job that's driving me crazy anyway," he joked. "Whatever you decide, you know

I'll help you any way I can." Tim got up and walked over to her.

"You've been so terrific to work for, Tim. I could never find another 'boss' like you. I owe you so much for getting me out here. I love it. My kids ... They've never been so happy. It would break Mike's heart to take him away from the beach. He wants to be a surfer more than anything else on Earth," she looked up at him, trying to smile at her son's ambitions, but there were tears in her eyes. "Why does it always have to be so complicated? How come no one ever tells you when you're growing up that it never stops being complicated?" Linda stood facing him.

Tim shook his head silently. He had no answer for that one. He put his arms around Linda and she hugged him hard. "I will really miss you. You've become my best friend," she said into the shoulder of his jacket, struggling unsuccessfully to hold back the tears that filled her eyes.

ᘐ

Okay, she told herself, as she sat at her desk at home that night after the kids were bathed and in bed. *So we've got another situation to figure out. What do I want to be when I grow up?*

ᘐ

Linda stayed with Harcourt for some months after Tim was gone, but it wasn't the same without him there and she felt that soon it was going to be time for her to move on, too.

I hate getting dressed for work, I love jeans, T-shirts and tennis shoes, she thought as she brushed her teeth before bed, watching her own reflection in the mirror. *I hate driving on the freeway when the rest of the world is doing the same thing. I like to work before the sun comes up and I'm ready to quit when the sun goes down, even if it isn't five o'clock. I hate having to eat lunch because it's noon. I love breakfast at two o'clock in the afternoon. I hate being away from my kids for so many hours a day. I love watching them grow up, becoming so much themselves. I'm in awe of their funny, separate individualities. And I hate working for someone else. I push myself harder than anyone else could... What I do like, is writing.*

No, Linda *loved* writing. She loved to play with words. She liked to make them tell her stories, to get them to communicate what she was thinking to other people. And, ridiculous idealist that she was, she wanted very much to fix things.

Where am I going to get a job doing that? she thought.

➳

Linda knew that if she could find work that she really wanted to do, instead of moving papers around for someone else, she would bury herself in it.

Using the connections that she had made in the publishing industry — while still on the payroll at Harcourt, so that with Dan's bit of child support they could survive — she began submitting some of her articles to different editors and the response was surprisingly encouraging. Much of her writing was perceptive, provocative and well-researched, and it dealt with controversial, current issues.

Maybe, she told herself, *just maybe there's a market for what I love to do best. If I can just find a way to get my foot in the door and get a share of the freelance market. At least enough to handle the bills. Another piece of the puzzle of life to find and then put into its proper place.*

➳

For years she and Cathryn and Nick had managed to stay in contact with one another, even if it was only by way of Christmas cards every December. In the beginning, there were also letters a couple of times a year, filled with news about houses and jobs, and even some children stories.

Cathryn was too busy teaching and squeezing in courses for her Masters, she said, to start a family. And Carrie, in the beginning of their marriage, told Nick that she *couldn't stand the idea of being fat for months,* even though Nick was longing to have children. After some years, she relented and they had two sons. Nick was ecstatic with joy at being a father and he sent Linda snapshots of two little boys whose eyes looked so much like their father's, that she felt a nostalgic pulling in the area of her heart.

But the months in between the letters grew longer and longer and finally turned into years.

And now, for the past week, for no reason that Linda could

discover, whether she was busy working in her office, or talking to the kids, or reading a novel, she kept feeling her attention drift to Cathryn with a nagging apprehension, and sometimes to Nick, with a vague, fragmentary thought that she could not quite grasp.

She found herself day-dreaming, reminiscing, remembering things that she and Cathryn had done together. The first time they went skiing, if one could call it that, on the table-like surfaces of the Midwest, in Lisle, Illinois, where they fell in the snow and laughed so hard at each other's awkward snowplow that their sides ached. Then, feeling as if their fingers would freeze, they pulled off their gloves and captured the moments on bouncing, fuzzy, home movies.

Each memory drifted away and in its place Linda felt a gnawing concern that would not go away, a sense that something was wrong, something that was happening now, something bad that had to do with her old friends.

Linda tried to tell herself, *There isn't any reason for me to feel anxious, nothing's happened. There's nothing at all to attribute this feeling of uneasiness to, or my nervousness, the shivers across my shoulders when I start thinking about Cathryn.*

Cathryn had never revealed much about her life with Edward when she wrote, She carefully did not complain. But it was still evident to Linda that she was troubled, that there were problems, that their marriage was stormy. Linda got the idea that it was because of Edward that Cathryn stayed so far away from her family. From Cathryn's early letters, Linda knew that Edward had discouraged her from returning to Chicago to visit her parents and her brothers, in spite of innumerable invitations, pleas and offers of plane tickets. Worse, he did not welcome visits to their home. In her letters, she always made excuses for him and justified his behavior, but Cathryn's husband virtually disconnected her from every caring person she had known before him, and Cathryn allowed him to do so.

From the very beginning of their relationship, Edward had been possessive and jealous. "Look," he told her, "I have a lot of work to do and you need to finish school. There isn't that much time left for us to be together and I don't want to waste any of it." He held her lovely hands in his and leaned close to her. "Cathryn, I want you near me every spare second. Nothing is more important than us."

Her heart pounded in her chest hearing the intensity in his voice and seeing it in his dark eyes. Part of her felt flattered, but though Cathryn would not acknowledge it, a small bit of her was apprehensive. Edward was so unwilling to share her with anyone else. He kept his arm around her possessively or held her hand tightly in his wherever they went. Cathryn was swept away with what she saw as protectiveness in his actions, but then there was so little free time for Linda and Nick, for Steve or even her mother. Edward had her account for her every moment.

Edward was usually careful not to criticize Cathryn's friends, or her family, and he remained polite but distant with them. Every once in a while, though, Cathryn thought that she heard something in his comments, in his reactions, that was not quite right, almost sarcastic. "What hasn't your father succeeded at?" he questioned sardonically one night. "Sometimes it seems as if he's already done everything there is to do." His voice was quiet and subdued, the look in his dark eyes was unpleasant. Cathryn made excuses for him again, attributing it to his strong feelings for her.

He just thinks he has to compare himself to Daddy, he doesn't have to do that for me. He's just worried about being able to give me all the things he thinks are important. I love him, I don't care what things we have, she told herself.

The first time that he met her parents, Edward recognized that though they were cordial, they were not pleased about his relationship with their daughter and that they would never be happy about their marriage. He didn't care.

I'll have what I want, I'll show every one of them, he promised himself.

∼

Linda's hands were still, her fingers rested lightly on the keyboard. She couldn't remember ever having felt so confused about putting her thoughts on paper.

Funny, she thought, *earning my living by expressing myself with written words.* She typed a few sentences quickly, then leaned back, gazing thoughtfully at the screen. Tiny lines deepened at the center of her forehead.

What can I say to her that will make her call or write back right away and assure me that she's all right, that the peculiar thoughts I've been having are nothing more than my imagination going off in weird, inexplicable directions? she thought. *We'll both laugh and it'll feel wonderful to hear her voice again after so long. We'll meet for a long lunch by the ocean, maybe at the Chart House on Coronado and we'll make up for all the lost time.*

Linda tried to remember when the last letter was written, who wrote it and what was said. *I wrote to Cathryn after I left Harcourt, didn't I? My letters never came back and yet, I never got an answer from Cathryn after the last one, or didn't I?*

She abruptly deleted the sentences on the screen. Feeling confused and frustrated, she saved the salutation to Cathryn and turned the monitor off. She didn't even have a recent phone number and maybe the address she had wasn't a current one. Her fingernails bit into her palms as she doubled her hands into fists. She was angry with herself for letting Cathryn slip so far away. Still, unable to chase away the troubling, anxious rumble deep in her abdomen, Linda told herself again that she was being silly.

I don't really have any idea at all what's happening with Cathryn after all this time. I am just imagining things. Maybe, she thought, *I'm just looking for an excuse to call Nick. Ah, Nick…*

ॐ

After some years, Nick had abruptly decided that he could no longer practice law, completely shocking everyone around him.

That must have been three or four years ago, Linda figured, *when he just suddenly stopped being "the lawyer."* She had been startled to hear the news of him leaving the firm, not really believing it was true, even when her mother heard it from a friend in Florida who had used Smithson, Ellingsworth and Naples for legal representation for years.

Nick's communications to Linda, like Cathryn's, had been sporadic and somewhat restrained. His few letters and cards didn't tell her much about what must have been pretty difficult times. She called him when she heard about him leaving the firm, but he didn't sound like the same Nick. His voice was measured and careful. "Let's not waste time on unpleasant stuff in our few calls or letters, okay?" he said coolly. "Sometimes things just don't work out the way you think they're going to," he said, his voice resigned, dispirited. Many times after that, Linda had wanted to pick up the phone and call him.

Carrie, she told herself. *Carrie, Carrie, Carrie.*

Still, an image of Nick's warm smile and soft mouth, his laughing eyes and gentle, caring ways remained close, always so close. Sometimes, in a nostalgic, quiet mood, Linda closed her eyes for a moment, listened to some plaintive, but impassioned music that played in her head. Then she would see him with his arms invitingly outstretched towards her, but then moving imperceptibly away, before she could touch him, until he just disappeared into a light and indistinct void in the distance.

Her eyes darkened. The thought of Nick, though tantalizing, mesmerizing, was always saddening for Linda. She told herself at least a thousand times, *All it is, is the memory of a first, important crush that feels as though it will never go away, never end.* And then she pushed it away, but it always came back.

Carrie Martin. Carrie Martin. Mrs. Carrie Martin. Mrs. Carrie Nicolas Martin. Linda, for God's sake, make sense!

Yet she still wondered what it would be like to see him again. After all the years, she still felt a rush, a faster pulse and heat in her cheeks when she let herself think of his smiling eyes. Or the strength of his hand when he held onto her own hand and kept her from walking away, just for a moment, on that far off last time they had all laughed together.

ॐ

Stop … stop it. Just stop, damn it!

Trying to pull herself out of her memories, Linda turned to

the stack of paperwork that waited on the desk behind her. She was editing the rough draft of an article that she had written. In it she was questioning the sanity and results of medicating young children in school, in an apparent effort to improve or modify their behavior. Though it was becoming a common practice employed in schools with youngsters who demonstrated an excessive amount of energy, or what was more commonly referred to as *hyperactivity*, Linda was totally opposed to it.

She was appalled by the method of dealing with high energy levels in young children with drugs like Ritalin, and she had pounded out a scathing and fractious article denouncing such treatments and supporting her viewpoint with research of the subsequent results of those drugs on the children who had received them.

"Just a cursory glance at the warnings, precautions, adverse reactions, and the note on drug dependence in the *Physicians' Desk Reference*," she wrote, "makes one wonder how any person in his or her right mind, could see this as a sane way of handling a child who is too active, or has too much energy for the existing school system." She insisted, "Change the system. Don't alter the minds of our innocent children with potentially dangerous, although legal, drugs."

Linda met with children who had been treated with the drugs and she saw firsthand the less publicized, adverse results that she had read about. She wrote from profound emotion. Believing that the real problems were not being addressed, and that tremendous damage was being done to children too young to defend themselves against such *treatment*, and whose families were too uninformed or too ineffective to prevent such actions within the school systems, Linda wanted to bring the issue to the attention of more people with her article.

The topic made her adrenaline flow and for a little while, the unwanted memories of Cathryn and the disconcerting thoughts of Nick subsided. Linda got caught up in her cause.

Some critical problems in our society need to be looked at and handled, fast. People need to be more aware of what the so-called authorities are promoting, she determined.

She had read some very startling statistics in a newsletter: "Since 1960 there has been a 560% increase in violent crime, there has been a 419% increase in illegitimate births, a quadrupling in divorce rates, a tripling of the percentage of children living in single-parent homes, more than a 200% increase in the teenage suicide rate, and a drop of almost 80 points in the SAT scores."

And, our schools just keep getting worse and worse, Linda lamented, uncomfortably remembering inner city classrooms that she had visited in Chicago and Los Angeles.

And, yet, she found her thoughts returning to Cathryn, no matter how absorbed she became with her work.

Something just feels so damn strange, Linda considered again, chewing on her thumbnail for a moment, then reaching for her cup of coffee as she turned back to the unfinished article.

༈

If Cathryn had been out on the street and not sitting within the confines of the three bedroom home she shared with her husband and dog, she would have looked like one of the pathetic, homeless beings who habitually live outside on the downtown streets of cities like Los Angeles and San Diego.

There were smudges of dirt on her face. Her once lovely hands, hands that could have been photographed for hand lotion ads, were bruised and red, the fingernails ragged and grimy. There was an almost blank expression on her face, her eyes were wide and vacant, except for a glimmer of apprehension or fear.

She looked exactly like a homeless person, a street refugee with nothing but misery etched on her face and the clothes on her back, with a collection of grimy possessions in a grocery cart or plastic bag close by and cautiously guarded. Cathryn looked like that, except for the possessions. She looked as if she had nothing and no one in the world who cared for her.

༈

Though appearing destitute and worn beyond her years,

Cathryn did have something left. She had a lot of money, an enormous amount of money, in fact. Technically and legally, she was very wealthy. Her father had earned it, and the portion that was designated for his only daughter had been cleverly and secretly hidden from Edward. Cathryn was never told about the terms of her inheritance should her father die, and she had no idea that there was so much of it. Years ago, Cathryn had appeared to have everything that any person could want. Inside her head, however, were confusions, uncertainties, and private lost battles with adversaries that no one else could see but her. But to look at her or speak to her back then, one saw the impression she tried so hard to give, that she was extraordinarily lovely, happy, comfortable and in love.

Then she married Edward and Cathryn gave him the right to affect her life and future in a way that no human being should have over another.

Three

A dangerous doctor...

WHEN SHE WAS YOUNG, besides being so pretty, Cathryn also had a sweetness and intelligence about her. She was oblivious to her own beauty and that made her even more attractive to other people. Her family adored her. The only daughter after the birth of three sons, she could have grown up wretchedly spoiled from all of the attention that she received from her protective brothers and caring parents, but she didn't. Cathryn developed into a sensitive and appreciative child.

But, later, as a gentle, lovely, young woman, Cathryn attracted more attention than she knew how to handle. In her early teens, prettier and shapelier than others her age, she was more embarrassed than flattered by the inquiring looks, comments with sexual overtones and probing suggestions she received. She was uncomfortable and wanted to withdraw from the scrutiny, the searching looks that caused unwelcome feelings of fear in her abdomen and rose through her body. Instead of making her feel attractive and confident, the attention made her feel troubled and confused. Unable to deal with this uncomfortable anxiety, Cathryn stumbled onto a prevalent but profoundly destructive practice.

Cathryn began to compulsively eat her discomforts away. Not often, at first. Every once in a while when she was in the house alone, after she ate an ordinary meal, she would still feel empty. Some peculiar non-physical hunger remained and she felt unable to stop feeding herself. She would rummage around in the refrigerator and cabinets, and embarrassed, fill herself with the food that was least likely to be missed. Sometimes she grabbed several slices of bread and butter, then handfuls of Cheerios or leftovers from dinner, something that she could tell Anna she had fixed for lunch. The need to feed the insatiable, perplexing hunger grew more demanding. She began stopping on the way home at a grocery store, a fast food restaurant, a bakery, or all of them.

Each time, after she hurriedly prepared, and secretly ate the food, she carefully rid the kitchen of any remnants of her orgy. She cleaned the counters and put everything away, then she took the bag of wrappers and containers outside to the trash, and buried it beneath the rubbish.

For several precious moments in the beginning, the eating numbed her and took her attention off of whatever was really troubling her.

But this emotional over-eating conflicted with an enormous fear of becoming fat and unattractive. One day Cathryn overheard a conversation at school — the girls were talking about forcing themselves to throw up. Cathryn went into the bathroom and forced herself to vomit. This had a pathetically bittersweet result. Cathryn found that by putting her fingers down her throat, she could undo what she had done by stuffing her body with too much food. A few minutes after feeling the horrible discomfort of a distended stomach, a stomach that felt as if it were filled with lead, Cathryn could feel thin, light and empty again.

Cathryn became what was later to be identified as a bulimic. More and more often, she felt irrationally compelled to overeat and then she felt equally driven to rid her body of the food she had just ingested. She tried frantically to hide her behavior from everyone, fully believing that she was the only one on earth who was so crazy.

Cathryn tried repeatedly, in dozens of ways, to get her eating under control. She tried whatever the current fad diet was, and she could make it last for a few days or weeks. Sometimes the only control she felt she had was when she stopped eating completely and she would go for days at a time without any food at all. At the same time that Cathryn couldn't allow herself to gain weight, she couldn't find a way to stop stuffing herself with food, and those times became more and more frequent, whenever she was tense or upset or frightened or bored or lonely or scared or stressed or pressured or too happy or too sad.

⁓

Her parents began to realize what she was doing, but they did not yet know how incredibly tormented she was becoming in her virtually unseen struggles. Each of the solutions that Cathryn came up with seemed to become the next problem for her. No matter what she tried, no matter what resolve she mustered up, no matter what plan she made to change her pattern every Monday morning, she could not find a sane way to handle food, one that enabled her to feel thin, in spite of the times that she felt she had to overeat. At those times Cathryn simply felt that she had no choice.

As the dilemma grew more involved, Cathryn found herself constantly hiding her horrible secret from her parents and her brothers, and even from Linda. She became more uncomfortable with any attention that she got, and as food became a kind of drug for her, the vomiting became obsessive. More distraught, feeling frenzied, she tried not to eat anything at all for longer and longer periods of time. But whenever she allowed herself any food at all, the compulsion to stuff herself would begin again, and she would as secretly as possible carry out the rest of her destructive procedure. Forcing the food and damaging digestive juices up through her esophagus, irritated her throat, caued the glands under her jaws to swell, and began to erode the enamel of her teeth. Worse than the physical injury that she was doing to her body, the mental anguish overwhelmed her and she had no idea where to go for help. She couldn't let Linda or anyone know what she was doing, and she was constantly terrified that someone would discover her horrible secret.

After she overate, now almost daily, she would force herself to vomit, and then she scrubbed away at any evidence in the kitchen and the bathroom. Finally, she would shower and wash herself from head to toe, opening windows and spraying Lysol and bathroom cleaner. Even though the thought that someone could easily discover what she was doing was so horrifying to her, Cathryn couldn't make herself stop.

Some days she only drank tea and chewed on ice cubes, refusing to eat any food at all. No matter how carefully she tried to keep others from knowing, her parents saw, of course, and grew more alarmed. At night Cathryn dreamed about eating too much and sometimes she had dreams about starving herself.

Anna and Joseph quietly consulted different doctors without telling Cathryn, hoping to get some advice that would help their daughter. Most of the doctors wanted to give Cathryn appetite depressants, or they suggested simple diet plans.

No, this can't be the answer to whatever is making her so unhappy, Anna thought.

ॐ

One night Cathryn found herself walking slowly along the dark hallway from her bedroom in the middle of the night, her fingers lightly trailing along the wall, carefully not making any noise that might awaken her parents. She went downstairs, through the large foyer, past her father's study, through the kitchen and into the pantry, where she stood still staring at the shelves of food.

I haven't eaten anything for ten days, she thought. *I'll just make an egg and a slice of dry wheat toast. My body needs something. I'm too tired. No, it's not tired, I'm too weak. Just a couple of eggs and one piece… two pieces of dry toast. I can do that and go back to bed. I know I can do that.*

But as she stood at the refrigerator, her hand gripping the handle of the freezer door, the now familiar battle raged within her. She had no moderation left. It was as if a war were constantly being waged in her head. Her blood pumped through her blood vessels too rapidly, her eyes darted from the refrigerator in front of her to the table, to the doorway and back again. Her pulse raced.

She could feel a pounding in her chest and she heard it like thunder in her ears.

Don't! a tiny voice screamed. *Please, please, PLEASE don't do this. It messes up EVERYTHING. Pleeeeeze. No! Don't! Please!* The sobbing, frantic, tiny little voice spoke, but Cathryn knew it would stop once she put food into her mouth. Then the battle would end.

Just eggs and toast. I can handle that, she told herself again. But before she finished wiping the last bit of egg up with the last corner of the dry wheat toast, she knew that it wouldn't work. She wanted more. No, she *had* to have more.

And, then, as quietly as possible, Cathryn took the loaf of wheat bread from the freezer and made more toast. Two, four, six slices, spreading thick chunks of sweet whipped butter on them, ravenously devouring them, trying to satisfy an insatiable hunger. One that had nothing whatsoever to do with any physical need for nourishment.

She grabbed a handful of cookies that she didn't even really like and stuffed them into her mouth anyway. Then she tore into a plate of cold barbecued chicken and ate it, skin and all. That was something she would never do if she didn't plan to throw it up. She followed that with a bowl full of nuts and raisins and then a huge piece of apple pie that she defrosted in the microwave with a mound of ice cream. The ice cream made her cold and she shivered, standing in the kitchen in her pajamas and slippers. She quickly boiled a pot of oatmeal, covered it with butter and salt and ate it all, right out of the pot, burning the roof of her mouth in her rush. Her stomach hurt and she felt ashamed of herself once again.

She felt so ashamed.

Are you satisfied, you idiot? I can't believe you did that. You are such a worthless idiot. Her fingers pressed against the ache of her swollen tummy.

But while the angry voice in her head continued to disparage her, Cathryn went from the refrigerator to the pantry and then to the cabinets. She needed something else, she needed some more to eat before she finished off the third huge glass of Ginger Ale that would help bring the food back up from her stomach. She reached for some crackers.

⌇

Then she was in her bathroom, her head bent over the toilet bowl, the smell and sight of the partially digested food that she had already thrown up, reaching her nostrils and bringing tears of revulsion to her eyes. The water was running in the sink in a futile attempt to keep her parents from hearing the sounds of her gagging and retching as she pushed a wadded up hunk of wet toilet paper deep into her throat. The glands at the sides of her throat swelled up, and tiny purple lines appeared in the sensitive, clear skin around her eyes that were already puffy and red with her efforts to vomit.

Tears ran down her cheeks and mixed with bits of regurgitated food on her face, and as she straightened up for a moment, Cathryn saw her reflection in the mirror. The pain she felt at the sight of her face brought agonized, racking sobs of despair from her throat and she was certain the noises would not be concealed by the sound of the running water. Abject hopelessness overcame her and Cathryn's almost perfectly formed lissome body slumped to the bathroom floor, as if her slim frame could no longer support her weight. Remorse flooded over her. As she slouched down, she grabbed a damp washcloth from the sink and buried her face in it, sobbing.

⌇

"NO! NO! PLEASE, NO!" she woke herself up with her own scream piercing the darkness of her bedroom. She bolted upright in bed, perspiration sticking her pajamas to her skin, her face wet with tears. "Oh, God, no, please, no, no, no…." she sobbed, grabbing the pillow and pressing it against her face so that her mother and father would not hear her anguished crying.

After a few minutes, she calmed down and moved the pillow away. She looked around the dark room slowly, not certain where she was or what had happened. She looked at the clock on the night stand, it was three-thirty in the morning. She was in her own bed. Her hand went to her throat and she swallowed hard, her throat wasn't sore. Her glands weren't puffed up the way they were after she puked her guts out. She put one palm against her stomach, it felt flat.

"My God, what a nightmare," she breathed, relieved, shivering in the cool air. She got up and went to the bathroom and then got back in bed, scrunching down into a small, trembling ball under the covers. *Thank God it was only a dream.* Now tears of relief fell from her eyes onto the pillow and after a little while she fell asleep again.

In the master bedroom down the hall, Joseph pulled Anna close to him. His wife was sobbing. "What are we going to do for her, Joe?" Anna asked, her voice shaking. "What can we do for her? I can't stand her pain anymore."

"Anna, Anna, tomorrow I'll make some calls. I know Cathryn doesn't want us to interfere. But, tomorrow I'll make some calls. We have to do something. This is enough. I promise you, it will be okay. I'll make it okay."

Joseph did not know how he would make it be okay, though. He kissed his wife on her damp cheek and he fell asleep, still holding Anna close to him. He did not know how he would help his daughter this time. He had never felt that way with anything that had happened to his family before.

Finally, three days after the night that their daughter had awakened screaming from a nightmare in which she thought she had stuffed herself with food, and twelve days since she had eaten anything except tea and ice cubes, Anna and Joseph insisted that Cathryn see a psychiatrist.

And that was a tragic mistake, perhaps the worst so far in the life of the very beautiful Cathryn Silberg.

Cathryn began to see a well-known and highly respected psychiatrist by the name of Dr. Aaron Krauss. He was supposed to help her with her *eating disorder* and periods of depression. But her problems, instead of lessening, grew considerably worse.

Dr. Krauss was fifty-four years old. He was an active, well-built man, who played tennis and golf several times a week. At home where he lived with his wife of twenty-five years, he rode an exercise bicycle. He looked younger than his actual age. He was tall, with thick, graying hair and dark-rimmed glasses. His demeanor projected self-assurance and confidence and Dr. Krauss exuded authority. In fact, he gave the mistaken impression to many who came to him for help that they could trust him completely.

After her first self-conscious, nerve-racking moments, seated at the edge of a pale blue, overstuffed armchair in his quiet and insulated office, Cathryn did just that. She didn't know what else to do. Frightened and completely confused by her own bizarre behavior and her apparent inability to do anything about it, she was ready to try anything, even this.

ॐ

The nightmares grew worse. One night Cathryn dreamed that she was sitting in front of the TV, mechanically putting food into her mouth, not caring what it was or how it tasted, slowly chewing and swallowing one thing after the other for over an hour until her stomach was so badly distended that it felt as if it might burst. She could barely stand up, so strong was the painful pressure in her abdomen, and finally, she went to the bathroom to throw up, but her stomach would not respond. The tearing, sharp physical pain grew worse, and no matter what she did, she could not force the food back up out of her stomach, as if it were protesting the long months of abuse.

Panic-stricken, Cathryn went to her room and tried to lie down, but her insides hurt worse. It felt as if they were ripping apart. Thinking she might even die, Cathryn screamed for her mother, "MOM, PLEASE HELP ME!"

Cathryn was in an ambulance on the way to the emergency room of the hospital, screaming, "I'm so sorry, I'll never do it again. I swear I'll never do it again…" when she woke up with Anna at her side, trying to calm her down.

"Sh-h, honey, it was only a bad dream. Everything is all right." Her mother wiped her tear-stained face with a damp, warm wash-cloth. Then Anna put her arms around Cathryn and stroked her silky hair. Joseph stood at the doorway to her bedroom in his pa-jamas, his face troubled and tired.

⌁

Cathryn's parents genuinely believed that Dr. Krauss would help her and together they begged Cathryn to continue to see him, to give him a chance, at least for awhile. So she went to his office and she sat timidly in the big chair, answering his questions hon-estly, trying to tell him everything. Her hands fluttered a little in her lap and she dropped her chin, ashamed and embarrassed, while she recounted how much she ate, how she hid the food and the trash from her family, how she forced herself to vomit and how unbearable her life felt to her.

When she began to cry, Dr. Krauss handed her a box of Kleenex, stared intensely at her troubled, young face, still so beau-tiful in spite of her sad and reddened eyes, and he said, "There, there, everything will be okay. Tell me more about how you felt then."

⌁

And, so, at his urging, Cathryn relived her worst experiences, her terrors, her losses, her unpleasant feelings about looking falsely happy to others, of disappointing her parents, and of her utter ineffectiveness to change it all. As she spoke, each one of her un-comfortable feelings was right there in that room with her again. She felt the conflict through her abdomen, her chest felt constricted and the blood pounded in her temples while her palms grew damp.

But no matter how much she talked about it, Cathryn didn't understand how Dr. Krauss' questions, her answers or his advice could change or help anything. When she left, she often felt even worse than when she had arrived, and every once in a while there was the tiniest hint of that weird uneasiness in her stomach again, the kind that had to do with men and sex.

But what else was there to do?

᷒

Dr. Krauss knew what else there was to do. He gave her medication the very first time that she went to see him in his plush office in Highland Park, the affluent suburb just north of Evanston. Cathryn was terrified and unhappy before her appointment, feeling totally out of control and not knowing how she could ever get her life to be the way it appeared to other people. At the end of the first hour, Dr. Krauss opened his desk drawer and gave her some medicine. "To help with the feelings of depression," he said. Then he smiled as he put the small plastic bottle of tablets into her hand and patted her on the shoulder.

Cathryn took one of the tiny tablets as soon as she got home. But, afterwards, she felt uncomfortable about trying to handle her frenetic emotions with medicine. She didn't feel relaxed at all. Cathryn decided she didn't want to use the rest of the tablets. She didn't mention the medication to anyone, not even to her parents, and she put the bottle away under some sweaters in her dresser drawer. Something about the little, reddish brown tablets made her uneasy.

What do they do in my body that changes what's going on in my mind? she wondered. But she kept the bottle close at hand, hidden in her drawer, for a very long time, just in case.

Cathryn established a routine. Once a week she brought her problems to Dr. Krauss, continuing to hope that in their conversations, somehow, he would miraculously handle them for her.

But, still she could not identify the nagging, uncomfortable sensation that she frequently felt when she was alone with him in his office, when he looked at her in a certain way that seemed strangely familiar. And it made her uneasy, but she didn't know why.

᷒

The appointments with Dr. Krauss eventually became a darker secret for Cathryn than her bulimia had ever been. Though the meetings and conversations were not giving her the help she desperately sought, she kept going. She had promised her parents, and she couldn't think of anything else to do.

But now there was something even worse than the eating and vomiting that she needed to keep anyone from knowing about.

⠀ᴓ⠀

After several weeks of seeing Cathryn, listening to her stories, watching her beautiful, yet vulnerable face become contorted with the painful emotions of her recollections, Dr. Krauss began walking her to the door of his office at the end of the hour. But before he opened it for her, he would put his arms gently around her and hug her close to him.

At first she was surprised and startled, but then Cathryn thought, *He knows what he's doing, for God's sake, he's a well-known, respected Highland Park psychiatrist. He knows what he's doing.*

So, she rigidly leaned against him, and then hurried from his office, only to return for her next scheduled appointment, truly believing that the help she sought was within that room, instead of within herself.

⠀ᴓ⠀

After listening to Cathryn tell him about the events of her week and how she succeeded or failed to handle the compulsions with eating that arose, Dr. Krauss continued to evaluate each situation, giving Cathryn his suggestions, ways to handle each incident. When she was ready to leave, he put his arms around her and drew her into an embrace that continued to confuse and bewilder her. Then he told her, "I will see you next time," and he opened the door for her.

⠀ᴓ⠀

Cathryn met Edward during this period of time, and as she began seeing more of him, she talked about her growing infatuation for Edward with Dr. Krauss. Spending time with Edward joyfully took her attention away from eating and vomiting, the episodes lessened somewhat, and she happily reported this to Dr. Krauss.

But the confusions in her therapy sessions continued and Cathryn was becoming more troubled. The brief hugs at the end of each hour gradually developed into longer periods of time with Dr. Krauss pressing her body against his and holding her there, as if this was perfectly normal behavior between a therapist and his patient.

Cathryn's uncertainties about herself — her sexuality, her ethics, her attractiveness — whirled furiously in her mind. Her physical attraction to Edward was very strong, but Edward was deliberately keeping her at a distance. There was nothing attracting her in that way to Dr. Krauss, and, yet, he was bringing her physically closer to him.

Momentarily Cathryn lost her own viewpoint about right and wrong, what was correct and what was incorrect. Failing to trust her own judgment, she allowed herself to be swept along by the determination of others. And that was her next tragic mistake.

꒰

Lying in bed at night, she thought about her doctor's oddly sexual behavior. *This doctor is educated and respected. He must know what he's doing. But is he supposed to act this way? He's my therapist.* She puzzled in the dark, alone, feeling as if she were going mad. She came to realize that she could not bear the sexual situation that Dr. Krauss was creating between them. She tried hard to explain it away, telling herself, *He's my doctor, I'm depending on him for help.*

While Cathryn was struggling with her tremendously strong attraction to Edward, he, too, was forcing her to confront her sexuality, but also in a way that was strange and confusing to her. Edward seemed to delight in deliberately and subtly arousing her, but then abruptly stopping, moving away from her, smiling, telling her they would wait a little longer, leaving Cathryn dizzy, feeling aroused, unfulfilled and as if she had done something or felt something that was terribly wrong.

Strangely, though, with her attention and her emotions so sharply shifted to her sexual desires, desires that blazed higher and hotter every time she was near Edward, her need to eat and throw up diminished. And, the nightmares stopped. Because of this, Cathryn was reluctant to question exactly where her new confusions were coming from.

If I tell Mom and Dad that I think Dr. Krauss is coming on to me, making sexual advances for God's sake, they'll think I've completely lost my mind. Dr. Krauss has treated so many people they know, and they all rave about him. He's practically an institution in Highland Park. He's been practicing there for over twenty years. Who would believe me if I said anything about this? Besides, he hasn't done anything wrong, not really.

Cathryn was at Edward's apartment late one night. He turned on the stereo, held her and touched her, teasing her into a burning frenzy. Then he stopped. Before he took her home, Cathryn begged him to really make love to her. He told her again, "Not yet, not just yet," with a strange satisfied expression that was not quite a smile.

Now, in the familiar armchair in the corner of Dr. Krauss' office, she trustingly struggled to explain to her therapist how physically drawn to Edward she was, how much she wanted to be with him, how important his opinions were to her and how she wanted him to make love to her. She dropped her chin and averted her eyes as she stammered, "I...I...I've never f...felt like this about anyone before."

Dr. Krauss, smiling, almost imperceptibly narrowed his eyes. There was a fleeting, flashing expression in them that was not at all happy, but rather irritated and annoyed. As Cathryn timidly raised her chin and looked up at him, the displeasure that was there a moment ago disappeared, and Dr. Krauss slowly nodded his head at her, as if he understood what she was telling him completely.

"But, it's close to the end of our hour," he told her, getting up from his chair. Cathryn thought that there was still plenty of time left but she obediently stood and slowly moved toward the door, pictures of Edward with his mouth and fingers on her lips and body still whirling in her head.

Dr. Krauss put his large, strong hands on her shoulders and gently turned her towards him. He raised her chin with one fingertip and kissed her on the mouth, so lightly and so gently that

Cathryn felt off balance and completely uncertain.

Am I turning some genuine expression of caring and affection into something sordid and ugly? Maybe this is all in my head, all my fault.

But now as she turned towards the door, Dr. Krauss put his hands against the small of her back and pressed his fingers into her body firmly, and brought her so close to him that she could smell the scent of soap on his skin. She felt the heat of his body and then against her belly, she felt his pulsing hardness against her. Realizing that he was sexually aroused, Cathryn became terrified. She quickly pushed herself away from him and pulled at the doorknob in a panic, her eyes wild and frightened.

He stepped slowly away from her, but he leaned his hand against the door holding it closed. His eyes were strangely warm and soft as he smiled down at her.

"Cathryn, Cathryn, you are so lovely and so frightened of your own feelings. Don't be afraid, Cathryn, I am here only to help you, I promise you."

And then he reached for her and took her back into his arms, in a warm hug that was so innocently affectionate, so non-threatening, that it could have been from her father. She looked up into his smiling, gentle eyes and she truly believed that she was imagining or creating the horrors herself. Cathryn never spoke one word about the incident with Dr. Krauss to anyone.

Cathryn continued to see Dr. Krauss because she was too afraid to stop. Superstitiously, she believed that if she didn't keep her appointments, the binges, her compulsion to vomit and the horrible nightmares would come back again.

In a week, she went back to see him and again told him of her fears and dreams and her growing passion for Edward. This time, Dr. Aaron Krauss got up out of his chair before the hour was half over and he moved towards her. He walked across to where she sat and took her hands in his, gently, but insistently, pulling her from the chair.

"Dear Cathryn, let me hold you for just one minute." She stood up at his command, as if she were hypnotized, and he put his arms around her and held her closely against him without moving, until the confused emotions of her own sensuality rose in her body. He continued holding her tightly against his chest, while he slowly stroked her lower back with his fingers, and then the beginning roundness at the top of her buttocks. He felt her relax a little against him and he brought his hands slowly around to her sides, still holding her tightly, closely. He looked down into her beautiful and very frightened eyes.

"I wouldn't hurt you for the world," he whispered, lightly touching her cheek with his mouth. "I promise you Cathryn, I will not hurt you," he said quietly, touching her lips softly with his own.

In spite of herself, she felt her mouth responding to his, she felt her body leaning towards the hardness of him, and then he tightened his arms around her, pressing his mouth harder against hers. He brought his right hand slowly around to just below her breasts, barely touching the swell of her breast just below the nipple with his thumb, in a very slow, deliberate stroking motion. Cathryn felt as if she could not breathe, her heart was pounding, she felt an overwhelming, heated, aching, longing between her thighs.

"Oh God, no," she sighed, pulling her head back with a little gasp.

He put his hand behind her head and drew her to his shoulder, still holding her tightly against him. She was aroused and confused, but at the same time there was such comfort in his certainty, his strength. She allowed herself to be held by it and she did not struggle.

He felt her relax in his embrace, again his mouth sought hers, slowly determinedly tasting her innocent and passionate sweetness, savoring it. The wave of Cathryn's passion rose stronger in her body. She felt him slowly move his hand down her side, along her jeans where they followed the curve of her hip, and he pressed his hand against her, between her legs, rubbing her slowly, hard, with his fingers. Her knees were weak, but she pressed upwards towards him, closer into his embrace. She wanted him to keep rubbing against her like that.

More, God, more, more, she thought.

Her hips undulating, responded to the rhythm of his hand. His tongue was barely inside her mouth, gently, investigating, then pressing. Hotter, fuller waves of passion washed over her. She wanted him to keep touching her and she wanted to run away at the same time. Suddenly she ripped herself out of his arms and pulled back away from him.

"I can't do this," she whispered, tears coming to her eyes.

"It's all right, Cathryn, I understand. It's all right," he soothed, putting his arms around her again, but holding her a few inches away from him. "I care about you very much. I just want you to remember that," he told her. He gently patted the tears on her cheeks with a clean, white handkerchief. She looked up at his face, feeling the confusion engulfing her like thirty foot ocean waves, causing her to sink down and down.

"I know. I know," she said in a muted voice. "I have to go."

"Yes, of course. I will see you at four o'clock on Thursday," he proclaimed. He opened the door and she stepped through it, tears in her eyes, not seeing or understanding anything at all, but knowing that when Thursday came she would come back to see him again.

Four

The evil of ECT...

PARTLY TO RESOLVE HER new problems with Dr. Krauss, Cathryn decided that she would marry Edward. She persuaded herself to believe that marriage would take care of all her problems, the compulsive eating, the vomiting and the starvation. Being married to Edward also would give her a solution to what was happening in her meetings with her highly respected psychiatrist. She would agree to become Edward's wife, he would finally really make love to her and she would belong to him and that would be the end of it.

&

Cathryn's father, Joseph, had come to the U.S. as a poor immigrant from Germany. He settled his young family, a wife and his first son, in Chicago. Then he went to work with furious intention to pay back the relatives who had helped him get started in his new country.

In his business ventures, Joseph had the proverbial Midas touch. He could do nothing wrong.

In the very beginning, he borrowed some money and opened a tiny wholesale jeweler's store on the third floor of the Maller's Building on Wabash Avenue. It sat in the middle of bustling downtown Chicago, next to the roaring, rattling noise of the elevated train tracks. The building, teeming with wholesale jewelers, had been nicknamed "The Den of Forty Thieves" and Joseph Silberg ultimately proved himself to be the hero, Ali Baba.

With a fervor to succeed, unusual honesty and energy, Joseph made the tiny business grow. People liked doing business with him. They trusted him in a field where trust was not easily earned, and in a few years the store expanded beyond the expectations of its founder.

Eventually Joseph brought his two older sons, Martin and Keith, into the business, while his youngest son, Steve, finished school. Martin and Keith were still very young, but they, like their father, were ambitious and hard-working, and the business continued to grow. They moved to the fifth floor of the Maller's building where they rented half of the enormous space for their own use, while other jewelers, who often came to Joseph for advice and materials, clustered in smaller shops in the remaining area.

After some years, Joseph was content to let his two older sons carry the burden of the business while he investigated other enterprises. He bought some shares in AT&T, and the stock split shortly afterwards and rose. It split again and still rose. The financial gain kept increasing. Joseph invested some of this money in other stocks, with the knack and foresight to choose smaller, unknown companies that subsequently grew rapidly and rewarded him with handsome dividends.

With this new wealth, Joseph looked for still other ways that he could make his money grow, viewing it as the challenge of a game provided by his adopted country.

One day Joseph had lunch with a longtime friend who told him about a plan to develop land out west in an area called Laughlin. Joseph had never heard of it, but he decided to fly to Nevada to see the arid, flat property along the Colorado River, which, as recently as 1970, was nothing more than a nameless bait shack. It was far removed from anything that Joseph considered civilization, and it showed no evidence of growth in the near future, but Henry Rogers was a good friend and Joseph wanted to help him if he could. He invested in Henry's development project for the land just before Laughlin emerged as the newest gambling mecca in the entire country. The homes that Henry built were sold as fast as he could put them up.

In the early eighties, Joseph, still fascinated with the complexities of the land development game, decided to take a look at another new area. He took Steve with him and they flew to the northernmost part of San Diego County. What they found was another empty, flat, arid space called Rancho California, just east of the old cattle and cowboy town of Temecula.

Joseph decided to go forward and invest, and his judgment was correct again. The area mushroomed over the next few years and Joseph earned more money than he could easily spend during the rest of his lifetime. He began making financial plans for the futures of his three sons and his daughter while he continued to find other advantageous investment projects. Steve, now absorbed with land development, soon proved that he was as good at finding locations in which to invest as his father.

Joseph began to relax a little and he read constantly. He and Anna did some extensive traveling while their sons worked, steadily increasing their family and wealth. Eventually, Martin, Keith and Steve were all married, and they had children for Anna and Joseph to enjoy, while their only sister grew further away from all of them.

In his heart, Joseph never held Cathryn responsible for the estrangement between them. He blamed it on her husband, whom Joseph had sized up from the first moment. He told Martin "Edward is arrogant, domineering, hungry for power and motivated by money. But he wants someone to hand it to him, he doesn't think he's supposed to work for it.

"He's a misguided son of a gun, with no purpose, no identity, no ethics. Cathryn is too naive to see these things."

In his mind, he prayed, *Dear God, if our only daughter would just find a way out of the mistake she made when she fell in love with that man, that miscreant who separates her from her family and the dreams that we will always have for her.*

Joseph knew positively that there was one thing he could do that would affect the mistake that Cathryn had made. He could control her access to his wealth. Cathryn would never have considered the idea of a prenuptial agreement when she married Edward, and she would never have believed that Edward could have any interest in her father's fortune.

Cathryn believed that when she and Edward were married they would be together forever. Joseph saw things concerning Cathryn and Edward differently, however. He decided to take specific steps towards the righting of the iniquity.

လာ

Joseph could control the disbursement of his fortune to Cathryn and he could keep it out of Edward's hands, if his lovely daughter was too credulous to see the flaws in the decision she made. Joseph had an elaborate trust set up, in which his money was stringently, cautiously doled out directly to Cathryn. Joseph planned it so that the rest of what he intended to be her share of his amassed wealth was withheld from her until certain specific requirements were met.

The terms under which Cathryn could receive her portion of Joseph's estate — whose value, as a result of her father's skill, prudence and lack of extravagance, had grown to several million dollars — were very specific.

Joseph was not going to allow Edward to hurt his daughter and use her money to do it. He would not allow Edward to benefit from the money that Cathryn was entitled to inherit, not under any circumstances. Joseph didn't discuss this with anyone except his trusted lawyer and friend, Don Castleman. Neither his wife, Anna, nor his three sons knew to what lengths he had gone to protect his daughter from Edward.

It was agreed between the two of them that under any and all circumstances, Don would see to it that Joseph's wishes were followed exactly.

လာ

After Cathryn married Edward and they moved to California, it finally became evident, even to her, that she had made a grave mistake. Once he was Cathryn's husband, Edward made little attempt to mask any of his darker characteristics. Sullen and angry, frequently losing his temper and shouting, he frightened her at first, and then his behavior merely caused Cathryn to stay out of his way as best she could.

At some level of awareness, she finally knew that she had married him to overcome her inability to deal with the attention she received from men.

But there was one positive change for her now that she was Edward's wife. Her compulsions towards bulimia subsided. Despite Edward's stormy and unpredictable disposition, Cathryn still felt protected by her marriage. If another man even glanced at her for more than a moment, she flashed the band on her left hand with an expression that demanded, *How dare you?*

However positive that one aspect of her relationship was, the rest of it revealed itself as destructive and ugly. Edward was not going to allow Cathryn to be influenced by her wealthy family, though he certainly would have liked access to the entire income that her complicated trust rationed out to her. But his father-in-law, whom Edward envied and hated for his successes and his power, had evidently found ways to avoid that happening, for now.

I can wait, Edward thought.

Edward, obsessed from the very beginning with preventing Cathryn from getting away from him, first insisted that they move across the country to California. Once there, he objected to her frequent phone calls back home, constantly telling her, "I'm trying to establish our independence from your father's money, and how can I, if you keep calling long-distance, running up our bills, sabotaging the budget I've painstakingly struggled over?" He didn't hide his enormous displeasure when her mother, father or one of her brothers called, and there was very little time when she was ever in their house alone, without Edward's inhibiting, stultifying presence.

In the beginning, Cathryn would do absolutely anything to try to please her husband.

჻

Edward, seeking his illusive power, went from one unsuccessful business venture to another, finally settling bitterly into a mediocre position in the city's planning department. Meanwhile, Cathryn taught school, and for a while she did well. She was happy working with the children. Her efforts and enthusiasm were appreciated and eventually she was promoted to an assistant principal's position in her school district.

Instead of being pleased, Edward, jealous of everything his beautiful wife had and did, was irritated by her accomplishment. He became critical and verbally abusive to her about her work. Finally, with Cathryn crying and upset, he taunted her about how absurd she would look, running back to her family and admitting that she had made a mistake.

"I can see you telling them," he sneered, "that your perfect marriage is a failure."

Cathryn suffered with her marriage, trying ceaselessly to make it make sense. But life was becoming a living hell. Edward argued with her constantly. He found fault with her cooking and he criticized how she dressed. In his attempt to control and direct her life he succeeded in one thing. He made her more confused and unhappy as time went on.

෴

One day Edward wouldn't stop yelling at her. He berated her for a long time about how incapable she was until she couldn't stand it anymore. Cathryn felt crushed and broken inside when she went to her room and pushed things aside in her dresser drawers until she found the tiny brown plastic bottle that Dr. Krauss had given her the first day she was in his office. She had never taken the rest of the tablets but had kept them hidden away.

Now, in the bedroom of the home she shared with Edward, she studied the label on the bottle.

Tofranil, she read. *One tablet every four hours.*

She stood there with the bottle in her hand, remembering her visits to his office, how the room looked, the sound of Dr. Krauss' voice, and then she felt the heated memory of his mouth and hands on her body. She shuddered. She didn't know if the tablets could still have any effect, but after staring at the bottle for a long time, she opened it and quickly swallowed four of the small pills.

What's the difference? Tears were streaming down her cheeks. *Damn Edward. Damn Dr. Aaron Krauss,* she sobbed to herself. *Maybe now something he did will help,* she thought. *Maybe now.*

࿐

The continuous fighting was making Cathryn feel as if her life was being ripped apart. She was afraid and ashamed to tell her parents what a mess she had made out of everything. As long as the little bottle of tablets lasted, she found some solace in the numbness that they caused in her. Edward didn't know that she was taking the pills, but he knew that some of her fight was gone and he liked that. He believed that he was winning. And as Cathryn became more passive, Edward became louder and more abusive.

࿐

One Saturday night they argued about something so insignificant that Cathryn couldn't even remember what it was later on. She was crying softly, her head bent and her lips and hands trembling. Edward sat in his chair, smirking and said cruelly, "What's the matter, Princess? Are you going to call your daddy now?" She pressed her hands to the sides of her head covering her ears, but he kept on in a belittling, sneering voice. "Go ahead, call and tell them how mean and nasty your husband is."

"Enough, please, stop," she sobbed. She ran from the room and Edward watched her go into the bedroom where she began desperately pushing the clothes aside in her dresser drawer until she found the medication. She put the last three tablets into her mouth and then she looked up, startled to see him standing in the doorway watching her, smirking, his arms crossed on his chest. The small plastic bottle dropped from her hand.

Cathryn stood motionless, her arms outstretched and her hands frozen in the space in front of her, terrified of what her husband might do next, but Edward only smiled at her for a long, silent moment. Then he said soothingly, "God, Cathryn, I've been such a jerk. I'm sorry. I love you. You are so beautiful. I just get worried I could lose you and then I act like an idiot. It's not going to be like this anymore, I promise." He put his arms out towards her and with tears falling from her eyes, she went to him. "I'm so sorry, baby, I'm so sorry," he said, holding her trembling body close to his.

☞

The next morning, at his desk at work, Edward picked up the telephone and called an acquaintance of his, a doctor who had been anxious for months to have the city change the zoning on a property he owned. Edward looked down at the empty brown plastic bottle, turning it over in his hand, while he explained that his wife had run out of a prescription medication she took occasionally "for her spells of depression."

"Can you prescribe something to calm Cathryn down, Jack? She's been a nervous wreck." Edward put the bottle down on his desk and smoothed his dark hair back with his free hand, glancing at his reflection in the glass door of the cabinet next to him. His mouth curved into a smile, but his eyes remained dark and unwavering.

"Yes, Jack, that would really be helpful, a terrific favor. Thanks, Jack."

After work Edward stopped and picked up a refillable prescription for Valium and had it filled, the first of many times to come, at the drug store across the street from the City Planning Department, before he went home to have a quiet dinner with his beautiful, young wife.

Once home, he put his arms around Cathryn, who smiled up at him timidly as she took a roast out of the oven. Edward kissed her cheek tenderly. Then he went to wash his hands, an eldritch grin spreading across his face, reflected in the mirror looking back at him, as he dried his hands on the bathroom towel. He walked slowly up the stairs into his office, went to his desk and put the receipt for the medicine in a box and then he put the box into the bottom drawer of the desk and closed and locked it. He was still grinning strangely to himself.

☞

Though Cathryn couldn't stand the bitter fighting anymore, the idea of turning to her family with the situation that she found herself in was not an alternative for her. When Edward, calm and caring, suggested that perhaps if she took some medication for her upsets, things would go better for them, Cathryn wearily and compliantly began to numb the fears, anxieties and tensions that were overwhelming her.

After several months, Cathryn became unable to function without the pills. With Edward's eager help, she developed a physical and psychological dependence on the drug he had gotten for her. When she tried to go just days without it, she experienced uncomfortable body tremors, harsh muscle cramps, sweating and sometimes vomiting, even if she had eaten very little. This was more than she could stand.

Life feels better with the pills now, she told herself. Or so it seemed.

However, even this change didn't stop Edward from provoking arguments. And eventually Cathryn made yet another mistake, one that would eventually affect her ability to live her own life. Permanently.

♂

It was 7:20 in the morning. Edward was showered and dressed for work and he was sitting at the kitchen table watching her, a cup of coffee in his hand. Cathryn was at the sink, her hands immersed in hot, soapy water. Her eyes were red from crying. Edward had begun their morning with complaints that the house was dirty, sneering at the way she was dressed in jeans and a T-shirt, and now he was snarling at her about how much money she spent on groceries. She made a small sniffling sound.

"For Christ's sake, Cathryn! You're not even working."

That's how you wanted it! she raged inside her head, but fearfully, her lips made no sound at all.

"You're home all day. Can't you even do a decent job with that? What the hell are you crying about now?" He slammed his coffee cup down, spilling the hot liquid on the table, his face contorted with anger.

She had already taken two Valium. Her hands were shaking, but she wiped them on a dish towel, and holding onto the counter, trying to be calm, with her back to him, she said despondently, "I can't go on like this anymore. I want to go back to Chicago to see my family."

Cathryn turned slowly away from the sink towards Edward, who was glaring furiously at her and she said to him, "We're both miserable. I think we should get a divorce." Her voice was wooden. She leaned against the sink.

He didn't say anything. He was quiet for several minutes, sitting across from her in his chair, staring into her eyes and puffing on the pipe he held in his hand. His eyes were very dark. Cathryn could see the blood pulsing in the veins at his temples and his left hand was clenched into a tight fist. Cathryn felt her heart pounding as if it would burst from her chest. Her knees were weak and she pressed her body back against the sink for support. Then Edward's face softened a little.

"Cathryn, we have to work this out," he told her, his voice quiet and even, but terribly strong. "I can't be without you, do you understand? Tell me exactly what it is that I need to do to make you stay and I swear, I'll do it. If you go back to Chicago, I know I'll never see you again and I would kill both of us first." He paused for a moment and then he said, "I mean it, Cathryn. I would kill both of us."

He said the words so quietly that at first she thought she didn't hear him correctly. She looked over at him, tilting her head to the side, thinking, *He's very upset, he's joking.*

But the expression on his face was harder and colder than she had ever seen it before. His eyes, though narrowed and dark, had pinpoints of light in their very centers that seemed directed at Cathryn with the intensity of tiny, high-powered search lights. She wanted to turn away and run from the room, but her muscles felt like loose rubber bands and her vision was blurred with tears. Her body felt out of her control. Even though she wanted to turn away, her eyes remained fixated on his as if she had no choice.

For the first time, Cathryn realized how much danger she was in from her own husband. Chills went up her back and arms and she shuddered, staring at him in disbelief, unwilling to see the madness in his eyes. But it was there, and she knew, finally she knew.

Edward wasn't kidding with her. He meant what he said. He was really threatening her. She knew in that instant that he could do something insane. He could hurt her or himself or both of them.

Her mind, dulled by the medicine, tried frantically to formulate a plan, something that she could say or do that he would believe. She knew that she really had to get away from him. And, while her mind worked furiously trying to think of a way to leave the house peacefully and be away from Edward once and for all, her husband had already made up his own mind about how he would make absolutely certain that she would remain with him forever.

๛

Like Loki, the God of strife in Scandinavian mythology, Edward was cunning and wicked but handsome and witty. Like Loki, the Gods seemed to like him for his cleverness and he often helped them with their problems. Unlike Loki, Edward remained unchained and he was able to act out his destruction.

๛

Edward urged Cathryn to take three more Valium and to lie down. "We'll work this out," he told her, watching her long eyelashes flutter softly. He pulled a blanket over her shivering body and she snuggled up under it.

"…slipping further into my place where there are no rough edges, no sharp corners…," she mumbled, looking up quizzically at Edward as if he were a stranger. *Now it will be nice if he just goes away and leaves me alone,* she thought, closing her eyes.

Edward left for work soon after and as he drove out of the driveway, Cathryn sat up, walked shakily over to the window and watched the car disappear down the street. Then she got back in bed and reached for the telephone to call her father.

I'll tell him everything, she vowed. *I'll beg him to help me.*

But her hands were shaking and she was horribly frightened.

First, I need to take some Valium and I'll clean up the house a little, she decided, her stomach aching and her small flash of courage quickly dissipating.

"Did I finish the dishes?" she asked aloud.

I'll call in a few minutes, she told herself, turning over and pulling the pillow closer. *I just need to get my thoughts together first, so I don't sound so nuts. That'll be better. Then I won't upset them.*

⸙

Cathryn took another Valium and leaned forward to stare at her reflection in the bathroom mirror. Her face was pale and there were dark shadows under her eyes. She drifted absently about the house, picking up towels and clothes for the laundry, washing the dishes that she had left in the sink. A floating, detached feeling from the drug took over and she sat down on the couch and turned on the TV.

She drifted in and out of sleep for the next few hours and when she woke, she took more Valium from the bottle on the coffee table, washing it down with cold coffee from breakfast. She forced herself to get up off the couch, barely managed to wash her face, comb her hair and put a frozen casserole into the oven before five o'clock. When Edward came home less than an hour later, he kissed her cheek and she smiled at him from the dreamlike safety of the drug.

Where there are no sharp edges, she thought — and then Cathryn dreamily went about fixing her husband a drink before dinner.

⸙

"Dear God, Edward, don't do this to me," she pleaded. "DON'T DO THIS TO ME. I DON'T WANT TO GO. Please let me stay here, please don't make me go. Please, please, please! I don't need a hospital. I won't do it again, I'll stay in the house. I'll do whatever you say," she begged. "I don't want to go to a hospital. I'm scared. Please, Edward, please stop! Don't do this to me," she sobbed from inside the bathroom where she had fled from him, but where he now held her captive. She pounded on the inside of the door with the palms of her hands, while tears streamed down her face and her hair fell wildly into her eyes.

Edward held onto the doorknob, barely leaning his weight away from the door on the other side. Cathryn was unable to open it. Summoning every bit of her strength, she pulled and yanked at the door, but she was no match for Edward. Well over six feet tall and more than two hundred pounds, he easily held her in the small bathroom until her hysterical, agonized pleading grew louder.

Furiously, he pushed his shoulder against the door, and at the same time he tightened his hand and turned the knob. Startled by the door opening, Cathryn fell backwards against the sink and struck the corner of the cabinet with her lower back. She was stunned with pain for a moment. Her face was wet with tears and the little bit of make-up that she wore was smudged about her eyes. She instinctively raised her arms in front of her face as he came close to her, his face livid with rage.

"You will do as I say," he fumed an inch from her face. "You will learn that you will do exactly as I say and exactly when I say it. Do you understand me?" he hissed at her.

She slumped to the floor sobbing and he stopped for a moment, clenching both fists, suppressing a strong desire to kick at her soft, pathetic body. He reached into his pocket and took out a small bottle of pale blue tablets.

"Take these now," he commanded, pushing the Valium into her mouth with his fingers. She coughed and spit them back and he slapped her hard across the face. "You stupid little bitch, you don't get it, do you? I will tell you what to do and you will do it." His face came close to hers. He was furious. The blood vessels in his neck popped out as if they might burst.

He's going to kill me right now, she thought. The room whirled around her as he grabbed her hair, pulling her head back with one hand. With the other hand, he opened the bottle again. Edward spilled four of the pills into her mouth. Then he glared into her eyes and held his fist in front of her face, daring her to defy him again. She sobbed and swallowed the pills.

Just seconds afterwards, Edward knelt by her side and pulled her into his arms. Suddenly he was gentle and his voice was pleading. Softly he told her, "Cathryn, Cathryn, it will be okay, I promise. Baby, you know I love you. I need you. You can't leave me, baby, not ever. I couldn't stand losing you. Everything's going to be fine, I promise. You know I'll always take care of you no matter what. You belong to me, baby. You're just confused, upset right now. I'll make everything all right. I promise. Just relax, let the pills calm you down. The hospital will help, that's all, it's just for a few days, honey. You'll see things more clearly, as they really are, that's all. I promise. You've been under so much strain, but we can fix everything. They'll make you feel better, honey, that's all," he crooned to her, while she sobbed in his arms. Cathryn began to drift.

Maybe he's right. Maybe he's right, after all. Isn't Edward always right about everything? she asked herself as she began to slip deeper into her world without any sharp edges.

వ

Edward was positive that he was right when he had told her to quit her job. "So we can spend more time together and we'll go to Europe on my vacation," he had explained. The pressure that Cathryn felt was too much for her. She was trying desperately to cope with Edward's unrelenting abusiveness at home and at the same time attempting to appear confident and in control at work. She didn't argue with him. Cathryn just did what he told her to do, she sadly gave notice to the school district.

As Edward had promised, he took her to Europe. It was a horrible ten days full of conflict and misery. Nothing made him happy and he fought with her constantly. Cathryn sent pictures to her parents and one of the two of them in front of the Louvre to Linda. She wanted to show her family and her friend how happy she was, how well they were doing.

Cathryn's memory of their day at the Louvre, perhaps the most beautiful piece of Louis XIV architecture in existence, remained distinct and painful. She had tried hard to look happy and care-free when a passer-by offered to snap the shot of the two of them together. Earlier, she and Edward had spent the morning in their hotel room arguing heatedly over how stupidly she had packed their things. Then, when she took some Valium, Edward stopped berating her. He had become caring and kind again, as if the medication had an effect on him as well as on Cathryn.

"I'm going to take you to see Venus de Milo and the Mona Lisa. Da Vinci worked on that painting for four years," he told her blithely, as if nothing upsetting had taken place between them. Cathryn was still trembling inside, but she nodded her head in agreement to Edward and smiled as bravely as she could at her husband.

۰۲

Cathryn tried to open her eyes, but she couldn't. They were too heavy. She felt as if bags of wet clay were pressing against them, holding them closed. She kept struggling to raise her lids, and, finally, through her lashes she could see that she was in a hospital room. A doctor stood by her bed. Edward was there. She could hear him, sounding attentive, a concerned husband. He didn't notice that she had awakened from her deep, drugged sleep.

"She's been having these…these spells more often, Doctor," he was saying. Cathryn tried to shake off the drowsiness that enveloped her, but she was too tired. Her arms felt weighted and too heavy to move. There was an IV set up next to her bedside, and with great effort, she moved her heavy eyelids a little and watched the tiny drop of liquid trickle into the plastic tubing and make its way down towards her arm. Then her eyes closed again, but she didn't sleep. She could still hear Edward's voice as he spoke to the doctor. It sounded anxious, but muffled and far away.

"I'm worried about her all the time. I don't know what I'd do without her. I'm worried she's going to keep hurting herself. The medication isn't controlling her upsets any more. It doesn't seem to be doing anything.

"She left the house yesterday when I was at work and the police found her wandering alone in the parking lot of the train station! She didn't have her purse with her and she wouldn't tell them where she lived. She said she didn't have a home. She's getting worse. You need to help us before she gets hurt again. Last night she fell on the stairs and hurt her back. She was upset about something with the dog and she slipped. I heard her crying from downstairs. Please, you've got to help my wife, Doctor," he begged.

Cathryn listened to his voice, afraid to speak and too numb to cry. A nurse came in with a syringe and put something into the tube of the IV. Cathryn saw what she was doing and tried to struggle up from the lack of sensation, the heaviness she felt. But, in a few moments, the medicine trickled down into her arm, flowed through her blood stream and dulled her senses.

Nothing matters very much right now, anyway, she thought. *If they would just leave me alone. Everything's so soft, like cotton,* she smiled to herself. *Everything is comfortably far away, even Edward. His voice is so tiny. Tiny little Edward. They can't touch me, floating, floating… Can't even touch me here. So nice, so soft.*

ॐ

Time went by with one day blending into another for Cathryn. She didn't know what day of the week it was or if it was morning or night. There were consultations with different doctors and Edward was almost always close by watching her with his dark, brooding eyes.

"I can't leave her alone, Doctor. I'm the only comfort she has when she gets into these depressions," he explained, sounding sadly noble.

The soft feeling was slipping away and Cathryn began to feel a panicky sensation. She felt certain that something was going to happen. She opened her eyes and looked around the room frowning, her mouth felt dry like cotton and there was an unpleasant medicine taste in her throat.

What are they doing now? I want to go home. God, I just want to go home…

When she spoke, her words didn't make sense. Her voice

sounded like someone else's. The soft, cotton feeling was gone.

I want it back! she thought, panic tearing through her.

Terrified, Cathryn asked the nurses to bring her more medication in stumbling words that were slow and slurred. They couldn't understand what she was asking them for and they told her to rest, that everything would be all right.

"I-don-know-how-I-fell," she tried to tell them. "Rex-wus-makin-too-muz-noise-Eward-duzn't-lik-that-tried-to-git-him-to-be-quiet-afraid-to-walk-on-the-sidewalk-feels-better-when-I'm-in-the-street-peopul-don-stare-at-my-face," the fuzzy words tumbled out against one another.

Then Cathryn started crying and she said she wished that she were back home with her brothers, with her mother baking in their warm kitchen.

I'm freezing cold! she screamed silently, trying to move her drug heavy arms.

The nurse patted her shoulder in response and left her alone. Cathryn saw her mother taking bread out of the oven, bringing it to the table. Cathryn had rarely been sad or cried back then.

Never so weak, so lost then, she told herself.

"My mother made wonderful bread," she told a doctor. "My brothers helped her more than I did." One doctor wrote on his chart while another held a light to each of her eyeballs.

More words tumbled out of her mouth or they wouldn't come at all. The doctors looked at one another and rubbed their chins thoughtfully and wrote on their charts. Most of the time Edward was there, standing attentively by her side, a worried and concerned expression across his face. But when Cathryn looked at him, she saw a warning in his cold, dark eyes that no one else seemed able to see. It frightened her terribly and so she closed her eyes again.

⁂

Then she slept. At least her eyes were closed. But she could see them all anyway.

They're there, waiting for me to say something. There's nothing to say. Nothing to say that will change anything.

༓

When she woke up again, two figures in white robes were wrapping something tightly around her wrists and ankles, binding them. She was in a small, cold room with white, square tiles from the floor to the ceiling.

Wait! What are you doing to me? her mind screamed, but the words roared inside of her head and only a garbled, mumbled sound came from her lips. Whatever they had given her had taken away the control she had over her own body. She couldn't form words with her lips and tongue.

The two figures in white robes tightened a band across her chest.

Stop, please, stop, don't do this! she heard some tiny voice within her begging, but Cathryn could not speak and the figures in the robes did not stop what they were doing.

Then, groggy from a shot that a doctor gave her, Cathryn felt the protest, the fight, seeping out of her and she stopped caring what they were doing. With the last vestige of fight within her, she pushed against the straps one last time, pushing back against being constrained.

"There, there, Mrs. Kent, just relax," a woman in a white gown and mask said. Cathryn could see the woman's eyes through her drugged haze and they were dark gray and unsmiling. Her words did not sound gentle. She reminded Cathryn of Edward.

Someone else dressed in a white robe, whom she could not see except for his arms and hands, forced a foul-smelling bit of rubber between her teeth and though she tried to turn her head to the side so that she could dislodge it and spit it out at him, her head was no longer under her control.

Someone gave her yet another shot, and though Cathryn thought her eyes were still open, the room darkened. Just before her eyes squeezed shut against her will, a white-robed figure with very pale, watery blue eyes, placed the electrodes on either side of her head and suddenly the excruciating pain went from the edges of her brain to the center and out again. Her head bounced up furiously and then flopped down and up, again and again, as if it belonged to a rag doll. A bit of drool escaped the corner of her mouth and fell along the rubber piece and onto her cheek.

She was no longer conscious.

ॐ

Everything is soft. The colors are soft and the sounds are soft. No rough edges anymore, she thought, relieved.

She was a little girl again, sitting on her father's lap. "My little, shiny-haired angel," Joseph murmured. "My angel cake," hugging her to him. Cathryn could smell the bit of shaving cream scent that clung to his skin and she pressed her tiny body closer to his chest. She loved her father so much. He was a quiet and gentle man, and he called his wife and children his five million dollars. He told her that he was the luckiest man in the world. And looking down at little Cathryn on his knee, Joseph Silberg believed that this was true.

"Please, Daddy, read the book to me some more," she begged. "Quick before Mommy calls us for dinner. I want to hear some more."

He looked at her big violet eyes, round with excitement, and he wondered if anyone would ever be able to refuse this beautiful child anything at all. She leaned comfortably against his chest and looked at the page intently, mouthing the words along with him as he read to her from *The Wizard of Oz*.

ॐ

When Cathryn awoke, she was in her bed in the hospital.

Everything is so fuzzy, she thought. *Looks like Edward sitting next to my bed reading a newspaper. He doesn't know I'm awake, he didn't see me move. That's good. All I want is to be able to go home, really home, to my real home. Daddy? Where are you, Daddy? I'm sorry about all the trouble. I'm so sorry, Daddy? Can you hear me, Daddy? Daddy?*

She closed her eyes and slept a long time.

Five

Caregiver...?

THE HOUSE WAS VERY QUIET. She sat on the floor outside the closed door to Edward's office. She leaned towards it and listened again. *He still isn't saying anything.* The sunlight streamed through the hall window onto the floor by her feet.

Why isn't he saying anything? Cathryn's eyes darted towards the bedroom, to the guest room, then back to his office. *Something's wrong. He isn't making a sound.* She couldn't hear the familiar tap of his pipe on the edge of the ashtray. *Why doesn't he ask me to bring him coffee or tell me to go and do some shopping? He's at his desk. I know he's planning something, but what?*

There was a feeling throughout the house that was different, Cathryn was positive of that. Something was missing, but she didn't know what it was yet. Still, it felt as if it was something very important. Even her dog was very quiet, lying motionless by the window of the dining room on the floor below.

Rex, you're a good dog. You're quiet and well-mannered, better than some humans, that's for sure. You're a gentleman.

She could see him lying there from where she sat in the loft above the living room.

He's so good, so well-behaved. She smiled down at him, but he didn't move at all. A chill went up her back and across her arms.

Maybe something's wrong with Rex. She was suddenly frightened. She still didn't get up, but now she stared hard at the dog's rib cage for a long while, until finally she saw the slight motion of breath going in and out of his body.

I have to give him some cottage cheese. She couldn't remember the last time when they had eaten anything.

Why isn't Edward hungry yet? Soon he'll start snarling at me to cook something.

She knew that she should get up off the floor and get a meal going before he came out and started in on her, but she could not will her body into motion.

Something's gone from the house, the air feels so light, it feels nice. What is it? she wondered. *Doesn't matter. I'll just rest here on the floor where it's nice and quiet. I'll wait until he decides to come out of there.*

The sunlight was creeping closer. It was on her legs now, warming her. It felt pleasant and soothing.

၃၅

Her eyes flew open. It was dark outside now, and she was very cold.

She rubbed her eyes hard with the heels of her hands making splotchy red marks appear.

The house was dark with only a bit of light peeking in through the spaces around the blinds on the window. A thin yellowish cast splashed from the streetlights onto the wall. She was still sitting on the floor, her back pressed against the wall, wearing only a T-shirt and sweat pants.

He hates it when I wear these sweat pants. He'll have a fit when he looks at me. He'll sneer first, and then he'll start to complain, and then he'll say, why do I have to be such a slob. I'm not a slob. Everything he wants me to do takes too much energy, more than I can deal with right now. I just need to rest.

It was hard to remember when she didn't feel like that about Edward.

Rex came up the stairs sensing that she had finally woken up. He put his head under her hand and then gently nuzzled her face.

"Rex, you good boy, you must be starving," she whispered to

the dog. "Come with me, baby. We'll get you something to eat."

She and the dog went slowly down the stairs, being very careful not to make any noise. Ignoring the chairs and table just next to the kitchen in the dining area, Cathryn took a carton of cottage cheese from the counter and she sat heavily down on the floor, her back up against the kitchen cabinets. The floor was dirty. There was a thick layer of dog hair everywhere. She didn't pay any attention. She rubbed Rex's head and the back of his neck.

He likes when I do that. She smiled. The dog's round brown eyes looked appreciatively up at her and he licked his tongue against her hand.

When she put the carton down for him, Rex gobbled away at the cottage cheese, finishing it in seconds. He licked at Cathryn's hand again. Then he went into the hall bathroom to drink some water out of the toilet bowl and then back to his rug by the dining room window.

Cathryn's eyes went to the stairs. She thought she would hear Edward's explosive voice any moment, but still nothing happened.

Maybe he went out when I was asleep. No, he would've said something — he would have been loud and angry, or quiet and nasty, but he would've said something. He always does.

God, it's strange and quiet in the house. Whatever went away earlier, before I fell asleep, hasn't come back into the house yet.

She sat on the floor in the dark, dismal kitchen and she was smiling now. *Maybe it will never come back,* she mused. *Maybe I can just sit here on the floor until Rex wants to go out in the yard. That would be all right with me. That would be fine. I don't have any energy.*

ॐ

She stayed awake most of the night. When she felt very cold again, she crawled slowly on her hands and knees into the living room and pulled an old, torn afghan off of an armchair. Then she curled up next to the couch on the floor and started to feel sleepy again.

I have to remember not to make any noise, she told herself. *I can't make a sound or the house will explode, like always, like it does every single time.*

Hours later when her eyes opened again, Rex was curled up next to her. It was early morning and nothing seemed to have changed. Nothing had disturbed her for a long while. She needed to go to the bathroom, but she wasn't going to take a chance.

It's safe like this if I'm very, very quiet. That's the most important thing. I can't move around too much, can't make any noise.

She felt a warm, wet sensation as the urine left her body and saturated the old, worn, gray sweatpants. Cathryn didn't care. She pulled the afghan tighter around her body and fell asleep again.

When she woke up a little while later, she told herself again that the only thing that mattered was that she was very quiet, but she wasn't certain why any more. She thought that she heard someone whispering to her, "Shhhh-h-h…don't make any noise. Shhhh-h-h." She looked around slowly, but she couldn't see who was talking to her in that tiny, hushed voice. It looked like she was alone with Rex but she knew better. Every once in a while when Edward wasn't in a room with her, she could hear that tiny little hushed voice.

Nothing's moving, she thought. She looked around, but she didn't see anyone else downstairs with her. The front door was closed.

The hushed voice stopped speaking to her. *I don't have to think about that now.*

Her eyes shifted to the windows at the front of the house where occasionally a car went by, and she wondered when Edward would leave for work. She thought about crawling into the closet next to the living room, but she knew that he would really become enraged if he had to look around the house for her. She sighed deeply and closed her eyes again.

৵

Rex woke her the next time by putting his muzzle under her chin against her neck. Startled, she sat up abruptly and hissed at him, "Don't touch me you dirty animal. Don't you touch me." The dog ran bewildered into the dining area and looked back at her from where he tried to hide under the table, his body trembling.

Cathryn was terrified. She clutched the blanket to her chest and began sobbing, "Please don't touch me. Please don't. I'm sorry, I'm sorry, I'm sorry." She continued crying uncontrollably, begging, "Please leave me alone. Please, please…." She pushed her body as close to the couch as she could. She pressed her fist against her mouth in a frightened attempt to muffle the sounds she was making, staring in front of her into a space that held a demon that only Cathryn could see.

"Please don't hurt me again, please, please," she cried, still trying to muffle her sounds.

Through the tears that poured down her face, her eyes remained riveted on the staircase. She knew that he would come downstairs any moment and he would be angry and mean because she had disturbed him. He would punch or slap her and hiss instructions at her.

Or else he'll be sweet and tell me that everything is going to be all right, just like he does when I get upset. But later, it's always different.

And, Cathryn never knew which reaction she would get from Edward.

She sat like that for almost an hour, sobbing and moaning softly, with her eyes glued to the stairs and her ears straining to hear any sound coming from his room upstairs. Nothing. She felt as if she were going crazy.

What's he going to do now? Why is he taking so long? She listened. She took a deep breath and held it while she listened again. Still nothing.

꘡

Finally, she couldn't wait any longer. She grabbed the end of the couch and pulled her stiff body to an upright position. Rex watched her cautiously from under the table, his tail wagging and his body shaking again. Slowly she moved towards the staircase.

I'll be very quiet. I won't do anything to upset him.

Like hell, you won't! someone shouted in her head. *Why don't you just scream at him to get out of here and leave you alone?*

What I really want to do is to rip at his face with my fingernails.

The thought made her clench her teeth together hard, and she sneered a little, and then she shivered with fear.

She went up the stairs one at a time, almost down on her hands and knees, her ragged fingernails digging into the worn carpet as she pulled her body along. Her hair was a tangled mess around her puffy face. Her eyes were dark and full of her terrors. Her shoulders slumped forward as she moved up the stairs slowly, carefully. She couldn't stand waiting for him any longer. She had to find out what he was doing.

What day is it? Is it still October? Isn't this the house in San Diego? Where is he? What's he going to do when he finally does come out of his damn office?

Cathryn got to the top of the stairs. Rex crept forward a fraction of an inch from beneath the table, watching her, waiting.

It's still so quiet, she thought. Even the muffled sounds from outside the house stopped. It seemed to her as if the entire Earth had paused in all of its many motions, waiting with Cathryn to see what was going to happen next.

The door to his office was still closed. She was next to it now, and, again she listened intently for any sound, not even daring to breathe for a moment. *Nothing. Still nothing.* She wanted to run back down the stairs and out the front door, but she knew he would bring her back.

He always brings me back. Always so calm and self-assured and always so right. Making me feel as if I missed something, something that was so obvious. But then he'll tell me that he'll help me see it, that we'll straighten it out. For years and years and years and years, he's been telling me what to do and what not to do. How to dress, how to talk, how to move, how to please him. I hate him. Tears welled up in the corners of Cathryn's eyes.

Edward had dictated Cathryn's days and ruled over her nights for a long time.

~

It had been a long time since he had reached for her with any emotion save anger. But even back in the early years of their marriage, Edward delighted in confusing her sexually rather than satisfying her.

With every touch, each kiss and caress, he slowly and deliberately aroused her to a point where she felt that, in another second, she would happily explode into a million smiling pieces. Then, abruptly, he would stop. He would look at her then, with a cruel, meanness glaring from his eyes.

"What? What's the matter?" she stammered, struggling back from the heated intense place where he had left her alone. "What did I do?"

"Nothing. Come here." And then he pulled her to him and he used her body to quickly satisfy himself, her timid mouth, her soft breasts, her smooth thighs. Sometimes he turned her roughly onto her stomach, jamming his hardness between the tightness of her buttocks, causing her to cry out with the tearing pain. Edward always had his orgasm, and he always left Cathryn unsatisfied, confused and miserable.

Each time, he left her frustrated and wondering what she had done wrong, questioning whether her own passion and excitement were somehow wrong. When she tried to ask him to explain, he pressed her gently to him, telling her that he was very tired. Then Edward would turn over and go to sleep, leaving his lovely, innocent young wife not just unsatisfied, but in a sexual turmoil that was so overwhelming, she had no idea how to resolve it.

Cathryn was certain that it was her fault. *I've done something wrong again,* she told herself. *Only, I don't know what.* She cried silently, her face pressed deeply into the pillow so he would not hear.

అ

Now Cathryn looked towards the hall bathroom. A thought occurred to her.

There's one thing I can do while I wait for him to come out of his office. I can get some Valium before he opens the door and comes out into the hallway. He likes it when I'm nice and calm. Yes, that's a good idea. I could take some Valium and maybe some of the Haldol they gave me in the hospital, and when he comes out of his room, I'll smile and be calm and quiet, the way he likes me. That's a good idea.

But then she thought about how the innocent-looking, small, pale green, Haldol tablets made her body feel. She could hear Edward's screaming echoing in her ears from the times when she didn't want to take them. He had gone to so much trouble to get them for her. The memory made her press her hands hard against her head.

But he doesn't understand how it aches in my knees, how my head gets so numb, the horrible burning in my joints. No, it won't work. He'll be upset with my crumpled clothes or tell me my hair is a mess anyway. It won't do any good. Nothing does any good anymore.

Should I just take a shower before he comes out? she wondered. But the thought of having to move her body into the bathroom in order to clean and clothe it was more than she could bear. She slumped against the wall and down to the floor again.

He still isn't making any noise in there, or else I just can't hear him. That's okay, too.

Hours passed. Rex came hesitantly to the bottom of the stairs and lay down, watching her, waiting. After a while the air began to feel heavier, and it was hard for Cathryn to take a breath.

I'm going to choke, she thought. *Oh God, no, not now!* She gasped a little, putting her hands against her throat. The doors and walls and ceiling spun crazily around her head. She fell forward, bumping her head on the staircase railing. She stayed there for a long time, not moving, her head pounding, but slowly she could breathe again. After a long while, she began to get hungry. It was almost dark outside again.

I don't care anymore what he does. I'll get some dinner for Rex and me whether he likes it or not.

With tremendous effort, she pulled herself to her feet, staring at the closed door.

Stay there, she thought. *Stay there forever, if that's what you're going to do. I'm hungry. I'll eat with Rex.*

She started for the stairs very slowly and went down them carefully, one at a time, listening for Edward behind her after each step. Nothing. Cathryn tiptoed into the kitchen with Rex at her feet, his tail wagging. She took an opened loaf of bread from the cabinet, and, slowly, mechanically, toasted eight slices, jumping a little each time the toaster popped up. She found a stick of butter in another cabinet, stuffed into a coffee cup. She put great mounds of butter on each piece of toast and took the plate to the table, not noticing the melting butter dripping from the plate onto the floor as she walked.

Rex sat at her feet and watched her. She tore each piece in half, gave him some, and perfunctorily stuffed the rest into her mouth and chewed it. She stared back into the next room towards the staircase. There were smudges of butter on her face and some in her tangled hair. Rex went back to the toilet bowl and got another drink. Cathryn drank, too, from a cup of coffee that had been sitting on the table. There still was no sound upstairs and the house was getting dark again.

She put her fingers around the doorknob of his office door and turned it just the tiniest bit. Nothing. She turned it a little more and the door squeaked slightly. She stopped. Nothing. She pushed the door halfway open now and took one step into the room. There were no lights on in the dark room, but there were little streams of light from the street lamps outside, coming through the dusty blinds and making thin, wavering shapes on the opposite wall. Her eyes got used to the darkness after a few minutes. She stood absolutely still, peering into the room and listening for Edward's outburst of anger.

Her husband often slept on the bed in the room that he used for his office instead of coming to their bedroom. Cathryn didn't mind that, but he wasn't on the bed now. Instead, he was lying on the floor next to the desk, with just his head resting against the chair leg at a weird angle, as if he had slumped wearily out of the chair onto the floor. He wasn't moving at all and she knew at once that he wasn't asleep because his eyes were wide open. He didn't move when she began screaming, "EDWARD! EDWARD! EDWARD! EDWARD!" There was a sickening stench about the room that made her stomach convulse. She thought she was going to vomit.

Rex had come halfway up the stairs behind her, but now he jumped, turned and ran back downstairs, bumping into the wall and yelping as he tore around the corner of the landing. He tried to hide under the table. Cathryn screamed Edward's name again and again. She stood in the doorway screaming it over and over, not moving from the spot where she first saw him lying on the floor. Fifteen minutes passed and all she could manage to do was to scream his name, her hand still frozen on the doorknob.

߷

The police found Cathryn and Edward just like that when they answered the next-door neighbor's hysterical telephone call and forced open the front door. There wasn't a single light on in the dusty, smelly house. Cathryn continued screaming at Edward's inert body even as two policemen ran up the stairs towards them. She wanted to talk, or cry, or move, but Cathryn couldn't say anything except his name. And she couldn't make her fingers let go of the doorknob.

One of the policemen, who after twenty years on the streets, had just about seen it all, calmly took out his radio and called for an ambulance. Then he forcefully, but gently, led Cathryn away from the doorway, down the stairs and over to the couch. Keeping one arm around her shoulders, he pushed aside the stack of old newspapers and clutter, and spoke in a tone that expected no disagreement whatsoever.

"Just sit there, ma'am, we'll take care of everything."

He firmly positioned her on the couch, his wide hands firmly on her shoulders. Cathryn got very quiet and looked up at him with the same expression on her face that might be found on the face of the survivor of an airplane crash or a bomb explosion. She had a good deal of medication in her blood system but she was also in shock. She sat completely still, her eyes wide and staring, not crying, not speaking. Then her body began to shake and someone put a blanket around her.

Later the ambulance attendants carried Edward's sheet-covered, strapped body down the stairs on a stretcher. Cathryn saw the shape under the sheet bounce up a fraction of an inch with their steps as they came down towards the living room and she began shrieking his name again, "EDWARD! EDWARD!"

A young man wearing a light green lab jacket with a stethoscope stuffed in the pocket, came to her side and spoke softly and reassuringly, but to no avail. Cathryn didn't hear what he was saying. All she could see in front of her were Edward's eyes, staring at nothing, as he lay crumpled on the office floor, like a discarded puppet. Every few seconds, she screamed his name again. Her eyes focused on no one. The image of his body lying on the floor of his room, in the house they had lived in together for years, floated close to her. All she felt was terror, and Cathryn didn't know if the terror was because he was gone, or because she felt he would come back.

☞

She jumped to her feet suddenly as they moved Edward's body out of the house and the medical assistant came over and quickly gave her a shot. She slumped back onto the couch like a rag doll, silent again, with the smell of decaying flesh filling the room and burning in her nostrils.

Cathryn's husband had died almost instantly from a massive heart attack more than two days earlier. He had fallen to the floor of his office and had remained there ever since. Cathryn leaned back on the couch. She noticed that the lights were on in every room now and she squinted her eyes against the brightness.

Rex came warily out from under the table, his entire body quivering anxiously, and he lay by her feet, trying to push his back side as close to the bottom of the couch and the comfort of her legs, as he could.

☞

Both of Edward's parents had died within a few years of the newlyweds' move to California, while they were still living in Napa Valley. Edward had inherited half of what they left, but his parents had spent most of their money themselves. He had one sister with whom he had not spoken for many years, over some long forgotten disagreement. In his own will, Edward left a dollar to her, his only living blood relative.

When she was asked, Cathryn said she had no other family. The long separation from her parents and her brothers for so many years made this seem true to her, at least at that moment. Other than Rex, she felt quite alone.

Two people whose names and telephone numbers were listed as emergency contacts in various papers of Edward's were contacted. They came and helped Cathryn as much as they could through those first days and nights. Margaret and Jack Ketterman, a married couple who also worked for the City Planning Department, both took a week off from their own jobs and stayed in the house with Cathryn most of the time. They helped her sort out the bills that were due, which were neatly arranged on Edward's desk. The basic procedures necessary to handle everyday life were a meaningless blur to Cathryn, and she let Margaret and Jack do whatever was needed while she sat and stared robot-like into space, waiting.

Margaret and Jack were horrified to see the condition of both Edward's home and his wife. "I can't believe he lived like this with her," Margaret whispered to Jack, looking around at the dirt and clutter.

They brought food and persuaded Cathryn to eat. Margaret gradually straightened up the messes they found and she did some laundry and shopping. She and Jack waited while Cathryn showered, and Margaret helped her put on clean clothes. They made phone calls for her and they handled the funeral arrangements. Jack helped with the paperwork that was needed to give Cathryn access to Edward's benefits from the City. His will left her the house and mortgage, a monthly income of two thousand dollars, plus another eleven thousand dollars in mutual funds from the small inheritance left by his parents and pieces of Cathryn's on-going allowance that Edward had invested.

Cathryn was heavily sedated by the doctors after Edward's death, and, later, as before, by her own hand. Eventually Margaret and Jack went back to work. They called often to check on Cathryn.

"Are you doing okay? Is there anything you need us to bring you?"

"No, Rex and I are fine," Cathryn told them calmly. Rex lay at her feet. A small, brown prescription bottle was on the table in front of her next to a cold cup of coffee.

Days and weeks passed. Cathryn lived a quiet, uneventful routine. There was no one there to tell her what to do or when to do it and often she didn't do anything at all. When she got very hungry, she looked for food. She drove to the grocery store a few times, but her appearance continued to deteriorate and she felt people staring at her. She became irascible, mumbling at them, "Mind your own damn business."

It's like him to win, to have the last laugh, she fumed. *What am I supposed to do? He always told me everything I was supposed to do, except what to do when he died.* At that thought, she laughed out loud in the empty house and Rex looked up at her curiously.

Sometimes it was too difficult to get out of a chair, so she stayed in it. Sometimes it was too difficult to shower, so she put it off for another day. Sometimes the bathroom looked as if it were miles away, so she ignored her body's needs and unknowingly, or uncaring, urinated or defecated in her pants. Sometimes she couldn't face having to get up to open the door for Rex, so he would whimper quietly for a while and when he couldn't stand it any longer, he urinated fearfully, self-consciously, where he stood by the sliding glass doors in the kitchen. The house reeked of unpleasant odors, the strongest of which was that of decaying flesh, and Cathryn believed it was still there, clinging to the walls and furniture, trying to suffocate her. Some days, no matter what the weather, she left the windows and doors wide open so that she could breathe.

On other days Cathryn believed that Edward hadn't died at all.

He's still in the house, waiting to see what I'll do next, she told herself.

When Margaret called to see how she was doing, Cathryn sometimes said, "He'll be back in a few days. He's giving me some time alone so I'll be happy to see him again," she reported, smiling knowingly, smugly. Then she laughed, expecting Margaret to understand the little joke that Edward was playing on her.

ॐ

More time passed. Cathryn got into her little red Toyota and drove through the neighborhood with Rex, but that got her into more trouble. Her driving was erratic and she had a habit of turning towards the empty space next to her while the car was moving, and talking to a passenger only she could see.

"I know you're very busy. Why did you decide to come with us?" she said aloud, with Rex watching her from the back seat, his tail wagging and his head bobbing. She didn't understand when the police stopped her. She thought they were bothering her for no reason, but they told her that she couldn't drive anymore and they took away her license. She could still take walks with Rex, though. She loved to walk up and down the quiet, rolling residential streets with him.

Rex is my best friend, he's my only friend, she thought. He often got thirsty while they were out walking. Cathryn, seeing an open front door, walked up, went through the screen door and took her dog into a stranger's kitchen to get him a drink. The startled occupants patiently directed her back home.

Late one afternoon, an elderly neighbor sitting in his living room in a house two blocks away, was so terrified when Cathryn suddenly appeared in his home with her disheveled appearance and her bizarre actions, that he made a frantic phone call to the police who came and brought Cathryn back to her house. She was loud and abusive to the two young policemen.

What do they want me to do when my puppy needs water? They're all crazy anyway. I want them to leave us alone.

"Go away and leave us alone!" she screamed after them, her eyes flashing and her hair standing out from her head in all directions.

I want everyone to go to hell and leave me the hell alone. But they won't. They're always bothering me, even now when it's finally so quiet.

✣

Papers, cups and socks kept disappearing. Cathryn, convinced that strangers were coming into her house and taking her things, began locking the doors and windows. But, still she found things missing almost every day. She sat at the kitchen table listening for the thieves, her eyes narrowed and her fists clenched. But they stayed away when she was awake watching for them. Finally, she thought of a plan to stop them. She decided that the only way she could keep the strangers from getting into her house and stealing her belongings was to put butter on the window sills.

They'll slip and fall if they try to rob me again, she thought smugly.

So, Cathryn patiently let the butter soften on the kitchen counter in the sun and then she took one of Edward's shirts and spread the oily butter across each of the window sills in the living room. Then she went into the dining room and did the same thing.

Not upstairs, they can't reach up there, she decided. She stood back, looking at her work with satisfaction, a crooked grin spreading across her face.

I'm smarter than they are, she thought. *Edward will see that, too. I know he's watching. Not all of the time, but enough to see what's going on, to realize that I'm handling things fine without him.*

She knew that she had to get rid of the checks that were coming in the mail. Someone was sending her checks that were not hers, and if she was right, and Edward was still watching her, it would make him furious if she took money that was his.

Maybe Daddy's watching me, too, to see if I can finally be trusted. Edward's waiting until I don't expect him to be in the house and then he'll come back. If I've made any mistakes, he'll be unforgiving and full of rage.

So, Cathryn sat at the kitchen table tearing the benefit checks from the City Planning Department into small pieces. She threw the pieces into the trash can at her feet.

✣

Margaret and Jack continued to try to help Cathryn. During the years they had worked with Edward they had heard him tell, with evident pain, how mentally unstable Cathryn was. According to him, he had been a tolerant and patient husband to the very beautiful young woman he had married, even after she tragically turned out to be psychotic. He had tried everything he could think of to help her.

What a shame, Margaret thought, when Edward told her quietly and sadly that Cathryn had needed hospitalization. And, that the various medications didn't help. That even the shock treatments had only made her passive for short periods of time, and then her uncontrollable, unreasonable behavior would begin all over again. Edward had had his hands full. He had tried everything to help his wife while he was alive. It seemed as if Edward had truly protected Cathryn and cared for her over the years. To Margaret and Jack and a few other outsiders, Edward had been a saint in his marriage.

A woman like Cathryn was so fortunate to have someone like him in her life, Jack believed.

ॐ

This belief held amongst his closer acquaintances, in spite of the fact that Edward had been instrumental in estranging his wife from her family, that he had had her committed to psychiatric hospitals and that he had caused her to be subjected to electroconvulsive shock treatments three different times, before she was thirty-five years old.

Coincidentally, though neither Margaret nor Jack could have known, each of those three episodes took place shortly after Cathryn made the mistake of hysterically blurting out to her husband, in pathetic desperation, "I can't live like this any more. I want to go home, please! I'm so unhappy. Please, Edward, I just want a divorce."

ॐ

Cathryn let Margaret or Jack take over when they were in the house, but after they left she stopped payment on the checks that they mailed for her to her mortgage company, or for her utilities. On most days, Cathryn didn't trust anyone except Rex.

Then she began to call them in the middle of the night, agitated, frantically telling them that Edward was still alive, that he was in the house, that he wanted to kill her.

"He's here, he's here right now! I know it! PLEEEEASE help me! He's angry! He's so angry!" she cried. More than once, Jack quickly drove the few miles to her house late at night and walked from room to room with Cathryn, turning on lights and looking in closets, until she finally took some of her medication, calmed down and wanted to go back to bed.

But they couldn't keep going on like that much longer. Eventually, Margaret and Jack saw that they had taken on more than they could handle. Once all of the paperwork was taken care of to the best of their ability, they began turning off their phone at night. They continued to visit and call Cathryn, but they couldn't face her terrified phone calls in the middle of the night.

୬

One night Cathryn couldn't get through to them. Their phone rang and rang and no one answered. She didn't know what else to do and as she became more terrified. It was like when she was a young child and she would convince herself that there was a dangerous monster waiting in her cellar. Although she managed to creep cautiously down the stairs into the dark, dank and threatening space to retrieve a toy, when her mission was accomplished, with her heart pounding uncontrollably, she still had to get back up that never-ending flight of stairs and out of reach of the imagined creature. A creature who became so real and terrifying, who was about to get its murderous, outstretched, giant, bloody claw-like hand upon her.

Now Cathryn flew out of the house, just like that child who had raced two steps at a time up out of the dangerous, frightening cellar, and she ran across the street and pounded hysterically on a neighbor's front door.

She was so troubled and incoherent that her dismayed neighbor called 911. The police, though used to calls regarding Cathryn Kent, were growing tired of the commotion she was causing. This time Cathryn found herself, once again, in a psychiatric ward, for help.

More medication was immediately administered to calm her down. More consultations with doctors were held to sort out the many differing opinions. These were followed by a diagnosis of different terms that did not open the door for any successful handling: paranoid schizophrenia, dementia praecox. More questions, more observation, more discussion, more theories. Then, still more medication and a marked degeneration of both her level of awareness and her self-determined will.

But they always told Cathryn that they were going to help her.

༄

A few weeks later she was released from the Tate Psychiatric Hospital. Instead of being brought back to her house, Cathryn was placed in a board and care facility in Leucadia. The Wilson Home was located in a quiet, dusty, not very well kept neighborhood, just a few miles from the beach.

Jack explained to Cathryn, "It has something to do with your hospitalization insurance and the number of days that you can be in a hospital under your coverage." Jack also told her, "The hospital is very expensive, it charges $950.00 a day even without the doctors or the medication."

Cathryn looked at him and began laughing. The figure was absurd to her. *That horrible place? He's joking with me,* she thought.

"The doctors don't want you to go back to your house and live alone right now," he told her.

Cathryn didn't understand, but she really didn't care. They told her that she could have Rex with her in the home and she decided that would be fine.

I'll take a break. There won't be so much for me to do.

And, maybe Edward, or her haunting memories of him, would leave her alone if she were not in their house.

In a fairly lucid moment, she called Steve and assured him that she was fine, that she hadn't been feeling very well, but that now she was doing much better. Cathryn neglected to tell her brother that her husband was dead, and she didn't tell him where she was living. She simply said she would call again soon.

Steve said, "Your voice sounds funny…"

Cathryn replied, "It's just from the medication I'm taking. It's supposed to relax me."

He wanted her to come back to Chicago to see her parents. "Dad's been really sick, they want to do more surgery on his colon. Mom's having a rough time of it."

Cathryn promised that she would come back soon. Steve asked, "Do you want me to come out to California to see you right away, and then we can fly back to Chicago together?"

Cathryn answered, "No, Steve, not just now. It will be better a little later on. I'll call you, I promise." Her throat felt raspy and the words formed very slowly.

᠅

Cathryn drifted in and out of clear states of mind.

Edward, my husband, my savior and my captor, is gone. At least it seems like he is.

She thankfully didn't feel his presence very much in the house in Leucadia. But what she had suffered at his hands, and from her treatments over the past years, was not easily reversed. Cathryn had moments when she was surprisingly perceptive and aware, when her mind and brain weren't affected and altered by the harsh medications — supposed cures with a long list of frightening contraindications and side affects.

No longer under Edward's oppression, Cathryn began thinking how she could salvage and straighten out her eviscerated life.

I need to stop taking my pills. But I'm so tired and all the things I need to do take so much energy, she thought.

Without the medications she had grown to depend upon, life seemed insurmountably difficult to Cathryn. But each day when she woke up in the Wilson Home, she resolved not to take the medicines and she attempted to get through the day without them, though she rarely made it for more than a few hours.

Life is too painful, too difficult and too ugly without their help, she thought, her mouth twisting cynically.

One thing's for sure, she thought as she looked into the mirror in the room she shared with one other woman, *my family cannot see me yet. Not like this.*

༄

Sylvia managed and ran the board and care home with her ex-husband, Barry. Unfortunately, as is sometimes the case in some businesses, they were two people whose rapacious natures outweighed their sense of benevolence.

Nine residents lived in the six bedroom home with Sylvia, Barry and two staff members who were there during the daytime. Five of the residents weren't ambulatory and they spent most of their days staring at televisions from their beds or wheelchairs, in a sad, apathetic state of existence. They were men and women in their seventies and eighties who had virtually been discarded and forgotten. Few relatives or friends came to see them. There were two others, brothers in their late sixties, who were gray, weary and bent, looking years older than they were. They had been in a serious car accident together and life's circumstances had made them almost inseparable. Apparently they didn't have any relatives with whom they were in contact, so day after day they rambled from room to room, both using canes, smoking continuously and arguing over cigarettes or which television program they would watch next.

There was also Nancy, Cathryn's thirty-four year old roommate, who had written brilliant poetry at one time, but then had spent several years in and out of psychiatric hospitals. She had been subjected to a long series of debilitating ECT treatments which had damaged her brain and destroyed a portion of her memory forever.

Nancy, like the Nobel Prize winning author, Ernest Hemingway, might have asked, "Well what is the sense of ruining my head and erasing my memory, which is my capital, and putting me out of business? It was a brilliant cure but we lost the patient."

༄

Nancy took Haldol and her other medications regularly. She never really came out of her drugged state, but shuffled from place to place, trying to stay out of everyone's way. Unlike Cathryn, Nancy Leigh Stevenson was usually very quiet, and rarely bothered anyone at all for any reason whatsoever.

Sylvia's experiences taught her that life was easier when her residents took their medications faithfully. While taking the various drugs, they were seldom argumentative. Instead they were very quiet, passive and obedient. Sylvia took enormous care to see to it that as soon as Cathryn arrived, she consumed every bit of the allowed prescriptions that the hospital doctors sent with her.

Sylvia and Barry believed that this would keep everything peaceful around the house, and they would continue to receive their monthly maintenance checks for each of their residents. Those checks were what kept a roof over the heads of the two Wilsons.

⌇

Most of those checks happened to be issued to the Wilson Home every month by the same person, a private conservator named Karen Brauning. Most of the residents in the Wilson Home were also Karen's clients and she earned a percentage from each of their estates for her services as she paid their bills each month.

Many of these elderly or disabled residents did not have anyone who was willing to take on the responsibility of handling even the basic administrative needs of an incapacitated relative. This was true even though some of these people still had substantial assets. Those were the clients that Karen most desired; the more they had, the more she gained.

But Karen Brauning did more than just pay the bills — she decided where her clients would live and just about every other thing that would happen to them.

Six

Enforced care–…

CATHRYN WAS SHAKING. Her eyes were wide with fear as she backed up towards the wall behind her.

"LEAVE ME ALONE!" she screamed. "Get the hell away from me! Get OUT of here!"

She was looking at something in front of her that Nancy could not see. Terrified by Cathryn's outbursts, Nancy ran out of their bedroom into the hallway. Cathryn was becoming even more upset. She was mumbling incoherent words and a bit of saliva bubbled at the corner of her mouth. She waved her hands wildly in front of her body.

Then she turned and quickly climbed into her bed, yanking the blankets up over her head. She had done everything she could think of to get them out of her room, to get them to stop tormenting her. She had yelled and stamped her foot, but they wouldn't leave her alone. They took her comb out of her dresser drawer and hid it somewhere to irritate her, to drive her mad. Now they were pulling on the blanket, trying to get her to get out of her own bed.

"Stop it! Leave me alone!" she shouted, pulling the blanket tightly up over her face. Then she screamed a bloodcurdling screech from under the covers. There was no one to be seen anywhere near her bed.

The short, heavy-set woman cowering in the hallway stopped as if she were frozen like a child in a game of "Statue" when Cathryn screamed. Nancy's entire body was quaking with her own fear. Even in Nancy's drug-induced, trance-like state, Cathryn's ravings unnerved her badly. Hurriedly, Nancy took two steps back into the bedroom, grabbed her stuffed bear off of her own bed, pressed it to her chest and fled, tears streaming down her face.

Behind her, Cathryn raged again, "Damn you! You took my clothes and ruined them! Get the hell out of here! Do you HEAR ME? Leave me ALONE!" The room was empty, except for the angry woman huddled under the blankets, who now had begun shouting obscenities at her invisible adversaries.

She pulled the blanket tighter around her head, and then suddenly she was very quiet. For ten minutes she lay perfectly still. Slowly, she got out of the bed, smiling conspiratorially, as she went into the bathroom and closed the door carefully behind her.

She was very quiet as she deliberately twisted, unscrewed and pulled pieces of the toilet loose from inside the tank. Cathryn stuffed the parts into the pockets of her jeans. Then she leaned her weight against the toilet and shoved it back and forth, back and forth, until it loosened a bit from the floor. She went back into the bedroom. There was still no one there.

The house was quiet except for the muffled sounds of the TV in the living room at the end of a long hallway, across the patio. Cathryn went out into the side yard through the sliding glass door in her room. She walked over to the heavy fence and carefully took the parts of the toilet from her pockets. She reached up high and standing on her tiptoes, she dropped them over the fence onto the neighboring property. Then she went back into the bedroom, grinning to herself.

"Now they won't be able to put scummy toilet water in my food," she muttered to her own reflection in the mirror over her dresser, a strange self-satisfied and triumphant smile on her puffy, pale face. The toilet began to leak onto the floor, and after a few minutes, the slow stream of water spread out into the hallway.

༄

Sylvia Wilson had had it. After operating her board and care facility for eight years, she knew what had to be done. Angrily stuffing dry rags into a bucket, she thought, *This woman is too crazy. There's no keeping her under control. There's no way to handle someone like Cathryn except to sedate her so she won't drive everyone else crazy.*

Cathryn hated how the Haldol made her feel. She hated the weakness and rigidity in her muscles and joints and the tremors that racked her body. Her hair kept getting thinner, clumps of it clinging to her comb and brush, and she hated the uncomfortable dryness in her mouth. So she protested taking her medications and a constant battle went on between her and Sylvia.

At first Cathryn tried to explain how she felt to Sylvia. "I want to be able to see things more clearly," she said. "Everything is fuzzy when I take the pills."

But Sylvia wasn't interested in her objections. She didn't care. Sylvia knew one thing was certain: the medications made the residents controllable and very quiet, and that's how she wanted it.

Some months ago, a friend of an elderly resident visited the home. The woman had tried to tell Sylvia what the medications could do to a person's perceptions, how they could harshly affect their bodily processes, even while they calmed them down and made them seem so quiet and peaceful on the surface.

The woman brought a copy of the *Physicians' Desk Reference*, and she tried to show Barry the contraindications it listed for the various anti-depressants that were administered routinely in the Wilson Home.

"There are a lot of possible side effects," the woman told them.

Neither Sylvia nor Barry Wilson wanted to hear what she had to say. "She can save her preaching for someone else," Barry scowled later.

What choice is there? Sylvia thought, furiously mopping at the water on the wet, slippery hallway floor. *How dare anyone try to tell me that what I do in my own home, with my own business, is not right?* she fumed. *I'm licensed! What do they know about handling sick, old people? When do they have to put up with demanding nerve-racking behavior day after day? It's all right for them to preach and question. They go home at night leaving their relatives for me to look after! I have to live day in and day out with these people. My life's become a hell since that damned Cathryn arrived and started carrying on about not being medicated.*

I need to keep them all quiet if I'm going to get anything done and that's what the medicines do, she stormed to herself. Sylvia dumped the bucket of grimy water into the bathtub and glared at the broken toilet, her face flushed with anger.

The other patients in the house are too old and feeble to get into trouble, or they're medicated and manageable like Nancy, Sylvia reasoned. *It's easier to take care of someone who sits and stares at the TV all day. Even their voices are weak and soft compared to Cathryn's harsh and demanding shouts.*

Yes, Sylvia had had it. But she knew what to do. She'd simply go to Dr. Murdock, tell him it was an emergency and get him to give Cathryn a shot of something, whether she liked it or not. *No one has to clear anything with anyone that way,* she smiled smugly, pleased with her cleverness. She wiped at the puddle of dirty water under the sink. Sylvia didn't want to lose Cathryn as a resident and jeopardize the income from Cathryn's insurance, but she knew that she couldn't go on this way with the woman so out of control.

Yes, first a call to Dr. Murdock and then a call to Karen Brauning for some help with this one, she promised herself.

Barry agreed with Sylvia completely.

"I'd like that Cathryn a lot better if she would just fucking shut up once in awhile," he muttered crudely to himself. He was standing in the hallway, leaning against the wall, staring absently at his ex-wife's soft, fleshy round bottom while she was on her hands and knees, wiping up the water with a rag. After a few minutes, Barry turned and went out to the garage to get a wrench.

Sylvia's ex-husband lived in a small, shack-like cabin at the rear of the property. He did some maintenance on the grounds and on the vehicles they used to transport the residents.

Barry usually handled upsets within the house much differently than Sylvia did. He simply smiled in a salacious, leering way. He liked to keep a bottle of Tequila in his dresser and he also had a water pipe in his room that he told Cathryn and Nancy he used for "a special Japanese tobacco."

Barry wasn't particularly eager to do the chores that Sylvia constantly found for him, but he did get pleasure out of taking the two younger female residents for rides to the store or out for lunch. And, it got them out of Sylvia's hair when she was busy cleaning. He wasn't beyond leaning his arm or thigh against the softness of their plump bodies, or talking them into coming back into his small, dingy room for a drink after dinner. He knew, of course, that alcohol wasn't supposed to be mixed with the kinds of medicine that they were taking.

But one little drink or two won't hurt anyone, he thought. *Anyway, they like drinking with me,* he told himself, smiling an unpleasant, lubricious smile that was frighteningly like the expression one might see on the face of a larger animal that has its prey cornered, instead of on the face of a human being.

Barry liked telling Cathryn his crude jokes. "She's a pain in the ass, but she still has enough brains left at least to get them, not like that numb ass Nancy," he mumbled. Barry was amused when Cathryn got self-conscious or laughed nervously. He liked how her cheeks got flushed whenever he pulled at her bra strap or made a rude comment.

Even though she looks like a mess, Barry thought, digging through a toolbox, *she's sure still got some looks under that tangled hair and chubby face and body.* He rubbed at his crotch with the fingers of his left hand and then he dumped the tools out of the metal box onto the ground, searching for the right wrench.

But the disturbances that Cathryn was making kept getting worse.

"If she needs to be doped, then we might as well get it done," Barry told Sylvia, smiling his weird, crooked smile, as he stood in the doorway watching Sylvia bend over to dump still another bucket of grimy water into the tub.

Essentially, Sylvia's ex-husband was morally corrupt, self-centered and unreliable, with a little mechanical ability and much less ambition. He had always been one of those lazy and unsavory men who live best off of the efforts of other people. Sylvia tolerated having him around mostly because he kept out of her way. And, when she pushed him hard enough, he sometimes fixed things that were broken.

One of Sylvia's aides had heard a rumor that Barry had lost a pharmaceutical license for improperly dispensing prescriptions years earlier. Though from the looks of him, it was difficult to believe that he would have ever been able to attain such a license in the first place. More gossip that circulated was about Barry having been jailed for performing illegal, and not very clean, abortions in the early sixties.

Once, when Sylvia took Cathryn shopping for groceries with her, Sylvia said confidentially, in a mean, critical tone, "I wouldn't be surprised if Nancy gets pregnant, she keeps hanging around Barry's room."

But as long as he kept up the repairs around the house, and the vehicles were running reasonably well, Sylvia would let him stay.

Especially if he stays out of my way and keeps his hands off me, she thought with irritation, feeling his eyes on her body.

～

Sylvia finished cleaning up the water from the broken toilet and she put the soaking wet rags into the bucket. She watched Barry, clad in grimy overalls and a ripped sweatshirt, as he tightened parts inside the tank. She wiped her hands on a towel and went into her room. Sylvia picked up the phone and dialed Dr. Murdock's office.

～

"Doctor, she runs out into the street. We can't watch her every second. Yesterday a car screeched out front and it almost hit her! She needs to be quieted down so she can get some rest. She just won't take her medication, Doctor. I don't know what to do. Please, can you give her a shot or something? I'm afraid she's going to hurt herself. You have to help her," Sylvia said in a whining, pleading voice.

～

That next morning Cathryn stood in an examination room, rocking from one leg to the other. She looked quite mad.

Someone was in my room all night, watching me, she told herself. *They kept moving my things around and laughing at me. They hid in the closet and behind the dresser and right outside the sliding glass door. Every time I tried to fall asleep, they laughed at me or pulled on my blankets. Every time, I had to scream at them again.*

Nancy had snored through most of the night, but Cathryn had dark circles under her wary, tormented eyes.

While the doctor listened to Sylvia, Cathryn's eyes narrowed and became muddy and dark. Her matted hair was sticking out wildly on both sides of her head and she kept clenching and unclenching her fingers.

I want to put my hands around someone's throat and feel soft flesh under my fingertips, she thought. Cathryn felt that she had never been so angry before in her entire life. But she said nothing.

It won't help to tell them anything. She pushed her chin out.

Suddenly she realized that Sylvia and Dr. Murdock had stopped talking. They were both looking at her. Cathryn's eyes darted quickly from Sylvia to Dr. Murdock, then back again to Sylvia.

The doctor had been standing next to the window patiently listening to Sylvia voice her complaints. Now he crossed his arms over his chest. Cathryn stood against the wall, pressing her back against the cold whiteness, listening and watching them.

Of course I stopped taking your drugs, Cathryn said to herself. *I don't want you near me with your damn little pills. They're evil. They make my joints hurt and my knees so sore I can hardly walk anymore. And that's the only thing I can do in your damn home,* she thought. *It won't do any good to tell this doctor anything. He doesn't care if I don't want to sit still on a couch like the half-dead people in that house, staring into space or the stupid programs on TV all day.* Cathryn wanted to shout in Sylvia's face, but she didn't. She just stood there, shifting her weight back and forth from one leg to the other.

I won't be obedient, follow your instructions, wake up and sit down and smoke and eat when you tell me to, Cathryn thought angrily. Dr. Murdock continued staring hard at her. Cathryn began to feel very anxious. She pressed her fingernails into the palms of her hands and then she opened her hands and spread her fingers against the cold wall behind her.

They make zombies in that house and I'm not going to be one. They won't get me. I'll get them, Cathryn thought, tightening her fists again at her sides.

She continued rocking back and forth, from one leg to the other. Dr. Murdock watched her closely. At the same time, she watched him. For a moment, her eyes darted to the cabinet on the wall of the examining room. She wondered what instruments he kept in there and what he did with them.

"Cathryn, I want to give you something that will help," the doctor told her.

Before the sentence was out of his mouth, Cathryn lunged towards the corner of the room and away from him like a startled animal. But she knew that she was trapped in the room with the two of them. Cathryn began to shiver.

"This will just take a second. You'll feel much better. This will help you."

ॐ

She no longer saw the doctor in front of her. Instead, Cathryn saw Edward standing over her as she lay on the floor near their bed. He was attempting to smile, but she knew he was furious, and the expression on his face was ugly and frightening. Her stomach still hurt from where he had pushed her hard, into the room, with his fist. She tasted blood inside her mouth where her tooth had cut into her tongue when he shook her arms so hard that she thought her head would fall off.

"This will help, honey. I promise. This will just take a couple of seconds and you'll feel much better." His voice was strained, he held his arm tightly around her shoulders. His mouth curved in a small smile, but his jaw was set and his eyes were dark and menacing.

Cathryn saw the tiny blue Valium and the orange Thorazine tablets in his hand, then she closed her eyes and felt him pushing them into her mouth with his thumb. She tried to clench her jaws shut before he could do it, but Edward was very strong. She gagged on the tablets, then she felt them dissolving, moving down her throat and through her body, as Edward held his fingers tightly on her chin so that she couldn't open her mouth and spit them out.

A feeling of nausea overtook her and the room went black, then everything got softer and lighter. *It doesn't matter anyway,* she thought. *Doesn't matter anyway.*

༄

Dr. Murdock had her cornered between the wall and the examination table. *He's not nearly as big as Edward,* Cathryn noticed, tilting her head to one side.

Briefly, she glanced out the window. Two floors below the traffic was moving steadily past the building. People rushed by busily in different directions on the sidewalks. No one looked up.

For a moment Cathryn's thoughts drifted to the space outside the window. *What would it feel like just to fling my body through that window, out into the sunshine and space? What if I could fly away?*

In that instant, Dr. Murdock reached out for her and grabbed her arm. He pressed a small swatch of antiseptic-soaked cotton against it and quickly jabbed the needle into soft flesh.

༄

Her shrill, agonized scream of terror died in seconds within the four walls of the small examination room. As the doctor inserted the syringe into her upper arm, the rage left Cathryn almost instantly. The clear, innocent-looking liquid passed into her body, in the name of help.

༄

For days, Sylvia was happier than she had been in a long time. Now, while she scrubbed out the toilet bowl with a brush, there were no insistent demands coming from Cathryn, demanding food or a cigarette or some other damn thing. Cathryn just sat quietly in a chair out on the patio, staring into space, smoking one cigarette after another and smiling. Two hours later, she still sat there, staring and smiling.

"Come in for lunch, Cathryn," Sylvia called cheerily. "We're having tuna sandwiches, your favorite."

"Okay," Cathryn replied meekly, slowly raising her body out of the chair. She walked carefully towards the kitchen door. Her body felt like drying, stiffening mud. Mud that might soften or crack and crumble. She had a thought that seemed ridiculous. It made her giggle out loud and she realized that she had never liked fish, not any kind of fish. She sighed and smiled, *Oh, well, let's go and have a nice lunch, a nice, lovely fish lunch.*

Barry stood at the kitchen doorway, leaning against the wall, grinning at her as she walked past him. "Come and see me later," he said, staring at her from behind his thick eyeglasses. "We'll have a drink together, celebrate." He winked at her, his lewd grin spreading across his unshaven, lined face.

Cathryn stopped and stared at him for a long time. "Okay, Barry, I'll come and see you later," she finally murmured docilely, sounding a little like one of those dolls that play a mechanical-sounding, programmed message when you pull the ring on a string.

Sylvia put the plate of potato chips and tuna sandwich in front of her, and Cathryn slowly began to eat. She had fed the other residents earlier, enjoying Cathryn's inactivity as long as possible.

Then Sylvia went into her bedroom and closed the door. Holding a business card in her hand in front of her, she dialed Karen Brauning's telephone number. Karen's answering machine message played, and after a second Sylvia heard the beep.

"Mrs. Brauning, please call Sylvia at the Wilson Home" she said, in a fawning, obsequious voice. "I have someone here I think you'll want to meet as soon as you can. Thank you so much." She hung up the phone, smiling, satisfied. Her troubles would end now and Karen would be very pleased. Sylvia might even earn some extra money, a kind of bonus for handling things so cleverly.

Seven

The attorney and the judge–…

"LINDA, PLEASE, HELP ME-E-E…" a small, terrified voice cried. Then it fell away, drifting off as if its owner were falling down a long, empty elevator shaft.

Linda bolted upright in bed, startled out of a troubled sleep. Still groggy, rubbing tired eyes, she peered around the room trying to see where the voice had come from, but there was no one there. Her T-shirt was soaked with perspiration and her heart was pounding so strongly, she was sure she could hear it. It was very dark in her bedroom. Only a tiny bit of light from the lampposts outside by the trees filtered into the room through the small spaces between the verticals covering the glass door.

Linda got out of bed and moved the verticals aside with a trembling hand. She looked around outside under the trees.

Maybe someone's out there and that's what I heard, she thought. *Maybe I was dreaming. It sounded like someone called my name.*

Everything was quiet and still outside in the parkway.

It's the middle of the night, for God's sake, what's the matter with me? A dream? My imagination running wild? But, she couldn't go back to sleep. The voice had sounded so real.

Linda got up, changed into a clean, dry T-shirt, splashed warm water on her face and rubbed it dry with a clean towel. Then she crawled back into bed, wondering about Cathryn again.

In the morning I'll do something, she decided. Feeling drowsy and perplexed, Linda tucked the thick comforter around her body and pulled the pillow closer to her. *I definitely have to do something,* she told herself solemnly.

ℑ

Karen Brauning was pleased to receive Sylvia's call. After she listened to the message on her machine, she didn't waste any time. Karen prided herself on taking action immediately.

Sitting around and moaning about things is Dick's style, not mine, she sneered about her husband.

She had been sitting at her desk arranging appointments in her book for the coming week when Sylvia called. She didn't feel like talking to her husband or anyone else just then, so she sat there listening as Sylvia left her message.

"That's some good news," she said aloud as Sylvia hung up. "A new client in one of my established homes. Another sick or elderly person I can be of service to. Good."

Karen's lips formed a sort of smile with her lips pulled back baring her small teeth. The top teeth pressed against the bottom ones, and, the resulting expression on her face was one of cunning and perfidious greed. Karen's short, narrow fingers drummed steadily on the desktop for a moment, the calculating wheels of her mind spinning rapidly.

She picked up the phone and reached for the pad of paper in front of her. Karen began making the arrangements, which in a short period of time would result in an increase in her income.

To earn her money, she handled the finances of other people who did not care to do so, or who could not be bothered with such matters. It was ridiculously easy. Of course there was always the paper work to get things started, and she usually had to move quickly in case there was someone around who might think about complicating her plans. But this was her territory, no matter who the client happened to be or what his or her circumstances.

That's one of "Karen's laws," she thought, smiling a peculiar, predatory smile once again. *What's mine is mine.*

She penciled a note into her book to remember to send Sylvia a gift. *That annoying and complaining little woman has been extremely helpful these past few months,* Karen reflected, tapping the pencil on her desk. It was true — Sylvia had been instrumental in bringing more than one lucrative client to Karen's attention.

ॐ

Karen Ethel Brauning was a short, small woman in her early forties, with dark hair and very pale skin. She had dark circles under her eyes that made her look as if she wasn't getting proper nutrition or enough rest, though she was rarely up and out of bed before ten. It was another of "Karen's laws" to leave Richard to handle the morning chores. Karen Brauning detested mornings.

Although her features were not really unattractive, and she certainly liked to dress well, Karen Brauning was not a pleasant person to look at. Her small, dark eyes were rather vermin-like and she very rarely smiled. When she did, it was that same peculiar, furtive, calculating expression, with her small teeth bared and set against one another.

Her demeanor, sublimely social and artificial, made most people in her company feel uneasy and very cautious. People were not drawn to her at all, and Karen didn't give a damn whether they were or not.

The truth about Karen Brauning was that she would attack anyone with a temerity that was unnerving, including those close to her, if it served her purposes. She gave off a sense of danger that oozed through her attempts at a pleasant facade. Karen often felt bitter about some things that had befallen her in life, but she was not the type of woman to sit by and do nothing to change them.

She didn't believe that her husband, Richard Edgar Brauning, was comparable to her in intelligence or abilities. He was, nevertheless, an adequate husband. Albeit he did make too much noise at the wrong times. He was somewhat brash and indolent, and he hadn't been very successful at earning an income even close to Karen's.

Richard Brauning's physical appearance was weak. He had a soft jaw line and a puling, complaining manner. Though Karen would not come out and say it, Richard was almost useless to her in bed. It was not Richard's sexual competence that kept Karen with him.

If it takes him twenty seconds to come, that's a long time, she had once sneered derisively to a carefully selected confidant.

But that didn't really matter much to Karen. Her greatest satisfactions did not come from Richard's abilities, nor were they determined by his inabilities. Richard was not a necessity in Karen's life. He was a convenience.

"Karen's laws" declared that Karen get what she wants, even while her husband thrashed about nearby, in his own little universe.

The Braunings lived in a comfortable two story home, in a pleasant-looking neighborhood and they both drove new cars. Karen's was a silver Lexus and Richard, or "Dick," as most people knew him, drove a dark blue Buick Regal.

It turned out to be very fortunate that they had extra room in their house, especially now. Their fourth bedroom had recently been remodeled to become Dick's new office. This was convenient for both Karen and Dick, though his move to the new office space had come about because of some very difficult and exasperating circumstances.

༄

Dick Brauning had been an insurance salesman when Karen met and married him. He was not terribly intelligent, nor industrious, but he was very lucky for a short while. An older, successful agent in his firm had suffered a sudden heart attack and someone was needed immediately to follow up on his long-standing and lucrative accounts. Dick found himself in the right place at the right time, and because of this, plus a loquacious embellishment of his own abilities, he acquired those accounts shortly after he began working for the company.

The money was coming in nicely when he met Karen, who was unequivocally impressed with both his leased 500 SL and his very generous spending whenever they were together. They were married within the year, while the money was still flowing into their bank account at a rapid rate.

But, Dick, being neither a caring nor particularly efficient agent, found it to be an annoying chore to continuously service his clients. To Dick Brauning this was a subordinate activity to collecting and cashing his commission checks.

"Jesus Christ!" he complained to Karen, his voice filled with disdain and irritation. "They want you to show up at ten o'clock at night or early Sunday morning, just because they've got a question or a problem. These people think my life is based on their goddamn aches and pains and their goddamn household crap! I'm sick of all of them."

Karen didn't answer him.

Karen knew that when Dick raved on and on, he didn't hear anyone else. She walked into the kitchen and fixed a drink for each of them. Dick continued grumbling nastily at his absentee adversaries, the same people who were supporting his lifestyle, while he accepted the glass from his wife. The phone rang again.

"Aw, shit," he muttered. "Let the service get it, I'm gonna watch the game. They can wait until Monday like the rest of the frigging world." Karen picked up a magazine and walked away from him into her office.

It didn't take very long before the complaints multiplied and several long time customers of Dick's rather prestigious insurance firm began to make noises about going elsewhere.

Dick's boss called him into his office in an attempt to resolve the problems that were reaching him with alarming frequency. Typically Dick became defensive and loud instantly.

"What the fuck do these people want from me, for Christ sake?" he stormed, ignoring what Mr. Palmer was trying, calmly, to explain to him.

Instead of suggesting actions that he might take to remedy the disturbing circumstances, Dick grew more argumentative with his boss. It was his style. Mr. Palmer became very quiet, somewhat amazed at the reaction he was witnessing from his employee.

Ultimately, Dick was dismissed with severance pay when Mr. Palmer realized that there was no one there worth salvaging. Dick had lasted exactly twenty-one months with his first and last established and reputable insurance firm.

For many years, Dick went from one company to another,

working in sales and telling himself that that's where the real money was. He was certain that people were suckers and that he knew how to handle them.

But without even the smallest degree of sincerity in his business dealings, along with such an obvious voracity to collect paychecks, and never mind servicing his clients, Dick rapidly disenchanted his employers and most of the other people with whom he dealt.

In the meantime, Karen was working successfully as a secretary in a law firm. She was earning a good salary, but more importantly, she was making significant connections for their future. When she wasn't at work she watched her husband's struggles with tolerance mixed with exasperated dismay, but she did a fair job of encouraging him in spite of his failures.

However, Karen Brauning consistently put her real energies where she felt they would give her the best return.

ॐ

Karen and Dick Brauning had sex infrequently. Ordinarily Karen had other things to do, and though he pouted and protested occasionally, Dick pretty much accepted what he received from his wife. One night in bed he was feeling particularly prurient and he reached over hungrily for his wife's small, pear-shaped breast as she leaned back against the headboard, her face buried behind a legal journal.

"I've got to finish reading this article, Dick," she said querulously swatting his hand away from her flannel-pajama covered chest, without so much as a glance in his direction. Karen stiffly tucked the covers tightly under her hip, immutable, leaving no room for discussion or argument.

Dick pulled the blanket up under his chin, his lower lip jutting out for a moment. "You've always got to finish reading some damn thing or other," he complained, but not loudly enough to get Karen angry.

Get her pissed and I'll never get laid, he thought. She completely ignored his muffled, fractious ire and turned the page of the magazine she held.

"Shit. I can't sleep," he muttered, climbing out of their bed. He went into the kitchen and fixed himself a drink.

The hell with her, he thought, *I don't need her shit.* And it was true, he didn't. Dick went into their small den, closed the door and stuck a video that he had tried unsuccessfully to get Karen to watch with him, into the VCR. He watched two young blond girls with huge breasts and effective tongues bring some gloating guy with an enormous penis to orgasm.

Dick watched esuriently, his lips parted and moist, his chest heaving. Soon he was pretending that it was those tongues, and not his own hand that was causing his muffled groans and then the explosion into the towel that he had brought with him into the den.

◦

Eventually Karen did get pregnant and the couple had a child. They both vowed soon afterwards that they would have no more. The noise and commotion caused by their new daughter was more than enough parenthood for both of them.

Dick Brauning, basically a resentful and angry man, had convinced himself that he worked as hard as the next guy, but that he was always unappreciated by the mediocre people who happened to be his employers. He hated being told what to do by people whom he saw acting self-important because they owned the business.

He complained continuously to Karen, "I'm getting pushed around by people who are stupid." One night he swore to his wife, "I'm going to find a job where I can push back, God dammit!" He had a glass of scotch in his hand and the ice clinked against the glass as his fingers shook and his voice got louder.

"For God's sake, Dick, do something and stop making so much noise about it," was his wife's piqued, unsympathetic reply as she got into bed, turned off the lamp, and turned her back to him. Within minutes he could hear her even, little snoring sounds. Gripping the glass tightly in his hand, he wanted to smash something badly. He realized that he had better get out of their bedroom.

While Karen was fast asleep, Dick sat at their kitchen table glaring at the newspaper. Despite the effects of the alcohol he had been consuming for the better part of the evening, an ad for law enforcement trainees caught his eye. He refilled his glass from a bottle on the counter and read the ad again.

I'm still young, he thought. *I'm in good physical shape. Maybe wearing a badge and a uniform would help straighten out some of the stupid morons I run into every day.* The idea brought a rare smile to his face.

And so Dick Brauning became a cop.

ॐ

Some cops are decent, and sincerely want to enforce laws in order to protect good people. They want to stop people from getting hurt and from hurting one another. But, there's another type: the cop who needs to be in charge, who has to control and stop others for perverse purposes.

Dick Brauning did not become one of those decent, conscientious cops. His irascible nature was so close to the surface that he was recognized as volatile, and more often, as an embarrassment to the force amongst many of his fellows. It was painfully obvious to them that Dick got his greatest pleasures from enforcing his own will, even if it was jaded by personal issues, a hot temper and a cruel anger.

He received several reprimands during the years that he remained on the force. Few of his fellow cops wanted to work with him or even be around the man. Instead of raising Dick Brauning's sense of responsibility and integrity, wearing the badge and uniform gave him reason to become louder and more arrogant, often nothing more than a bully. With the continuing complaints, Dick Brauning became even more volatile.

After some time, he made one too many nasty, aggressive mistakes, and, rather abruptly, he was no longer a law enforcement officer. But he left the force with compensation, and, so, he really didn't give a damn when he had to turn in his badge.

ॐ

When his little daughter asked him, "Why aren't you a policeman anymore, Daddy?" Dick felt a fierce, rekindled anger.

He told her, "It doesn't matter, Leslie. Things just happened. But don't worry, honey, I'll fix them. You'll see." He picked her up and kissed her on her mouth, a little too hard and a little too long.

"You're daddy's best girl, aren't you?" he asked, holding her in a hug that was too tight and uncomfortable for Leslie. She squirmed in his arms, but he wouldn't release his grip on her.

"Tell me you love me and I'll let you go," he said stubbornly.

"Down, Daddy, put me down," Leslie frowned, tears coming to her eyes.

"Go play then," he scowled, abruptly letting her go and roughly dropping her to her feet. "Just go play, dammit," he snapped at the child as she ran out of the room.

~

The seething, cancerous acerbity within him grew. He was angrier than he had been ever before. Dick Brauning was obsessed with finding a job where he could tell others what to do, where he would have work that put him in charge no matter what.

~

Thus an idea formed in the Brauning household. Actually, it was Karen, with her many helpful connections, who went to work on it and helped her husband pull it off.

Some time later, with Karen's help and other measures, Dick Brauning made it through law school and became an attorney.

The reaction of one of his estranged former associates was, "God help that profession now."

Dick moved into a small office space belonging to the law firm of Ronald Hardwick, an older, established attorney friend of Karen's, who owed her several favors. Ronald had managed for many years to eke out a decent living handling personal injury cases and minor real estate transactions. He agreed to rent space to Dick and to push some work his way.

The law offices were located in the southernmost corner of Vista, an area rife with gang disputes and crime. Drugs were exchanged on street corners in the shadows and cars and homes were broken into and robbed more than anywhere else in North County.

There, at the end of a gray, dismal street, amongst buildings decorated with graffiti, was Dick's new office. The windows of the small one-story building bore heavy iron bars and the sign outside read, "Law Offices." Under that sign was another that read, "Credit Bureau." It belonged to a collection agency next door that specialized in pursuing debtors with a vengeance. The personnel often enlisted the aid of the adjoining law firm, or at least its letterhead, to give their demands more force.

Though it wasn't the most prestigious beginning for a new lawyer, it looked as if Karen Brauning's husband was going to have another chance to put himself in charge.

However, even this seemingly golden opportunity was short-lived. Within the first few months, a number of upsets occurred between Ronald, a normally easy-going man, and Dick Brauning, who seemed to stimulate turbulence and animosity wherever he went. Dick, believing that other people were continuously preventing him from finding his proper position in life, was, even on his best days, an argument waiting to happen.

Ronald's assessment of the situation was that he couldn't work with someone on whom he couldn't rely to do what had been promised. What made it worse was that Dick Brauning seemed to enjoy lying about why he didn't perform as he said he would.

Ultimately there was a big blow up about some particular legal matter and Ronald called it quits, Karen or not. He told Dick to pack his personal belongings and get out of the office.

Dick fumed back at him. "I wouldn't work another second with such an unreliable bastard, anyway. You say one thing one minute and then you change your mind! I didn't do a damn thing that you wouldn't have done yourself and you know it. You're being a pompous ass. You'd be the first one to save your own ass and we both know it!" he shouted across Ronald's desk.

At the reception desk down the hall, a dark-haired secretary turned the volume down on her radio and smiled happily.

Ronald tightened his fists at his sides and clenched his teeth together, but he didn't say another word. *This guy is unbelievable,* Ronald thought to himself. *How even someone like Karen lives with him is beyond me.*

These unpleasant circumstances resulted in Dick Brauning moving the next phase of his new career into the fourth bedroom of their middle class home.

ॐ

Karen didn't care very much that Dick went from job to job during most of their marriage, as long as he did what she needed and stayed out of her way. Besides, now it appeared that he was finally going in a direction that could actually be helpful to her own ambitions. She didn't care that he was often such an egregious ass in front of people. He did much more than she did to keep the house neat, and he never gave her a hard time when she asked him to run an errand or take Leslie somewhere. Karen was busy making a lot of money and Dick helped in his own way.

Karen was a basically dispassionate, opportunistic person. She knew how to take advantage of her husband's virtues and she found other arrangements to offset his less desirable attributes.

ॐ

Eight years ago Karen had accidentally stumbled upon the work that she now pursued relentlessly. A legal secretary in the law office where she worked was chattering enviously over coffee about a new car her friend was buying.

"I'm giving these clowns notice," she joked wryly. "Terry's going to train me as her assistant. All she does is manage money for old people and she's making a fortune." The conversation got Karen's attention.

In the very beginning Karen had recognized how incredibly easy it would be to produce an income that would make her salary in the law firm look ridiculous. And, she would no longer have to answer to arrogant, narcissistic lawyers all day. Karen was still amazed that a career as a private conservator was such a well-kept secret, and for her part, she intended to keep it that way.

She had finally found a tremendous need in society for her knowledge and her talents.

Of course, you need the correct connections, she reflected, *and not everyone is good with figures. But when your income depends directly upon how well you handle someone else's money and their other assets, you can get good at it fast!* she thought, an expression crossing her mouth that was more of a smirk than a smile. In managing other people's money, Karen had turned out to be an extremely adept student, especially when those people were elderly or incapacitated.

Karen enjoyed the additional bonus of working at home and not having to deal with her clients unless she chose to do so. She was not particularly fond of elderly or sick people who were always complaining about something or other. This aspect of her work was a plus, and most of her duties could be handled by computer, fax, mail, and telephone.

Of course there were the court appearances, but that wasn't very complicated. Not with the help of Judge Jerome R. Humphrey, Superior Court, Department S, Escondido.

Karen and Judge Humphrey had hit it off immediately. This was understandable, as they were both rather cold, calculating and pompous individuals. In fact, in their somewhat aligned careers, Karen Brauning and Judge Humphrey might be called truly Machiavellian, as they steadfastly placed political expediency above morality. Also, they smiled at one another more than they ever smiled elsewhere. It was whispered that Karen Brauning and Judge Humphrey were both arrogantly self-righteous concerning their positions and their powers.

And, Karen's clients? Karen handled them for their own good always, by whatever measures she and her good friend the Judge, deemed correct. After all, Jerome Humphrey, though he was not well-liked or admired, was someone to be reckoned with in his realms of authority, on the bench and at home. He was known around the courthouse as a man with a rather narrow mind and an ostentatious, self-important, God-like manner. Nevertheless, each day, properly robed, he sat upon the bench, pontificating and authoritatively dispensing justice, exactly as he saw fit.

Eight

A conservator...

LINDA BEGAN TRYING TO TRACK Cathryn down in earnest. She called her mother, Lois, in Boca Raton who then made phone calls to Cathryn's brothers in Chicago. When Lois finally reached Steve, he gave her the telephone number that he had for the Kents' house in San Diego. Lois gave it to Linda and Linda began calling. There was no answer. The telephone simply continued to ring. Linda tried calling in the morning, in the afternoon, and then again in the evening.

No answer, no answering machine. What gives? she wondered.

She tried again. Still nothing. She dialed the number just before she went to bed, and then again in the middle of the night when she woke up to go to the bathroom.

No answer, nothing, just the continuous, maddeningly, measured sound of the phone ringing over and over, again and again.

She checked the unlisted number with her mother and asked Lois to verify it with Steve. "See if he has any other numbers for the house or Edward's work or anything else," Linda said, rubbing the back of her hand wearily across her eyes. "Mom, this can't be right. They've got to be home some time. Call Keith or Steve again and make sure this is the last number they had for Cathryn, okay? And find out how long it's been since they've heard from her by letter or phone. Jesus, this is getting too weird, Mom. Something's really wrong."

"Honey, I will. It doesn't make any sense that they haven't talked to her for so long. No one seems to know what's going on there," Lois replied.

She told Linda that she was reluctant to alarm Joseph and Anna, that she preferred to talk to the brothers. Cathryn's parents, both in their eighties, were not doing well physically and Joseph was worse than Anna. He had undergone two surgeries for colon cancer. But the constant worrying that Anna did about her husband was taking its toll on her as well.

Moreover, for nearly twenty years their only daughter had been their greatest heartache.

❦

Linda was puzzled by the unanswered calls. She checked with the operator to see if there was something mechanically wrong with the line, but it was okay. It just didn't make any sense to her.

No answering machine? she wondered. *They're probably the only ones left in the world without one.* Linda hoped that they were just on a vacation or a trip somewhere. But the feeling that something was terribly wrong would not go away. She continued dialing the number over and over again with no response.

Then Lois called Linda back. "The number is the right one as far as Keith knows. He hasn't talked to Cathryn in over a year but Steve heard from her once, not too long ago, and she didn't say anything about a new telephone number."

Linda kept calling, mechanically dialing the number every once in a while, becoming used to the unanswered ringing.

Then one afternoon the ringing stopped and a woman's voice said, "Hello?"

Linda was so startled to hear someone's voice instead of the steady, uninterrupted ringing, that she hesitated a moment, her mouth open.

"Hello?" the woman said again.

That's not Cathryn. She sounds older, Linda thought.

"Hello, I'm trying to reach Cathryn. Is she there?" Linda asked urgently.

"No, I'm sorry. She isn't. Who's calling?" the woman sounded worried and anxious.

"This is Linda, her cousin. Who is this?" Linda asked.

"Margaret Ketterman. God, I'm so glad you called," the woman sounded relieved. Her voice was shaking as if she were about to burst into tears.

✧

"Where is she, Mrs. Ketterman? I want to see her as soon as I can," Linda said. "I knew something was wrong. I knew it." Her voice trembled, there were tears in her eyes and her cheeks were flushed.

"Just 'Margaret', please? Look, Linda, if you haven't seen her in a long time, you are going to be shocked. She's gone through a lot. More than you can imagine, more than should happen to anyone. Let me explain what I know."

"Of course," Linda said. "*Please.*"

✧

An hour and a half later, Margaret was sitting across from Linda in a booth at a Denny's in Del Mar, just off the freeway. Margaret nervously twisted the corner of her napkin. She barely touched her coffee as she told Linda about Cathryn and Edward and about the past year.

Margaret was a pleasant looking woman, slightly plump, but neat and well-dressed. She appeared to be in her late fifties with dark hair that was beginning to gray swept up behind her head in a thick bun, giving her a distinguished, confident look. But her voice quivered. Her eyes were dark with worry and her mouth trembled sadly as she spoke. She looked from her napkin to Linda, then up at the people passing by their booth. For a moment she was quiet, thoughtfully remembering, and then she looked out of the window on her right and back again to Linda.

"Both Jack and I worked with Edward for a long time," she explained. "We saw Cathryn every once in a while, usually when he brought her to a business dinner. She was incredibly beautiful then, but she always seemed nervous, uneasy. It was as if she was always anxious to go home, even when they first got there. That's the thing I remember the most. She was always so nervous. I couldn't understand it. She looked as if she had everything a woman could want. She was so pretty.

"He was a devoted husband under horribly demanding circumstances. He described Cathryn to us as high-strung and extremely nervous. Unfortunately," she related, "Cathryn had a nervous breakdown just after they were married, and since then her condition's been continuously monitored by doctors and controlled by medication."

"'Her family,' he said to us, 'never wanted to be involved in our problems and we've pretty much been left to our own devices.' He had to hospitalize her more than once, 'for her own safety,' he said. I remember him keeping his head down and his voice was very sad. 'She's doing much better now, though,' he told me once and he had brightened up a little. That was a year or two ago," Margaret said.

"We hadn't seen Cathryn for a long time. Edward had stopped bringing her to business dinners and parties. He told Jack that she couldn't leave the house except when she had a doctor's appointment or needed to bring Rex to the vet. He said that she was too terrified to go anywhere after dark, even with Edward, and, so usually he stayed home with her.

"Then, without any warning — he had never been sick all the years we knew him — Edward had a heart attack and died instantly, right there in the house. He was dead in his office for two days before Cathryn found him.

"She must have just gone completely off the deep-end with his death," Margaret said. "She was all alone in the house and no one knew about any family on either side, except a sister he didn't have anything to do with anymore, so no one was contacted. We never even found a single piece of paper or a letter or anything that indicated where any family was, his or hers."

Margaret's eyes were cloudy and damp as she remembered how troubled she and Jack had been, how they had wanted to help Cathryn, but, having never dealt with anything like this before, they felt frustrated and helpless as her condition worsened. Linda sat quietly listening, and when Margaret paused, Linda waited patiently for her to continue. The ache in her chest felt like cruel fingers pressing against her heart and lungs. She sighed deeply but said nothing.

After a few moments Margaret went on, "Jack tried so hard to straighten out her affairs. He called Edward's lawyer and met with their CPA, and finally he felt they had things in some sort of order for her."

Margaret took a sip of water, but instead of putting the glass back down on the table, she held it a few inches from her face, looking into the water as if she could see something there, remembering.

"But Cathryn thwarted us every step of the way. Sometimes she called and stopped payment on the checks he had just persuaded her to write for the mortgage on her house! He was afraid that she would lose it, but we didn't know what else we could do. Sometimes it was as if she understood everything that was happening, as if she had some weird plan of her own, something that had to do with her and Edward, something that Jack and I couldn't figure out at all. Sometimes she just seemed so crazy, as if there were no plan or reason for anything at all. Just madness. Not rational, not sensible, not understandable.

"We tried, but she managed to get herself into so much trouble in her neighborhood that the police were called once too often and she was put back in a mental hospital. Tate is the name of it. This time there was no Edward to retrieve her when they got her sufficiently quieted down, and so she ended up in a home, just for a while, the hospital people told us."

"But, why?" Linda interrupted. "She still has resources, doesn't she? Did Edward leave her anything? What about the house? She has family! They care about her very much. They never stopped.... Jesus...," Linda's voice broke. Margaret could barely hear her. Linda pressed her napkin against the corners of her eyes to stop the tears and she blew her nose.

"What? Well, let me tell you the rest. For some reason Cathryn eventually decided to tell the hospital people about us, about Jack and me. She even remembered our phone numbers at work and at home, and she gave them to a social worker. Sometimes she's amazing," her voice drifted off for a moment. She looked at Linda and continued, "The hospital social worker called and we went to meet with her. She explained that Cathryn needed to have an LPS conservator before they could release her from the hospital."

"What's that?" Linda asked, puzzled.

"They gave us a lot of paperwork on it. I brought it for you." Margaret pulled a manila folder out of her bag. "I have more things for you in my car. Anyway, the letters stand for the Lanterman-Petris-Short Act. By establishing a conservatorship, the Court grants authority to another person to see to it that someone who is found to be disabled, or who can't provide for their own food, clothing and shelter, has their basic needs and necessary mental health treatment provided for them."

Linda looked at her helplessly, her mouth opened a bit, but no words came. *What horrible shape can she be in for this to happen to her?* she thought. A chill went up her arms and she shuddered.

"Anyway, she had to have an LPS conservator, before the hospital would release her. And they said that she couldn't live alone in the condition she was in. We just couldn't handle the responsibility of something like that, so she was given a court-appointed attorney, a court-appointed LPS conservator and she was placed in the Wilson Home in Leucadia, with pretty much everything taken out of her control." Margaret stopped and took a deep breath, then she looked up at Linda.

"You must be mistaken," Linda gasped a little. Her voice was muted to a disbelieving tone that didn't sound at all like her. "This can't be true. This can't be happening, not to Cathryn," she whispered, her voice filled with pain. She bent her head down a little, and tears that she could no longer stop fell to the table.

ॐ

An LPS conservator is, ostensibly, someone who accepts the duties and responsibilities of assisting a fellow citizen at a time when that person is unable to effectively meet his or her own needs.

And that is what occurs in many instances.

However, the rights of a person deemed "gravely disabled" are greatly diminished by this action. Such a person is determined, by statute, to be "unwilling or incapable of accepting treatment voluntarily" and, so, the determination that they should be medicated, hospitalized or further treated is taken out of their hands and given to another human being.

God help the disabled person if that other human being is acting on anything other than genuine caring for the individual.

༣

The laws that determine who that other human being can be are very specific. In the State of California that decision is based on probate law, "Article 3, Establishment of Conservatorship, Section 1820, Filing of petition." This code states who may request to be the conservator. It clearly gives the disabled person, himself, a voice in the matter. Also, any relative of the proposed conservatee is able to file such a petition and preference is given by law to suitable family members or friends. But despite these first two points, the decision of who is selected to hold someone else's life in their hands is ultimately up to a judge's discretion.

And that is the reality of it.

༣

"We went to see her as often as we could," Margaret continued, her eyes staring out the window at nothing in particular, as if she could see it happening again, or perhaps as if she could feel how Cathryn must have felt. Her voice was subdued. Linda leaned forward to hear her. "She was so bright and pleasant one minute and so psychotic the next, we just didn't know what else to do. God, Linda, we *wanted* to help her."

Gradually, Margaret and Jack withdrew, because they really *didn't* know what else to do, and — not because they didn't really care, but because they were overwhelmed by the circumstances and the legal procedures — they abandoned Cathryn to the care of the authorities and the legal system.

༣

What Linda didn't discover from her conversation with Margaret was what took place later, when Cathryn continued to cause problems in the Wilson Home and pushed its proprietor one step too far.

Sylvia Wilson went further than just seeing to it that her most troublesome client was medicated by Dr. Murdock into docility and submission, traits that were not at all native to Cathryn Silberg Kent. Sylvia, intent on winning the whole game with Cathryn, not just a round or two, had hurriedly contacted Karen Brauning, private fiduciary, estate and trust administrator, guardian and conservator.

For Cathryn, this was yet another mistake of great magnitude.

ॐ

Sylvia had reached her limit of torment from Cathryn's erratic behavior. She was more than familiar with Karen's expertise in these matters. In the past, whenever Sylvia had a problem with any of the residents who were under Karen's authority, Karen would promptly step in and the upset would be taken care of immediately, usually with just a few phone calls, and usually with a hospitalization. The result was always a very calm resident.

When one of these formerly troublesome or disruptive residents was returned to the Wilson Home, Sylvia didn't get a moment's aggravation from them.

Sylvia didn't really like Karen Brauning. *Karen is peculiar,* she thought, *haughty and aggressive, especially for so small a woman.* But Sylvia couldn't deny that Karen was very effective. Now Sylvia couldn't wait to get her involved in Mrs. Cathryn Kent's life, so that Sylvia could have some peace around her own home again.

ॐ

Karen Brauning descended upon her new opportunity much like a vulture descends upon its prey.

ॐ

The encyclopedia states that vultures eat dead animals. That's how they survive. They have blunt claws, which are rather poor weapons for seizing and carrying off their food, and so they normally dine right there, where the animal has ceased to live. Though they are ugly birds, with naked heads and dark feathers, they are useful, for they eat dead bodies. If they didn't, these dead bodies would decay and become health dangers. It's interesting that the vultures, themselves, do not carry disease.

They are birds which have a graceful, soaring flight and they sail through the skies in broad circles. Because of their sharp eyes and keen sense of smell, they can spot dying or dead animals from great distances.

॰

After learning from Sylvia that Cathryn had some resources, and that there was equity in the house she owned, but could no longer live in by herself, Karen began the paperwork necessary to become Cathryn's conservator over both her person and her estate. Everything she did was carefully correct and legal, and it was all perfectly documented. And, now, she even had her own in-house attorney, literally, who could prepare the necessary documents for her and then go to the courthouse to file them.

Dick Brauning took this opportunity to bend the truth a bit, as needed. His questionable probity was finally becoming useful.

Karen took each subsequent step carefully, methodically, but quite rapidly. It was necessary to move quickly before any previously quiet or distant relative could voice any objection.

"It means we have to file a confidential report with the Court stating that any family that exists is ineligible for the position as conservator. Either they reside out of the county, out of the state, or they have failed or declined to come to Cathryn's assistance in time of need," she reminded Dick. "Any relatives," Dick's report later read, "were either unavailable, incapable or completely inadequate, as demonstrated by their lack of actions in the past."

The rest was relatively easy. Karen and Judge Humphrey had worked on similar cases together many times before.

Jerome Humphrey, a venal and small-minded magistrate, was also very concerned with his image. He was absolutely certain that Karen Brauning would work within the exact framework of the law, even if some truths of the situation were altered slightly or even omitted. The judge knew that he could count on Karen to be extremely thorough. He was fond of the woman and had been for some time.

After all, she's much like myself, he thought. *She's cunning and resourceful. And an attractive woman,* the judge mused as he looked over the document that had reached his desk that morning.

༃

Jerome Humphrey watched Karen walk out of his office later that day, a small smile stretching across his thin lips. He noticed how her skirt pulled just a bit across her hips, and he wondered, for a moment, if she was exaggerating her sway from side to side for his benefit, knowing that he would be watching her exit.

So self-assured, so capable, so in control, he thought. *So different from Eleanor.*

Eleanor, the judge's wife, was doting and devoted, but as exciting to Jerome Humphrey as a peanut butter sandwich.

But, Karen, he thought as the door closed behind her, *She's thrilling in some inexplicable, almost dangerous way, with her sharp tongue and pointy little breasts.*

The judge was smiling broadly now. He was also beginning to get an erection.

༃

Karen Brauning's petition was accepted without question and she was appointed Cathryn's temporary conservator of person and estate by Judge Jerome R. Humphrey.

Karen proceeded to handle Cathryn's financial affairs; in other words, to pay her bills. By law, she was to be compensated for her services. She was now entitled to receive a portion of the existing estate, according to the hours that she spent dealing with Cathryn's situation. Additionally, any time that Dick spent preparing needed documents and running errands would be paid for by the estate. Karen was delighted to discover, when going through Cathryn's bank records, that her new client received some sort of trust payment every month.

This is better than it looked at first, she grinned to herself. *And not a word from any family. This is going well. Yes, it's going very well.*

꒳

And, it *was* going well for them. It was a wonderful system for Judge Humphrey's friends, Karen and Dick Brauning. It was not so good for Cathryn, who, after one phone call and one meeting with Karen, during which she refused to sign anything, became Karen's newest client, whether she liked it or not. Like a pawn on a chess board, or a lump of clay, to be moved about at Karen's direction.

It was now up to these uncaring strangers to decide whether Cathryn would be hospitalized or not, whether she would be medicated or not — with or without her consent. They would determine where her money would go, what she could buy, where she could live, whether or not her house would be sold, and, sadly for Cathryn, even what could happen to her beloved Rex.

Nine

A visiting day...

WHEN LINDA LEFT MARGARET after their meeting at Denny's, she was miserable. She felt as if constricting bands were pulling tightly around her head and abdomen with a hurting, steady pressure. When she thought of her cousin, she was filled with a frightening agitation. And it grew worse, like a gas creeping, flowing into every part of her. Her days had been filled with a foreboding, a strange presage that was very slowly divulging itself.

But after she finally saw Cathryn, her agony was greater than she would have ever thought possible.

⁓

The morning after the meeting in Del Mar, Linda drove to the address of the Wilson Home in Leucadia that Margaret had given her, parked her car on the street, and walked up the driveway to the front door. All the curtains were closed. An insect-speckled yellowish night light over the door was still on, though it was after ten o'clock in the morning. She rang the doorbell and waited. Inside the house she heard the murmur of voices from a television program. There were no other sounds.

Linda had driven down the freeway that morning along a coastline heavily shrouded by a dull and gray, overcast sky. It looked as if it might rain, but that was unlikely for southern California this time of year. It was the end of September and the days ordinarily remained warm and spring-like, with bright sunshine and shimmering, tepid ocean waters.

The neighborhood surrounding the Wilson Home was peculiarly quiet, except for a dog in the distance somewhere down the block, repeating a pathetic whining sound. Linda looked around the dismal front yard. It was overgrown with weeds. She tapped lightly on the door.

"Coming," she heard a woman's voice call from inside.

The door opened and Linda introduced herself to Sylvia Wilson, who was wiping her hands on a small towel. The two women looked at one another for a moment. Then, with an uneasy smile, Sylvia said, "Let me take you to Cathryn. She likes to sit outside on the back patio."

"Thanks," Linda replied. Her heart was pounding now, the memory of an awful photograph of Cathryn that Margaret had shown her, clear and distinct in her mind.

They walked through a small living room where two older men sat on a couch watching TV. One of them didn't turn away from the screen. The other stared hard at Linda and nodded his head slightly when she said, "Good morning." The room smelled of age, disinfectant and stale tobacco. They passed through the kitchen where a heavy-set Mexican woman at the sink turned and bobbed her head at Linda as she followed Sylvia through the kitchen and out onto the patio. Linda managed to smile weakly, but the woman had already turned back to the sink.

Cathryn was sitting in a chair on the patio, her back to the house, gazing out into the yard, smoking a cigarette. She didn't turn or move at all as Sylvia and Linda approached.

"Look, Cathryn," Sylvia said loudly, in a voice that was stiff and solicitous, "Your cousin Linda's come to see you."

"Linda?" Cathryn's lips slowly formed the word. She didn't get up and she didn't turn her head. But Linda was in front of her now, and then down on her knees before the chair. Her arms went around Cathryn. Linda struggled to hold back the tears that were filling her eyes as she hugged Cathryn tightly to her for a long moment. Then she leaned back and looked into her friend's eyes. Cathryn sat very still but her eyes looked directly back into Linda's. They were gray and blank. She didn't say anything.

"Would you like some coffee?" Sylvia asked.

"That would be great," Linda answered, her eyes still riveted on Cathryn's lined and puffy face. Sylvia left them alone.

ৎৎ

Linda pulled a chair close to Cathryn's. After several minutes, there was a flicker of recognition, and then a sparkle of light shone in Cathryn's eyes. Tiny laugh lines slowly appeared at the corners of her mouth and she tilted her head to one side, thoughtfully taking in Linda's features. Linda reached over and held Cathryn's soft, furrowed face between her fingers for a moment. "Oh, Cathryn," she sighed deeply.

"Well, what are *you* doing here?" Cathryn asked slowly, her voice a low monotone, as if it took great effort to speak. But her lips still smiled the tiniest bit. Then she took a deep drag on her cigarette and blew the smoke away. Aside from the movements necessary to get the cigarette to her mouth and draw in enough breath to get the smoke deeply into her lungs, Cathryn barely moved.

"I just found out where you were," Linda told her. "I just found out about Edward. I met your friend, Margaret Ketterman, and she told me where you were. I'm so sorry it took me so long." Linda's voice broke and tears filled her eyes again.

Cathryn didn't seem to notice. "Margaret isn't my friend," she said absently without emotion. "She and her husband work in Edward's office. Rex is my friend." At the sound of his name, the gentlemanly little dog waddled obediently over to Cathryn from where he had been lying on the grass, patiently waiting for her attention. With his tail wagging, Rex looked directly up at Cathryn with big brown, loving and sorrowful eyes. Cathryn absently patted his head and he sat down beside her. Then he glanced over at Linda before he lay down at his mistress' feet, his head on his front paws.

Sylvia returned with two cups of coffee. She handed one to

Linda and put the other on the table next to Cathryn's chair. She dropped a few packets of sugar and Nutrasweet next to the cup. Linda thanked her and Sylvia walked away. Cathryn looked out into the yard while she smoked the cigarette almost down to the filter. Then she lit another one from it and stubbed the butt out in an ashtray on the table. The two women sat silently looking at one another, each of them with her own thoughts, in her own separate and very different universe.

༣

Though Margaret had shown Linda a recent photograph of Cathryn and had described her behavior in detail, Linda still was not prepared for the enormous mental and physical deterioration that she saw in her cousin. She watched as Cathryn stared for a long time at nothing.

She's sedated, too calm, as if she's a million miles away, Linda thought. She looked at Cathryn's clothes. She was wearing a faded, worn, denim shirt, baggy, stained jeans and scuffed, graying tennis shoes. Her hair was unevenly cut and her fingernails were ragged. *I don't believe what's happened to her,* Linda thought painfully.

Except for the initial light in her eyes, Cathryn was almost entirely unrecognizable from the beautiful young woman Linda had known. Linda's insides felt knotted and aching. She gripped her hands in her lap, her fingers entwined so tightly that her knuckles began hurting. Her eyes grew moist as she watched Cathryn in the chair beside her, focusing her attention now on some vacant place in the yard, until she shifted her eyes, momentarily, to her cigarette, or to her dog. Each movement she made was painfully slow and careful.

In the brightness of the morning, her hair looked snarled and dull and there were deep lines across her forehead and at the corners of her eyes and mouth. Her clothes were shabby and too tight across her breasts and hips. Her body and face were bloated out of proportion.

After several silent minutes, Cathryn turned towards Linda and asked, "Who have you seen in the family?" in a voice that was unnaturally subdued and polite.

As Linda answered, there was only a dull, glazed look in Cathryn's eyes in response.

ॐ

After a while, Linda decided to take Cathryn for a ride, thinking that maybe, away from this place, she would feel more comfortable, more able to talk.

They drove along the beach and then stopped at Coco's and ate apple pie. Linda mentioned Nick and their wonderful Bahai Temple picnic, hoping to rekindle the light she had seen earlier. But watching Cathryn's tired, blank expression, she thought, *What have they done to her, for God's sake? How could this happen to someone like her? And what am I going to do? What can I do?*

Linda shivered and pulled her sweatshirt closer around her body, even though the restaurant was comfortably warm.

It's like trying to talk to someone who isn't even there, Linda thought, her fingertips pressed lightly against her lips as she looked across at Cathryn lighting still another cigarette.

ॐ

Later, feeling strangely exhausted so early in the day, she took Cathryn back to the Wilson Home and walked slowly, wearily up the walkway with her. Just then, a stocky, harried woman in her early thirties, came rushing out of the front door with a purse clutched in one hand and a teddy bear under her other arm. She stared hard at Linda, but nervously, purposefully, avoided Cathryn, as she hurried across the driveway and got into a car that was parked there. A strange-looking man, whose mouth was smiling but whose eyes behind thick eyeglasses were not, sat at the steering wheel. He had been sitting there, slumped in the seat, quietly watching Linda and Cathryn for several minutes.

"Hello," Linda said, but Nancy didn't answer, and the man just grinned weirdly at her and started the engine. He backed the car slowly out of the driveway and leaned out the window. "See you *later*, Cathryn," the man said, with a leer. Linda felt a chilling shiver go up her arms.

At the doorway she told Cathryn, "I'll be back to see you soon."

Linda put a little booklet in Cathryn's hand.

"To read, when you feel like it," Linda told her. "Just a peaceful, hopeful, little piece I came across. I liked it a lot."

We used to share things like this all the time, don't you remember? Linda thought, watching Cathryn's face and the absence of any emotion as her fingers closed on the book.

Linda asked, "If there's anything you need, I can bring it next time."

Cathryn thought for a minute. "More cigarettes," she said, "if you bring anything else, people in the house will steal it from me."

"Are you sure? Do you have enough clothes? Shampoo, things like that?"

"All I want is more cigarettes. But can we bring hamburgers back for Rex the next time we go for a drive?"

"Yes, sure," Linda said, fighting with her tears again. She put her arms around Cathryn and hugged her hard. "I'm glad I found you," she whispered.

Cathryn smiled vacantly for a moment. Then she turned away and was gone into the house to find Rex. And to light yet another cigarette and sit out on the patio in the same chair in which Linda had found her.

Linda walked back to her car feeling dazed and a little frightened. She had to call her mother, or Cathryn's brothers, or Nick, or someone.

From inside the house, someone moved the curtains aside slightly at the front window and watched Linda as she got in her car and drove away.

⁓

A few days later, when Linda called the Wilson Home, Sylvia answered the phone. Linda told her that she wanted to see her cousin again, but Sylvia said, "Cathryn was so bad after your visit, we had to have her hospitalized again."

Linda was instantly alarmed and puzzled, "I don't understand. Cathryn wasn't doing much but sitting quietly in a chair when I saw her." *She was about as subservient as a person can get,* Linda thought. *What the hell is this now?*

Sylvia responded, her voice cool, "Sometimes Cathryn *is* very peaceful, but day to day her behavior is unpredictable."

Linda saw that there was no point in questioning Sylvia further. It wouldn't change anything, and, besides, she didn't like or trust the woman.

She reminds me of a small rodent, an oily, small rodent, she thought miserably.

So Linda went to find Cathryn again, this time in the Tate Psychiatric Hospital.

⌒

It was a beautiful, sunny, blue-skied day, when Linda turned off the freeway, drove another mile through the rolling hills of Poway, and finally pulled into an expansive parking lot in front of the modern one-story, sprawling building that housed the Tate Psychiatric Hospital. She got out of her car, locked the door of her little, old, but reliable, champagne colored BMW, and turned towards the building. She stood still for a moment, aware of the quietness, wondering at the lack of people or activity around her.

She crossed the asphalt and went down a walkway of grey stone steps with colorful foliage on either side and pretty flowers that looked strangely out of place. Five or six cars were parked in the huge visitor's lot, but there were no other people in the parking area or near the front of the building. The entire area was eerily quiet. Linda approached the main entrance and hesitated there for a moment, standing in front of a darkly tinted glass doorway. She couldn't see inside. Finally, she took a deep breath and walked through the doors into the psychiatric institution.

The reception area was also very still and quiet, reminding Linda of the atmosphere of a funeral home. She looked around. There were two huge, identical arrangements of artificial flowers. One was perched on a long, low glass table in front of two dark wood chairs in the small waiting alcove on one side of her, and another on the long counter that separated the receptionist from the visitors. The air smelled stale, artificial and heavy with furniture polish.

The receptionist asked Linda to sign a "guest list." Then she gave her an adhesive-backed "Visitor's" tag, which Linda circum-spectly placed inside her pocket, instead of sticking it onto her shirt. She thought, *How odd that just a piece of paper stuck on a person's shirt could determine if they'll be locked up in this building, or if they'll be allowed to leave.*

A peculiar, agitated sensation rippled uncomfortably up through her abdomen.

༉

Linda had fully believed that she was prepared for the visit. After all, this wasn't her first trip to a mental hospital. On two separate occasions years ago, when they were all teenagers, she had gone to visit friends, Joyce and Brent, who, because of conflicts at home and school, smoking dope, cutting classes and that kind of thing, had been subjected to brief stays in the psychiatric ward of the gigantic Michael Reese Hospital in Chicago. Thinking about it now, she could remember the strong medicinal smells and the faces of terribly troubled-looking young people. What she had forgot-ten was how terribly uncomfortable she, herself, had felt, looking into the despair and the apathy that she had seen on their faces. Linda soon found that she was not at all prepared for what she saw in her next two hours in the Tate Psychiatric Hospital.

As a teenager, Linda had been meek, but terribly optimistic, almost to the point of not seeing any danger, trouble or evil, even when it was right there, right in front of her eyes. In those days she still had some faith left in all the *systems* and in people in posi-tions of authority.

A friend with whom she had once worked had dubbed her "Alice in Business Land." It was true. Linda had continuously failed to see transgressions around her, instead preferring to believe that people and things were good, whether they were or not.

The only problem with that, she realized finally, *is that if you don't look at something exactly as it really is, you never become able to do a damn thing about changing it.*

When she had gone to see Joyce and then Brent, they were being given sedation and this was a shock to her. Even back then she hadn't realized that shock treatments and lobotomies were still being done. Joyce and Brent had vacant staring eyes and a numbness about them, the same kind of empty expression she'd seen in Cathryn's eyes.

Back then she hadn't even truly realized how inhumane, savage and barbaric such practices are.

But this time it was different. This time Linda saw it very clearly.

Too clearly to ignore it again.

ॐ

With those past experiences strangely more vivid today than when they had happened, she walked through the heavy, double oak doors which remained locked until the receptionist pushed a button and a buzzer sounded.

A long hallway extended before her with closed doorways and signs on either side. She walked slowly, passing a pharmacy, examination rooms, a cafeteria for the guests who wore the name tags and who could come and go, and maintenance rooms. She kept walking. There was a strong chemical smell in the air, and the funny, muffled murmur of sounds far off down the long, empty hallway.

There were no other people in the hallway, like the parking area, and there were no signs telling where Cathryn's "Unit" was, so Linda kept walking. Up ahead she saw a large round desk where several staff in white jackets were moving about, holding clipboards in their hands, talking to one another, joking, and answering phones and pagers.

Just behind the busyness of the desk, beyond a locked door, stood Cathryn. She was gazing into space and concentrating hard on how she would get her next cigarette from someone.

It's 2:35 P.M., they'll make me wait to smoke until 3 P.M., she thought agitatedly.

Later, when she tried to explained this to Linda, Linda couldn't understand the logic to the smoking rules. They seemed to exist just to arbitrarily restrict one of the few liberties the patients apparently still had.

Again, Cathryn's hair looked as if it hadn't been washed. Today she wore a yellow shirt that was stained and denim shorts that were frayed along the pockets. The seams strained from the extra weight she carried and on her feet were dirty, torn tennis shoes.

She looked forlorn and lumpy. *Cathryn used to love good leather shoes with matching purses,* Linda remembered. She was thinking about how many pairs of shoes her cousin had once owned and wondered idly, *Who's wearing them now? What did she do with all of them?*

Linda walked up to the desk, gave her name, and she was buzzed in through the locked doors just as Cathryn noticed that she was there.

"Oh, you got here!" she exclaimed, her face brightening. "Did you bring me cigarettes?"

※

They went for a walk outside, through the doors of the small, crowded dining room. They could go about twenty yards along a sidewalk with high chain-link fences on one side, and the walls of the concrete hospital building on the other. Then a high stone wall abruptly ended the pathway. Linda put her arm around her cousin's shoulders as they walked and asked, "Are you doing okay?"

"Yes," Cathryn said too brightly. "The food is pretty good and I get plenty of rest. I saw Dr. Dubowsky and he said I would be here a little longer." She sounded like a small obedient, well-mannered child.

"Do you see him every day?" Linda asked, but Cathryn turned just then, startled by a loud thudding noise. Someone was pounding against the thick window next to them. Linda turned and saw a boy, about ten years old, pressing his cheek against the window, who held up his middle finger, and twisted it in a lewd, vulgar gesture towards the other smaller boy who stood at his side and shared his room in the hospital. Then he pressed his tongue obscenely against the glass at the two women, and the younger boy began laughing hysterically. Their voices were barely audible through the thick glass, but what Linda did hear was nasty and crude as they swore at each other, pointed at Linda and Cathryn, then swore and laughed again.

"My God," Linda gasped, "what could kids that young have done to be put in here?" A pain stabbed behind her forehead and she rubbed her temples, frowning. She almost never got headaches. Linda turned away from the window.

Now Cathryn was calmly puffing away on her cigarette, "I have no idea," she said. "Did you bring me a whole carton?"

"Yes, I did," Linda answered, feeling very tired. Her shoulders slumped heavily and she felt too weary to walk any further.

Where's my energy lately? she wondered.

↘

They went back into the building and sat down in two lumpy upholstered chairs in a small lounge area. A TV game show was playing in a corner way above their heads, to no audience at all. At the other end of the room an elderly woman sat motionless in a big leather chair. Her mouth was hanging open and her head leaned back against the chair at an odd angle, looking almost disconnected from her upright body. Her eyes were wide open but vacant, and she was staring absently into the space above her.

While Linda's attention was drawn to the old woman, a young hospital attendant walked by them. He was very tall and walked with his shoulders hunched over. He wore dark tinted glasses that slipped down on his nose. He kept pushing them back up. His hair, oiled and spiky, jutted out here and there from his head. His green scrubs were too short on his long legs. He wore graying tennis shoes with laces that were dragging along the floor. The loops were dingy with accumulated dirt.

Linda looked up at him and asked, "Hi, how long have you worked here?"

"A few months," he answered, stopping in front of them. "It's not very busy right now, but it usually keeps you going."

"What's the matter with that woman?" Linda asked, her voice wary.

The attendant looked over towards where she motioned, saw the woman staring from the chair, and said, "Oh, her. She was depressed, wouldn't get out of bed. We gave her medication, but she still wouldn't get out of bed, wouldn't do anything."

"How does the medication change that?" Linda asked him, her discomfort making her feel quarrelsome and contentious now. He shrugged his shoulders. Obviously he had no idea.

Linda wondered how people could work in hospitals and help administer treatments they had no understanding of. She hesitated before she asked the next question that occurred to her. But as she looked at the almost lifeless creature in the chair, her own head hurting and her heart aching, she had to know.

"What caused her to look like *that*? Is she sick? She looks barely alive." Her voice trailed off.

The young attendant smiled, "Well, she stayed depressed so long, we had to give her ECT."

Linda felt her stomach lurch. *Does anyone actually believe that putting electrical current through someone's brain really helps them?*

Now she felt overwhelmed. Her breakfast of coffee and wheat toast rumbled threateningly with the rolling convulsions of her stomach. Trying to push away the nausea, she looked at the hospital attendant. He still had a grin on his face and his expression was repulsive to her. She felt even sicker, but she forced the feeling down and glared up at him.

"And, now what?" she demanded, unable to keep the hostility out of her voice.

He wasn't at all bothered by her attitude. *Don't matter to me — I don't care what this bitchy lady thinks. She doesn't sign my pay checks.* He shrugged it off. He was just passing time. *Another hour and my shift's over.* He was almost sneering at Linda now. *Fuck you,* he thought.

"Well," he said nonchalantly, "the treatment's done in sets before we get results. She'll get a set of three treatments a week, then we'll see." He picked up a tray from a table, walked past the woman without so much as a glance, and went back out into the hallway.

As unwanted tears sprang to Linda's eyes, she became irritated with herself. *Damn*, she thought, wiping the tears away. To Linda, crying was irrefutably a sign of her weaknesses. She sat up straighter, pushed her chin forward, drew her shoulders back, and looked over at her cousin. Cathryn's eyes were glassy and disoriented. Linda stared hard at her. Cathryn was making some strange, rhythmical, involuntary movements with her tongue, mouth and jaw. She would pucker her mouth, puff out her cheeks and then make some strange chewing movement. Occasionally her upper arm and shoulder jerked in an involuntary movement, as if an invisible source was playing tricks on her body.

What in God's name is this? Linda wondered now.

ॐ

Yet, somewhere beyond Cathryn's numbness, her pain and agony, the physical manifestations — apart from all of the effects of the past years, the treatments and medications — Linda saw, or at least *hoped* that she saw, that the human being that was truly Cathryn, was still there.

Linda's most fundamental, most vital impulse was to continue to try to reach Cathryn. In spite of everything that had happened, Linda loved her and would always love her. She knew intuitively that the pain that her friend had experienced up until now was nothing compared to the agony and hopelessness that could come, with no promise of relief, for the rest of her years — nothing left but to become more of a vegetable, to be institutionalized again and again.

I can't let that happen, Linda told herself.

"Cathryn," she said softly, taking the other woman's limp hand in her own, "did you ever read that little booklet I gave you at the Wilson Home? You know, the one that says that man is basically good, that we *can* change the conditions of things around us."

Her words were wasted. Cathryn was medicated into an oblivion that was not to be reached. She stared at the cigarette in her hand, looking as if she hadn't heard Linda speak.

A single tear escaped from Linda's eye and fell silently onto her cheek. She brushed it away, annoyed.

ॐ

Later, at home on the floor in front of her couch, Linda pulled out the *PDR,* and as she read, she became more horrified. It listed adverse reactions that a person could have from taking Haldol, and the other so-called anti-psychotic agents, the major tranquilizers that were commonly doled out every day in mental institutions, the places that are entrusted to care for their patients.

What they're really doing is controlling them, she thought. *They are being made manageable in the most economically expedient way.* Her headache was gone, but now her stomach ached horribly as if it were being squeezed in a vise-like fist.

‿

Several days later, Cathryn telephoned Linda from the one pay phone in the hallway that the patients were allowed to use. She sounded better, brighter, more like Cathryn.

"The doctor asked whether I preferred to be medicated in the mornings or at night and I told him that I prefer *not* to be medicated," Cathryn laughed, and Linda smiled at the familiar sound. But then Cathryn's voice became serious, and she told Linda in a hushed voice, "I've decided not to cause any problems so that I can get out of here and home again."

Linda said, "What do you mean, 'not cause any problems'?"

Cathryn explained that the day before she had caused an upset by asking for a cigarette too early, too many times, and she was forcibly placed in an isolation room, and the attendants threatened to put her in restraints if she didn't settle down.

"It was horrible to be alone in there. When I pounded on the glass, they told me to stop or they'd keep me in there another hour. So, I decided I'd better be very quiet," she said to Linda, turning from the pay phone for a moment to see who was nearby and might be listening to her conversation. She looked carefully up and down the long hallway.

There was no one there expect one man, about thirty years of age, who was sitting in a chair against the far wall, having an unintelligible, garbled conversation with someone who was not visible. He waved his hands in front of him and then he got very quiet, making strange rhythmical, involuntary movements with his tongue, his mouth and his jaw, puckering his mouth, puffing out his cheeks, some strange chewing movement. But no words, no sound came from his lips. There was a bit of spittle at the corner of his mouth and a widening circle of dampness at the crotch of his baggy trousers. Every few minutes, his upper arm and shoulder jerked in some involuntary movement, just as Cathryn's had a few days ago.

"TIME FOR MEDS," the nurse's voice crackled loudly over the PA system. "THE MED CART IS IN FRONT OF THE REC ROOM. PLEASE GO TO THE REC ROOM *NOW!*"

‿

Linda was appalled by what Cathryn told her. She asked Cathryn if the times she had been hospitalized before were like this, and Cathryn answered, "I don't want to talk about that now." Her voice drifted off and the dark memories of those earlier times came closer, despite her desire to stave them off forever.

Linda felt as if she could almost feel Cathryn's troubling memories, as if for a moment they were her own.

Dim, horrible pictures. Cold people in white jackets. Being moved from one place to another. Being drugged and feeling numb, disconnected and lost.

Linda told Cathryn that she understood, and then she said, "Cathryn, no matter what's going on, I'm thinking about you all the time and I love you. I want you to remember that. I'm here now. I'm *not* going away. I swear, Cathryn, I swear." Linda paused, her voice shaking, her trembling hands holding the phone tightly.

Cathryn answered in a whisper, "Linda? I wish I could talk to you every day."

God, why didn't I do something sooner? Linda thought, her heart aching and heavy.

‿

The next morning the ring of Linda's telephone woke her out of a deep, but troubled sleep.

"Linda, ARE YOU COMING TO SEE ME?" Cathryn yelled, her voice raspy and demanding. Either the cigarettes, the medications, or both, made her words slurred and harsh.

Linda rubbed her eyes and turned to the clock on her night stand.

"Cathryn, it's not even five-thirty in the morning," she protested sleepily.

"I don't have any cigarettes," Cathryn complained. "And I don't have any socks or underwear. There's no one here who does anything," she continued, her voice getting louder and angrier.

Eventually Linda got her to calm down, telling her that she would get there sometime during the morning, that she would help her handle whatever was wrong, and, "Yes, I'll bring more cigarettes."

Finally she hung up the phone. Cathryn was satisfied for the moment. Linda pulled the blanket up to her chin. She wasn't looking forward to spending the morning back in that psychiatric hospital.

Jesus, what am I going to do?

At twenty minutes to seven she sighed, untangled herself from under the comforter, got out of her warm bed and headed for the shower.

༄

Margaret had given Linda some of Cathryn's things: photographs, two sets of keys, several purses, and a few other personal items that she had gathered from Cathryn's house. After a short visit with Cathryn that morning, Linda decided to go look at the house.

Maybe there would be some answers to her questions there, in those rooms where Cathryn had lived with Edward. Anyway, someone had to do something about the house sitting empty.

It was that house that had been the setting of Cathryn's unhappiest years. It was where she must have begun her pathetic plunge into the existence that she was living today.

༄

It was a long drive. The morning had been cloudy and gray, and even though it was mid-afternoon when Linda pulled into the driveway of the house that had been Cathryn's home with Edward, the overcast hadn't burned off. Both the day and the structure were dim and dreary. Two tall, overgrown pine trees prevented any light from reaching inside the windows. They cast huge, swaying shadows back and forth across the "For Sale" sign that was wedged in between the mailbox and the sidewalk on the sadly neglected front lawn.

Once inside the front door, Linda stopped abruptly. She was startled to find the house completely unprepared for visitors, especially prospective buyers. It was filthy and smelled of urine and damp dog hair. Most of the furniture had been sold, stored, or given away by the Kettermans, but piles of newspapers, magazines and other debris remained in untidy stacks in the living room and kitchen.

The house, like Cathryn, looks like an abandoned project, Linda thought.

She stood at the bottom of the stairs looking up, listening, wondering, *What went on here between the two of them? If these walls could talk,* she thought, *what tales of misery would they tell?*

After a few minutes, she forced herself to walk up the stairs. She went slowly into each room looking around at what was left there, and wondered again, *What really happened between Edward and Cathryn?*

She didn't go into Edward's office until she had walked through the rest of the upstairs. The only sound was that of the dusty floor creaking beneath her feet. And then it was quiet, quieter than a deserted cemetery.

Margaret had described the house to her in some detail, but even if she hadn't, Linda would have known in which room Cathryn's husband had died.

༄

The paint on the walls of Edward's office was darker than the rest of the house, a dismal gray. The curtains over the blinds, partly open, were heavier and darker than in the other rooms. On the wall to the left, in a heavy, ornate frame, was a large, imposing picture of an unsmiling, stolid looking older man. His lips were pressed tightly together and his eyes were dark and unfriendly. He was sitting stiffly upright, dressed punctiliously in a starched white shirt, conservative dark tie and jacket.

Edward's father.

Next to the photograph was Edward's framed university degree. On the floor below, there was a small stack of framed certificates. The door to the room was halfway open.

Linda pushed the door open the rest of the way. It felt as if the air had been sucked from the room when Edward died there and had never entered it again. The room was stuffy and musty. Other than the single photograph on the wall and the certificates, the room was empty and dim. The house was still and quiet. Linda stood at the doorway looking around, the air uncomfortably heavy and warm around her face and body. She felt the dampness of perspiration between her breasts and her palms were moist. She turned away, wiping her hands on her jeans, her heart beating hard in her chest, and hurried back down the stairs.

Behind her, the silence of the empty room was suddenly broken by a loud, thundering, rattling of the window pane, as a single, strong wind gusted hard against the side of the deserted house.

Halfway down the staircase, Linda shuddered.

⟡

Next to the garage there was a small, narrow storage room. Linda shoved the door open. The door creaked, its warped bottom and side rubbed against the concrete below it and the misshapen wooden frame along its perimeter. It was damp and dark inside. Linda walked through the doorway and tiny, flimsy cobwebs, disturbed by the movements of her body in the long unused space, came apart, flickering uncomfortably against her face and bare forearms. She shook her head, brushed the spider's thin traps away from her, and wiped her hands on her jeans again.

After a few moments her eyes got used to the dimness, and with the gray light coming through the open doorway, she began looking through the boxes that she found there. She opened one. It was filled with pictures, diplomas, and Cathryn's high school yearbook. She closed the top, rested her hands on it and sat there on a dusty crate, staring at the box.

Maybe I will find something that untangles all this for me, she thought. *Something that will help me understand how she's been so destroyed. She was so beautiful, so able. Maybe she made some wrong choices, but what did she ever do to deserve what she's getting now? How did it happen?*

The small storage room smelled like mold and the light was

so poor that Linda decided to take the box back into the deserted house.

The house where Cathryn and Edward had lived — where Edward had died, and, it seemed, so did most of what was once Cathryn.

༄

The afternoon remained damp and gray with the sky overcast and cloudy. It wasn't the typical spring-like weather that San Diego County enjoys most of the year. Linda stared out of the dining room window at the clouds overhead.

I wish it would rain hard, she thought. *A really heavy rainstorm is the one thing I miss about the weather in the Midwest. I wish it would pour for days. After a good rain storm it always seems as if everything's been washed clean.*

This house is so quiet and eerie. As if unseen presences are watching.

Linda wanted to get out of there before it began to get dark.

It felt to her as if the emotional battles that had gone on between Edward and Cathryn were still reverberating within those walls. And that struggle between strength and weakness, good and evil was continuing. And the ultimate outcome had not yet been determined.

༄

Linda sat down at a small, rickety desk in the dining room, holding two pictures in her right hand. She stared at the beautiful young woman in the older photograph on the left. Cathryn was smiling happily back at her. The picture was taken just after she started college at Northwestern and just before she met Edward.

There was a haughtiness in the expression on Cathryn's face in the early photo. Proud, confident, daring. The look on her face seemed to declare that whatever it took, Cathryn could face the world and twist it gently and competently around her little finger. Linda stared at the photo. She saw life, beauty and strength in her cousin's eyes.

Then she looked at the other, more recent photograph that Margaret had given her just before her first visit with Cathryn, and a feeling of nausea slowly uncoiled within her stomach. The expression on the only slightly familiar face in the second photograph was distorted and ugly. Cathryn looked trapped and beaten, but still angry.

How does someone as lovely as she was come to such a horrible ruin?

She had no answer at all.

⨯

The circumstances that Linda uncovered through her conversations with Margaret and her visits with Cathryn, instead of helping her to really understand what had taken place, made no sense and made Cathryn's situation more confusing. Linda didn't know what to do next, except now she was certain that she would call Nick.

She felt that he needed to know about this. He would *want* to know.

⨯

It soon became apparent through Linda's conversations with her mother, that Cathryn's family, after having been separated from her for so long, was not prepared to confront Cathryn's dilemma.

"Joseph is eighty-nine and he's had colon surgery twice in three years. He's dying, honey. Anna is old and frail herself. They wouldn't be able to come to California even if there was something they could do. Steve and Keith and Marty have tried to call Cathryn so many times, they don't try much anymore. They've *tried* to get her to come back to visit. They've wanted to come and see her.

"When Steve was in California on business several times, he couldn't even get Cathryn to return his calls," Lois told Linda. "Joseph's illness is getting worse and Anna is upset over his condition and so weak herself, she has all she can do to cope with Joseph's needs."

"Pretty grim back there, hmm?" Linda answered quietly.

Each of Cathryn's three brothers, after listening to their sister's defense of her marriage to Edward, after her alienation from them for so many years, had finally tired of trying to encourage her back to the family, of trying to help her. She had turned them down so many times, that the distance between them, became habitual. And now, tragically, they accepted it.

ॐ

The walls of the room around Linda looked as if they were moving ever so slowly. She felt a sensation of heat expanding within her chest and perspiration suddenly dampened her forehead. Linda put the two photos down on the desk and rested her chin in her hands. Her eyes were moist.

The face in the second photograph stared back at her defiantly, as if not to be put off so easily. The woman in the picture looked beyond old, though she was only forty-one when it was taken just months ago, shortly after Edward's death. There were no remnants of the beauty or the strength of the young girl. Anger and pain remained. Lines etched deeply into soft flesh spread harshly across her face. Beneath her eyes there was a dark, shadowy puffiness. Her hair was in disarray, heavy and matted with dirt and oil. The striped shirt she wore was stained and wrinkled.

Where are all her beautiful clothes? Linda agonized. But the pain she felt had nothing to do with the loss of Cathryn's possessions. It was the loss of Cathryn that cut so deeply into Linda's heart.

Instead of the strong, slightly raised chin in the earlier photograph, there was a look of defeat and anger.

Linda blinked the tears back. Cathryn looked as if she would rather become a rock than deal with the unreasonable demands around her. There was no light in her eyes any more. Only somber darkness in her tortured, agonized, dulled gaze.

Linda bent down and picked up some framed things from the box, wiping the thick dust aside with her fingertips so that she could read the print. In the small stack she found diplomas, a certificate from an honor club in college, an Illinois State Scholarship certificate, a teaching degree, and a letter of promotion to Assistant Principal.

She put them on the desk and as she did, she caught a glimpse of her own reflection in the glass of one of the certificates and she stared at her own eyes looking back at her. She didn't look anything at all like Cathryn anymore.

⤳

The affinity that Linda felt for Cathryn transcended everything that had passed. There was a time when each of them knew what the other was thinking, before they even had a chance to put the thoughts into words. So often they had witnessed some incident or other, and had turned towards one another laughing, the same reaction having taken place in each of their minds at the same instant. Nick had shared that with them, a telepathy of sorts. Life had been such a joy to them in those days.

⤳

Linda — in awe of her pretty cousin when they were small children, when the few years difference in their ages had seemed so great — read the same books that Cathryn read, was enchanted by the same poets, worshipped the same movie stars and got emotional over the same music that brought tears to Cathryn's eyes. They shared clothes and secrets, and developed a kind of code of honor that they unconsciously followed. If there was a boy that Linda liked, Cathryn wouldn't give him a glance, in deference to her friend's feelings. And Linda was the same when Cathryn's eyes were filled with a starry dreaminess over someone or other.

⤳

What held Linda, Cathryn and Nick together as friends in those early years, was an honesty, a caring for one another, a sense of responsibility and personal integrity.

It was this same unseen but real bond of caring that pulled them towards one another again now, despite how the paths of their lives had diverged.

⤳

Linda looked at the older photograph once more. She remembered seeing the same one of a young Cathryn before. It had been one of her aunt's favorites. The only picture Linda could remember of Edward during all the years was a small snapshot of the two of them taken when they had gone to Europe together. Behind them was the Louvre. Cathryn was looking up at Edward as he stood stiffly at her side, not touching her, a pipe in his hand as usual. The passer-by who snapped the picture for them was just far enough away from the couple for the sadness that was so evident in Cathryn's eyes that day to be almost indiscernible in the photograph.

చొ

Linda turned in the chair and looked out into the backyard.

Not too long ago Cathryn sat in this same chair, she thought, *probably watching Rex chase a squirrel across the yard, while she drank her coffee and wrote a letter.*

Today the yard was desolate, empty, overgrown with weeds and strewn with dry branches that had fallen from the tall pine tree near the fence.

Stories that Linda had heard about her cousin over the years drifted back to her as she sat in that chair. Stories that circulated around the family while Linda was still in Chicago, before she moved to San Diego. She had heard proud and happy reports about Cathryn winning honors in post-graduate studies, of Cathryn becoming the principal of a school when most of the other women in their family were struggling to raise small children and prepare large meals.

Then later there were other tales, in hushed but angry, indignant voices, about how Cathryn's husband kept her away from her family, how he had managed to persuade Cathryn not to go back to Chicago even to visit.

In whispered voices, elderly aunts gabbled about Cathryn's so-called mental illness, and then about Edward having to put her in a hospital.

"Nervous breakdown," they said, with no explanation of what that really meant or how it came about.

It had never made sense to Linda. She never believed that it was the whole story.

Linda and Dan's marriage had failed by that time. Linda was a divorced and somewhat harried single mother. Cathryn's sporadic letters were too casual, as she tried to gloss over her day to day existence. Linda wrote back, giving her the details of her own difficulties and struggles. Cathryn's responses to Linda's news were clever and perceptive, but the paragraphs about her own situation were brief and vague. It seemed impossible to Linda that she could have been put in a mental hospital and confined there.

Why? Linda had wondered then, but she had done nothing to find out.

⬧

A car horn honked loudly on the street bringing Linda abruptly back to the room, to her cousin's desk, back to present time. She looked slowly around the room feeling troubled, still unable to make any sense out of what had happened. She started to feel a little dizzy again. Glancing down at the photos, as if she *had* to keep looking at them even though she didn't know why, a vague feeling came over her again that her search would eventually reveal what had happened.

Then, Linda hoped, she would know what needed to be done to salvage Cathryn's life, before it was too late.

⬧

Linda found a locked metal container at the very bottom of the cardboard box. It was the size of a large shoe box and it was buried under piles of photographs and diplomas. She picked it up and shook it. She tried one of the smaller keys that Margaret had given her, but the lock was old and rusted, and it came apart in her hands. She opened the top. The box was crammed full of hundreds of prescription slips for medications that Cathryn had been taking over the years. There were stacks of them, each stack had a tape around it. Each was marked with the appropriate month and year, all in Edward's heavy, careful handwriting. Linda stared at the pieces of paper. She pulled a rubber band off and began reading through them.

Every single one was for sedatives, tranquilizers or barbiturates. All medications that Edward was giving his wife to keep her quiet and docile and with him forever.

Linda was astonished. She realized that she held in her hands a macabre record that Edward had kept, for no apparent reason.

What in God's name was the matter with him?

～

She walked out into the back yard to get some air. The house was too stuffy and warm. The neighbor to the south was outside with her two small sons and a new puppy. She smiled timidly over the low fence and Linda walked over and introduced herself.

"Kind of a dreary day, but we had to get the puppy out," the young woman smiled nervously. "Would you like to come in and have a cup of coffee?" Nicole Wrightwood asked.

"That would be really nice, thanks," Linda answered.

A few minutes later, they sat in her kitchen over steaming cups of fresh coffee. With her children playing on the tile floor, Nicole said that she needed to tell someone what she had witnessed at Cathryn's house. She had been so upset by it all for a long time. She began describing the frequent, loud, abusive arguments that she had overheard through open windows and doors, over the past years.

"They argued a lot. I don't think he ever hit her. He just sounded so nasty sometimes. Mostly I could hear him, mean and angry. When I heard your cousin crying, I'd close my windows. They had arguments and he threatened her about medicine. He kept telling her she *had* to take this or that. I could hear him scream at her. And I heard her crying.

"We … we never knew what to do," the gentle young woman offered feebly. She had tears in her eyes.

Many, many times, evidently, Edward had forced Cathryn to take the pills or tablets, in spite of her tears, pleas or promises.

～

For a long time afterwards, Linda sat by herself in the almost barren house, at the small desk, the photos spread out in front of her, and she wept. Deep, racking sobs of anguish burst loudly from her throat and echoed in the emptiness of the house. This time there was no chance of holding back her grief.

Linda knew that life was not supposed to be this miserable.

Ten

Enter Nick ...

I T WAS A LONG, LONELY DRIVE home and well after ten o'clock at night when Linda pulled into her garage. She walked into the house and dropped her keys and purse on the counter. Although it was two hours later in Chicago, she reached for the phone and dialed Nick's number. She pulled open the sliding glass door and walked out onto the little deck beyond her office and sank into a chair. Wearily, she leaned her head back against the cushion and dazedly looked up at the star-filled sky above, while she listened to the phone ring somewhere in Nick's apartment in Chicago.

His answering machine came on. After his voice, she heard the beep and she started to leave a message just as Nick picked up the phone.

"Linda! I don't believe it's you," he exclaimed. "Are you okay?"

"I...I'm okay," she stammered, in spite of herself. "But, Cathryn.... Oh, Nick...." Tears welled up in her eyes and the words stuck in her throat. *Damn tears, the weakness, the feeling of helplessness, the utter exhaustion.*

"Tell me," Nick said softly. "What's going on?"

Linda took a deep breath, while Nick waited silently, patiently.

She looked out into the night at the few stray clouds and the brilliant stars. The dim lamplights cast a warm glow onto the deep green foliage of the macadamia trees. She took another deep breath and began to tell him the story.

She heard the disbelief in his voice change to dismay as she related where Cathryn was living, and what had happened to her over the past years.

They talked for over four hours that night, and, finally, at two o'clock in the morning, four o'clock in Chicago, they said good night. As she crawled into bed physically exhausted, Linda felt that her wavering strength had been vivified somehow by connecting again with Nick. Nick had an idea, a plan that he could start to work on right away. *Nick always has a plan,* she remembered, pleased. Linda fell asleep right away. She slept soundly that night without dreams. It was the first decent night's sleep she had in weeks.

⚬

Linda hadn't held anything back. She described her consternation at seeing Cathryn, how horrifying it was to see the physical and mental deterioration. She told him about the Wilson Home, how strange the place felt to her, and how Cathryn had ended up in the mental hospital again immediately after her visit.

What Linda did not know was that her first visit had been just days after the medication that was administered by Dr. Murdock at Sylvia Wilson's request. That one shot had virtually turned Cathryn into a well-behaved zombie for several days.

⚬

Nick had asked some questions that Linda couldn't answer about the series of events – legal and otherwise — which had taken place. So, in the next few days, Linda politely, but determinedly, questioned Sylvia and Barry. She made telephone calls to the hospital inquiring about Cathryn to the staff and the social workers. Slowly, Linda began to unravel the legalities of it all and the various motivations behind those legalities. When she learned of the existence of Karen Brauning, a temporary conservator, she called Karen directly.

This was another mistake — one of substantial consequence — that was made on Cathryn's behalf. It alerted the enemy.

⚬

Karen sounded surprised and mildly interested to find out that Cathryn had a relative in San Diego.

"I wasn't aware of that," she told Linda. Karen's voice, though cordial, betrayed her instinctive defensiveness, and Linda heard the questioning caution, though she didn't understand what it was all about.

"She has family with some resources who are terribly concerned about her. There are decisions that we have to make about her house. It's in terrible shape right now. We want to help her. We've never seen her like this," Linda's voice broke.

At the other end of the phone, Karen was busily writing down notes as Linda spoke. She underlined "family" and "resources" and "house" heavily with a pencil. She pressed the pencil so hard under the word "resources" that the point broke and flew into the air. At that moment, Karen's expression and posture resembled that of a cunning feline that was being backed into a corner by an enemy, with its back arched, its hackles raised, and emitting a low, warning hiss.

This particular telephone call, during which Linda, characteristic of her approachable, amiable nature, said too much, would turn out to be the *casus belli*, the major event provoking the inevitable war.

৵

Linda learned that there would be a hearing. She called the Attorney Referral Service in San Diego and went to have a consultation with a lawyer named J. Harold Winston. They spoke for some time, with Linda giving the attorney as much information as she could.

"By law, now that your relationship and presence are known, you are to be informed of any proceedings, as are Cathryn's other living relatives. Karen Brauning has only a temporary conservatorship established, but she and her husband, who is also her attorney, are rapidly preparing the way so that Karen will be given permanent control of Cathryn's person and estate by the court."

Linda called Nick that evening and asked, "But why would it

be so important to them? They don't even know or care about her. They've got plenty of people in homes who they can represent."

"Linda, this is business to them. There is a promise of great financial benefit to them and *you* are getting in the way."

"But she has *family* who *care* about her," Linda protested.

"They'll find anything and everything wrong that they can, in order to hang onto a client with resources," Nick told her.

"But the attorney I met with today, Winston, told me that a family member has a certain priority and that the judge will ask Cathryn what she wants," Linda told him.

"I know. And that should help. It *should*," Nick emphasized. "Who is this lawyer? Does he know Brauning? Has he dealt with him or this particular judge before?" Nick questioned.

"I don't know. His name's Winston, J. Harold Winston. I got his name from a lawyer referral service. I'll find out tomorrow. God, this stuff makes me sick to my stomach."

"I think I understand," Nick said quietly. He paused, his gaze going to the sliding glass doors of his living room. He considered, ironically, how idealistic and naive he had once been, how he had truly believed that he could accomplish so much as an attorney — but that was before he opened his eyes to the hypocrisy and deception he found so prevalent in the practice of law – that was before his disaffection as a lawyer.

"Some day soon we'll talk about the legal system and its quirks. Right now, why don't you get some sleep? Do some more checking around before you retain this guy. See if you can find an attorney who knows this Brauning and who thinks he can handle this with him. Will you give me a call tomorrow night?" Nick asked.

"Mm-hmm," Linda answered, distracted, uncomfortable.

"Linda, you know I'll do everything I possibly can to help, don't you?" Nick offered.

"Yes. I just wish you were *here*," she blurted out. "I'm out of my league and I'm scared." Instantly she was sorry she said it. She shook her head to chase away the words. She was already relying on Nick and she hadn't even seen the man in *years*.

Damn it, grow up! she demanded of herself.

Linda had faced enough situations, had gone through enough turmoil over the past years to know that the tactic of relying upon someone else didn't work well for her. She had long since learned that she had to make her own decisions and live with the consequences of them.

And, now here was Nick, offering his help as naturally as always, with all the caring and warmth she remembered. Was she just leaning on him, unable to confront Cathryn's situation herself? She knew she needed his help – his legal knowledge and experience – but she also knew she had to face this herself.

She felt tears sting her eyes and for perhaps the hundredth time in recent weeks, Linda cursed whatever weakness provoked that reaction.

"I'll call you tomorrow night, around ten your time, okay?" she said quickly, upset with herself and wanting to be off the phone before he heard the weariness, the helplessness, the overwhelm in her voice, before he tried to do something about it for her.

"Okay. Talk to you then," Nick replied.

د

They hung up. She sat and stared out into the night for a long while. She almost couldn't remember what life had been like just a short time ago, before she had come face to face with this mess.

Well, I guess I just take one step at a time. Somehow, she thought, *somehow I have to help Cathryn.*

د

Nick put the telephone down in his small apartment on Lake Shore Drive in Chicago. He got up, crossed the living room, opened the sliding glass door and walked out onto a small terrace where he could see an almost full moon shining brilliantly over Lake Michigan. It was cool, not too bad for early fall, and there was very little wind coming off the lake.

He held onto the railing that ran along the edge of the terrace and looked up at the stars, just as Linda was doing at the same moment. He knew that he would be going to California soon. He knew that this conservator situation was worse for Cathryn than Linda understood. He knew exactly what could happen in that hearing. He also knew what the courtroom procedure would be, and he knew too well the type of characters who would determine Cathryn's fate.

And, he knew that he wanted to see Linda.

ॐ

God, how he had come to *despise* being a lawyer.

Nick had practiced law with some talented attorneys. His closest friend, Steve Styers, was one of the most straightforward and blunt men whom Nick had ever met. Steve was honest and decent, an amazingly ethical lawyer. Steve really believed that it was up to him, that it was his job, to ensure that justice was served. He didn't give a damn for politics in or out of the courtroom.

He was extremely effective, thorough in his research and brilliant in the courtroom, while still maintaining a measure of understanding and compassion that was astounding. There were no manipulated deals cut or strange compromises made within Steve's legal arena.

Steve Styers did *not* have a reputation for being nice or reasonable. In some circles he was known as ruthless, merciless, upholding the law as it was written, *period.* He did not represent clients in whom he did not believe, and Steve Styers seldom lost a case.

Nick had seen him back down to no one over the years, no matter what his adversary's wealth, position or power, even when professionally it might have been to his advantage to do so. Steve Styers faced up to attorneys and judges who were known for their unbending will and forcefulness, in his personal battle against recidivism — and it didn't make any difference to him on which side of the bench he found it.

Steve took them on willingly, without hesitation. Nothing mattered to him as much as the law, *exactly* as it was written. Nothing anyone could do to him or threaten him with effected a modicum of change in Steve Styers.

The friends he made, he made for life, but he made some

equally obdurate adversaries as well. Because of his strong beliefs and his unbending principles, Steve missed some career opportunities, the kind that generally go to more compromising personalities. But simply because Steve Styers was this kind of character, he had Nick's respect and affection forever.

Nick had met some men and women in the legal profession who had high integrity. They were people who believed in and supported the laws and those people that those laws were intended to protect. He had met the uncustomary lawyer, district attorney, prosecutor, public defender and judge, who with inordinate decency and determination, operated towards preserving a true justice system.

But, damn, they are rare, he thought now.

Jesus, Nick lamented, *they're such a small minority among the multitudes of those who don't seem to have a shred of decency in their entire being. I've seen too many money-hungry, nasty people in the profession, men and women who are so busy being impressed with their goddamned law degrees, and their ability to make big money, that they don't consider it necessary to act with some caring and ethics.*

Nick's personal struggle as he practiced law had continued.

It is as if their ultimate goals, the only ones that matter, the only ones towards which these people seem capable of working, are money and power, he protested. *Their twisted sodality manages to turn the legal profession into the one unique vocation that can charge exorbitantly for its time, whether it produces a beneficial result or not.*

Any street cleaner, waitress, or clerk, performs a service of benefit in order to receive the exchange of money. Who else on this earth is guaranteed an enormous hourly wage for talking on the phone or writing letters, when those conversations and those documents might or might not achieve what the client wanted in the first place? Who else gets paid for his time on the job whether he's producing something worthwhile or not?

No one, Nick thought bitterly. *No one except my esteemed colleagues.*

Suddenly, one day it made him so horribly sick to his stomach that he turned in his resignation, shocking his illustrious partners, to say nothing of the consternation that he caused his wife and her parents.

෨

Nick immediately began feeling like himself again. It was easier to smile and joke, and he found that he was regaining his former happiness. But Carrie wasn't at all happy with this turn of events, even though Nick was almost immediately offered alternative jobs. He accepted one as a consultant for a large electronics manufacturing company. The salary was almost as much as what he was earning with the law firm, but the prestige did not compare, at least not to Carrie's North Shore family. The unspoken, but much-hinted at possibility of Nick eventually becoming active in politics was out of the question now, destroyed forever by some idealistic nonsense of Nick's that the Clarks could not fathom.

No one in Carrie's family had paid any attention to the fact that Nick, himself, never had had a desire to play the political game in the first place. That was Norman Elliott Clark's idea, but Carrie thought her father's plan for their future was an excellent one.

"Nick isn't making any sense," she complained to her father.

She told Nick, "I don't understand what you're doing to us, Nick. You're taking apart our marriage. You have to realize that I can't live with you like this. This isn't what we planned. It isn't what I want."

The brief happiness that Nick had felt after leaving the firm was gone like dust in a strong wind.

Nick thought that she would get used to the idea, that she would change her mind. Or so he hoped.

෨

What Nick had not yet realized was that their marriage was doomed. And, this was certainly not just because he had decided to abandon the legal profession.

Nick had waited years for Carrie's agreement to have children and he was crazy about his two sons. A divorce meant at least some degree of separation from them, and that was a devastating proposition to him. The thought of being able to see them only on week-ends, vacations, at designated times, was his worst nightmare and suddenly he found himself in the middle of it.

⅍

Nothing, Nick thought, *prepares a person for life as it really is. First you're a little kid, and somehow you get the idea that you'll grow up, and at some point you'll be in control of everything. No one tells you it isn't like that, that it's a continuous battle to maintain your power of choice and self-determinism.*

Now Nick felt weary as he looked at the small framed photos on the coffee table in front of him. Jimmy looked back at him with his innocent freckled face, broad smile and missing front tooth. Next to it was one of Scott, with an expression that was more seri-ous and thoughtful, looking as if he had already had a glimpse of how complicated life could become.

For a while their marriage had continued. Nick went to work. He tried not to argue with Carrie about having given up practic-ing law. He went with her to more dinners at the Country Club than he could stand. But his heart wasn't in it. He lost weight and his sleep was restless. As he and Carrie drifted further apart, he longed for something that would make sense to him again.

⅍

But Carrie was relentless. "If you won't change your mind about this, I can't accept it," she declared unreasonably. When Nick tried to reason with her, to work it out some way, she exploded at him.

As it turned out, there was another factor affecting their rela-tionship besides Nick's career change. No woman in her right mind discards a man like Nick, unless she, herself, has been up to some-thing or other. And, indeed, Carrie had.

⅍

One of Carrie's closest friends finally elected to enlighten Nick. Susan Mettler convinced herself that she had to say something to Nick. *The poor guy has to know what's really going on.*

Yet there was one other factor which influenced Susan to come forward with her information, and that was the smoldering passion she had felt for Nick for some time. With diligent attention to her own purposes, Susan called Nick and arranged for them to meet for drinks after work.

"We really need to talk, Nicky," she told him. "It's important," she said, in her husky, too dramatic voice. "No, it can't wait, Nick. No, I *can't* tell you on the phone."

ॐ

Susan sat in a booth in a dim corner of The Owl in Northbrook, a trendy and expensive restaurant and singles' bar that was the most recent success amongst the affluent element of the North Shore.

When Susan insisted that they meet there, Nick had reluctantly agreed. He was tired. He didn't feel like company, and certainly not Susan's. Places like The Owl appealed to Carrie, not to him. He parked his car on the crowded street, foregoing the valet service, and sighed deeply as he walked up the entrance way.

The new club was decorated with tasteful artwork, lush plants, soft, supple leather booths, heavy mahogany tables and long bars with plush, comfortable high-backed stools. This particular night the place was alive with smartly dressed men and women. The food was superb and intriguing scents drifted through the rooms. The lighting was soft and clandestine.

Nick stood waiting for the hostess, looking around uncomfortably. He didn't feel like running into people he knew. He wanted to get this meeting over with as quickly as possible. He wanted to get home to see his sons before they were asleep in bed.

He wondered what Susan was up to. She had sounded serious and that was out of character for her.

His eyes took in the fashionably dressed men and women at the bar, in the booths, and walking past him, all promoting themselves to one another.

Why did I let her talk me into this? he asked himself.

Nick glanced at his watch as he followed the hostess to where Susan was waiting. He slid into the booth opposite Susan, thinking that he'd rather be at home in jeans.

"What's up?" he asked immediately. Susan had been a friend of Carrie's since high school, but Nick had never particularly liked the woman, and she was not someone he trusted. He looked at her apprehensively.

Susan Elizabeth Grandstone Mettler, with long, bejeweled fingers and manicured nails, looked at Nick for a moment, then reached for her drink and lifted the glass to her lips. She was obviously in no hurry at all. Her eyes smiled too warmly at Nick over the glass.

She's already buzzed, Nick guessed.

The waitress, a young, pretty blond, clad in an attractive, clinging, light blue silk blouse and matching slacks, came to the table to get Nick's order. "Michelob," he told her. He thought he saw Susan wince.

The blond looked politely towards Susan, who said curtly, "Another Glenfiddich, rocks." The waitress nodded and walked away.

Susan gazed at Nick, her fingers still wrapped around her almost empty glass. She leaned towards him, her expensive, heady perfume wafting about his nostrils. Susan was tall, fashionably thin with large, firm breasts, big round blue eyes and thick, dark hair that curled intriguingly forward around her face.

Nick looked at her thoughtfully. He was not at all interested in Susan, nor would he ever be. Susan Mettler, at first glance, was a very attractive and sensuous woman. At second glance, one saw a woman who was calculating and self-absorbed. *Susan,* Nick reflected, *may be the most self-seeking, self-indulgent, self-centered person I have ever known.*

She had had a lifetime of training, having been indulged by an extremely wealthy father throughout her thirty-five years. And then, in addition, by two even wealthier ex-husbands, neither of whom had lasted longer than three years.

She had no children, and that was perfectly fine with Susan. Children would only get in her way. Her life revolved around her sexual conquests, her accumulated money, and ways to entertain herself with it. She was very rich, very unproductive and not very happy.

Nick had watched her during the course of his marriage to Carrie. In and out of her own two marriages, Susan managed to keep a barely respectable distance from Nick. The fact that he was her friend's husband clearly did not put him off limits, and her manner was openly inviting. Susan made it perfectly plain, in dozens of ways, that she would thoroughly enjoy it if Nick would just put his hands on her.

One Sunday morning at their house, Susan had gone to change into a swim suit, while Carrie sat outside with the boys by the pool. Nick went into the kitchen for a cold drink and as he walked back towards his office, he had to pass by the guest bathroom where Susan was changing clothes. The door was wide open and Nick wasn't terribly surprised to see Susan standing perfectly still in front of a full length mirror, totally nude, watching him. She had a very beautiful body and she knew it.

Nick walked quickly past the bathroom, while Susan made no attempt to reach for a towel or her bikini, which were inches away on a dressing table. She merely smiled invitingly at Nick in the mirror, casually tossed her hair back off her shoulders and asked, "Wanna put some suntan oil on my back, Nicky?"

Nick was not tempted by her invitations.

Even if he wasn't married, he couldn't imagine being drunk or stupid enough to get involved with her. *Susan, the not-very-discriminating seductress,* he thought wryly. He usually handled Susan by joking with her or ignoring her.

But tonight he was not in the mood to indulge her. "So, what's up?" he repeated. She continued to lean towards him so that her breasts pressed against the thin, cream colored sheer blouse she wore under a perfectly tailored darker jacket and skirt. The delicate outline of the lace of her low cut bra, encircling her full breasts, was clearly visible.

꒰

It took two more drinks and too much small talk, before Susan stopped trying to seduce Nick from across the small table long enough to give him the information that she had called him about.

"Carrie's been having a little on the side. She's fucking someone else," she finally revealed, her words barely slurred from the alcohol. Susan could certainly drink.

Nick's fingers tightened around the beer bottle. His shoulders, feeling heavier than concrete, slumped forward and his heart ached. It wasn't even that he was very surprised by the news that Susan was obviously getting pleasure out of divulging. It was just that he was so damned disappointed.

༄

When Susan finished telling Nick every unpleasant detail she could think of about Carrie's on-going affair with Brad Levingworth, a well-known North Shore attorney of Carrie's social caliber, Nick gave up any tiny shred of hope that he had clung to for continuing to create their marriage.

It wasn't just that she was having an affair, it was the pretense which got him. He felt repulsed to his very core.

He was disgusted with Carrie, but, even more, he was disgusted with himself. He finally saw how phony and empty their marriage really was. It was a sham.

He stopped trying, stopped hoping, at that precise moment. Nick decided that he would give up everything they had even before Carrie got around to asking, except for one thing.

He would willingly give up everything; the house, the furniture, every damn thing, except for his sons. He would not give them up. Never.

༄

Within days after Nick's meeting with Susan, Carrie boldly demanded a divorce and asked for everything they owned. She carried on as if Nick had destroyed her life.

"I can't live with you any more. You've changed. You aren't the same person I knew. I don't understand what you want or what you're doing. Nothing that matters to *me* is important to you. I'm miserable with you, Nick! I want a divorce."

Nick simply said, "Okay, Carrie. Have the papers drawn up and I'll sign them."

He never even brought up Brad's name. *What difference does it make?*

He said okay to each of her unreasonable demands as long as he was assured of joint custody of his sons. She could have all the money and possessions.

He was so tired. All he wanted from her now was his time with Scott and Jimmy. She could have the rest.

~

Nick sensed the severity of Linda's pain about Cathryn, and though he knew that what she could accomplish at this point was rather limited – since no laws had been broken as far as he could tell — he couldn't help wondering what it would be like to see Linda again after so many years.

He remembered the warmth of her outrageous smile, how she always looked at him with trust and caring. She was probably the most sincere person he'd ever known.

~

Linda read over the section of probate law that Mr. Winston handed her concerning the selection of a conservator. Later, she talked it over with Steve, her mother and Nick. She needed to retain a lawyer, to go to the hearing and request that she, or another family member, be given the conservatorship. Not a stranger, not Karen Brauning who knew nothing about Cathryn except how to keep her housed and fed and pay her bills. And, how to keep her quiet and complacent.

Linda had consultations with two other lawyers, and finally decided on J. Harold Winston. She chose him because he was a quiet, unpretentious man who told Linda that he had worked both with and against Dick Brauning several times before, and that he felt that he could deal effectively with him.

"Of course," he added, "I can make no promises about the outcome, as the Judge will have the final say." Harold Winston carefully advised, "Judge Humphrey has the reputation of utilizing and enjoying this particular aspect of his profession a great deal, perhaps more than most."

And so, in her selection of an attorney to help her with Cathryn, Linda made yet another unfortunate mistake which would affect Cathryn's future.

‍ॐ

Mr. Winston proceeded with the paperwork that was needed for the hearing. He called Linda into his office after some time had passed. "This has been filed with the Court," he told her, handing her Dick Brauning's Petition.

She sat in an imitation leather chair in Winston's office, reading Brauning's paperwork in disbelief, the lines in her forehead deepening, her eyebrows arching, and suddenly she exploded, "This isn't true! This is *NOT* true!"

The impassive, dull expression on her attorney's face infuriated her. "This is *bull shit!*" she said, her face flushed with frustration and anger. She slammed the papers down on the desk in front of her.

"How does he dare lie like this to a *judge?*" she demanded.

Mr. Winston didn't move even a fraction of an inch. His expression did not change. The only evidence that Linda's fury had impinged upon his robot-like beingness was the rapidity of his pulse, which was actually racing to a dangerous level, and the minuscule beads of sweat that broke out just at his hairline at the top of his broad forehead.

‍ॐ

"The document is *untrue*," she told Nick that evening. "The way it's worded makes it sound as if all of Cathryn's relatives *deserted* her years ago. That they decided not to see her or care for her over the years. That they're not interested in her even now. That she simply cannot get the proper attention and help she so badly needs, if left to rely on her family. It emphasizes that a competent, impartial, private conservator should be appointed to look after her medical needs and to administer her existing resources."

‍ॐ

"How do we tell the judge that this is untrue?" Linda demanded of the pale-faced Mr. Winston at their next upsetting meeting.

J. Harold sat quite still behind his desk. His palms were beginning to sweat profusely and he wiped them on his slacks. He was now regretting having taken on this simple little conservatorship case. The Braunings were hard enough to deal with, and now he had this angry woman before him.

He chose to pretend some confidence. He carefully explained, "We can handle it all at the hearing. The concerned family members will be present. Your cousin, Cathryn, will be allowed to tell the judge how she feels about this. The Court will have someone impartial go to see her prior to the hearing."

Linda listened, but her anxiety was not allayed. Suddenly she knew that she had the wrong lawyer and that she'd made the wrong choice. But there was no going back, there was no time for that. She doubted that this man could deal with the Braunings, and she feared that he was simply stalling.

She clenched the papers in her fist as she stormed out of his office. She had to call Nick again. *Damn!*

⁊

Following her altercation at Harold Winston's, Linda's days settled into a deceptive calm for a little while. She went to the gym in the mornings, worked on her articles, and talked to her son and daughter almost every day. Nick checked with her a couple of times a week, trying to help lessen her uneasiness about the pending legal procedures concerning Cathryn.

⁊

Some families with only one parent come apart at the seams. Because of time, economics and other factors, children and a single parent often go in opposite directions. Communication lessens, and with it goes understanding.

Linda was very glad that her relationship with her son and daughter had not gone that way. She knew that she had made too many mistakes in their life together to be the *mother* in the sense of an authority figure. Instead, she was their friend. They talked about everything; finances, romances, friendship, ethics, politics and integrity. She found that being any other way with them was unnatural and uncomfortable.

The result was a very special bond. They were considerate of each other and they stayed close and in communication with one another. Julia and Michael had became Linda's closest friends, as well as being her daughter and son.

When they had some time, Linda met them for lunch. They were a tight little group, kids and mom, and they kept an eye on one another. They also teased a lot — Mike's specialty — and helped each other out whenever they could. Now, Mike and Julia listened and were supportive.

Neither Julia nor Mike were brought up by Linda to behave and comply for no reason. As a single parent, she had trusted them and relied on them to help and contribute to the household in any way they could from when they were very little. Instead of trying to bend them to her ideas of how they should be, as Dan may have done had they remained married, Linda found herself fascinated and enchanted with their individualities and the people they were becoming.

৵

Linda visited Cathryn once or twice a week, and the work on her articles kept her occupied as she moved through the days. Yet she felt drained, with little energy, and she was still hoping that Mr. Winston would find a way to turn things around.

Once in a while, in the early morning hours, before she got out of bed to go to the gym, disoriented images and pictures disturbed her sleep. After years of contentedly falling asleep just moments after snuggling up against her pillow, and waking up quickly, kicking the covers off, jumping out of bed with enthusiasm and energy, her nights were restless and troubled.

She woke up thinking the phone was ringing when it wasn't. She had vivid dreams of Cathryn back in Chicago, just before she left with Edward, with some sort of plea in her eyes. But when she opened her mouth, no sound came out. Cathryn's lips were moving, but Linda couldn't hear what she was saying, and as she leaned closer, Cathryn's face disintegrated before her.

Linda was awakened one night by a horrible bloodcurdling scream. Her face and chest were soaked with perspiration and her heart was pounding. She listened, sitting up in her bed. Everything around her was completely silent, except for the blood pounding through her body, banging loudly in her ears. She was certain that somewhere close by, someone had shrieked shrilly into the night.

But she knew it was only another dream.

৴

Cathryn called her to ask for cigarettes or dog food for Rex. Linda did everything for her that she could. She took her out for lunch, got her hair cut, walked on the beach with her, brought Rex to the vet, and bought carton after carton of cigarettes.

How, Linda wondered, *can she be smoking that much?*

All the time, Linda felt a growing apprehension about the presence of a stranger, a woman whose business was to put herself in charge of another human being's life, whether that person agreed or not.

৴

Then, finally, it was the day of the hearing during which a permanent conservator for Cathryn Silberg Kent would be appointed by Judge Jerome R. Humphrey.

Eleven

His Honor dispenses with justice—...

ON THE MORNING OF THE HEARING Linda felt some degree of confidence. She now had a pretty good idea of what had been going on over the past few months, of what was *still* going on at the Wilson Home. She was certain the judge would be interested in her information.

He just needs to hear the truth, she thought. *When he knows that Cathryn has family who love her and will take care of her, when he finds out what the board and care facility is really like and what they're doing there, he'll make the right decision. He doesn't know us yet. He's only got the Brauning's petition and that's filled with lies. Maybe we'll even be able to get the Wilson Home investigated and shut down.*

ॐ

Cathryn had told her about an elderly woman in the home who wasn't able to get off the toilet by herself, and who sometimes sat there moaning, "Please get me, please help me," for ten, fifteen or even thirty minutes, before Sylvia or one of her assistants helped the frail old woman back to her room.

She told Linda, "Barry drinks tequila at night in his little room," which was none of Linda's concern. But, also, "He likes to have a drink with Nancy or me." Both women were taking psychotropic medications, drugs that have an altering effect on the mind and are potentially dangerous when mixed with alcohol. That *did* concern Linda, very much.

But she heard different tales from Sylvia, who angrily reported that Cathryn, or someone, had poured the gasoline used for the lawn mower into the trash cans at the side of the house. And, someone in the house had changed the setting on the oxygen machine that Mr. Nelsen used at night.

"It *must've* been Cathryn. No one else wanders around at night," she accused.

When Linda confronted Cathryn with Sylvia's recriminations, Cathryn calmly looked into Linda's eyes and said softly, "I *didn't* do those things. Who sounds like the crazy person, Linda?"

Over the past several weeks Linda had spent hours and hours with Cathryn, slowly determining Cathryn's part in all of it, what she did, why she did it. Together, bit by bit, they looked at Cathryn's life with Edward: her terror of him, her fear of failing in her family's eyes, the various drugs and treatments. Sometimes Cathryn was so sedated that she didn't know what Linda was asking her about, but other times, her eyes, at their very centers, brightened and began to glow. It was as if Cathryn, herself, was really there, looking, seeing the past, and finally able to tell someone about it.

"I remember the exact second when that psychiatrist first put that bottle in my hand," she said, clenching her teeth in anger. "And, I remember so many years later when I found it in my dresser and decided to take them," she sighed deeply.

"I was afraid of him, you know? Edward could be very mean." Then the memories of her terror swallowed her up, her eyes grew glassy, and she didn't want to talk about it anymore.

"Hey, it's okay," Linda said softly. "Let's take Rex and drive down to the beach. There's going to be a beautiful sunset. Come on, Cath." She put her arm lightly around Cathryn's shoulders and waited for her to climb back up out of the swirling dark miseries of her past. Together they walked to Linda's car.

Linda didn't have any doubts in her own mind about who really cared about Cathryn and her well-being. She would tell the

judge. His decision would determine what was to be done to her —
for her — and by whom, probably for the rest of her life.

She met with Mr. Winston several more times and he continued going over the probate laws with her. He was more fumbling
than she would have liked, but he assured her again that he felt he
could communicate with the Braunings, and the judge, in Cathryn's
best interests. She didn't have the time, money or energy to find
another lawyer. Linda decided to rely on his help.

ৼ

Linda leaned towards her reflection in the bathroom mirror.
Her eyes looked tired. There was a grayish darkness around them
and her face was pale. Her normal southern California glow was
gone. The preceding weeks of restless sleep had taken their toll.
She put on a little peach lipstick and stepped back, frowning. It
didn't help. There was nothing to do except somehow get through
this day as best she could.

She called out to her mother, "Mom, are you almost ready?
We should leave in about ten minutes. I'll call Mark to make sure
he's on the way." Linda's only cousin on the West Coast was going
to join them and help if he could.

"Be ready in a minute," her mother answered.

Linda's mother was Cathryn's aunt, Anna's only living sister.
She had flown in from Boca Raton for the hearing when Linda
told her what they were facing. Joseph's cancer was worse. The
doctors weren't very encouraging about his recovery and Anna
was not in any condition to travel nor to face the situation swirling around her daughter. And, so, Lois had come to help if she could.

Each of Cathryn's three brothers had offered some financial
support when Linda spoke to them. But, after twenty years of frustrating separation, the oldest, Martin, told Linda, "I just don't see
how coming to Cathryn *now* is going to do anything for her. She's
never wanted us to interfere in her life before and I'm sure she still
feels the same way about it."

ৼ

Linda's mother had originally been in disbelief. "The court

can allow a stranger to take over my niece's affairs, direct her life? Be able to put her in and out of hospitals without her family having anything to say about it?"

"At least I can make sure this judge knows what kind of family he's dealing with," she had told her daughter earnestly on the phone.

Lois, a tiny, but strong woman, was seventy-one years old. She still remembered how she and her sister Anna were bewildered by Cathryn and Linda more than once while they were growing up.

"But we were lucky. You were good children, no real problems with any of you," she had told Linda the night before, leaning forward on the edge of her daughter's couch, squeezing her hands together nervously. Lois' eyes were moist and there were shadows under her eyes. It had been a long trip for a difficult purpose. Court involvement in Lois' life was unwonted, alarming and very intimidating.

⟲

She looked into the mirror in the bathroom of Linda's guest room, dabbing a little color onto her cheeks. Lois, with warm, dark eyes and short, wavy brown hair, still without a trace of gray, was an attractive woman growing older in a gentle, charming manner. Linda's mother was full of life. She walked three miles every morning, waving and greeting everyone in her path. And she still swam two or three times a week.

Once a week she volunteered as a teacher's aide in a first grade classroom, where the teacher gladly welcomed her help and the children adored her. At the end of the day she would go home comfortably tired, smiling with a renewed brilliance twinkling in her eyes. Her neighbors, mostly retired and becoming more and more sedentary, shook their heads in wonder, marveling at both her discipline and energy.

But today Lois did not feel energetic at all. Tremendously saddened by what was happening to Cathryn, she thought of earlier years. She remembered Cathryn as a child, the shining star of the family, the most beautiful and intelligent, with such a strong will.

How could her life have come to this?

Edward Kent. It was because of that man.

༚

Edward hadn't ever had much money, but he always had enormous ambition. He had been determined to move to California and to take Cathryn with him. His plan had always been to get out of the dismal winters of Chicago and move closer to his parents who were somewhat affluent now, and had been on the West Coast for several years. Once he finished college, Edward decided that it was time for the right wife, the right career, and time to rejoin his parents. After all, his mother and father had been the original impetus to his ambitions.

He believed that they would help finance his business plans. Even so, Edward's plans were growing at a far greater pace than any of Edward's actual achievements.

Lois remembered the day when she was at her sister's house and Cathryn brought Edward home for the first time. "Cathryn's eyes were positively shining with happiness," Lois told Linda as they sat and reminisced.

"I'll never forget how he looked around at their beautiful home. I can see his face as if it was just a few days ago. He looked around, kind of hesitating before he sat down, as if he might wrinkle or soil his suit by sitting on their furniture, which was so lovely and clean.

"He had such incredible arrogance about him. But your cousin just kept looking up at him as if she had brought home some deity." Lois' voice broke. Linda put her arm around her mother's slim shoulders.

After Lois had left Anna's home that first night, Edward had continued looking from Cathryn's beautifully glowing face next to him, to her mother and father sitting on the other side of a coffee table laden with fresh flowers, lovely silver pieces, and fragrant, freshly baked cake.

He had smiled a thin smile at Anna and Joseph. He would have Cathryn, but he *would not have these pathetically arrogant people in his life.*

Edward had lifted his coffee cup to his mouth, smiling his

strange half-smile at them again. These people did not fit in with his plans. But their daughter did.

⌐

The doorbell rang, startling Lois back to the present. "I'll get it," she called out to Linda.

"Hello, darling," she greeted her nephew Mark, reaching her arms up towards him. "It's been too long since I've seen you."

"How are you?" Mark asked, hugging the little woman to him for a long moment.

Mark Benson was Linda's only other relative in California besides Cathryn and her son and daughter. He was a pleasant looking man in his late thirties, with dark hair that was beginning to gray at the temples. Mark had never married. After Linda's divorce, Mark was frequently a comfortable addition to her young family. When an emergency arose or if Linda had to travel out of town for work, Mark often materialized to help out and to keep an eye on little Julia and Michael. After their move to San Diego, Mark was one of the few things about Chicago that was sorely missed by Linda and the children.

He had built up a successful practice as a CPA in Chicago, but, then, spontaneously, on a vacation to see California and visit Linda, he decided to stay. Mark, too, had had his fill of the Midwest's savage winters.

"I don't have anything keeping me in Chicago," he told Linda. Eventually, Mark established his business in Del Mar and he often spent Sundays with Linda and the children, when Julia and Mike were growing up.

Mark probably had never done a thing to hurt or upset anyone or anything intentionally in his life. Sometimes his help was a small loan. Sometimes it was being there for Julia and Michael when Linda worked, or when she needed to grab a few precious hours for herself.

When Cathryn, Linda and Mark were small children, their three families had vacationed together at a family home in Wisconsin, on the seashore of Lake Michigan. Cathryn, the oldest of the three, used to love to pretend that she was Mark's mother. He always indulged her, knowing that he would eventually be rewarded with freshly baked cookies or cake from Anna's kitchen.

But until just a few short weeks ago, Mark and Cathryn hadn't seen each other for over twenty years.

༄

"Well, it'll be good to have this day over with instead of anticipating it, hmm?" Mark said to Lois, his brows pulled tightly together.

"I can't wait, for all of us," Lois replied. "It's like a bad dream and I know it's been worse for you here. And Linda and Julia, seeing Cathryn all the time and trying to handle everything with this nightmare happening, with legal papers going back and forth." Lois shook her head. Legal procedures were matters with which she did not want to have to deal.

But, then, that was partly why people like Karen Brauning had a job in the first place.

༄

Julia had gone with Linda to see Cathryn several times over the past weeks. Sometimes they just walked on the beach. Sometimes they took her for a haircut or a manicure. When Linda had to go out of town on business one weekend, Julia was the one who thought of getting Cathryn some playing cards. Another time Julia brought her some oil paints and canvases, which had delighted her and caused her eyes to lighten and shine as they used to in the past.

Mark, too, visited Cathryn with Linda and Julia. The long years of separation from her family were melting away after so much time and tragedy.

༄

"I only hope this judge sets it right and that we can find a way to help her live a decent life out of hospitals," Lois said softly, her forehead drawn with concern, much like Linda's.

"Well, that's his job. Now he'll have a chance to do it," Mark answered. Their words were a little hesitant, but still hopeful. They fell silent for a moment, waiting for Linda.

Linda came into the room. "I'm ready. Thanks for being on

time, Mark. My stomach ache is bad enough without us being late."

༃

Linda was a pretty woman, but today worry was visibly etched on her face. She hadn't slept well again, instead tossing and turning with one bad dream after another.

She kept telling herself that the hearing would go well. She knew that she could communicate to the judge how much they all cared for Cathryn, and how desperately they wanted her life to be managed by people who cared about her. The judge could appoint either Mark or herself as the conservator. Then Cathryn would be safe.

Linda knew that Cathryn wanted them, not the Braunings, in that position. In fact, shortly after Edward died, Cathryn had named Mark and Linda as her beneficiaries, when Jack Ketterman persuaded her that she needed to make out a will. Money wasn't something that Cathryn paid much attention to; there had always been enough available to her each month for all of her needs.

Cathryn's memories of Mark were warm and fond. He was one of her favorite relatives, even on days when she didn't like people very much.

༃

There was an important factor affecting Cathryn's future which neither she nor any of the others were yet aware of. There was money – a substantial fortune, thus far hidden — waiting for her. Only her elderly, sick father, and his friend and attorney, Don Castleman, knew about it, and the stipulations under which Cathryn could receive her inheritance.

And this was something that Karen Brauning, with all of her extensive connections and interrogations had not been able to discover. Yet Karen was being extremely industrious in her endeavors to uncover what finances did exist. She secured bank records, diverted Cathryn's mail to her office, and from her temporary position as Cathryn's conservator, she took charge of all of Cathryn's assets and affairs that she could get her hands on. She was being very thorough.

༃

Linda was grateful that Cathryn would be given an opportunity to talk to the judge, to tell him, herself, how she felt about her situation. She felt confident that Cathryn would be lucid and that her testimony would be convincing. After all, it was her life they were deciding about today.

೧೨

Mr. Winston had gone over everything with her. Linda repeated it all to Nick when they talked in the evenings. She read the excerpt from the probate law to her mother, Mark, Julia and even Mike.

According to the law, when a conservator is found to be necessary, the decision is ultimately up to the judge. A relative is given some priority if there is someone willing and available to hold the position. Both Linda and Mark lived in the county and were able and willing to take on that responsibility.

The person's wishes were also to be taken into account. Cathryn had the right to express her preferences and there was no doubt she would tell the judge what she had been saying for weeks. She didn't want Karen Brauning to represent her in any way. She didn't feel that Karen had done anything for her and she didn't understand why she should have a complete stranger handling things for her. She would tell the judge that.

Linda smiled now. She was certain that there would be no problem.

೧೨

Nick, however, knew that there was really only one thing which counted and he tried to make Linda understand.

"The law states that the appointment of a conservator is up to the judge's discretion, Linda. He can decide any way he sees fit."

"But when he hears us tell our side, he'll see what's true," Linda said. "We're not just her family. We love Cathryn and we'll never stop caring for her and protecting her," Linda argued. She doubted that an impartial judge would hold the years of separation against them, not if he listened and understood what they were saying. Nick was worrying for nothing.

೧೨

In his petition to the court, Dick Brauning had characterized the family as uncaring and unconcerned about Cathryn. Representing Cathryn's temporary conservator, Karen Brauning, he had prepared his petition and reports with the specific intention of having Karen named as Cathryn's permanent, paid conservator.

In order to accomplish this most expeditiously, Karen had instructed him, "You must disclose anything reproachful concerning her relatives and any other potential candidates for the position. Even if you need to adjust the truth somewhat to do so."

The documents submitted to the court by Dick gave no information about Cathryn's parents' illnesses, or their physical inability to visit their daughter. He gave misleading and incorrect information about Linda's personal beliefs concerning medicine. "Ms. Clinten's beliefs do not allow for any medical treatment, under any circumstances," making it sound as if Linda would stand in the way of Cathryn receiving correct and necessary medical attention.

From the language of the document, no one would realize that Linda's only real objections had to do only with the *known* side effects of psychotropic drugs and their potential contraindications involving the brain and nervous system.

Dick reported to the court that, "The family failed to help Cathryn at the time of her husband's death, and at the time of her hospitalizations." Brauning went further, stating, "The family members were uncaring, choosing to ignore Cathryn's needs." That Linda "threatened the Wilson Home with lawsuits," that she "threatened to sue the doctor who put Cathryn on Haldol."

"I've never even *thought* about threatening anyone with a lawsuit in my whole life," she had sobbed to Nick. "I don't believe this is happening. I don't believe he can actually *do* this. Why can't I call the judge? Why isn't Winston calling Brauning a liar? I can't believe he can get up in the morning and look at himself in the mirror!" she cried, blowing her nose hard and throwing the documents in her hand down on the floor.

Nick felt the same frustration that he had felt so many times during his disappointing law career. He lay back against the pillows on his bed in his apartment and rubbed his temples with his free hand. He held the phone and listened to Linda's sad recounting and his own eyes were moist, remembering those ugly, horrible, frustrating times, while he waited for Linda to calm down a little.

He wished he knew of a way to ease her pain.

ↄ

After reading Dick's legal documents, Linda began having precisely the same feelings about the legal profession that Nick had painfully acquired during his years of practicing law.

She was outraged at the lies and half-truths in the documents.

"How could someone, an attorney — lie so blatantly to a judge?" she asked Julia. Her daughter didn't have an answer.

Nick, having dealt with this particular aspect of legal procedure until he was no longer able to continue to do so, had no difficulty understanding Linda's upset.

He told Linda as calmly as he could, "It *is* common practice, right or wrong, and there's very little you can do about it except present the truth in the courtroom during the hearing."

Nick's response angered and frustrated Linda even more. "First my lawyer tells me that there's nothing I can do about someone lying about me to the judge, and then *you* tell me that it happens all the time! Damn, Nick, I can't deal with this … this *system!*"

But what could she do? Call Cathryn and say that she was sorry? That she just couldn't deal with it? Tell her that it was really just too bleak, and so damn repugnant, and that she wished Cathryn would find someone else to get her out of the mess she'd managed to get herself into?

Unsatisfied to merely be understood and acknowledged by Nick, Linda stormed around her living room for a while. Then she sat down at the computer and pounded out a complaint to the State Bar of California.

She referenced the pending case and stated, "Richard E. Brauning, attorney at law, behaved unethically."

"He gave false information and left out pertinent information in his presentation of the facts to the Court."

Finally, she declared, under penalty of perjury, "Richard E. Brauning submitted many undocumented statements that are pure falsehoods to the Court."

A short time later Linda received a response to her letter and her mouth dropped open as she read it. The letter, signed by the State Bar Complaint Analyst stated that:

"The authority of the State Bar is limited by law. We can discipline an attorney, or recommend that he/she be disciplined, only for a willful violation of the State Bar Act or the Rules of Professional Conduct. The conduct of which you have complained does not fall within the prohibitions of that Act or those Rules. Consequently, we are closing your file on this matter."

Linda was stunned and disgusted. *What then,* she wondered, *are the Rules of Professional Conduct? Evidently, lying is not a violation of an attorney's professional conduct.*

Getting a close look at this glaring ineptitude in the legal system enraged Linda and made her feel sick to her stomach. The tiny, nagging, seed of fear in Linda was growing, and the single piece of paper that she held in her hand made her feel weak and even more frightened about what she was facing.

༠༠

Now, in her living room, Linda leaned down and hugged her mother, "You're such a jet-setter these days, Mom. Thanks for coming out." Linda's eyes were teary and so were Lois', but the two women tried to smile bravely at one another.

"Let's go," Mark spoke softly, putting his arms around them and walking towards the front door.

༠༠

Cathryn waited for them outside the front door of the home with a cigarette in her hand. She wore a red T-shirt and jeans. Perched on the top of her head was a red baseball cap that Linda had given her to keep the sun out of her eyes when she walked up and down the streets of the neighborhood with Rex.

"Oh, you're all here together," Cathryn smiled, childlike,

pleased to see them. They each hugged her, and then Mark directed them towards his car.

"Did you have breakfast, Cathryn?" Linda asked. "I don't know how long the hearing will take."

"Hmm? They made pancakes this morning and I had an egg," Cathryn answered, distracted, in an unnaturally cheerful voice, as though they were going on a picnic, instead of to a courthouse to determine her future. There was a distant look in her eyes and a strange, artificial gaiety about her.

"We're fine, Mom, relax," Julia smiled. "It's Grandma's job to make sure we all eat while she's here, not yours," she teased, squeezing Lois' hand affectionately.

～

Thirty minutes later they drove up to the courthouse and Mark let them off in front of the imposing building while he went to park the car in the crowded parking lot.

Linda felt the nausea rise in her stomach but she didn't say anything. They looked at one another, smiling bravely. Except for Cathryn.

Only Cathryn was oblivious to the seriousness of the morning. She was glad to be with her family and away from the Wilson Home for a few hours. She wasn't thinking of much except to wonder when they would get some more cigarettes for her. She didn't even care about the capsules Sylvia had given her at breakfast. She felt fine.

An insensate smile remained on her face as if it had been pasted there.

～

Mark held the door open and they entered the building through an electronic security check like those used at airports.

They were early. The door to the room designated for their hearing was still locked, so they sat next to one another on hard wooden benches in the corridor. Mark, Lois, Linda and Julia were quiet, absorbed in thought, while police officers, lawyers and clients filed past them in continuous, steady streams in both directions.

It was simple to sort them out. The police wore the badges, the lawyers carried briefcases. And the clients were the ones wearing intense, worried looks.

"I'd like a cigarette," Cathryn said to no one in particular, her eyes mechanically following the traffic as it moved up and down the corridor.

"Come out this door with me," replied Julia. "You have to be outside the building to smoke." She took Cathryn outside and waited with her while she smoked two cigarettes, one right after the other.

To Julia, Cathryn looked like an injured, trapped bird. Yet she was certain that somewhere inside, somewhere deep beneath the drugs, she understood what was going on and was frightened. But Cathryn continued to smile at her.

Cathryn did know that there were two people who truly cared about her. Linda and Julia always showed up, no matter what she asked for or when she asked for it. She took another puff on her cigarette, watching the smoke drift up and away as she slowly exhaled.

Suddenly, Cathryn laughed out loud.

"What's funny, Aunt Cathryn?" Julia asked gently, curious about what could be amusing to her today.

Cathryn looked thoughtfully at her niece. Julia's long, wavy brown hair lay softly against her face. Her lovely, almond-shaped, inquisitive hazel eyes looked directly at Cathryn. Julia waited while Cathryn took another drag on her cigarette.

"Everything, sweetheart," Cathryn replied. "Absolutely *everything*." She put the cigarette out on the concrete wall next to her, and without another word, she started back into the building ahead of Julia.

༄

The courtroom was hushed. When the judge was announced, everyone stood. Judge Humphrey requested that the family sit in the juror's box and so they lined up next to one another. Mark was at one end with Julia on his right and then Lois. Next was Linda and to her right was Cathryn, closest to the judge, who sat upon his imposing raised, wooden bench.

Linda looked at her cousin. Cathryn had attempted to comb her matted hair into place. She was also wearing a red wind-breaker with a torn pocket. On her feet were scuffed tennis shoes. She looked bizarre, and not very stable at all, in the rigid, uncompromising surroundings of Judge Humphrey's courtroom.

༈

Judge Jerome R. Humphrey, unsmiling and aloof, began his questioning.

The Court had appointed Carol MacInaugh to represent Cathryn, and Ms. MacInaugh briefly explained the circumstances of the past months to the judge and said that she had interviewed Cathryn just three days ago.

She stated plainly, "Cathryn does not want the recent, temporary conservatorship continued. Cathryn has asked that her cousin, Linda, be named to oversee her affairs and look after her welfare."

Ms. MacInaugh told the judge, "Cathryn does not want Karen Brauning to continue as her conservator since she feels that Karen has not performed for her."

Karen and her attorney turned and smiled assuredly at one another as Ms. MacInaugh made her statements. They looked smug, as if they had anticipated such dialogue and they dismissed it like the buzzing of a fly.

Linda looked at their faces. It seemed to her that they knew exactly what she'd say. Linda and Julia looked at one another, puzzled. *But, she's telling him the truth,* Linda thought uneasily.

༈

Mr. Winston was called on to answer the judge's questions next. He explained to him, "Linda Clinten is available to act as Cathryn's conservator, and there is also another relative who is completely qualified and willing to take on the duties of the conservatorship, to serve in this capacity for Cathryn's welfare.

"Mark Benson is entirely able and willing to take on the duties of a conservator required by the Court. In fact, he is also a beneficiary to Mrs. Kent's estate. He lives in the same county. Mrs. Kent would be agreeable to Mark Benson or Linda Clinten being appointed her conservator."

In spite of these positive remarks, Mark's composure was daunted by the judge's inauspicious, intimidating manner and by the unfamiliar surroundings and procedure. Mark cared about Cathryn and would do anything to help her. The judge looked at him authoritatively now and began to rapidly fire questions at him.

"Mr. Benson, *exactly* how do you feel about this situation? What *are* you prepared to do on Mrs. Kent's behalf?" Mark froze like a piece of ice, confused and bewildered by the judge's severe, oppugnant tone of voice.

"Well, I … I'm relatively new to all of this," he stammered a little. He didn't really know what the judge wanted to hear him say and Humphrey did nothing to clarify his questions or to help him.

In a loud, booming voice, Judge Humphrey harshly interrupted the bit of communication that Mark offered. "What *exactly,* if anything, have you *ever* done to care for Mrs. Kent?" By that time, Mark's hesitancy was worse, his words sticking in his throat.

Linda realized with a start that the judge was attacking Mark. He was challenging him with an accusing tone, as if he had done something wrong. Linda was shocked. A cold wave washed over her.

What's going on here? she thought, turning in her seat, feeling her heart pound.

Next to her, Cathryn was smiling and looking around the room in childlike wonderment.

Judge Humphrey addressed Lois next, passing over Julia as if she weren't there. Julia glanced over to Linda, surprise on her face. Linda patted her arm, trying to reassure her. *Don't worry,* her eyes said to her daughter, but her heart felt heavy and it had begun to thud with her own misgivings.

"Mrs. Manning," he asked, in a tone almost as severe as his communication to Mark, "Do you have something to say to this Court regarding the situation with your niece, Cathryn?"

Lois gathered herself together. She straightened up in her seat, determined to give her best effort. She wanted to tell the judge the truth about her family, and she wanted him to know how much they cared about one another. That they were all concerned about Cathryn's well-being. She truly believed that this was the important information on which Judge Humphrey would base his decision.

She began, "Linda and Julia have done so much to handle Cathryn's needs and they *care* about—"

Abruptly, in the middle of her sentence, the judge interrupted her declaring loudly, "Mrs. Manning, this is *not* about caring. THIS IS ABOUT MONEY!" Everyone in the courtroom seemed to catch their breath for a moment. It was absolutely silent. Lois was at a complete loss and couldn't even respond to his statement. She looked at him, frozen in disbelief, her mouth open.

For a moment that seemed to go on forever, Lois sat staring at the judge. Linda couldn't believe what she had just heard. Julia's jaw dropped, and she turned towards her mother, her eyes wide with incredulity.

Linda, next in the row of Cathryn's abettors, focused her eyes directly on Judge Humphrey's face and pulled her shoulders back, more than ready to have her turn. She was smoldering now. She was ready to speak her mind.

"Mrs. Kent," the judge began, in a surprisingly mild, gentle voice, looking directly at Cathryn. "How do *you* feel about this situation?"

Linda was stunned. Judge Humphrey had passed right over *her,* as if she didn't even exist. She couldn't believe that this was happening. Another cold wave swept over her entire body. All the tension of anticipation in her shoulders and along her spine began to melt away, her shoulders slumped forward, in despair and hopelessness.

All at once, she knew exactly what was occurring in the courtroom, and she could not call it justice.

༉

At the same instant, Julia knew, too. She and Linda didn't look over at Karen and Dick Brauning. If they had, they would have seen expressions of self-satisfied, swaggering, triumphant victory. They did not have to look at one another. They knew that the hearing was over.

Linda realized now that this was no impartial court. The judge's decision had been made long before they entered his courtroom.

⌇

Linda struggled desperately with her despair. This was impossible. Cathryn would tell him what she had been saying for weeks. Her face was flushed with anger.

He has to listen to her. He'll hear what she has to say. How she feels has to matter.

Linda forced her attention to what Cathryn was saying to this judge, the one person in that Courtroom who had been chosen to be the arbiter of Cathryn's fate.

⌇

From very far away, Linda heard Cathryn's voice. "Linda is the only one I can trust to do anything for me, to help me," Cathryn said simply. "I *don't* want Karen Brauning to be my conservator. There was a day when she came to see me at the Wilson Home and I got confused. But I never signed anything. I never put anything in writing. Karen Brauning said I didn't have to. I didn't sign anything and I don't want Karen to be in charge of me," Cathryn looked up at the judge.

"Thank you, Mrs. Kent," the judge acknowledged her. "Thank you all for your information," he said, looking down at the papers on his desk.

For a few seconds, the judge was busy gathering papers together. Then he looked up and declared imperiously, "This Court decides in favor of Karen Brauning to be appointed permanent conservator over Cathryn Silberg Kent, person and estate." He pounded the gavel on the table with finality, emphasizing his unquestionable authority.

The judge went on to direct the Braunings in the matter of handling Cathryn's finances. He gave instructions regarding the release of Carol MacInaugh as Cathryn's court-appointed attorney. He paid no attention to the five people on his left, four of whom sat absolutely motionless, stunned by his actions, their mouths open, staring at him in disbelief and dismay.

Linda didn't hear his instructions to the Braunings.

His justice was like a giant hammer, slamming, in slow motion, into their hearts. Linda knew that this outcome was her fault. She had chosen the wrong lawyer or not done something she should have.

She knew now that she had most certainly been out of her league, and that her concept of the world as a place of truth, honesty and fairness was imagination and wishful thinking. Her weak, but still hopeful thoughts of a few moments ago, had been dashed to dust when Judge Humphrey lowered his gavel.

Twelve

Judicial aftermath...

SOME INJUSTICES ARE HARDER TO experience than others. Those that are totally unexpected can cause the most pain — the wrongs that simply *cannot* happen. They make a feeling, caring human being feel as if some giant, invisible hammer, wielded by a non-sentient power, has come down from the sky and smashed one's very essence to smithereens.

Such obliquity had taken place in that courtroom that the disbelief they felt was shocking and absolute.

How could this actually happen in any halfway civilized society? Linda thought, futilely.

↬

Her thoughts and memories whirled. She remembered the first time in her life that she had to confront a courtroom, when she was divorcing Dan in Illinois, prior to the adoption of no-fault divorce laws by that state. She was put on the witness stand by her own attorney, who *expected* her to *lie* about her husband's behavior so that she would be granted a divorce based on his wrongdoings. Linda, highly idealistic and more than a bit naive at that time, became speechless before her own attorney. He had had to prompt her, to put the statements there himself and then ask her to agree to them.

"It's true, isn't it, Mrs. Clinten, that your husband came home very late at night on many occasions without telling you where he was?"

Linda gagged at her memory of that *justice.* Her face had gotten red and her palms became clammy and damp. She was barely able to nod her head. She couldn't form words with her mouth and tongue.

Dan was a decent man, in spite of the fact that they argued. They were going in opposite directions in life. He never did the things that that court of law deemed necessary behavior in order to allow them to end the marriage.

The legal system had lost its altitude with Linda somewhat from that day forward. However, today, she had foolishly expected justice, and, again, what had occurred had caught her completely off guard.

She cringed at her own naiveté. *When will I learn?* she wondered.

⁊

Finally, Linda stood up and began to walk slowly towards the door, her family following her out of the courtroom. She felt numb, like someone in shock and she couldn't think of anything to say. Her lawyer spoke to her, but she barely heard him, and she didn't understand what he was saying, nor did she care.

She wasn't even sure which side he was on. *What was so complicated about this hearing? How had it gotten out of control?* She felt deceived by him, deceived and cheated.

⁊

They walked silently down the corridor and filed out of the courthouse into bright sunlight. Suddenly, the numbness went away and Linda was angry.

Now what happens to Cathryn? Can the Braunings keep us from visiting her? Will they hospitalize her again? Linda's stomach churned.

She looked over at the others standing there, each of them visibly shaken, except Cathryn. They were waiting for Linda to do something, anything. But all she could do was cry, softly at first and then harder, and that made her even angrier.

Roughly wiping at her tears with the back of her hand, she walked over to a row of pay phones and dialed Nick's number. For weeks he had tried to bolster her morale, to give her support and advice so that she could handle the hearing. Last night he had called. "Just want to wish you success and justice, Linda."

She hadn't detected how difficult it had been for him to conceal his concern, the trepidation he felt about the potential outcome of the legal matter. Not until now.

Today Linda didn't want to tell Nick how badly it had gone. She didn't want to say that she had failed miserably on Cathryn's behalf. She didn't want to see how like Voltair's Pangloss she had been, ridiculously idealistic and optimistic. But the outcome wasn't successful, nor was it just. The judge hadn't let her say a word. He didn't want to know her or how much she cared.

What Linda did not yet know, however, was that Judge Humphrey and Karen Brauning knew each other well.

※

"I just need a few minutes to talk to Nick," she said over her shoulder to her dejected family. She knew she shouldn't need to hear his voice. But she was beyond that now. She needed a friend, and besides her family, he was the only one she had. Nick's phone rang three times… four.

Linda thought that she was going to get his answering machine now, when she so much wanted him to be there.

Julia watched her mother with deep concern on her young, clear face. Lois, too, was looking at Linda, wringing her hands in a helpless gesture. Mark stood with his arm around Lois' shoulder, subdued, quietly waiting.

Cathryn looked completely unaffected by it all, and kept smoking one cigarette after another. She asked, "When will we go for lunch? Can we get some more cigarettes?"

※

"Hello," Nick answered, out of breath.

"Oh, Nick, I'm so glad you're there." The torrents of tears started again, and for a moment Linda couldn't talk. Nick waited, just like the first night when she had called, until she pulled herself together and told him what had happened.

"Jesus," he said, "I don't *believe* it. He didn't ask you a single question? What did Cathryn tell him?"

Linda answered, "Exactly what she's been saying for weeks! That she does *not* want Karen Brauning." Gradually she felt her own strength seeping back, and her anger rising again.

"I'm *not* done," she told him. "This is *not* right and I'm *not* done with this, and I *never* will be until I make it right. I'm sorry to call you with bad news," she said.

"Hey, it's okay, I'm sorry it didn't go better," he told her. "Give me a call when you're at home, when it all settles down, we'll talk, okay? Linda, there's *more* we can do."

"Yes, sure. There has to be," she answered, her voice sounding beaten and not very hopeful. "Nick?"

"Uh huh?"

"The Braunings looked as if they knew *exactly* what was going to happen next. All the way through, from the beginning to the end," her voice drifted off. "I'm sorry to call you like this, but I'm glad you're there."

"Hey, it's going to be okay, Linda. I know what we can do next. There are some things that we *have* to do. I'll talk to you in a little while, okay?"

"Okay, Nick. Thanks."

In spite of Nick's encouragement, she had little hope at that moment. Linda looked at Cathryn, wondering if her cousin would ever forgive her.

Ironically, at that moment, Cathryn didn't look as if she cared at all. Linda smiled faintly at her cousin. The other woman smiled back.

"Can we still go for lunch?" Cathryn asked.

ॐ

But they didn't go anywhere for lunch. Cathryn was the only one who had any appetite after the outcome of the hearing. They took Cathryn back to the home, and she climbed out of the car realizing that it was lunch time there. She hastily waved goodbye to them, patted Rex on the head, and hurried eagerly towards the dining room, not even slightly aware of the anguish felt by the four people whom she left standing at the car behind her.

Linda watched her go, knowing that Cathryn did not realize to what extent her own future had been signed, sealed and delivered to a stranger. A stranger who would be paid a percentage of her estate for the rest of her life, just for paying her bills. A stranger who would move her around like a chess piece, from home to home, in and out of psychiatric wards at the slightest provocation.

And what if the medication failed to work? Would there be more shock treatments? Could Karen Brauning cause that to happen? Linda felt sick to her stomach. She leaned against the car, steadying herself so that she wouldn't throw up.

༘

When Linda had first begun interviewing lawyers, she encountered one who was supportive of the practice of ECT, electro-convulsive-therapy. She couldn't believe that anyone could still believe that this was a good thing.

"Sometimes electric shock is a necessary treatment," the lawyer had started to explain to her.

Linda's heart had begun to pound and the rapid flow of blood was a roar in her ears. Clutching the arms of the chair on which she sat in the lawyer's plush office, she leaned forward.

"Let me explain to you *exactly* how I feel about that, so there is *absolutely* no misunderstanding at all between us." She said this quietly, but with such force that the lawyer sat back in his own chair and listened.

"If someone believes that putting a strong, damaging electric current through a person's brain can in any way *help* that person, that it might somehow make them feel better, happier, *whatever* — then I suggest that they put their own head into the nearest wall socket. And then they can tell me how that can possibly help anyone."

༘

Linda could barely wake up enough to reach for the phone. It was 4:30 A.M. and she had only been asleep for two hours. A nightmare had wakened her earlier from a very sound sleep in the middle of the night, and it had been some time before she fell asleep again.

But now she wasn't dreaming, the phone *was* really ringing. She grabbed for it in the darkness and heard her cousin's voice, but it seemed very far away, just like in her dream.

"I called Karen. I just get an answering machine. She doesn't return my phone calls. She doesn't come here. She doesn't do *anything*. Sylvia won't do anything. I called the patient's advocate. *Nothing* happens. *No one* calls back. Linda, please, will you help me?" Cathryn cried pathetically.

"Cathryn, let me make some calls in a little while. Let me see what I can do, okay?" she offered, her voice still drowsy with sleep.

Cathryn's voice changed completely. "Okay, sweetheart, it's nice talking to you," she said gaily. Click. She hung up as abruptly as she had called.

Linda untangled her body from the sheets that were pulled away from the mattress. She had evidently been sleeping quite fitfully. She got out of the warm bed and went to the bathroom. When she came back to bed, she wrapped the comforter and flannel sheet tightly around her chilled body.

She was wide awake now, staring at the ceiling, not wanting to close her eyes just yet, clearly remembering the nightmare. Chills ran down her arms and she shivered.

God, I'm tired, she thought. But when she finally did close her eyes, she saw the same vivid picture of her cousin falling down a long tunnel, being tossed like a rag doll from one side to the other, terribly, terribly fast. Cathryn was caught in a dark, slashing vortex, falling further and further away from Linda, her arms outstretched over her head, an expression of pure terror on her face, and she was screaming Linda's name over and over again, in fear and desperation.

"LINDA... LINDA... LINDA... LINDA... LINDA... LINDAAAAAAAA..."

Huddled into a tight ball beneath the covers, Linda shivered and her teeth made little clicking sounds. She felt exactly as she had in the dream.

Powerless, ineffective, as if she were being held motionless by some unseen force, while Cathryn tumbled away from her before her eyes.

Her heart was pounding and her cheeks were wet with tears.

Thirteen

Teamwork and passion...

"LINDA, I'M COMING OUT THERE," Nick said quickly, his voice determined. "Listen, this is what we have to do, and the sooner, the better." Then Nick began to explain how they might still be able to fight back.

❦

Linda got off the phone with Nick feeling as if little, gentle sparks of life were gently touching every inch of her skin. She was smiling now, for the very first time since the hearing.

❦

When she saw Nick coming down the airport escalator, Linda's heart felt as if it were beating faster and harder than normal. She could hear a thudding sound at her temples. The temperature in the airport was comfortable, but her skin was burning with excitement.

He looks tired, she thought.

She felt an impulse to comfort and care for him, and then he spotted her, and it was as if more than twenty years had not passed by at all. As they looked across the distance at one another, Linda felt her pulse racing, and she felt just exactly the same as she had whenever she was close to him so many years ago.

He smiled down at her, stepped off the escalator, and in a few long strides he had her in his arms, while rushing crowds of people hurried in all directions around them.

"Hi," he said warmly, holding her away from him, looking down at her, taking in everything from the top of her head to her shoes.

"You look *great*," he told her, pulling her gently back into his arms again, into a warm, comfortable hug that encompassed her completely, separating her from the rush and noises of the bustling airport.

He was wearing jeans, a soft, blue denim shirt open at the neck, no tie and brown loafers; a brown leather duffel bag was slung over his shoulder. Linda had on jeans, too, sandals, a beige silk shirt with the sleeves rolled up just below her elbows, and a touch of lipstick. Neither one of them said anything for several minutes. They just looked at one another, smiling and then they hugged again, ignoring the bumping, jostling crowd around them.

"Let's get out of here," she said, finally.

Nick kept his arm around her waist as they walked towards the baggage claim area. Every few minutes he looked down at her, kissed the top of her head and laughed. Linda's face was glowing with happiness. Her eyes were sparkling and her mouth settled into a soft smile. The lines were gone from her brow. Her body moved fluidly and her shoulders relaxed as she walked alongside Nick.

༃

That night neither one of them slept. They sat out on the deck and talked, hugged some more, stared silently for long moments at one another, ate popcorn and, finally, began to plan their strategy. Nick would stay with Linda for a while, in her extra bedroom.

Nick asked, "Show me all the paperwork you've accumulated, anything that documents what's happened with Cathryn."

At first Linda protested, "Get a good night's sleep, we can do this in the morning." But Nick insisted on getting started on it. And, so, she grumbled but reluctantly dragged out two huge file boxes containing copies of all of the court papers, lists of medications that Cathryn had been given in the various homes and hospitals, hospital statements, Linda's letters to the Bar Association and her attorney, newspaper articles, excerpts from probate law and more.

Most of it was filed neatly, chronologically, in two thick, black binders, but from the moment the hearing had ended, she had apathetically piled the paperwork in a stack in one of the boxes.

Nick sat at her desk reading the contents of the first binder. He didn't say anything as he turned the pages, his eyebrows pulled together and his lips parted a little. Then he stopped, looked up and asked Linda, "Did you ever get an answer back from this first hospital, about what medications they put her on?" Linda told him what they had said, and he made notes on a legal pad that he took out of his suitcase.

Linda went into the living room, turned the stereo on very softly and played a CD, The Narada Collection. She brought his things into her guest bedroom and then she made a pot of coffee. She took two steaming cups into Nick, and they drank it black from mugs, just as they used to an eternity ago at Clayton's in Evanston.

༈

"Can you believe this?" he asked, his voice angry. Nick was holding up one of several statements from the Tate Psychiatric Hospital.

"Just how do they have the guts to put this in print?" He smashed the piece of paper onto the table with his fist.

It was a statement charging Cathryn for room and board, no doctors, no medical assistance, no medication. The statement read:

> ROOM AND BOARD Medicare (Blue Cross)
> 7 DAYS AT $950.00 RATE
> BALANCE DUE: $6,650.00
> For your convenience, we accept the following
> credit cards....

The statement estimated the insurance coverage, which would pay almost the entire amount, gave the hospital name, phone, and tax identification number.

"Nine hundred and fifty dollars a *day* for the privilege of being in a locked environment, told when and what you can eat, when you can smoke, when you can sleep? Jesus Christ, doesn't *anyone* see something wrong with this picture?" Nick exclaimed, his eyes staring incredulously at the stack of papers in front of him.

Linda was quiet. Nick's hands rested on the table, the papers were spread out before him, his face was flushed with anger. He looked up at Linda and saw tears in her eyes. He got up and went over to her.

"I'm sorry," he said softly, putting his hands gently on her shoulders. "You've gone through all this already, haven't you?" She nodded her head and looked up at him, her face tired and sad. She put her right hand on the hand he had on her shoulder and then Nick kneeled down next to her chair. He put both of his hands lightly on her hair, then with his thumb, he gently wiped away a stray tear that had found its way down her cheek. He kissed the tip of her nose and then said to her, "Let's get some sleep. You were right, we've got some work ahead of us."

"Okay," Linda sighed, exhausted.

It was almost six o'clock in the morning when they went to their rooms. But instead of falling asleep quickly, Linda lay in bed with her eyes wide open. As devastated as she had felt immediately after the hearing, she now had some hope. Nick was here.

Her thoughts kept her awake for a few extra, tantalizing minutes, and then, finally, she curled up and drifted off, a look of pleasure and peacefulness on her face, in spite of it all.

꒰

The next morning, the weather was glorious. Linda liked to sleep with the sliding glass door open in her bedroom, and today the soft, mild breeze coming off the ocean floated across her bare shoulders. The moist, salty smell played at her nostrils before she even opened her eyes. She breathed in deeply and when she turned over and looked towards the open door, the sun was shining through the verticals. Close by, the soft, bright, tinkling melody of chimes played in the wind.

She stretched her arms out across the bed for a long, luxurious moment, and then she threw the comforter back, got up, stretched again, and got in the shower. She dried her hair with a towel, put on a pair of cut-off shorts and a T-shirt, and very quietly, tiptoed past Nick's room, through the thickly carpeted house into the kitchen. She brewed a fresh pot of coffee, took a cup outside and curled up on one of the chairs on the deck, her face raised towards the bright morning sun.

༄

"Hi," he smiled down at her less than ten minutes later. "I didn't want to wake you up. How'd you sleep?"

"I don't remember, but it was nice," she answered, smiling back at him. "Want some tea? Coffee? Are you hungry?"

"Just coffee sounds great. I'll get it. Sit still. No food yet. I want to show you a plan I've been working on for us." He was barefoot, wearing faded jeans and a dark blue T-shirt, his hair still damp from the shower. The color rose in Linda's cheeks again as she gazed up at him in the brilliant morning light. She put her fingers absently over her rapidly beating heart and took a deep breath.

༄

"How long have you been awake?" she asked.

"Don't know, maybe an hour or so." He handed her the legal pad, went into the kitchen and poured a cup of coffee while she read his neat, orderly notes. She saw that he had written, step by step, exactly what he felt that they needed to do in order to reverse Cathryn's situation through legal channels.

As she read, she remembered what he had told her the night before, "The little skirmishes don't matter *if* we win the battle. And that's what we're going to do. We have to find a way to reverse this decision — legally — so that Cathryn can be helped as much as possible, so that people who really care about her have something to say about how she's treated. That's all.

"Well, also, we want to do as much as we can to put the Braunings out of business. It shouldn't be this easy to take over on a person's life, and totally disregard their feelings or what they want. In any event, she has rights. She should be heard, and her wishes must be considered by an impartial court.

"If she says she disagrees with someone being her caretaker, like she did at the hearing, that must be looked into, followed up on."

A look of amazement crossed Linda's face. Her eyes were wide with wonder and her eyebrows rose in surprise and delight as she read his notes.

∽

"You like it," he smiled at her, a look of pleasure on his face. But then Nick's expression grew serious. He knew that he really needed to enlighten her about what they were facing.

"What we're *really* up against," he said, "is going to be a little more brutal than you want, but there's no choice, Linda."

Nick took a booklet out of his suitcase. Linda read, "Dr. Caligari's *Psychiatric Drugs, Network Against Psychiatric Assault,* Berkeley, California, Third Edition (with Addendum), 1987." Nick showed Linda the excerpts that he had highlighted on the plane:

—"Psychiatric drugs interfere with neurotransmitter chemical function and have inherently toxic potentials."

—"We also want known our strong opposition to all forms of involuntary psychiatric intervention, including involuntary commitment, forced drugging, seclusion rooms, and restraints. We oppose the use of electrically-induced convulsions (electroshock or ECT) and the use of psychosurgery (lobotomy, amygdalotomy, etc.) under any circumstances. In addition, we do not endorse the use of psychiatric drugs, although we recognize the right of individuals to decide for themselves whether or not to use such drugs."

—"Almost all psychiatric drugs are depressants that slow down brains and bodies. The primary effect of drugs like Thorazine, Elavil, and Lithium is to place the user in a chemical straitjacket. These drugs 'control symptoms' by restricting the individual's ability to think, feel and act. Furthermore, this control often comes at the cost of discomfort, disability, and sometimes death.

—"Every drug or chemical that you take can damage your brain and body."

—"Psychiatric drugs are often misleadingly called tranquilizers or medications. This gives them an aura of promoting health and well-being. Unfortunately, that is often far from the truth in terms of their actual chemical effects. These drugs have the brain as their target, and because of the brain's vital role in coordinating and regulating all body organs and functions, drug effects are felt from head to toe. The ability of neuroleptic-type drugs, like Thorazine, to cause permanent brain damage (called tardive dyskinesia) highlights the serious risk of damage inherent in the use of psychiatric drugs and reinforces the need to respect their dangers."

—"Psychiatric drugs can make people feel terrible and look weird. Because people getting drugged often have not been warned about these drug effects, they may interpret them as symptoms of some form of mental illness or of physical disease."

—"What psychiatrists regard as a beneficial drug effect is often experienced by those getting drugged as quite distressing and disabling."

⌁

Linda read the excerpts carefully, holding the pages so tightly that her knuckles were white, as she painfully digested the words.

Nick told her about the existence of involuntary commitment laws, enacted years ago, which allow psychiatrists to decide who is mentally ill, and then which give them the right to incarcerate those people without their consent.

"Not too long ago," he went on to say, "in New York State, there were five bills pending to make involuntary commitment even easier. This is the same state that passed a law in the eighties labeling membership in a new religious movement a *mental disorder* and gave the psychiatrists the power to seize members and *impose* psychiatric treatment on them. Fortunately, that law was vetoed. Today, if some psychiatrists have their way, every member of every church will have the mental health *benefits* necessary to profitably *treat* them against their will. It's so crazy in this area sometimes, that it's hard to even look at what's actually going on.

"I keep asking myself, how did *so many* people buy into the false belief that this is help?"

꒐

Linda put her head down, her hands hid her face and muffled her words. "I can't stand this," she whispered. "I don't want to be mixed up in this any more. I can't stand what's happened to Cathryn and I can't stomach dealing with lawyers and courtrooms." Her muffled voice trailed off, and once again tears fell from her eyes to the table.

"It's too late, little girl," Nick said gently, in a soft, clear voice. "You've taken on the bad guys and I'm afraid there's no backing down if that's what you believe in, if that's what you meant to do. What's the alternative, Linda? Give up? Walk away? Pretend you never saw what a horrible, lying mess it can get to be? Could you live with yourself if you did that? Come here," he reached out his hand and she took it. He led her over to the couch and pulled her down beside him, his arm holding her tightly against his warm, strong body.

"It's a crazy planet, isn't it? How come no one tells you what it's like when you're growing up? How come they just let you keep getting older, thinking that one day it will all make terrific sense and all the other stuff will just smooth out?"

He lifted her chin with gentle fingers and looked down at her pretty, tear-stained, face.

"Was it John Milton who said, 'The world is too much with us, late and soon, getting and spending?'" he asked her.

"I don't remember. Yes, I think so," she sniffled.

He handed her a clean handkerchief and she blew her nose loudly. She leaned her head against his chest, relaxing a little.

I wish I could stay right here forever, she thought. Nick put his hand on her chin again, but this time as he lifted her face to his, he touched his lips lightly to hers in a soft, gentle kiss.

Then, with his arms still holding her, he said, "I'm starving. Come on, I'll buy you breakfast." He got up and pulled her to her feet and back into his arms, where he held her for awhile, until the deep pain faded from her face.

꒐

It was almost four o'clock in the afternoon. Linda took him to her favorite little restaurant by the beach. They each ate an enormous omelet. Then they went for a walk on the sand, their arms around each other, walking comfortably, naturally, as if they had been walking that way together for a long time.

‿ৎ৲

At the same moment, while Nick and Linda walked along the ocean, Cathryn was feeling trapped. She wanted a cigarette. Her fingers tightened into fists and loosened as she shifted her weight from one leg to the other.

It's five-thirty, she thought, *and they won't let me smoke again until after dinner is over. Damn them.*

She went to the pay phone and called Linda's number, but when the answering machine came on, she angrily slammed the receiver down. She paced up and down the hallway, clenching her fists, glaring at the other patients. Her knees hurt. She felt miserable and trapped.

‿ৎ৲

In another small town close by, Karen Brauning sat at her desk. She felt a little hungry and she glanced at the clock. *Five-thirty.*

Let Dick figure out something for dinner. She stretched her arms out in front of her for a moment, reached for a cigarette and looked down at her desk. There was a stack of literature in front of her. She was trying to decide what other actions she could take to support the President.

She had read and reread many letters from various colleagues, institutions and politicians, all supporting the President's mandate for mental health care. This, Karen believed, was the key legislation that would ensure that the government could expand funding of the type of treatment that Karen's clients received, and from which Karen so greatly benefited. Karen, herself, had written many letters, spoken with several groups, called local politicians, and faxed her thoughts on the topic to Congressional Representatives and Senators.

Now she was waiting, almost holding her breath, hoping for

the passage of the legislation. The funding for this mental health coverage would give the psychiatrists with whom she worked unlimited funds to treat every man, woman and child in the country, while the citizens and their employers would pay the price for it.

She had read somewhere that recently a Kansas City psychiatrist was arraigned on fourteen counts of insurance fraud in pretrial hearings. Also, another psychiatrist, somewhere in Utah, was under investigation by the Utah state licensing board for sexual misconduct and abuse of patients.

As if that wasn't enough bad publicity, there was the NME bust, where FBI agents had raided a psychiatric hospital in San Diego, seizing documents and files as part of a nationwide search of the hospitals owned by that chain.

According to the newspapers, the FBI said that it was investigating possible criminal misconduct by the NME, the nation's second-largest chain of private, for-profit psychiatric facilities. One source told that the NME was suspected of defrauding Medicare, MediCal, the military health Insurance plan known as CHAMPUS, and private insurance companies of three to five hundred million dollars.

Karen did not like it when mental health got this sort of publicity. She sat there, chewing on her lower lip. And, even worse, there was the popular national TV show which had recently taped a program dealing with enforced incarcerations and insurance fraud.

Karen threw the clipping about the TV show onto a stack of papers, her cheeks flushed and her eyes bulging out with anger.

Yes, both Karen and Dick Brauning would do anything they could to get the President's mandate for mental health care pushed through the system. They *had* to. Their income, their life style depended upon it.

༄

In the following weeks, Nick and Linda went almost everywhere together. But, first they went to see Cathryn, who, under Karen Brauning's direction, had been put back into the psychiatric hospital, again.

This time Rex was boarded in a cage in an animal hospital while his mistress was treated. Living in a space three feet by four feet for weeks, with unhappy animals squealing and yapping around him, bewildered the gentle little dog. He began spending his time curled up in one corner of his cage, trembling, waiting patiently for his exercise time, but mostly for the day when he could again snuggle up at Cathryn's feet.

The bills for Rex mounted quickly, but that was not a problem for Karen Brauning. And Cathryn didn't know that her beloved pet was not at the boarding home waiting for her.

꒰꒱

As strong as Nick had been for Linda so far, he was visibly shaken when he saw his old friend in such despairing ruin. Cathryn recognized him right away. A smile came to her lips that was so reminiscent of that long ago, lovely, young girl he remembered, that for a moment, he couldn't say anything at all. Nick stood there, unconsciously squeezing Linda's hand until it hurt. When he slowly put his arms around Cathryn and held her firmly against his chest, he was fighting back tears, while Linda stood off to the side doing the same.

"What are *you* doing in California?" Cathryn demanded, throwing her head back and laughing. Before Nick could say a word, she continued, "And, with *her*?" She motioned towards Linda, her eyes twinkling with pleasure. Then, quickly, "Where's Carrie? And, for God's sake, who's holding down the fort with the Chicago courts while you come out here to play, hmm?" she challenged, smiling at him, teasing, like the old days, a million years ago.

꒰꒱

They took her outside to a small courtyard where she could smoke, and where Linda and Nick could escape the smells of medicine and disinfectant that burned sickeningly in their nostrils.

The sight of one patient after another, looking barely alive, shuffling along aimlessly, sitting in chairs lined up along the walls of the inside hallway, their faces impassive and blank, was heartbreaking.

Linda and Nick watched them, and they saw an absence of light in their eyes and little purpose to their movements. But worse was the lack of caring from many of the hospital personnel as they dealt with those sad and tormented souls, barely answering their questions or responding to them with cool, unfeeling indifference. *It's only a job,* their attitudes seemed to say.

"But, I just want to go home," one frail, old woman wailed pitifully from her chair, as she reached out to a nurse who walked by. "I want to be in my own bed, please. Will you call my son? Tell him I want to be in my own bed. I don't like it here. I just want to go home, be in my *own* bed. Why can't I sleep in my own bed?" She started to cry softly, like a small, frightened child.

The nurse said, "There, there, Mrs. Hemming, let go of my sleeve or we'll have to get you a shot. You'll go home, honey, when the doctor says you can." Her voice was annoyed, she had things to do. Feigning a smile, she brushed off the tiny, clutching, weathered fingers and walked away.

Linda told Nick, "I feel like I can barely breathe inside this place."

She showed Nick an article she had found, an exposé of some European hospitals.

"It's about Italy," she told him, "where the situation concerning some psychiatric hospitals there is being exposed. There were investigations recently," she read, "which included 'a member of the Italian Parliament and teams of cameramen and reporters from two national television programs and one national newspaper.'

"The conditions they uncovered were 'little better than concentration camp conditions. Film crews documented filthy and decaying facilities with patients sleeping on the floor naked or semi-naked, primitive shower and toilet facilities, crumbling walls and broken windows, stifling heat with no air conditioning. At night, patients were locked in cramped cells with no furniture, no windows and no way to call a nurse.'"

Linda said sadly, "And while we applaud ourselves for being so advanced technologically, we are so deficient spiritually that it makes me feel like puking.

"'The outraged Italian public,'" she went on, "'called for regional and parliamentary investigations, which are now on-going and causing major changes in that country.'"

Linda wearily rubbed her temples and sighed. She wondered what it would take for Americans to confront the abuses happening in their own psychiatric hospitals. *What would it take for the public here to become outraged?*

She looked into the empty faces of the patients who sat silently, staring into space in the courtyard surrounding them.

She felt the emptiness, the futility of their existence. *They have already lost so many of the things we take for granted.* She wondered how many of them had been abandoned to the system by their overwhelmed families. Pathos welled up in her heart.

With another sigh, Linda turned back towards Cathryn and Nick. The two of them were looking at one another and talking softly. *It has been too many years,* she thought.

Nick's hand rested gently on Cathryn's wrist as the three of them sat at a round metal table together, again.

ॐ

After Cathryn was stabilized with additional medications or new doses, Karen moved her again, but this time to a different board and care home. Cathryn called Linda, and she, Julia and Nick went to see her.

This time they were told, "Cathryn isn't allowed off the premises for a month, according to her conservator." They were shocked and upset. They had wanted to take her away someplace for a couple of hours.

"No, you can't take her out for lunch without Mrs. Brauning's okay."

When they got home, Linda was still so angry that she called Karen's office without talking it over with Nick. She intended to demand an explanation of Karen's actions, but she got her answering machine, left a message, and an assistant named Sonia called back a short time later.

The woman told Linda, "When a client is moved to a new residence, it's advisable to give them several weeks to adjust before taking them off the grounds."

"Why?" Linda demanded.

Sonia, in a cold voice, replied, "If you have further questions, you should have your attorney contact Ms. Brauning's attorney." She gave Linda Dick's office number.

❦

"What is *with* them?" she protested to Nick later that night.

"They're protecting what they feel is their territory. Looks like it's going to get a bit nastier now. It would be better if you didn't talk to them anyway. We'll be better off using a different approach."

Nick, in a low, calm voice, told Linda what he felt they must do next. "We don't have any choice anymore."

"You aren't serious?" she asked, her eyes wide and incredulous.

❦

The next time that Cathryn called, Karen had moved her again, to still another home that was even further away from Linda. They went to see her again, this time with Mark. They were given permission, after Linda signed a form, to take Cathryn out for lunch and to a grocery store for a few things she wanted to have in her room.

Cathryn told them, "I don't know why I've been moved, but every time I am, more of my things are missing. I don't know what medication I'm being given or how long they'll keep me here." Her speech was slurred and she walked hesitantly, carefully. When she stood still, she shuffled her feet from side to side, changing the weight from one leg to the other.

Cathryn talked to them about the place Karen had placed her in this time. "There are four rooms for women in my wing, four beds to a room, one bathroom between each of the two rooms. Eight women share a bathroom."

"For one hundred and five dollars a day!" Nick was livid with outrage. "Most people don't care, I guess, especially if the financial burden is handled by insurance or Medicare."

"This is *criminal*," Linda answered.

﹏

By the time the afternoon was over, Linda felt drained. It left her feeling exhausted and dazed.

These places in which people like Cathryn are housed, Linda thought with anguish, *are pathetic and useless. At best, some of them are kept relatively clean, but their sole purpose for existing is to house human beings who have almost given up on life, who are waiting to die. Nothing productive is being done for them. For the most part, the staff is there just to keep them controlled, subdued and quiet.*

They're shuffled from one room to another and given innumerable rules that they have to follow, under the threat of still more freedom being taken away from them or even more harm coming to them. It's as if they've committed crimes, instead of being emotionally upset or troubled.

"Instead of leaving these already unhappy souls alone, or giving them some activities, some choices and some freedom of motion concerning their own existence — while taking care that they don't hurt themselves or anyone else, and waiting, giving them a chance to become a little less frightened of whatever demons are driving them into their emotional isolation — most of these places give them more demons to contend with, when they have already been so overwhelmed, so subdued," Linda told Nick. "I never would have believed that they were like this, if I hadn't seen it with my own eyes. Doesn't anyone pay attention to what's happening in these hospitals and homes?"

﹏

The only thing that alleviated Linda's excruciating agony over Cathryn at all was when she and Nick began their own private investigation into the matter.

﹏

"Let's go," Nick said. "We'll start with the local newspaper and library and then go to the courthouse. On the way, we'll have a look around their neighborhood. Ready for this?"

Linda sighed, "As ready as I'm ever going to be." She bit her lower lip and looked up at Nick.

He smiled, put his arms around her and kissed her lightly on the lips, but a look of uneasiness crossed his face. The kiss, heartfelt and spontaneous, was a bit unsettling for both of them. At the same instant, they moved apart uncomfortably and left to go to the Escondido Union Newspaper office.

ౕ

For weeks now, Linda and Nick had been operating off of an unspoken, tacit pact.

We'll keep our relationship exactly where it was, Linda thought. *Good friends, long-time friends, and along with that, this quest to help Cathryn. That's what's important right now. And we're temporarily sharing my home in order to accomplish our purpose.* Linda told herself over and over that that was all that was happening. That it was that simple.

And, for Nick it was the same. They had more than enough to deal with in trying to help Cathryn. They didn't have the time or energy to complicate matters. And he thought constantly of his sons, Scott and Jimmy. He could see their faces, bright eyes, red cheeks, and he was anxious to get back to them.

ౕ

But it wasn't that simple.

The truth was, Nick was enormously attracted to Linda and he kept wanting to pull her closer to him.

She was so alive, so real, so open. He thought about what she'd handled by herself; raising kids, moving across the country, and now helping Cathryn.

He realized that he had never known anyone less demanding and less pretentious. Nor had he known anyone warmer.

Working with her day and night, Nick began to know her moods and needs. The attraction, the electricity between them grew until it was impossible to ignore. But just slightly stronger was Nick's determination not to turn it into a brief, heart-ripping affair for a few weeks, and then, with more wounds and injuries than either of them had before, limp painfully back to their former existence.

Alone in bed at night, Linda stared at the ceiling, but in her mind she saw an image of Nick's face, his eyes smiling back at her.

Something about him had always pulled her towards him. When he wasn't there, she could tell herself it was all her imagination, just her first important crush. *But now he's here and it's worse. He's strong and sensitive at the same time. Carrie must've been out of her mind to let him go.*

In a still unfinished article that Linda played with sometimes, she wrote about men and women and relationships. "…an area that has gone completely crazy during my lifetime." She wrote a notation in the margin, "I am so tired of hurting from loving … I know one thing for sure, this is not how it is supposed to be, this isn't loving … "

As for Nick, his whole world and all of his plans had exploded so violently with Carrie, that it left him with a painful emptiness that wasn't healed. Lying in his own bed at night, he still sometimes found himself trying to figure out what he could have done differently and what would've made it work out.

Nick and Linda both knew, without a trace of doubt, what they did *not* want at this point in their lives. Because of all of their determination to avoid what they did *not* want, they each managed to construct some sort of a protective barrier, a façade.

But it was, after all, only a façade.

༈

There was disappointment on Linda's face as they left the newspaper office. Her smile was gone, the tiredness ringed her eyes. They had gone there in search of an index that would help them locate any articles that had been published recently, mentioning either the conservator, her attorney husband, or the judge. But it was a small neighborhood paper and it didn't have an index.

But, the buxom, young redhead behind the wide reception desk, gazed dreamily up at Nick, and went out of her way to be helpful. She gave him a card on which she wrote the name of the newspaper's librarian and his telephone extension.

"Maybe he can help you more," she purred.

Linda stood by the entrance way, watching. Nick gave the redhead an appreciative smile, and they left for the public library. Linda giggled a little at the embarrassed flush in Nick's cheeks, and his hurried exit.

"Very funny," he retorted, taking her hand in his. He opened the car door for her. She smiled again at his discomfort from the girl's attention and got in the car.

෴

The library did have an index for the local paper, and also for The San Diego Union. They were able to locate and scan through several newspaper columns. They did find some mention of the judge, but the articles were not about anything that would serve their purposes. Nick made copies of two articles.

"Just in case," he told Linda, and they went back out to the car.

"I'm fascinated," Linda told him. "There are so many things that I didn't even know existed before all this started. You're responsible for increasing my shrewdness. Not a word I would've used to describe myself before this mess."

"Naw," Nick teased, shaking his head from side to side slowly, "sagacious, perspicacious, astute even, but shrewd, *no way.*" He was shaking his head and smiling down at her, and she looked back at him thoughtfully, her head tilted to one side.

Linda looked into his gentle eyes, her lips slightly parted, her hands entwined in her lap, then she turned away.

෴

They went to the courthouse next. The task was laborious and time-consuming. They had to scroll through the computer index of all the cases in the Superior and Municipal courts. Then once they found a name they were looking for, they had to get the case number. The cases were sectioned off by date, by court and by type of case. Reading the darkened screen took some getting used to for Linda.

"How do you know about all this?" she asked Nick.

"Private detectives use this stuff all the time, it's public record," he told her. "That's why they charge so much. They spend a lot of time traveling to courthouses, finding case numbers and then going through all the pertinent files. Sometimes you get lucky."

After they got a list of case numbers with Richard Brauning's name on them, they went to the clerk and asked to see the files. The clerk explained the codes to them, "Several of these cases were filed downtown and you'll have to view them there. You can see these four cases if you go outside the courthouse and upstairs to the department next to the law library," the clerk told them, marking off the numbers with a pencil.

"Thank you," they both said, turning away.

It was some hours since they had begun their search. Linda walked quickly, but with some effort, to keep up with Nick's long legged stride, her shoulders slumped forward a little. She was really tired. Worse, she didn't feel very hopeful anymore. She worried that they would not come up with anything that would help.

But Nick went ahead with single minded perseverance, tenaciously, like a bulldog. He took her hand in his as they went upstairs and down the long, musty hallway, past the law library.

And, finally, they were rewarded.

ॐ

When they were back in the car talking about it later, they laughed so hard that Linda's sides ached. Someone had made a mistake, but by the time it was discovered, it was too late. Nick and Linda had been able to read an entire confidential report, and now they understood an aspect of Dick Brauning's character that would have stayed hidden from them forever, if not for the error.

They had gone into the office, according to the clerk's directions, and handed the case numbers that they wanted to view to the woman behind the desk. She came back with three of them, gave them to Nick and told him, "The fourth one is on microfilm. If you want to look at it, I'll get it for you."

"Yes, please," Nick said politely. Linda stifled a giggle, remembering Nick's stories about charming secretaries in law offices so that he could get his hands on documents without having to go through all the usual red tape.

The clerk went to get the microfilm and Nick turned to Linda conspiratorially, "What are you laughing about?" he whispered, leaning toward her, his eyes soft, as if he might kiss her right there.

"You've got to look less like a spy and more like an attorney," he cautioned her teasingly, his voice getting even quieter as the clerk returned with the plastic container in her hand. Linda kept her hand in front of her mouth to hide her amusement, while Nick, in a serious, appreciative tone, thanked the clerk for her help.

"Come on, you silly little thing," he grabbed Linda's hand and led her away from the counter to a machine where they could review the court case film. Linda giggling more now, followed behind him.

꒜

It took them over forty-five minutes to go through twenty pages or more of court documents on the screen, searching for any reference to Dick Brauning. Apparently, the case they had their hands on was about a complicated real estate venture that appeared to have been grossly and illegally mishandled, but their man was not the culprit. Instead he appeared to be one of those allegedly harmed by the crime. Nick rewound the tape and Linda returned it to the counter.

They found a small table and sat down with the other three files. Nick began to read one, while Linda studied another. The case that Nick had in his hands was turning out to be another dead-end, and after about fifteen minutes, he yawned and looked up at Linda. She was reading intently, carefully, through each page in the file, and all at once her eyes widened and she said, "Nick, *look* at this!"

꒜

The case that Linda had in her hands was a lawsuit that had been brought against an off-duty policeman, Officer Brauning, by an elderly woman. The police officer had been speeding down a residential street late one afternoon and the woman had yelled at him to slow down. In her irritation, she had thrown a rolled-up newspaper towards the car from her own front porch.

The officer, who had his wife in the car with him, screeched on his brakes, jumped out of the automobile, and according to the documents in the file, began hollering at the woman and threatening to arrest her. The woman did, in fact, call the police herself, but Officer Brauning, becoming even more irate at this, actually had her handcuffed and arrested. The elderly woman eventually won her lawsuit for the unlawful arrest, and she was awarded eight thousand dollars in damages by the court.

Linda and Nick looked at each other. "Well, this is quite an interesting story about our boy's character," Nick said.

Linda was engrossed in a page that she hadn't finished reading yet.

"Hmm?" she said to Nick, not looking up. "What did you say?" she asked absently. Nick repeated what he said, but Linda still didn't really hear him. She asked, "Can we make a copy of this to take with us? This is incredible!"

"Yeah, sure. The clerk will copy it for us. What've you got there?"

"A psychologist's report, someone who treated the woman because of all the stress after this happened," Linda said.

"What?" Nick was amazed. "What's *that* doing in there? Let me see that." He began to read the pages that Linda handed him. "My God," Nick said. "'*The patient recounted that Brauning looked like a madman, someone who was on drugs, when he yelled and screamed and threatened her in front of her house.*' This isn't supposed to be open in the file, it's a confidential report," Nick exclaimed.

"I'm going to get the clerk to copy these pages. We can *use* this!" Linda said getting up and walking boldly over to the clerk at the counter.

Nick sat back in his chair, watching her and smiling to himself. She certainly didn't look scared or intimidated now.

The clerk's reaction was similar to Nick's, only she was much louder and much more dismayed. "This is *not* supposed to be part of the file, where did you get this? *Why* wasn't this sealed?" the woman demanded.

"I have no idea. It was in with the rest of the file," Linda told her truthfully and shrugged her shoulders.

The flustered clerk's eyelids fluttered as she shook her head rapidly from side to side, pinching the file closed and holding it out of Linda's reach.

"Can I just copy down the psychologist's name?" Linda asked, reaching her hand towards the file.

"No, this is a mistake, *no!*" the clerk said again, clutching the file tightly against her broad chest.

"Well, okay, sorry, thank you," Linda replied, holding back a smile. She walked back to where Nick sat grinning at her and she said, "Who cares? We both already know Betty Tyson's name and how she feels about Mr. Brauning."

Linda was smirking, her eyes bright. She couldn't wait to find some more dirt on the Braunings. *Maybe we can turn this around,* she thought.

ᴔ

The last file was equally revealing about Richard Brauning's character and his abilities as a law enforcement officer.

Evidently a crime of sexual molestation was committed on a fourteen year old girl and two policemen investigated the matter. The two officers were given a suspect's name. Using a Department of Motor Vehicles printout by a name only, they prepared a declarant in support of an arrest warrant. The warrant was issued with no further investigation, such as contacting the suspect's employer, father or roommate to confirm identity or whereabouts.

While at home getting ready for bed with her new husband, the plaintiff was abruptly arrested on child molestation charges and taken to jail. Her husband posted bail right away. The couple retained legal counsel, and within a very short time a cursory investigation established that the plaintiff was *not* the proper defendant. Only their names were similar.

However, it was fifty-three days and several court appearances before the case was dismissed and the plaintiff's innocence was made known.

One officer in particular, Dick Brauning, was found to have

contributed to the situation resulting in arrest and prolonged prosecution. The plaintiff was awarded fifty thousand dollars in general and punitive damages.

"Nice work, Dick," Nick said as he finished the file.

❧

"Hey," Nick told her a little later, "we've earned the right to take a break. These court files were quite a find.

"We get some time off. Jesus, it's almost four o'clock," he said looking at his watch. "Are you hungry? I'm starving." Linda had been so agitated earlier that she hadn't been able to eat anything at all. She was famished.

"Let's go to your little cafe," Nick said. "If you don't eat something pretty soon, I'll have to carry you home."

"Sounds fine to me," she smiled.

"Which?" he asked, teasing. "Food, or me carrying you home?"

"Either," she answered softly, smiling back at him. "Both."

❧

Afterwards, they left the cafe and walked down to the beach again. Nick took Linda's hand in his. They walked along the sand watching the funny little sandpipers scurry from one spot to another. The undulating ocean swept stones away with a loud rustle. The sun was setting in a burst of orange flame. They watched each other.

"What are we going to do?" he asked her, his voice serious.

"What do you mean?"

"About you and me?" Nick said.

Suddenly Linda was afraid. She felt a jabbing sensation in her chest and she shivered. She didn't answer him, but turned to look away out over the ocean.

Nick put his arms around her, drew her to him and rested his cheek against her smooth hair. She loved the feel of his lean, strong body holding her.

"Let's just stay right here forever, okay?" she whispered against his shoulder.

After a while the sun went down, disappearing into the water behind them, a huge, brilliant, melting, fiery orange glob. The sky was streaked with color and seagulls flew over their heads.

ॐ

They drove back to her house and were just one step inside the door when Nick turned towards her, put his hands on her arms and looked into her eyes.

She stood there frozen for just a split second, then she leaned towards him.

She felt warm all over. She took a breath, sighed, and at once her resolve, her promises, her plan, her analytical handling of this exact scenario — which she had gone over and over in her mind in the past few days — all went to hell.

She was in Nick's arms and he was kissing her hair, her forehead, her cheeks, the corners of her mouth, gently at first, happily, then deeper, intensely. These were not the affectionate, controlled kisses that they had shared before.

Nick's hunger for her, once released, was so intense, he felt as if he wanted to devour her with his mouth. His strong hands pressed her body closer and closer to his own. Their restraint during the past weeks broke down completely. The façade crumbled, leaving them with an enormous burst of raw passion for one another.

She looked up at him, her eyes misty with tears of pure joy. She had waited such a long time for this moment.

He held her away from him, his hands on her shoulders.

"You are beautiful, Linda. You are even more beautiful than I remembered. Inside and out," and then his arms drew her to him again. But this time he just held her in a very firm, warm hug, his arms enfolding her, making her feel happy and safe and cared for.

She stood very still, as if her body were suspended in space. Neither one of them moved for a long time. Then he began to stroke her silky hair and she pressed her hands harder against his back, brushing her lips back and forth across his warm cheek. She reveled in every touch, every sensation, loving the faint smell of soap on his skin, the feel of his fingers on her arms, the warmth and strength of his body against her own.

"Oh God, you feel too incredibly wonderful," she whispered, her hands moving slowly, deliberately along the muscles of his lean back, while the blazing heat of her desire for him overtook everything else.

❧

Nick took her to bed. He held her hand and led her to his room. He turned the lamp on very low and turned towards her slowly, as she stood still watching him. He lifted her chin up towards him and kissed her mouth gently, and then with greater and greater passion as if he would never stop. His hands slid along her back, then down her hips and he brought her body still closer to him. He slowly, deliberately unbuttoned her shirt and slid it from her shoulders. He leaned down and kissed her throat, her shoulders and the sensitive, smooth skin just above her breasts, his mouth soft, exploring and deliberate. He pulled his own T-shirt over his head and dropped it to the floor. His fingers slowly, softly traced the lines of her back, her shoulders, her arms, her face, as he watched her expression. Linda was trembling.

He put his arms around her and gently, firmly, leaned her back across his bed and he lay down beside her.

"What was I thinking about twenty years ago?" he asked her, his lips brushing back and forth across her shoulder.

"I don't know," she laughed, tears of happiness spilling onto her cheeks, "but I know what *I* was thinking about."

She pressed her mouth against his, tasting his lips, his tongue and she pulled his body still closer to her own.

❧

For a moment Nick held his naked, strong body close above hers, he slowed and paused, his eyes on her face, and then he entered her. He moved up just a little, but not away, and then again, *so* slowly, until he was touching her so deeply, so perfectly, as if he could feel everything that she felt, as if her body was somehow registering its sensations within his own and his movements were measured exactly for what she was feeling.

Linda felt herself slipping away into an incredible, intense orgasm that enveloped and shook her entire being. At that moment, feeling her intense release begin, Nick pressed his body even closer, closer to her, and he said, "Oh God, jeesuz, jeesuz … " as he came, as she came.

Good God, glorious, delicious, Linda thought, pressing her face into his warm shoulder, trying to feel and smell and taste and hear everything of him all at once, while her hands against his back held him to her.

"Good God…" she breathed, softly, her eyes bright with delight at the exquisite blending of pleasure.

$\backsim$

They made love for hours that night. And, finally they fell asleep in each other's arms in the bedroom where Nick had slept for weeks. The fresh, salty scent of the ocean was on the cool breeze that came in through the open window and danced across their bare shoulders. Linda snuggled closer and Nick pulled the blanket up around her, his arms holding her body tightly against his.

As she fell asleep in Nick's arms, Linda was feeling only the wonderful sensation of being cared for and loved.

Fourteen

Their crimes...

NICK WAS FAR FROM FINISHED with his investigation of the Braunings and the honorable Judge Jerome R. Humphrey. Because Karen and Dick Brauning had so violently attacked Cathryn's family members with untruths to the court that had gone unquestioned, Nick was convinced that any one of the three, and most likely all of them, had some serious hidden crimes of their own. He was determined to find out what these were. Then he and Linda would be able to take the next step in their defense of Cathryn's rights.

He telephoned Dick Brauning's former law office and audaciously gave his real name and former profession to the woman who, for a brief time, had been Dick's secretary. He told her honestly, "I've got a client who may have been dealt with unfairly by Mr. Brauning. Every once in a great while, I find that when someone says that about an attorney it turns out they're right," Nick chuckled pleasantly.

After a few minutes of conversation, Cathy Lange was laughing comfortably. She told Nick, "I'm not exactly a member of my former boss' fan club."

Nick let her know that neither was he. He asked Cathy, "Look, I don't want to keep you from your work. Can I buy you lunch or a cup of coffee, somewhere near your office?" Cathy, her dark eyes sparkling with curiosity, thought, *This could be interesting.*

"Sure," she said. "Twelve-thirty okay with you?"

"Perfect," Nick answered, smiling.

֍

Nick met Cathy at a small, busy Mexican restaurant on the main business street of Vista, just a block from the law office with its barred windows. Cathy Lange was an attractive woman in her late thirties, with long, dark brown hair, big brown eyes and a rather hard, no-nonsense face. She had worked for Ronald Hardwick for over six years. As she told Nick, "I've seen and heard a lot."

֍

"Yeah," Cathy told Nick, scooping the rice and beans together on her plate with her fork, "Dick got the job in the first place because his wife has known Ronald for a long time. She arranged a favor or two for him through her connections with some judge." Cathy put a forkful of the steaming food in her mouth.

Nick asked if she remembered who it was that was involved in the favors.

"Naw, can't really remember his name, doesn't matter," she said with finality, but with her eyes twinkling. Nick recognized that Cathy would not discuss the circumstances or the judge's name with him because her loyalty to her present boss was inviolate. In spite of the circumstances, he was pleased.

"Ronald and Dick knew each other before, too, when Dick was a cop in this area. He and Ronald evidently bumped into one another more than once." She cut a large chunk of chicken in half with her fork, put it in her mouth and chewed, thoughtfully.

"Ronald helped Dick with his stress disability claim," Cathy said, matter-of-factly.

"What?" Nick cut in abruptly. "What kind of claim?"

Cathy explained, "Dick always seemed to be running into trouble on the force. He's a hot-head, arrogant, pushy, that type, you know. And he kept pissing people off. Finally, it looked as if the department was going to find a way to dump him anyway, so he started going pretty wacky, and, eventually, he or his wife, or someone, came up with the idea of him being off-loaded because of stress and that's what they did. I guess he saw a shrink and was taking tranquilizers and stuff." Cathy dipped a chip into the bowl of salsa and held it in mid-air for a moment.

"The guy leaves the department with a record of improper arrests and a lot of other screw-ups, and then gets paid for it! What a system." Cathy shook her head and ate the chip.

Nick was pushing the food on his plate around with a fork. Now he picked up his cup of coffee, nodded agreement to Cathy and encouraged her to continue.

"When he was in our office, he was really an arrogant bastard. Not fun to have around at all. On top of being demanding, he was always making slimy remarks about women, acting like he was looking down my blouse or up my skirt. The guy is really disgusting.

"When he and Ronald started getting into it, I was glad 'cause I never liked him. He'd interrupt what I was doing like I was his personal slave instead of someone who'd been working for Ronald for years. He isn't a particularly nice guy, and he belongs where he is, at *home*. His wife is a piece of work, too. She handles him real well," Cathy laughed.

"How so?" Nick encouraged again.

"Karen is a real little ball-buster. She doesn't take any shit from anyone. From what I've seen, she's the one who calls the shots and she tells him what to do and he does it," Cathy paused for a moment, remembering an incident.

"One day Karen called the office from her car phone, and Dick had me put her on hold. He was just talking to a guy on the phone, laughing and joking, while he made her wait. I kept going back and telling her he was still busy, and finally she got really pissed when I told her who he was talking to, and she knew it was no big deal. Well, when I went back to tell her he was still on the other line, she had already hung up and was on her way here!

"Man, she came in that front door like a hurricane and didn't say one word to me, just stormed down the hall and into his office and he was still laughing and joking with his buddy. Karen went over to his desk and pushed the button down on the phone and disconnected the call! Then she marched back and closed and locked the door and really gave him hell. She kept her voice down and I couldn't hear exactly what she said, but I sure could feel the way she said it. He must've almost peed his pants!" Cathy laughed out loud again.

They finished their lunch, and then a little while later Nick shook Cathy's hand and thanked her warmly out in front of the law office. "Hey, I really appreciate you taking the time to talk to me. Maybe someone like your former boss should be slowed down, if he treats people the way you describe."

"Boy, would that make me happy!" Cathy said, grinning.

Nick thanked her again, got into Linda's car and drove to the Escondido City Hall, which housed the Police Personnel Department. Before he went inside, he called Linda from a pay phone to tell her how it had gone with Cathy.

"You charmed her into submission and she told you all the firm's secrets," she teased him.

"Nope, actually the lady's too ethical for that. She's got a lot of complaints about our boy, though. Guess he wasn't such a nice boss, and she was happy to tell me about that. I hope the police department is as helpful," he said. "How's the article coming?"

"Fine. I read it to Julia and she did her usual editing job on me," Linda laughed. "My daughter believes in a very direct approach. A bit more work, but I think it's going to be a decent product," she told him.

"I miss you," he said. "I should be back in a couple of hours. I want to drive past their house and see what I can find out about trash pick-up and a couple of meaningful license plates, then I'll be back home."

"Sounds fun," she said nervously. "Nick, be careful, okay? I'll be right here."

ॐ

Later they compared notes. While Nick was finding out about Richard's past at the law office, Linda had been busy as well. A trip to the courthouse had been quite revealing.

"Nick, listen to this!" Linda said excitedly, "Karen Brauning and her husband have been involved in dozens of conservatorship hearings in the past eight years. And in whose court do you think *every single one* of these was held? Judge Jerome Humphrey's! Interesting, eh?"

༄

Early the next morning, Nick pulled Linda's warm body close to him and kissed her on the nose, his eyes twinkling. "I'm enjoying being a sleuth," he smiled at her. "Maybe I should change professions, do this full-time."

"Right," Linda answered with a touch of sarcasm. Gently, she pushed him towards the garage door, putting her car keys into his hand.

"Okay, okay, I'm going." He kissed the tip of her nose once more and was out the door.

༄

First he went back to the Police Personnel Department at City Hall. The day before he had asked to see documents that were part of public record regarding former police officers, and he was told by a short, gray-haired woman that his request needed to be in writing. "Only a salary range, class or title and approximate dates of employment will be verified. It's not the department's policy," the clerk said, sounding like a tape recorded message, "to disclose information concerning a person's reason for leaving, his job performance, medical condition or sick leaves." She stuck her chin and her chest out as she spoke, reminding Nick of the Little King and he pressed his lips together so that he wouldn't laugh.

Nick was back at the same clerk's desk again, only this time with a formal letter that he had prepared, explaining that he was considering employing Richard Brauning, who was formerly with the Escondido Police Department.

The letter gave approximate dates of Brauning's employment, salary range, medical and sick leave data and a glowing report of achievements as a police officer, ostensibly told to Mr. Nicolas Martin by Mr. Brauning during the course of an employment interview. It was, in fact, a brief history hurriedly put together by Nick and Linda the night before, with whatever data they had to hand. And, just as Dick had done to them, they had filled in the blanks for their own purposes.

Short of Nick being a federal government agent who was requesting the information for a security check on Dick, there appeared to be no legal way to get specifics from personnel files. Some days later, when he received a response in writing, very little of the information he provided had been verified or responded to in any way at all.

He telephoned the Department's Personnel Analyst, a cordial, soft-spoken woman named Elaine McPherson. Ms. McPherson told Nick that she was sorry that she couldn't provide him with more specifics on Richard Brauning's file. But when she said the name, Nick thought that there was a certain amount of vilification in the tone of her voice, now that she had had a look at the particular file in question. She said *Richard Brauning* with something in her voice that sounded like contempt.

Nick was guessing, and it was only an intuitive hunch, but he was getting the idea that the Escondido Police Department had not been laden with remorse over the loss of Officer Brauning.

ᘓ

On another hunch, Nick stopped outside a Denny's and he telephoned Steve Styers from the pay phone.

"What I need," he explained, "is a San Diego cop who can poke around and find out what happened with this guy, just the basic story, nothing elaborate," Nick chuckled. "Know anyone like that out here, Steve?" There was silence for a moment.

Then Steve's enthusiastic laughter bellowed from the phone. He had been sitting with his feet up on his huge oak desk when Nick called, but now he swung them to the floor and turned his chair so that he could see out of the enormous picture window that took up one entire wall of his office.

The Law Offices of Steve Styers were located on the sixty-third floor of the East Towers Building, a high-rise that was built in the shape of a three leaf clover. It was located on the edge of Chicago's Outer Drive with Lake Michigan bordering it on the east. Sparkling frost clung to the perimeter of the window. Down below, the icy water shimmered, reflecting beams of sunlight back up against the building. Seagulls flew past the window in what looked like a team maneuver. Steve, fascinated, watched them soar out of his sight.

Then he responded, "You don't ask for much, do you?" He laughed heartily again. "Hey, Nick, it's good to hear from you, even if you are always asking for favors, ya jerk!" They laughed warmly at one another, as close as always, though separated by half a country.

Steve admired what Nick was trying to do, he respected and shared Nick's ideals. He said, "I hope you nail these bastards if they're fucking with people, damn it."

ॐ

Steve told Nick that he would get back to him. Nick hung up the phone and stood there for a moment feeling a little odd, a queasy, uncomfortable sensation invading his gut.

He knew that he was going to have to decide what to do about Linda. She was settling into his heart in some gentle, wonderful way. But then there was the question of his sons back in Chicago. He could not live apart from them. He just couldn't.

ॐ

And, then there were his own parents, married for over forty-five years and still kind and caring to one another. Both his mother and his father still wanted him to bring Scott and Jimmy for brunch or dinner every single Sunday. But they never demanded anything of him. He missed them all.

ॐ

Nick leaned against the phone booth. He looked up at the clear, blue sky and considered how freezing cold it would be in Chicago soon. After a few minutes, he shook off the confusion, nostalgia, homesickness, or whatever it was that was creeping over him. It was time to get back to work, to get some results.

He walked back to Linda's car and drove to the courthouse. He stopped at the Information Desk and asked directions to Judge

Humphrey's courtroom. Nick, dressed in a suit and tie and carrying a briefcase, looked very much like one of the hundreds of attorneys who hurry in and out of those courtrooms all day long. He found the courtroom marked "S," walked directly inside, and sat down as comfortably and naturally as if he had impending business there.

Seated next to him, in the next to the last row of seats, were two men wearing suits and a woman in a dress and hat.

"Good morning," Nick nodded to them as he sat down in the aisle seat. He noisily took a small stack of papers from the briefcase, rumpled them around, and looked up at the judge on the bench. The judge was looking down, studying some paperwork himself. Nick stared hard at him for a moment or two and then put the papers back into his briefcase, shut and locked it, stood up and left the courtroom, smiling and humming quietly to himself.

Now Nick knew exactly who Judge Humphrey was and what color tie he was wearing. Dark blue with a single gray stripe. No one paid any attention to him as he left.

❧

Nick sat behind the wheel of the little BMW in the parking lot for a few minutes. He got out of the car and walked around the front entrance, and then a few more feet along the side of the formidable, brick building. Then he went back to the car. He could see no other convenient way to get to the parking area, other than through those front doors. He walked back to Linda's car and sat there, patiently waiting, with the stereo on very low, his eyes on the doors. He didn't want to miss the judge's exit to his car.

❧

At ten minutes after four, Judge Jerome R. Humphrey, minus his robe, wearing a suit and dark blue tie with a single gray stripe, came striding through those front doors, with what looked like two young attorneys following nervously, subserviently in his wake, bobbing their heads, and scurrying to keep up with him. Without slowing down or turning his head in the slightest, he appeared to be telling them something, something which they hastily scribbled down into notebooks, as they attempted to run alongside the judge.

He got to his car, a lovely, rich, cream colored Jaguar and tossed his briefcase into the back seat. Then he dropped behind the wheel.

"That's all of it. Handle it," Nick heard him say sharply to the two young men who stood almost at attention at the side of the car. The judge pulled the door closed hard and drove off.

Nick followed the car out of the parking lot. He would have no trouble spotting the vehicle again, nor the license plate which read "HH JRH."

"HH," Nick mused. "'His Honor'? What an ego," he said aloud.

～

Later, Nick opened the door from the garage and immediately saw Linda's tear-stained face. He dropped his briefcase and took her into his arms. "What's the matter?" Nick asked anxiously.

"Joseph died. My mom called a little while ago. He died last night and Anna isn't doing well at all. The boys are with her, but they're really worried about her heart. Mom's going to Chicago tomorrow morning and the funeral is Wednesday. Oh, Nick, I feel so bad for Joe, for Anna, for Cathryn, her brothers, for us," her voice broke off in muffled little sobs.

～

Nick called Don Castleman, Joseph's friend and attorney. Nick and Don had met years ago, introduced by Steve, when Nick was a brand new attorney. They had liked one another right away. Don was another one of those old-fashioned attorneys, a basically caring and ethical man who also happened to practice law. He had admired Nick's professionalism when Nick was with Smithson, Ellingsworth and Naples, and yet Don had understood Nick's decision to leave the firm. They had dealt with one another on several different cases, and despite the difference in their ages, they had become friends and they trusted one another.

Don asked, "Are you representing Cathryn in some way, and if so, can you come to Chicago and see me about the trust?"

Nick briefly told Don what the circumstances were concerning Cathryn.

"I think it's really important for us to have an informal meeting, as soon as possible," Don said, his voice somber. He paused for a moment, and then added, "There's an awful lot of money involved in this, Nicky."

"I'll fly back tomorrow." He looked over at Linda and added, "With Linda. She'll want to be at the funeral and we'll both come to see you Thursday morning, if that's okay."

Linda nodded at him, with a small, trembling smile, appreciatively. Her eyes were still red from crying. She sat curled up in the corner of the couch now, like a small child, nervously chewing at the cuticle of her thumb.

"Yes," Don told him, "around ten o'clock Thursday then. Take care, Nicky."

"Thanks, Don. See you Thursday," Nick answered and hung up the phone. "Ready for Chicago?" he asked, turning towards Linda.

"No, not really," Linda told him, "but with you there with me, I think I can handle it." She was thinking about the funeral, the family she hadn't seen for years, the legal mess surrounding Cathryn, Nick seeing Carrie and his sons. She completely forgot to consider that it was November and that her home town would probably be freezing cold.

"I guess I'm just a little tired," she added. Nick didn't answer, but his strong, warm arms reached out and drew her close to him.

$\backsim$

When Linda and Dan had dissolved their marriage, Linda had plummeted briefly into the steadily growing society of what she liked to call, the *screwed up* singles.

Though busy with the demands of her work, and two small children, she was still motivated by a strong, normal longing to connect and share her life with another person. Compromising her own reality, though, she found herself seeing what she wished the other person and the relationship to be instead of what was actually there. And, this always led to hurt and pain.

A friend, Lisa, also newly divorced, had persuaded her to get out more, to go to clubs, places which were, in reality, meat market singles' bars, where the loneliness and desperation were so evident on the faces of the men and women there, that Linda often went home feeling lonelier and worse than when the evening had begun.

It wasn't her style to sleep around, to fall into bed in casual relationships, but she did it for a time and she found herself confused and lonely. In a pathetic attempt to find some caring company, she made mistakes and she continued to make them for a while.

Then suddenly one day, sanity returned. Linda felt as if she had blinked hard and could at last take a good, clear look at what she was doing, and she didn't like it. The casual, transient sex made her feel stupid and even more lonely than before. It became clear to her that she would only be happy following her own code of behavior, and not trying to live someone else's.

And so, she had avoided relationships for a while. For a long time she put her energies into Julia, Michael, her home and her work instead.

⤳

Before the trip to Chicago, Linda had to take some of her material to Los Angeles to meet with her agent, Kyle Williams. She wanted to take the train so that she could do some editing on the two hour trip. Nick dropped her at the Amtrak Station and he carried on with his investigation.

The meeting with Kyle went well, and by two-thirty Linda was on her way home. She loved the train ride. Sitting comfortably next to the window, her feet up on the empty seat facing her, Linda wondered what it was about trains, even a commuter train, that felt so romantic to her. With the rattling, shaking from side to side, creaking, whistle-blasting atmosphere of the train, she was scarcely able to keep her attention on the papers in her lap. She kept looking out the window, gazing at everything the train passed, listening to that warning-announcing-wistful sound of the train whistle, and thinking about Nick.

And, so, after all these years, she was in a relationship. Again. But this one was different. There was so much open communication between them and so much caring. And, she realized, she didn't feel stupid. She felt in love.

ॐ

It was impossible for either of them to be making love and ignore the issue of where they were going with their relationship. When Linda got back from L.A., they compared notes about their day and got something to eat. That night they stayed up until the sky began to lighten at dawn, just as they had on the first night Nick arrived in California. They talked, this time about themselves, about each other.

"It's really hard to be away from the boys. And for some reason, it's still important for me to be close to my parents." Nick said softly.

"They matter to me. Guess I feel like I owe them, or more that I want to be there in case they need me, like they've been for me," his voice was sincere, his eyes filled with emotion.

Linda told him what she wanted, what she needed and what she felt she had to offer. She didn't feel needy, the way she had when she was younger.

Nick was unusually quiet. Linda looked at him for a long while and still he said nothing. His silence felt like disagreement to her.

She got up, left him sitting on her couch, and went into the kitchen. She stood facing the sink, thoughtful. She wanted his hands on her, his arms around her, more than anything. But he had to want it, too. He had to want her.

She sighed deeply, resignedly, and then reached for the pot of coffee and was about to pour a cup, when Nick came up behind her. He wrapped his arms around her and pressed his face against her hair and the warmth of her neck. She felt a little confused and tried to move away. But Nick held her firmly in his embrace and didn't let her go. Finally, she relaxed against him. There were no words spoken, just a comfortable and caring embrace that somehow erased any upset, leaving understanding between them again.

And yet, Linda knew, even as she turned towards him, her arms reaching around his hard, lean body, that when they were done with the Braunings, when Cathryn was safe and secure, Nick would be on his way back to Chicago. She could hear in his voice how much he missed his sons. When he talked to them, he sounded so loving, so adoring, so devoted — the same way she felt about Julia and Michael.

∽

To say that Chicago's winter weather is cold is not quite accurate. That single word does not adequately describe forty degrees below zero with the wind chill factor. Linda had told Nick, "I'll be fine! I've been back to visit in the winter before, and I'm taking this monstrous warm, wool coat, boots, gloves, a knit hat and a scarf. Nick, quit worrying." When they arrived at O'Hare Airport, she laughed at Nick. "I'm warm, for God's sake, I'm buried under all these clothes!"

But, then they stepped out through the automatic doors, and when Linda inhaled, she felt as if she could barely breathe in the freezing cold air. In thirty seconds she was so cold from head to foot that it was hard to move. Nick looked at her surprised face and laughed, "You are so California-ized, you'd never last here. Your suntan is turning red!"

He pulled her close to him, kissed the end of her very cold nose and held her tightly. Under all the layers of clothing, disagreeable little shivers danced up her arms and across her back and shoulders. She shuddered, an uncomfortable groan escaping through her chattering teeth and numb lips.

Nick kept her as close to his body as he could as they made their way onto the warm shuttle, drove across to Hertz, and got settled into their rental car. Then he pulled her over to him again, keeping his arm tightly around her as he drove from the airport. He never loosened his grip until the efficient heater turned the interior of the car into a comfortable seventy-eight degrees and he could feel the muscles of Linda's hunched, shivering shoulders relax into a more natural position.

Linda snuggled against Nick's side, looked up at his profile, and thought how much she was loving this man.

⟡

The funeral was difficult and certainly no place to bring the details of Cathryn's situation. Keith, Martin and Steve were enormously grief-stricken over the loss of their father, who had been an ever-present and important part of their lives. It was a particularly poignant scene, the three sons standing protectively close to their mother, all clad in black. Three very successful, well-dressed businessmen, so saddened by the loss of a father who had managed to be a friend to each of them — ironically, something that he failed at with his only daughter.

The concern about Anna was great. The tiny woman who had immigrated to a new homeland, raised four children and stood by her husband's side through both very difficult and very rewarding times, could not stop crying, though she was barely making any sound. She stood as tall as she could, her shoulders drawn back, dabbing at the corners of her eyes with a white handkerchief, under the black lace of her veil. The tears continued to run down her pale cheeks as if they would never stop.

Sadly, Anna, who was physically weak before her husband's death, now looked like a small, frail, delicate, lost child. Surrounding her, towering over her, were her sons. Though they had known that this sad day would come, they were failing miserably at holding back their own pain from their loss.

The relief when the proceedings were finally over, and the formal mourning of Shiva finally began, was almost palpable in the room. Linda understood, more than she ever had before, how the presence of family and friends in the Shiva house, laughing, eating and remembering, could bring distraction and some bit of comfort to the bereaved. The ritual allowed for a change of mood. It was a time for family and friends who shared the loss to busily comfort one another just by their presence, and often without words. Now it was a time to get on with life, with living.

Linda was among family again and that was good. However,

the bit of happiness was dampened by the circumstances, both here and at home.

✣

The day after the funeral Linda and Nick went to Don Castleman's office. It was large and comfortable, but unpretentious. Pictures of Don's wife, children, and grandchildren lined two shelves of the heavy oak bookcases which covered an entire wall.

Linda remembered meeting Don briefly at the Silberg's house many years ago, and now, she found she liked him right away. Don Castleman, a short, stocky pleasant man with a firm handshake and a mellow voice, explained in careful detail and a straightforward manner what Joseph had hoped to achieve when he had asked Don to draw up a trust and will, many years ago.

" 'To protect my daughter, Cathryn, as best I can, from Edward Kent,' Joseph explained to me. Then I remember how he looked out the window behind my desk. Snow was falling very heavily that day and the wind was blowing so hard that the glass shook and rattled. Just weeks earlier, Joseph told me he had called Cathryn and begged her to come home for the holidays.

" '...to share Rosh Hashana and Yom Kippur with us, with your brothers and their children, Cathryn, please,' Joseph pleaded with her.

"Cathryn told him that she could not, 'Such a trip isn't possible at this time, Daddy,' she said. 'No, Dad, please. I can't. I just can't right now.'

✣

"Joseph looked back at me then. His face was so weary and so sad. 'This is something that I must do for her, something that she will not understand for a long time, if ever,' he told me. His voice broke and he bent his head and cried for a long time," Don told Nick and Linda.

"Joseph Silberg didn't fail in many things that he attempted in his lifetime," Don said, tears glistening in his eyes now.

" 'My only daughter, we love her so much, we've lost her', he told me and tears kept falling from his eyes and his aging hands were trembling. I walked over and put my hand on his shoulder, but there was nothing I could say."

৵

Nick and Linda were astonished to learn the terms of Cathryn's inheritance and the amount of money that was involved. They sat across from Don, and simultaneously, their jaws dropped open as Don explained the details.

According to Joseph's will, Cathryn had to divorce Edward and attest that she was no longer subject to his will or decisions.

Because of his death, the inheritance would now surely become hers.

"Cathryn Silberg Kent is worth over five and a half million dollars," Don told them.

৵

If Karen finds out about this money … " Linda said, looking from Don to Nick.

If Karen was able to find out about Cathryn's trust and inheritance, Don would be obligated to disclose the details to her, as the conservator.

Karen would have her and her millions of dollars as well.

৵

There were legal means, of course, to reverse the decision of the Court, of Judge Jerome Humphrey. But, if Karen knew about the money and moved swiftly, she would be in a position where she could use Cathryn's resources to fight every point of opposition from the family. She and her husband had altered the facts before and they would do so again. Karen would be able to wage a lengthy and an entangled legal battle with almost unlimited funds. And she and Dick would, of course, be paid for doing so.

"I can't slow this down very much," Don told them soberly.

They were in Don's office for over two hours. When all three of them were satisfied with a strategy that they would follow, they went over their plans carefully, and then discussed the procedure completely again. Linda and Nick thanked Don profusely. They made arrangements to keep him informed of their progress and they said their good-byes.

At first Don extended his hand to Linda, but then he hugged her warmly to him instead, emotion visible in the softness of his features. Don, a gruff, old, seasoned attorney, had tears in his eyes again. Linda hugged him back gratefully, a tremulous smile on her mouth, below her own moist, glistening eyes. "Don, thanks so much for helping."

✧

Nick and Linda stayed in Chicago for eight days. The Shiva, following tradition, lasted for seven. Nick went to see Scott and Jimmy several times, while Linda spent time with her mother before she flew back home to Boca Raton.

Lois and Linda, spoiled by the temperate climates of Florida and California, were not anxious to travel any further than they had to in the sub-zero temperatures, chilling slush and slippery ice and snow. They visited with family and friends during the days of the Shiva at Steve's house in Glenview, where Lois was staying so that she could be with Anna as much as possible. Anna's home was with Steve and his family now. The condominium that she and Joseph had lived in together for the last, difficult years would be sold.

On the last day, Linda and Lois spent several hours alone together. They went to see a movie and then they had a long, leisurely lunch with glasses of White Zinfandel, in a warm, cozy restaurant with a huge, blazing fireplace not far from Steve's house.

With the comfortable warmth surrounding them, they looked outside through the restaurant's windows and saw dainty, graceful snowflakes floating to the ground. The gray sky and severe cold were made a little more palatable by the whimsical, light snowfalls that came and went during the day. Everything began to take on the bit of magic that comes when a dreary, dark, gray concrete city is transformed to a winter playground, with its darkness hidden under a blanket of soft, clean, white snow.

The dark, sprawling branches of the huge trees overhead

looked as if they had been frosted with the snowfall, *like dark pieces of cake,* Linda thought, remembering another snowfall, many years ago.

"Mom, I'll miss you," Linda said softly. They had had this conversation before. Linda was always trying to convince her mother to live closer, to move to San Diego. But, Lois was happy, independent and satisfied in a community that had sprung up rapidly in southern Florida, accommodating the influx of retirees who had escaped, at last, from the brutal cold winters of the east coast and the Midwest where they had spent most of their lives.

"I would've thought you would be tired of looking at me after my vacation to see you, and now this one, so close," Lois kidded, her voice drifting off, her eyes dropping for a moment. She looked up at Linda. Neither of the two trips had been a vacation for either of them.

"No, Mom, I'm not tired of looking at you," Linda answered. She leaned towards Lois, put her hands gently on the softness of the older woman's face and said, "I love you. I'm glad you're my mother, I'm glad I have you."

Fifteen

Chicago winter...

NICK STOOD AT THE DOORWAY of Jimmy's room, and with the light from the hallway, he watched his younger son's chest rise and fall with the easy breathing of untroubled sleep. In his left arm, Jimmy cradled the new football that the three of them had broken in earlier that afternoon. Nick looked around the large bedroom, taking in the expensive oak bedroom set with two dressers, two matching twin beds and an entertainment center that held a stereo, TV, VCR and computer. Neatly arranged on two of the shelves was an impressive array of videos, CDs and disks. On another, was a collection of boy's stories in handsome leather-bound editions, with gleaming, embossed gold titles.

The mirrored, closet door was open part way, and Nick could see a row of shelves with shirts, sweaters, jeans and socks, neatly ironed and folded by Carrie's efficient Venezuelan maid.

A bit of moonlight drifted through the oak shutters that covered both the windows and the French doors. The doors led out to a raised deck and stairway down towards an enormous pool, and the rarely used but constantly maintained tennis court.

Nick leaned against the doorway, his arms folded across his chest. Materially, they would have everything imaginable. He had always provided well for them, but never quite up to Carrie's standards. But, then her parents had no problem filling in what they saw as the gaps.

Scott's room was almost a duplicate of Jimmy's, except that Scott had opted for bunk beds with a ladder. His penchant for motorcycles was apparent in the intricate models that he and Nick had worked on together, which were now neatly lined up in racing formation on two of his shelves. There was an extensive book collection about the repair and maintenance of bikes, and framed bike posters covered the wall behind his bed. The posters had been a concession for Carrie. They didn't follow her decorating scheme, but together Nick and Scott had somehow won that one small argument.

Carrie came up the stairs soundlessly behind Nick. She pulled roughly at his shirt sleeve, motioning him away from the doorway and downstairs into the den. She wanted to talk. Reluctantly, Nick began to close the bedroom door and turn to follow her, but first he took another long look at his son's precious and innocent face.

༉

"Is *this* how it's going to be?" Carrie demanded, her displeasure and anger turning her pretty features harsh and severe even in the subdued lamplight. She had turned on Nick as soon as he followed her into the room, and now she stood rigid with her arms folded across her chest, one foot slightly in front of the other.

Nick recognized this as a typical Carrie pose. He sighed and closed the door behind him. He had had a terrific day with the boys. He knew Carrie would not miss an opportunity to spill venom before he left. But he didn't want her to wake Scott or Jimmy with her upset, whatever it was about.

"What is it, Carrie?" Nick asked softly, with another weary sigh. "What is it *now?*" He sank into a chair and she took a step towards him, but stopped when he glared up at her. Carrie knew just how far she could push Nick, and she intended to do so at any given opportunity, but only to that exact point.

"'What *is* it?'" she mimicked sarcastically. "'*What is it?*'" her voice grew louder, crazier. "You disappear for almost two months and you come back as if nothing unusual has happened. You think a few phone calls and gifts will make them understand and everything will be all right?" she gestured towards the upstairs, their peacefully sleeping children. Her face was becoming even more distorted with her ridiculous sense of injustice.

"What is the *matter* with you?" she demanded.

In the next few seconds, Nick made a decision. He drew in a deep breath with his eyes fixed on Carrie. He slowly let it out.

⟳

He and the boys had had a wonderful day. It had been a clear, sunny morning, but very cold, even too cold for more snow to fall. They had gone to their favorite pancake house on Green Bay Road for breakfast. Then they played touch football in the park, despite the cold and remaining bit of snow and slush, until their faces were bright red and their clothes were soaking wet. When they went back to Nick's apartment, they took steaming hot showers, and watched movies on the floor in front of the couch on top of big, fluffy pillows.

They were all starving by then, so Nick called and ordered three different kinds of pizzas. Before he brought them back home, they shared a quart of cookie dough ice cream, passing the container back and forth, each armed with a spoon. They laughed and tumbled around on Nick's living room floor, in between taking huge mouthfuls and giggling at one another.

⟳

Now, Nick looked at their mother dressed in a soft, green, silk shirt, skirt and perfectly matching heels.

She was wearing her favorite jewelry. Delicate earrings and matching bracelets with tiny braided strands of gold, set with brilliant emeralds and diamonds that were made exclusively for her. Once again he considered how far apart their importances were.

Carrie was even thinner than she had been the last time Nick saw her. Instead of adding to her attractiveness, though, it seemed to give her a sharp, angular look.

⟳

Scott was born with Carrie's coloring and features, and he had looked like a tiny, masculine image of his mother for years. But now his hair had darkened, and his eyes had changed to the same deep green as Nick's. Jimmy, on the other hand, had been a replica of Nick from birth, except for his tangle of thick, blond hair that he had gotten from his mother. They were both tall for their ages and growing rapidly. Both were strong, good-looking, little boys with gentle hearts, like their dad.

⌒

He knew that he could not stop Carrie's sharp tongue and critical attack – he'd never been able to before.

But, now a degree of sanity, a measure of strength that he had never felt in all the time he had spent with her, flowed through him. He stood up, his face angry, and he took two deliberate, menacing steps towards her. Carrie moved back just a little, revealing her wariness. Nick was within inches of her face and there was not the slightest hesitancy in his actions, nor in his voice.

"Knock it off, Carrie, *now*," Nick told her, his voice low, steady and powerful, with each word measured, exact and forceful.

"We're not going to go over this again. Not *now*. Not *ever*. I did something I felt needed to be done. It has *nothing* to do with you. It has *nothing* to do with how I feel about my sons. You and I are divorced. It's done.

"I'm not spending the next fifteen years fighting with you. I've had enough of that for *two* lifetimes. You will *not* tell me how to live *ever* again. You will *not* spoil every moment I have with them with your insane sense of whatever it is that makes you feel you can govern and control everyone around you.

"Go do whatever it is you do, Carrie," Nick said, tired and disgusted. "I'm going home. I'll call the boys tomorrow night." Nick turned and walked from the room.

Carrie didn't say anything. She stood motionless.

Nick had never spoken to her in that manner, in that tone of voice. Nick had never sounded so strong.

Carrie's ridiculous, ill-conceived anger was gone. She was obviously shaken. For a very *brief* moment, she even felt regret.

⌒

When Nick caught up with Linda again, he was thoughtful, subdued.

"Had a great time with Scott and Jimmy," he told her, "but Carrie has a hard time not being a bitch with me, and when she does that around the kids, it rips me up. Besides, it's just so damned hard to be a part time father, to see them once in a while." Nick's voice faded, his eyes were sad and glistened a little as he spoke.

Linda listened, but said nothing. *When your children are an enormous part of your reason for existing, that's just how it is.* And it was a feeling that Linda fully understood.

જી

Nick went to see his parents and that was good. He and Linda took them out to dinner. She hadn't seen them since college. They went to a good Italian restaurant and drank Merlot and ate crisp salads, flavorful eggplant parmigiana, creamy turkey tetrazzini and warm garlic bread.

Over spumoni and coffee, his mother and father chatted about Nick's antics as a young boy. They enjoyed telling Linda how he had worked so industriously at a newsstand with his uncle when he was only eight years old. How he had played hockey so well in Toronto. They reminisced about his love for an abandoned German Shepherd puppy he raised, and his persistence and salesmanship when he begged them for a pet snake. They all laughed.

Linda liked Nick's parents, who were soft-spoken and obviously very fond of one another after forty years of marriage. They were an affable couple, and gracious towards Linda. By their words and the warmth in their eyes, Linda knew that they loved and respected their son very much.

જી

After eight intensely emotional days, Nick and Linda flew back to San Diego. They sat close to one another, talking very little on the flight to Dallas and then on the connecting flight to Lindbergh Field. Nick kept his arm around her shoulders, and most of the time his hand rested comfortably on hers. When they hurried through the busy airport at Dallas, he held her hand tightly in his.

The warm, gentle sunshine that they felt as soon as they came off the plane and walked out of the airport delighted Linda, as it did every time that she came back to the San Diego area. Especially now, after the harsh winter chill of Chicago. As always, the strong, comfortable feeling that she was really home filled her with happiness.

Nick was impressed by the sparkling beauty of the San Diego area, Mission Bay, Balboa Park, Coronado. But, he teased, "The weather is so nice so much of the time that it knocks out any challenge. It makes the population of Southern California *very* complacent."

"Give me complacency over frostbite any time," Linda retorted. "I put in my years in Chicago's winters. It's someone else's turn."

But, often for long periods of time, Nick was quiet, absorbed and thoughtful. His mood caused Linda to retreat. It seemed to her as if he was trying to erect some barrier of monumental proportions around himself, a formidable barricade. His attitude seemed to say, Do not advance — don't touch, for God's sake — don't question me and *please* don't cry. Sometimes he seemed almost angry, but not really, not at her. It was a kind of gloom that was Nick's way of withdrawing as a defense. But against what?

Nevertheless, just his hand on her, his fingers lightly touching her hair or her shoulder, and Linda was alive with desire. Nick was not as easy to reach when dark, thoughtful shadows and memories filtered across his eyes. Those memories dimmed the present.

Then, for a while, they put aside their personal issues concerning life in Chicago versus life on the West Coast, and they went back to their real battle.

ॐ

Steve called with some good news.

"This is just hearsay, rumor, okay? But sounds like your man wasn't very well liked. Probably the department was thinking about getting rid of him, even before the stress retirement thing. Cops aren't too fond of attorneys ordinarily, and it looks like Brauning was working on that, or at least talking about it for awhile before he actually left the force. Usually cops see lawyers as their enemies. Anyway, I get the feeling that Brauning is a real bastard and not particularly missed by his fellow cops.

"Looks like he was able to leave the way he did," Steve went on, "because he either knew someone, or had an important relative somewhere, or else the guy's got some dirty laundry on someone. Maybe all of the above. People are a little reluctant to talk about the guy. Know what I mean, Nicky? Interesting, hmm?"

"Yeah, definitely interesting," Nick said. "Hey, man, I owe you one."

"Hell, Nick, you owe me more than that, you bum," Steve said, trying to sound gruff, but not really succeeding, then laughing his deep, hearty laugh.

"How much longer are you gonna stay out there in *la-la land*?" Steve asked.

"Haven't gotten that far yet. Hey, I'll keep you posted, okay?"

"Yeah, Nick. Take care of yourself and watch your ass, my man. Let me know if I can do anything. Go get 'em."

༈

And, so, Nick did. And, his trash detail was the most comical part of their plan to handle what they came to refer to as the *gruesome trio*—the Braunings and their friend the judge.

Nick called the city and found that the trash was picked up in front of the Braunings' home and office on Tuesday mornings. He bought a pair of gray work overalls, black work boots and a navy and white bandanna. Then he stopped shaving for four days. He rented a small pick-up truck from a local gas station and early Tuesday morning, well before the scheduled trash pick-up time, Nick posed as a trash man for the Brauning's block.

However, the only stop he made was at their house. He casually dumped the contents of three trash cans into the pick-up, covered the heap of garbage with a tarp, placed heavy pieces of rock at each corner, and went merrily on his way. Once again, no one paid any attention to him.

༈

It took three Tuesday mornings of Nick brazenly posing as a trash man, dumping garbage from only one house into the silly little pick-up that looked nothing like Coast Waste Management's actual vehicles, before he and Linda found anything more significant in the rubbish than unpleasant smelling remnants of what the Braunings ate for dinner, Dick's spelling errors and Karen's catalog orders.

But when they found it, it was well worth the extra long showers that Nick needed to get the smell of the garbage off of him. They were as happy as the day the clerk accidentally gave them the confidential report.

It was merely a crumpled, rough draft of a memo to Judge Humphrey from Karen. It dealt with a pending case of conservatorship and would have been innocent enough, had it not also contained a postscript that Karen certainly would have burned or shredded if she had had any idea that her garbage was being examined on a rather regular basis.

At the bottom of the typed memo, in pencil and in Karen's own handwriting:

J, please make Fri. nite work. It's been much too long. Luv, K.

⌇

"Why can't we just take this to the media?" Linda asked. "To 'Hard Copy', 'Inside Edition', 'The San Diego Union', 'The L.A. Times', damn it!" Her cheeks were flushed with anger and her fists were clenched.

Nick smiled.

"Take it easy, little girl. We could, only what would it accomplish? It's the *threat* of us doing something like that that will get us somewhere. And that's what we want. What we need now – what will really do the trick – is to uncover some of their deepest, slimiest secrets so that they'll know, with total certainty, that *we know* about them."

"But," Linda began to protest.

"Linda," Nick interrupted, "this note is inconclusive, circumstantial, and it doesn't really prove *anything*. It tells us that we're close, but not quite there. Just a little more time and we'll have them *for real*.

"I'm going to follow a car tomorrow night. Want to come with me? I've rented a new camera I want to try out."

"Absolutely," Linda declared, as bravely as she could. "I'll put my hair up under a baseball hat and wear your jacket." She smiled a little, but her stomach turned and her throat caught at the thought of what they were about to do.

"Whatta sleuth," he teased. "Ah, Sherlock would be proud of you tonight, my love," and he pulled her down on the couch into his warm embrace.

Sixteen

Finally…

I F SOMEONE HAD TOLD THEM how rough it was going to get, they would have laughed. Nick and Linda wouldn't have believed this could happen.

ॐ

Linda went with Nick that night and the next, and the next, and the next. The first time they waited in the parking lot, a good distance from the cream colored Jaguar.

"He's got a car phone," Nick noted absently, looking at the small antenna. Linda's hair was tucked up into a baseball cap and she was slouched down in the passenger seat of a nondescript, dark green rental car, with huge, round, dark sunglasses perched on her nose. Nick sat behind the steering wheel, wearing a baseball cap, too. His was turned backwards. He turned towards Linda and laughed, "Is this nuts, or what?"

The longer they sat and waited, the more nauseated and jittery Linda felt. Her fingers trembled slightly as she adjusted the sunglasses, and though the weather was mild and dry, her skin felt cold and clammy.

It was nerve-racking enough to sit in the safety and privacy of her home and dream up schemes with Nick, but to actually be lying in wait for a judge! She wondered if they'd both lost their minds.

Nick, humming softly, played with the buttons of the radio, changing from station to station. He joked, trying to get her to relax, "You look like my kid brother today." Linda smiled a little, but when she pulled the glasses off and absently rubbed her temples, her eyes were cloudy and timorous. Nick reached over and took her hand in his, surprised at how cold her skin felt to his touch.

A little while later, when Judge Humphrey finally came out of the building, got into his car and started the engine, Linda pressed her hand against her chest. Her heart pounded hard for a moment. Then she felt frozen, as if the blood had stopped pumping through her veins and arteries.

"Dear God, what *am* I doing?" Her voice was detached, terrified, and the color drained from her face.

Nick started the engine just after the Jaguar began to back out of its parking space. Then he turned towards Linda, put his hand on her shoulder and asked, "Are you okay?"

"*No*. I can't believe I'm doing this," she answered, her voice sounding strangely distant, as she sank down a few more inches into the seat. "*GO!*" she told him, "I'll keep my eyes closed."

But Linda kept her eyes wide open, riveted to whatever part of the cream colored Jaguar that she could see, as Nick carefully followed the car through the traffic, as it left the courthouse in Escondido and traveled south onto Highway 15.

It was rush hour and the traffic on the freeway was heavy. Eventually, being careful not to get too close to the judge's car, Nick lost it somewhere in the four lanes of commuters rushing anxiously to get away from where they had been, even though they didn't look very happy about where they were going. The stream of drivers' faces went by them on both sides, one after another, intense expressions, white knuckles gripping the steering wheels of their vehicles, as they followed one another too closely and too aggressively.

It was four-forty-five on Thursday.

◦

The next day, Friday, Nick rented a different car, a dark blue, medium sized Buick. For two hours, they drove down Valley Parkway, into the courthouse parking lot, spotted the Jaguar, drove back out again and then retraced their path. Each time they stayed as close to the exit lane out of the parking lot as they could, being very careful not to let the cream colored car slip past them. Then they again drove slowly into the parking lot, parked their car for a while, and repeated the same motions.

꒳

When a police car pulled up and parked next to them and a uniformed deputy got out, not three feet away from Linda, she was terrified. A too realistic vision of handcuffs and bars floated through her mind for a moment. Her window was rolled halfway down and she fully expected to hear, "Step out of the vehicle, please, ma'm," from the stern-looking, gun-bearing deputy.

Linda held her breath, waiting and thinking. *What do I tell him we're doing?*

At the same moment that the deputy slammed the door of his patrol car, Nick quickly reached into the back seat, grabbed a bag of potato chips, pushed the bag under Linda's nose and asked innocently, "Want some?"

The deputy dipped his head a bit, flashed an almost imperceptible smile at the two of them, and continued on his way into the building.

Linda took a deep breath and sighed with relief. Then she began to cry softly. Nick put his arm around her shoulders and pulled her closer to him, "Linda, Linda, you aren't cut out for this kind of work. Aw, come on, there just isn't any law we're breaking by sitting in a car in a public parking lot for a few minutes. They *aren't* going to arrest us."

Linda looked up at him, feeling a little relieved and very foolish. She started to laugh now. Her cheeks were wet, her eyes and the tip of her nose were red. They both laughed.

꒳

This time they managed to follow the Jaguar all the way to its destination. They watched as the judge pulled into the driveway of his affluent Rancho Santa Fe adobe home and the heavy doors of his garage began to open.

"Well, now we also know where the judge and his wife live," Nick beamed.

ॐ

Linda stubbornly insisted on going with Nick the next day and the next. On Saturday, they cruised past the judge's house but saw nothing. The main road wasn't very busy that afternoon and they couldn't keep driving back and forth in front of the judge's home, even though the car they were in now was a gray Corolla. Nick thought that they might be able to spot the judge, hopefully going somewhere, rather than coming back home. But it didn't happen.

If the Jaguar left its garage that day, it had done so when the two occupants of the gray rental car were out of viewing range.

On Sunday morning, Nick again tried to persuade Linda that she didn't have to come with him. But she raised her chin stubbornly and told him, in a quiet, but determined voice, "This is really *my* fight and even if it does scare the hell out of me, I need to do it. I need to confront this man any way I can. I believe he's unethical and disgusting. If this is what it takes to expose him as *unjust*, then it's what I need to do.

"Besides, Nick, I can't just dump my problems on you. If I do that, what do I do when you aren't here anymore?" she blurted out. This time she successfully held back the tears that threatened.

Nick didn't say anything. He nodded a little, put his arm around her and they walked out to still another rental car. This time a white Sentra.

ॐ

Late Sunday afternoon, after long, careful, watchful hours, they saw the judge's garage door begin to open.

They had driven first one way past the judge's house and then the other. They were trying to stay as close to the house as possible, but not so close that their presence would become obvious. It was another mild, sunny day, and they were spending it driving around a lovely, rolling, peaceful area, but the reason they were there dimmed their pleasure.

Nick tried to make it as comfortable as possible. He tried to draw Linda's attention to music on the radio, to the spectacular deep blue color of the sky, broken only by vivid, huge, fluffy cumulus clouds high over their heads. But Linda kept looking nervously back towards the house.

Nick leaned over and kissed her cheek. Then he gently traced the clear, clean line of her jaw with his fingers. Linda smiled a tremulous smile at him, and her eyes darted back towards the house again.

৴

Linda saw it first. She bolted upright in her seat, pointed over Nick's shoulder and cried out excitedly, "Look! Look, Nick! Look!" They were parked down the road, off on the edge of a wide shoulder, under a huge eucalyptus tree, when the Jaguar came down the long driveway and turned left.

He drove right past them, so close that they could see that the judge was in the car alone. He went by them, paying no attention to what must have looked like a tourist's car at the side of the road, parked under the trees with its occupants enjoying the country-like beauty of Rancho Santa Fe, where the golf courses are lovely, the estates opulent, and acres of beautifully kept, white-fenced grounds house priceless thoroughbreds.

Linda's heart jumped and raced. It was almost six o'clock at night. *Where is he going alone?* She thought she knew the answer to her own question.

Startled by something finally happening after the long hours of waiting, Nick sprang into action. He gunned the car into motion, spraying dirt and stones behind him as he took off in pursuit of the too familiar Jaguar.

Nick and Linda were both smiling now with renewed hope and enthusiasm. They drove along a good distance behind the cream colored car as it sped along the curving, tree-lined, narrow road. The judge was in a hurry, it seemed, but he obviously knew the road well. There was no hesitation as he drove fast, turning each corner smoothly.

Nick glanced over at Linda. He was glad to see that she didn't look frightened now.

Instead, Linda had a fierce look of determination on her face. Her jaw was set and her lips were pressed tightly together. She was leaning slightly forward in the seat, with one hand on the dashboard in front of her, as if her very posture would keep them from losing the car that was now more than a half-mile in front of them.

The Jaguar went around a curve and disappeared from sight. Nick accelerated and they spotted it again. He took his foot off the gas pedal and they slowed down. Then around another curve and the Jaguar went out of their view again. Nick pressed the pedal down hard and the little, white Sentra lurched forward in response. Their chase was on.

 ✺

Judge Humphrey, having a proclivity for exceptional Scotch, especially when it looked as if he would be spending the night at home with his wife, had an errand to run. He didn't pay any attention at all to the car that was following behind him.

Though Eleanor Marie Humphrey had tried desperately to please her husband, as usual, and had suggested every other type and brand of liquor that they had in their well-stocked bar, nothing would do but for him to go after a particular brand that they did not have on hand.

"No," he told her, "I'll go myself, you needn't bother. I'll be back shortly."

Jerome Humphrey pulled into the parking lot of a small, specialty shop several miles from his home. The store specialized in liquor, gourmet foods and gift items. In order to accommodate and cater to the unpredictable, pampered and wealthy residents of Rancho Santa Fe, it was open long and unusual hours.

The judge got out of his car, looked around for a moment, and then walked over to the two pay telephones at the corner of the building. As he dropped coins into the slot, a white Sentra drove by quickly. There was no other traffic.

The judge spoke on the phone for ten minutes, raising his free arm in the air several times, gesturing emphatically. His back was to the road, but he turned, glancing over his shoulder every few minutes. Then he looked at his watch, said something else into the phone and hung up. He went into the shop and came out a few moments later carrying two packages. One was a paper bag containing a bottle of Glenlivet Scotch Whiskey and the other was a tin of assorted gourmet nuts that Eleanor liked. He got back into the Jaguar and drove home.

A quarter of a mile past the shop, the white car pulled over to the side of the road. Linda and Nick had seen the tail lights of the Jaguar as it came out onto the road and headed *back* in the direction of the judge's house.

"I wonder who he called from a pay phone in the middle of nowhere," Nick smiled.

"And why wouldn't he just use his traceable car phone?" Linda asked grinning happily.

They drove home themselves. It had been a long day.

⤳

"Okay, okay, I give up," Linda said, with considerable relief that was much greater than her mild protest. "You tell me when you want company and I'll go with you, but tonight you've convinced me. I'll stay here this time.

"I'm going to take a long, hot shower, light some candles, burn some incense and listen to some peaceful, happy music, like Yanni. When you get tired of watching a car weave in and out of traffic or driving in and out of its garage, come back home and hug me, okay?"

⤳

Candles. She didn't know what the appeal was, but it was there. They were soothing. She burned them when she was listening to music, or reading, or watching a movie. The kids teased her unmercifully, telling her, "It's the nineties, not the sixties, Mom!" and that she was a closet hippie. When she brought out the incense, Julia and Mike groaned and laughed good-naturedly at her.

⤳

Nick smiled at her now, his green eyes glowing. "You're a cute lady, you know?" he said, putting his hands gently on the back of her head and drawing her closer to him.

"The shower and stuff sounds so nice, maybe I'll skip going tonight," his lips brushed against hers and she leaned her body towards him. They kissed, one long, slow, passionate kiss.

Nick moved a fraction of an inch away from her mouth. Softly he said, "Maybe I'd better go, or you won't get to that shower and music at all. But I'll be back soon, okay?"

Linda's eyes were misty, "Yeah, get out of here. Do something useful. Go to work," she told him in a soft, husky voice.

❦

Nick's task went on for almost three weeks. During that time Linda grew more anxious, and then more disappointed every time Nick came back with nothing more interesting than which cleaners the judge used, or where he stopped for coffee and a Danish on his way home.

"Jesus, Nick, doesn't he even go to movies or play golf? Except for last Friday, he hasn't even taken his wife out for dinner! Oh, Nick, this isn't going to work. Maybe he *doesn't* do anything wrong — except turn into some sort of Machiavellian monster in his little courtroom." She began to cry, her expression forlorn and cheerless.

"Maybe," Nick replied wearily. "Maybe this *is* just a wild goose chase." He knew they were running out of time. It wouldn't be long before Karen Brauning found out about Cathryn's money. Then she would have a fortune at her disposal with which to protect her interests. Suddenly he was unsure of himself, of his ability to turn the whole thing around. What if his hunches were wrong? This could take months, with Cathryn still in their clutches, moved from place to place and medicated into compliance.

But to Linda, he said, "Don't cry, please. We'll get Cathryn out of this, I promise." Nick wanted so much to reassure her. He was positive that the crimes of Karen, Dick and Jerome were there. He just had to find them. He had to, for everyone's sake.

"I promise, Linda," he told her, as he stroked her hair. But now his voice was shaky, and he hoped Linda hadn't heard it.

↷

Linda kept going to see Cathryn, never knowing what to expect when she got there. Some days Cathryn was so like herself that Linda began believing that the whole thing *would* get turned around.

We can take it back to the court and ask for another hearing. Maybe one day soon they won't be able to even say Cathryn needs a conservator, Linda told herself. She was remembering the alert look in Cathryn's eyes that afternoon, how bright and aware she had been.

↷

Then Linda's phone rang, piercing the silence of the room.

"I HAVE TO GET OUT OF THIS PLACE!" Cathryn shrieked into the phone. "I-CAN'T-STAND-IT-HERE-THEY'RE-CRAZY-IT'S-GETTING-WORSE-AND-WORS-S-E!" she screamed, her words running into one another.

Then suddenly her voice dropped to a raspy, conspiratorial whisper, "I don't know how much more I can stand. There's a crazy woman in my room now. She's stealing my combs. She stole my cough drops. They lock me out of the bathroom. They defecate all over the toilet seat. They're putting something in my food to make me gain weight. I *have* to get out of here," she hissed into the phone.

"I've *got* to get out of here." She didn't even sound like Cathryn. Her words were slurred and her harsh voice was snarling.

Linda listened, her head bent. She rubbed her forehead with her thumb and fingers. *Oh God, dear God, what am I going to do? What can I do?*

"Cathryn, you need to call Karen Brauning. You need to tell her that you…" Linda began weakly.

"THAT BITCH NEVER RETURNS MY PHONE CALLS! SHE WON'T DO ANYTHING FOR ME. IF YOU WON'T HELP ME, THEN GO TO HELL!" Cathryn slammed the receiver down with a crash that echoed in Linda's ears.

↷

Nick stopped using rental cars and wearing the baseball cap. He was getting pretty good at following someone without that person knowing it. He always kept the cameras on the seat beside him in an open canvas bag. Still, no one seemed to be paying any attention to him.

$\backsim$

It was Wednesday afternoon. Linda was going to having dinner with Julia, while Julia's boyfriend Peter was working late. Julia and Linda wanted Nick to come with them, but he felt that he had to at least make an attempt tonight.

"If it looks like another blank wall, I'll meet you at The Cove later," he told them.

Once more Nick parked the BMW along the street onto which the heavy traffic from the courthouse parking lot spilled, as it made its way to the freeways. He drank out of a carton of orange juice and was barely listening to a jazz station on the radio. His thoughts flitted from Linda to the boys and back to Linda again.

It was another clear, sunny day, and Nick wasn't particularly excited about the prospect of following the Jaguar home through rush hour traffic again, but still he felt that *maybe*, sooner or later, it would prove worthwhile.

$\backsim$

Finally, the Jaguar pulled out of the long courthouse driveway heading towards the freeway. But this time the judge didn't make the right hand turn onto the ramp. Instead, he kept going straight under the overpass.

Nick, startled out of his reverie, fumbled with the keys in the ignition, got Linda's car started, and barely managed to get out into the bumper to bumper stream of cars without losing sight of the Jaguar. He was so taken off guard that he almost turned right onto the freeway. But, at the last second he spotted the Jaguar going straight in the heavy traffic.

He realized, excitedly, that the judge wasn't heading towards home this time.

From the right-turn-only lane, he quickly rolled his window down, hit the left turn signal, motioned imploringly to the car next to him, and luckily squeezed back into the lane of through traffic, hurriedly waving his thanks to the driver behind him.

Nick headed under the overpass and continued to follow behind the cream colored car towards the Harbor.

‍‍‍‍‍‍‍‍‍‍‍‍‍‍‍‍‍‍‍‍‍‍‍‍‍‍‍‍‍‍‍‍‍‍ محمد

In a gut feeling, Nick had fully expected to see the scene that was now unraveling before his eyes. But actually seeing it stunned him and left him feeling light-headed. Even though there was a steady, pleasant evening breeze coming off the ocean and drifting through the open car windows, beads of perspiration lined his forehead.

His hands shook a little as he reached for Linda's Canon and checked the new lens he had gotten for it, a lens that would easily utilize all the remaining light. He hesitated as he put it back in the bag. Then he reached over and grasped the small video camera. One which was fitted with "a zoom lens that can capture moving images with as little as a candle light," the guy in the Carlsbad Camera Store had explained to him.

Now he held it to his right eye, with his finger on the trigger, and squinted his left eye closed.

When Nick pulled into the parking lot of the Boathouse Restaurant, the judge was nowhere in sight. But his Jaguar was neatly parked just past the main entrance of the building and slightly away from the heavier traffic. There were several empty spaces between the cream colored car and the next parked vehicle. On the other side of it, there was a large, concrete bordered planter area with a tall ficus and dense, deep green foliage. At the base of the tree was a myriad of brightly colored impatiens, marigolds and phlox.

Nick parked on the other side of a similar planter area, across from the Jaguar, and about thirty feet away. Leaning over the seat from the passenger side of the BMW, he now had a clear view of the cream colored car and the entrance to the restaurant. Most of the BMW was shielded by the abundant leaves of another ficus.

He wiped his forehead with a bandanna, took a deep breath,

steadied the camera on the back of the seat, and squeezed his finger again on the trigger. Through the viewfinder, he watched a miniature version of Karen Brauning as she parked her silver Lexus next to the Jaguar, adjusted her rearview mirror and applied some lipstick. She briefly touched her fingers to her hair and got out of the car.

Nick watched as she smoothed her beige linen dress down over her hips and glanced down at her nylons. Then she adjusted her purse on her shoulder, briefly looked into the window of the Jaguar, wet her lips with her tongue, smiled a little at her reflection and walked into the restaurant.

Nick watched. And the tape in the video camera turned.

For a moment, Nick zoomed in on each of the two license plates. The numbers and letters were clearly visible. The motor of the video camera whirred softly in his ear.

"Thank you, thank you, thank you," Nick whispered softly.

↫

Nick had become very resourceful as he practiced his craft of private detective. After Karen went into the Boathouse, he opened the cooler in the back seat. Linda had stocked it with several cartons of orange juice, a couple of sandwiches made with thick slices of turkey, apples and a small bag of cookies. Also in the back seat, in another large canvas bag, was a paperback Stephen King novel, *Drawing of the Three*, a magazine on physical fitness, a bag of almonds, his jacket, a tie and a flashlight.

Nick munched on half a sandwich and drank some orange juice. Then he went into the restaurant and walked over to the pay phone. He dialed Linda's number and got her just as she and Julia were on their way out of the house.

"I'm doing *fine*," he told her happily. "I'll see you later, but I'm afraid I'll have to miss dinner. I'm having a turkey sandwich," he said enthusiastically.

"What's happening? Nick, can't you tell me anything? Where *are* you?" Excitement rose in her voice as Linda sensed that, finally, he had *seen something*.

"Okay, fine," Nick said. "We'll talk more later, okay?"

She knew that she would have to wait for the details until Nick came back home.

"Damn! Why didn't I go with him?" she mumbled, putting the phone down and turning to Julia, whose mouth hung open in puzzlement.

"What's going on, Mom," she asked suspiciously. "What are you two up to, now? Where *is* Nick? Mom-m-m?" the final consonant of the word rose and fell with Julia's impatience.

"Come on, honey, let's go get some dinner and we'll talk," Linda said, turning toward the garage. As they got into Julia's car, Linda burst out, "I don't believe it! Maybe he's actually done it!" she laughed.

She didn't know what Nick was doing, but some wonderful, light feeling had invaded her heart the moment he had called.

I can wait, she thought. *Yes, for this I can wait.*

The smile broadened across Linda's face and Julia looked at her closely, more perplexed, shaking her head as if at a mischievous child. Linda glanced at her as Julia backed the car out of the garage, and the expression on her daughter's face made Linda laugh out loud again.

~

Nick couldn't see either Karen or Jerome from where the pay phone was located. He used the men's room and then went back out to Linda's car. Nick could wait a long time now. He could wait as long as was necessary.

~

The parking lot of the Boathouse was busy with continuous traffic in and out, and the area was well lit. After some time, Nick got so used to the sounds of people passing in and out of cars, in and out of the door to the restaurant, that when the judge and Karen came outside together, for an instant he was unprepared. But just for an *instant.*

He dropped a half-eaten cookie in his lap, quickly grabbed the video camera, braced it on the back of the passenger seat and aimed it at the couple as they walked to their respective cars.

For all intents and purposes Karen and Jerome looked like two business people who had just shared some time together over dinner.

The motor of the camera continued making its low, steady buzzing sound.

⌇

Cathryn sat defiantly on her narrow bed. She spit the pill out of her mouth at the attendant.

"YOU take the damn pill, if you think it's so wonderful. YOU walk around here like a damn zombie with your damn knees aching," she screamed at the woman.

"Cathryn, if you don't swallow this, and swallow it *now*," the stocky attendant said, her words measured and threatening. She stopped and bent over with some effort and retrieved the pill from where it had fallen. "Dr. Levin will order a shot," she declared.

"And, if you don't shut your foul mouth, we'll have to put you in isolation. Take your choice, sweetheart," the woman in a rumpled graying lab coat with a name tag that said, "Ms. Bette," told her.

Ms. Bette's thinly penciled eyebrows raised high above her small dark eyes. The red-orange lipstick she wore was garish, even in the dim light of Cathryn's room. She looked directly into Cathryn's eyes, with the arrogant expression of an unquestionable conqueror, and she waited.

For a split second, Cathryn's face darkened and crumpled. She looked as if she might cry, then her eyes flashed and widened with fury. She pressed her lips tightly together.

Her mind raged. She wanted to kill the woman. *I want to put my fingers around her pudgy throat and squeeze the breath right out of her. I could squeeze her grimy, thick neck until her eyes bulge out of her head, until her tongue protrudes out of her mouth and chokes her little bit of breath off! NO! No, I would lock her in a closet and starve her for days, then give her nothing but little pleated paper cups with medicine inside!*

Cathryn laughed shrilly.

I would give her pills to wake her up, pills to put her to sleep, but

*mostly I would give her pills to shut her fat face up! Yes, I would give
her pills that make her quiet and well-behaved, while inside her guts
would be screaming with agony, LET ME OUT! LET ME OUT! IT
HURTS! My body hurts. Can't you idiots understand? YOU ARE
KILLING ME, YOU BASTARDS! YOU GODDAMNED SOULLESS
BASTARDS! YOU ALL BELONG IN HERE! I HOPE SOMEONE
DOES THIS TO YOU ONE DAY, I HOPE SOMEONE HELPS YOU
THE WAY YOU'RE HELPING ME! I HOPE YOU ALL WIND UP
IN HERE FOR ETERNITY!* she ranted in her silent rage.

Cathryn looked wildly around the room. She looked over the
shoulder of the fat attendant who was smirking at her now. She
looked at the bars on the windows. She saw more grimy, fat attendants dispensing their "meds" up and down the hallway. She had
to call Linda. She had to take the damn pill and then this fat pig
would let her alone. She would call Linda.

*GIVE ME THE GODDAMN PILL, YOU FAT PIG, AND GET
THE HELL AWAY FROM ME,* she screamed silently in her head.

Cathryn reached her hand out for the medicine and Ms. Bette
chuckled, "Good girl, Cathryn," reaching out to pat her shoulder.

Cathryn pulled away from her as if she were a gigantic rattle-
snake. She swallowed the pill.

꒰

The judge and Karen walked over between their parked cars,
secluded a bit from the entrance to the restaurant. For the moment the parking lot was quiet. Karen looked around for a second, then she gazed up at the judge.

Evidently the two of them felt reasonably secure that they were,
indeed, alone, because as the judge opened the driver's door for
Karen with his left hand, and just before she sank down behind
the wheel, he leaned down and kissed her parted lips for a linger-
ing moment. His right hand slipped intimately down her left side
along the slightly clinging, linen dress, and rested knowingly, possessively, for just a moment, on the roundness of her buttocks. He
squeezed her flesh between his fingers and smiled at her.

Then Karen pressing her small teeth together, smiled, too. She got in her car and drove out of the parking lot. The judge watched her go, went around to his car and unlocked the door.

He, too, looked around briefly, appeared rather pleased with himself, and got into the Jaguar to follow Karen.

ॐ

The zoom lens of the camera brought the images of Karen Brauning and Jerome Humphrey as close to Nick as if he had been standing next to them.

ॐ

"Bingo!" Nick said softly, happily, while Linda struggled up from a deep sleep after picking up the ringing telephone. It was 4:45 A.M. When she heard Nick's voice, she was abruptly wide awake.

"What? Are you okay? Where are you? Tell me!" she said, her eyes suddenly wide open and her voice filled with hope and excitement.

"Hold on, I'm on my way home right now," Nick answered.

"Good God, Nick, don't make me wait!"

"Well, our *friends* didn't disappoint us," Nick began. "I'm on my way home, little girl. Make a pot of coffee and some popcorn, will you? We're going to watch a movie."

Seventeen

Mission accomplished...

"**M**Y OD," LINDA GASPED. "Oh, my God. I don't believe this! I *don't* believe this!" She scooted up right in front of the TV and sat on the floor. Her eyes wide and round, were glued to the screen. Nick pushed the rewind button on the remote for a couple of seconds, then he pressed play and leaned back on the couch.

"Watch this next part. You haven't seen anything yet," he told her happily.

There was a minute or two of blurred headlights, streaking street lights, and then darkness when Nick had tried to balance the camera and keep it focused, while he followed the cream colored Jaguar north onto the freeway towards San Clemente, instead of south towards its home in Rancho Santa Fe.

༈

Nick's heart was pounding expectantly as he drove and juggled the camera. His jaw was tense with anticipation and prescience. Any doubts he had had now dissolved. He *knew* he wasn't wrong. The weeks of waiting and watching were about to be rewarded. His fists were clenched tightly on the steering wheel. He knew that he was getting dangerously close to the judge's car on its surreptitious trip north.

Just then Nick saw the judge look up and check his rearview mirror. Then he reached up and adjusted its angle, watching behind him for a long moment.

Jesus! Maybe he recognized Linda's car!

Nick felt a cold sweat break out across his forehead, a chilling shudder went across his shoulders and down his arms.

Not now! he thought, *I can't mess this up now. We're so close. I know it!*

Nick quickly pulled over into the right lane, put on his turn signal, and headed towards the off ramp at Las Pulgas. But then at the last minute, as two other cars sped past him on his left, Nick turned off the signal and continued on the freeway, still in the right lane, letting several more vehicles get between him and the Jaguar. He never took his eyes off the cream colored car for more than a split second.

Nick's heart pounded and he reached his hand across the seat. His fingers lightly touched the comforting metallic coolness of the video camera beside him.

৵

Linda's gaze remained transfixed on the TV screen in front of her. She saw a huge parking lot, then the welcoming sign of a sprawling Radisson Hotel. The camera slowly panned the grounds. Lavishly planted and carefully manicured, they were parted by a lamppost lined driveway that curved up to a large, well-lit main building.

In front of the building and to the right was a guest parking area and brightly lighted, green mesh draped tennis courts. From beyond a fence, as the video camera neared the reception area, Linda heard the muted sounds of laughter and chatter. Then she saw water splash into the air from a swimming pool.

The Royal Radisson was located right on the ocean, and for a moment, as the camera turned towards the entrance way, Linda thought she could hear the sound of surf in the background. It was a still night, illuminated by starlight, a brilliant, full moon and the amazing capabilities and modern technology of a video camera.

৵

Cathryn's room was dark. It was late. Most of her fellow residents had robot-like, but peacefully, stumbled their way into their beds, and now slept the deep sleep of the drugged. If they were troubled or tormented, it was difficult to tell, unless one looked very closely. The woman in the bed at the far end of Cathryn's room appeared to be sound asleep, but she gnashed her teeth together in a scraping sound every few minutes. Then she sobbed once and her breathing became even again.

All the while, her eyes beneath their lids never seemed to sleep, even though her body was still. Her eyeballs under those lids darted from side to side, up and down, searching, searching, searching for *something.*

A thin, young man in the room across the hall, who never spoke at all anymore, lay on his bed clothed in a T-shirt, pajama bottoms and socks. A blanket was pulled up around his angular knees. His head was upright against the wall in back of him and he didn't move. Except his fingers.

His eyes were closed and a long, deep snoring sound came from his nose and throat. His thin lips were parted and a stream of drool dripped from the corner of his mouth. Despite the peculiar angle of his body, he appeared to be sleeping comfortably, save for the movement of his hands.

His hands looked like those of an old man, though he was probably not more than thirty-five years of age. The fingers were weathered and rough, the knuckles knotty and swollen, and the nails at the ends were long and ragged. His fingers moved continuously, clenching and opening, clenching and opening, against his worn cotton pajamas, the nails scraping harder and harder through the material into the thin flesh that covered his thighs.

Scraping, clawing, digging, as if on their own, they were trying to climb out of something.

The man in the bed next to him slept, too. But, as he slept, he babbled, drooled, shook and could not control his bowels. The room stank.

Down the hall, in the brightly lighted nurses' station, two female night attendants filled out detailed reports of the medications dispensed, and then they turned to the task of reading movie magazines.

A male attendant, a tall, dark-haired, wiry young man with reddened blotches of pustular eruptions on his face and neck, strutted down the hallway towards the station. He leaned over the ledge of the half door, and lewdly suggested to the younger, chubby attendant, "Hey, Margie, why don't you and me go clean up the rec room together and I'll get us some doughnuts after?"

He leered at her, leaning on the door with one arm, staring at her large, fleshy breasts that strained against the zipper of the lab jacket she wore. He licked his thick lips and salaciously rubbed his other hand up and down on his crotch. Margie giggled up at him, nervously pressing her thighs and knees together. She looked over questioningly at the older woman.

The gray-haired woman shrugged her shoulders and continued to read her magazine. Margie got up and followed her co-worker into the dark rec room down the hall.

↯

Cathryn lay in bed. She was very still, except for her eyes which were wide open and moving constantly. She could *not* close them. When she did, she saw Edward come back into the room and he was going to kill her. He was furious with her for leaving him alone and he held a huge knife in his hand.

Cathryn's fingers were numb with cold and shivers of terror ran up her back and arms. She clenched the edge of the blanket and pulled it up under her chin. Her eyes darted back and forth across the room and towards the hallway, where she heard one of the attendants giggling.

When she closed her eyes for just a second, Edward was right there, telling her what he was going to do, and she believed him. Except he said she wouldn't die, and she knew that he was lying.

You left me, Cathryn, he snarled at her. *I told you never to do that to me. You are mine forever and I will not let you go away from me. I'm going to bring you back, Cathryn, and I'm going to be certain that you never do this to me again. See this knife? I'm going to fix you so you can never do this to me again. Close your eyes, my darling, I'm going to take away your voice so you cannot lie to them about me.*

He swung the knife through the air just an inch from her throat. She heard the whooshing sound it made in front of her. She tried to duck further down into her bed, biting her lip so hard it began to bleed.

He was grinning madly at her and he began to laugh loudly at her trembling fear. *I'm not going to kill you Cathryn, I'm going to FIX YOU, GODDAMMIT, I'M GOING TO FIX YOU THE WAY I WANT YOU FOREVER!* he screamed at her pale, terrified face. *Then I'm going to fix you so you can never walk away from me, my beautiful Cathryn.*

His eyes flashed glaringly red at her, and she winced, horrified. He poked the sharp, stinging point of the blade at her knees and again slashed the knife through the air so she heard the whooshing sound of the sharp blade in her ears again. Cathryn pressed the heels of her hands against the sides of her head so she wouldn't hear him, so she wouldn't hear the blade coming closer.

But Edward shouted even louder, piercingly evil through her head.

You won't need to walk again, my darling, I will carry you where I want you to be. YOU WON'T WALK AGAIN, CATHRYN! he shouted menacingly at her, stabbing the blade at her heart and pressing the tip into her soft flesh.

Her eyes flew open and he was gone. But she knew that if she closed her eyes, he would come back and cut her throat. He would cut the tendons and ligaments in her legs and then stab and scar her body until her blood was everywhere, until she bled to death in his arms.

"NO-O-O-O-O-O," Cathryn's blood-curdling cry rang out down the hallway.

The gray-haired attendant heard the scream and slowly turned the page of her magazine, trying to ignore it.

"Damn nut," she scowled under her breath.

Cathryn screamed again, this time even louder. There were rustling, moaning, complaining mutters from some of the patients. The gray-haired woman sighed, exasperated. She put the magazine aside and walked heavily down the hallway, her fists clenching angrily. She would have to shut up the troublesome Mrs. Kent.

～

The video, after a considerable amount of bouncing, focused on the rear end of a parked, light colored Lexus. Linda could barely see the back of a person's head over the top of the driver's seat.

Then the scene blurred as the camera abruptly turned towards Judge Jerome R. Humphrey and zoomed in closer, just as he pulled open one of the large double doors that led into the entrance way of the registration area. Several other people walked in and out of the same doors for a minute and then the video film stopped.

There was a blank screen for a moment. When it started again the judge was walking towards the Lexus. But he continued on past it, his hand gripping a small object he held up in the air. Linda could barely see his profile. He seemed to be smiling to himself.

Linda sat in front of the screen, her mouth open, as she watched Judge Humphrey, followed at some distance by Karen Brauning, climb a flight of outside stairs and put a key into the lock of room number 235. The camera zoomed in on the numbers as the door opened, and then the Judge's hand flipped on a lamp with the light switch near the door.

He went into the room, closing the door part way. Karen followed him, stopping briefly at the top of the stairs to cautiously look around, never suspecting at all that a camera lens was zooming in on her face at that precise moment.

Karen slipped into room number 235, and as the door closed, Nick turned the camera towards a huge, ornate clock embedded in the stone work of the building next to the entrance way. It was 9:23 P.M. The picture blurred briefly as the camera returned to the door with the small metal numbers on it. After a few minutes the lamp light that could barely be seen in the tiny separation of the thick draperies went out.

～

The video film went on for a minute or so, and then there was another brief separation followed by a blank screen. When the video continued, the view once more focused on the clock. It was 2:30 A.M. Then nothing again.

Back onto the clock, 2:50 A.M. Now the camera turned slowly from the clock, to the door of room 235, just as it opened slightly. There was no light in the room behind her when Karen came out into the night. She paused under the dim night lamp between the window and the door to the room, glancing to her right and then to her left, before she walked down the stairs to her car.

She got behind the wheel and turned the rearview mirror towards her. Looking at her reflection, Karen smoothed her hair and put on lipstick. Then, she started the engine and backed the car out of the parking spot.

Nick turned the camera back onto the room. He kept it focused on the doorway for a long time, but there was no light, no motion. Everything was still and quiet. He waited over an hour, keeping the camera ready, but the judge did not appear.

Yawning and rubbing his eyes, finally convinced that Jerome was going to spend the night at the Radisson, having told Eleanor God knows what, Nick turned the key in the ignition of the BMW and drove to a Shell station. He filled the tank. Then Nick walked over to a pay telephone, dropped some coins in, and happily woke Linda.

꒰

Nick got back onto the freeway going south, heading for home, smiling a little.

People who do rotten things to other people, who attack falsely, who lie — they have committed their own crimes. Their own nasty, hidden crimes, he told himself.

꒰

"My God," Linda exclaimed again. "Nick, do you *believe* this?" she asked, her back to him and her face still turned towards the TV screen, even though the picture was gone and only the speckled, black and white image and loud, staticky sounds remained.

꒰

What Nick didn't see, and what the video camera, in spite of its high tech capabilities, could not record through the draperies, the door, or the walls, was a scene that would have sickened and angered them.

Within the lavishly furnished hotel room — with its king size bed, large screen TV, thick carpeting, double sink dressing area and floor to ceiling mirrored closet doors — the scene that Nick, had he been able to see into the room, would have witnessed and recorded, was the haughty Karen Brauning. Clad only in her panties, she knelt at the side of the bed before the seated judge, clad only in his arrogance and his passion, his right hand pressing eagerly against the back of Karen's neck and his left hand gripping his own white, fleshy thigh.

His head was tilted back, his eyes closed, his mouth open and he was taking very deep, fast gulps of air, as he held tightly onto Karen's hair, his fist tightening with the increasing heat of his arousal.

Karen's head was down below the judge's pale belly, her hands resting on his rather bony knees.

Quid pro quo, Karen. *One thing in return for another.*

But, neither Nick nor the video camera could see into room number 235 that night.

✼

After that, it was complicated, but not very difficult, for Linda and Nick to handle the rest of their mission. With their suspicions corroborated, the rest involved only the implementation of their counter-attack.

The Braunings and the judge appeared to have a serious conflict of interests that might certainly affect the fairness of decisions made in his honor's courtroom.

Their next steps were made simpler with a character like Steve Styers in their corner, albeit, half a country away. Steve's communication lines were, as he had already proven, quite extensive, but Nick and Linda were totally amazed by what he helped them to accomplish next.

✼

Karen let herself into the house through the garage door.

"Where the hell *were* you!" Dick demanded, slamming out of the den, where he had been watching another of his video collection. He heard the garage door open and close, and he had hastily ejected the videotape from the VCR.

Pulling the belt of his terry cloth robe closed tightly around his waist, he complained bitterly, "It's almost four in the morning! For chrissake, Karen, where *were* you?"

Karen looked calmly at Dick's flushed face.

Amazing he knows I was gone, she thought. *He obviously had himself well entertained between his booze and his hand,* she thought contemptuously.

"Don't start with me," she said in a dangerously quiet, warning tone, her expression icy, her voice filled with acerbity. Karen dropped her purse on the table, and turned to face him, a pernicious cast contorting her features.

"Don't even *think* about it. *Everything* I do helps you with *every* breath you take. Don't dare interrogate me, Dick, don't you *ever…*" She turned abruptly and walked away from him.

Dick went back into the den and picked up his half empty glass of scotch. He swallowed the burning, numbing liquid in two gulps and filled it again.

"Bitch," he muttered, miserably frustrated. "Goddamn bitch."

And, yet, in a few minutes, after the additional booze had fully entered his blood stream, Dick Brauning subserviently followed Karen upstairs, carefully apologized, and tried, unsuccessfully again, to put his hands on his wife's body.

჻

"You need someone in North County who is legally connected to a sister firm here," Steve explained.

"The phone calls need to be made from here and the mailing should originate from here, also. If it becomes necessary, and it most probably will. But the actual filing and so forth has to be done in Escondido, in Humphrey's domain, but only *well after* the calls," Steve said adamantly.

Nick made notes on the legal pad in front of him. He asked Steve questions about service of papers and listened intently. Linda watched Nick's face and hand, an expression of anticipation mixed with bewilderment across her face.

჻

The battle to expose and stop the bad guys continued for another next three weeks. But, for Linda, those three weeks were pure joy, compared to the previous, agonizing and terrifying three months.

She went to see Cathryn as usual. Only, now, when Cathryn was troubled, upset or complaining, when she saw or heard things that Linda could not perceive, Linda knew that there *was* hope. She believed, finally, that they *would* win. She was brighter and happier, and Cathryn sensed the change in her, and her own eyes began to lighten again.

They sat outside at the round, metal table. Next to them was an older man with a young couple. The three of them were busy chattering to an older woman who sat stone-like and expressionless in her wheelchair, staring somewhere over their heads. The three visitors went on as if the woman heard them anyway. They told her bits and pieces of news about relatives.

She never said a word to them. Her only movement was a grotesque facial spasm that twisted her features into a frightening mask.

Linda had found articles explaining such disfigurement:

"Many kinds of psychiatric drugs, including the major tranquilizers, can cause lasting, grotesquely disfiguring nerve damage known as 'tardive dyskinesia' or 'tardive dystonia.' The term 'tardive' means 'late-appearing,' 'dyskinesia' means 'abnormal movement of muscles,' and 'dystonia' means 'abnormal tension in muscles.' In tardive dyskinesia and tardive dystonia, which are permanent conditions, the muscles of the face and body contort and spasm involuntarily, drawing the face into hideous scowls and grimaces and twisting the body into bizarre contortions.

"These horrifying effects occur in more than 20 percent of persons *treated* with major tranquilizers, and currently affect between 400,000 and one million Americans."

‽

Cathryn turned her puffy, lined face towards Linda, reached for her hand and told her, "Linda, I'm glad you came back to me."

‽

"It will still take a little time," Steve said, solemnly. "It's like slow-motion. You draw this huge noose around the enemy and then their own actions cause the noose to grow tighter and tighter, until at last, they've virtually hanged themselves." His voice was grim.

Steve was right.

Two phone calls were made from Chicago, person to person, to the conservator and to the judge. Preferred mailing addresses were requested. At first this was met with denial, refusal, indignation.

"No, these are not necessary," came the calm reply. "The mailing can certainly be done directly to your office or home, if you prefer."

Nick had the video copied. The original was secured in a safe deposit box. He Federal Expressed the copies of the video to a contact in Chicago. From there, two copies were mailed in plain, brown wrapping paper, simultaneously: one to a seldom used post office box, registered in the name of the Honorable Judge Jerome R. Humphrey. The other was sent to one that had been hastily established in the name of Karen E. Brauning.

A short time after that, Steve's attorney contact in San Diego filed a Petition with the court requesting that the conservatorship of Cathryn Silberg Kent be transferred from Karen Brauning, to an appropriate, qualified family member residing in San Diego County.

It was immediately approved by the presiding Judge Humphrey and filed in the court on December first.

There was no contesting action put forth by either Karen Brauning or her husband/attorney, Dick Brauning, or anyone else, for that matter.

Linda Dawson Clinten became the duly appointed, qualified and acting conservator of the person and estate of Cathryn Silberg Kent, with Letters of Conservatorship issued to her on that same date.

༄

Linda was by herself, making a cup of coffee in the kitchen. She was very happy. Neil Diamond was singing on her stereo.

Barefoot, she spun around in a little dance in the small kitchen, raising her arms at her sides, snapping her fingers in time with the music, grinning widely, her head nodding to the beat.

"You — hold the light, yes you do, and *you've* got the right, yes, you do.... Don't you dare let go, oh no.... And we won't let go.... Oh, no...."

Yes, Linda Dawson Clinten was *very* happy.

ॐ

In a matter of days, Linda had Cathryn and her few belongings yanked from the most recent board and care home. This one was a large institutional facility with locked gates. Almost a hundred residents were housed in several connected buildings that smelled like harsh chemical disinfectants, pharmaceuticals, urine, and something resembling over-boiled potatoes.

Linda knew where she wanted Cathryn to live, at least for a while. She had located a private, state-licensed facility called Seguro, a ranch northeast of Los Angeles. It was a place where the owners/administrators, as well as every single staff member, believed in a gentle, rehabilitating recovery program for people like Cathryn.

Seguro's operating philosophy included excellent nutrition and a carefully analyzed program of supplementary vitamins and minerals. With guidance from nutritionists and medical doctors, a new person was helped to gradually come off of any psychiatric drugs with which they had any disagreement, or from which they were experiencing any unwanted side effects.

No medication was dispensed without an explanation of its content and how it worked in the body, towards understanding on the part of the person involved. After a short time, no psychotropic drugs were used at all by many of the people there.

Exercise and fitness activities, including swimming, aerobics, bicycling, tennis and hiking were available. But nothing was enforced or demanded of the people recovering there.

Productive projects for candle-making, wood-working, knitting, painting, sculpting and music lessons were all offered and readily available, in small, informal classes throughout each day, but nothing was mandatory.

07

Nick, Linda and Julia drove up to Seguro on Saturday morning, while Mark and Michael stayed with Cathryn. They stayed there as guests until Sunday afternoon. They were shown around the entire forty acres of grounds, traveling by jeep along the hiking paths, into the woods, along a small stream, and through fields of vegetables and almond trees. They watched the staff work patiently with people of all ages.

They ate in a comfortable dining hall where guests and staff alike had their meals at round tables with comfortable chairs. The room was filled with sunlight coming in through huge windows. There were large paintings on the walls of seascapes and snow-capped mountains. A huge case along one long wall displayed drawings, statues, poems, knit articles and other crafts done by the people who lived there. Their names were boldly lettered on gold-bordered cards which stood proudly by each item.

The food was wonderfully wholesome and abundant. Each meal was served buffet style with warm homemade breads, huge platters of salads, fruits and pastas, fresh juices, vegetables, eggs, cheeses and meats. Much of the food was grown organically right on the ranch. The staff and many of the patients helped with the planting and harvesting.

Later, when Cathryn first saw the buffet herself, she said, "Choices, choices, choices. So many choices." But she had smiled broadly, walking back and forth, deciding, choosing. She had piled her plate high and no one chastised her when she went back to get an extra banana to take to her room, though she had looked around nervously, flinching when anyone walked by her, waiting for a reprimand that did not come.

Linda, Nick and Julia stayed in a small, clean guest cabin, with two bedrooms and a fireplace, much like the one that Cathryn would live in, near the main house. Before they went to sleep, the three of them sat together on a soft, comfortable couch that faced a big picture window. For a long time, they stared up at a clear, star-filled sky, through the huge pine trees that surrounded the buildings.

"It's so incredibly peaceful and lovely. It's like being on another planet, compared to the homes and hospitals we've seen her in," Linda said, her voice shaky with emotion.

"Makes you wonder why, with all the resources poured into the mental health industry, there isn't more humane, compassionate care like this around," Nick replied.

Julia was sitting between the two of them on the couch.

"Mom," she asked, "what does 'Seguro' mean?"

"It's a Spanish word for 'secure, free from danger,'" Linda told her.

Julia put her head down on her mother's shoulder and snuggled her small hand into Nick's large grasp. He leaned over and kissed the top of her head, holding her fingers warmly in his own. Almost at the same instant, the three of them sighed deeply. Then they laughed.

ᣔ

On Monday, Nick and Linda drove to the ranch again. This time they brought Cathryn and Rex, and they quietly watched her look around, holding their breath, hoping that it would seem the same to her as it did to them. At first Cathryn didn't say anything at all. Then, gradually, she became inquisitive.

"What if I want to leave? How long do I have to stay? Can I call you when I want? Do I get my own room? Rex can stay with me?" she shot one question after another at them.

"What exactly goes on here in this place?" she wanted to know, her eyes darkening with suspicion.

"As far as I can tell," Nick said, "they *help* people."

ᣔ

"People like Cathryn, who come to Seguro, are cared for by four different shifts, twenty-four hours a day. If Cathryn wants to change her clothes ten times a day, walk in the woods at midnight, write letters to her family during lunch, or smoke one cigarette after another, she will never be thwarted or questioned.

"And, she will never be left completely alone," Joan Golden, the Chief Administrator of Seguro explained to them.

There were tears in Linda's eyes. She nodded her head as she listened. Nick sat by her side, shaking his head a little in amazement, as he hugged Linda's shoulders. Cathryn stood at the window in Joan's comfortable office, rocking back and forth from one foot to the other. She wore new baggy jeans, a bright red short-sleeved shirt, clean white tennis shoes, and she had a fresh, shapely haircut.

Cathryn wasn't interested in the conversation going on behind her. Her attention was on the view out the window in front of her, the tall pine trees and the cows that she could see in the distance.

"Cathryn will be allowed to roam at will, with enough supervision only to prevent her from either hurting someone else or hurting herself. There are no other restrictions," Joan continued.

"Cathryn," she said looking over towards the woman, whose face bore the expression of a young child, who, having grown up in the city, was seeing the wonders of the country for the first time. "If you have any questions about what I'm telling Linda and Nick, please tell me and I'll try to answer them for you." Joan didn't require a response from Cathryn.

"We're in a good position here," Joan continued. "We're small, state licensed, and while we do receive some bit of government funding, we aren't relying on it by any means. We're primarily privately funded, fortunately, and so our acceptance of a client is based on their need and what we feel we might be able to do for them to positively affect their lives. It *isn't* determined by their insurance coverage or their finances.

"Cathryn will be allowed to gradually come off the psychotropic drugs, to choose food when she's hungry, to sleep when she decides she's tired, wherever she is, to the best of the staff's ability.

"Everyone on our staff truly believes, that, perhaps one day, whatever is tormenting a person, causing any distressful or bizarre behavior, can dissipate to a greater or lessor degree. We believe, given time and patience and care, that a person can sufficiently recover from a distorted, torturous past, and be able to live near their family again."

Near the calming ocean, near us, in her own space again, with any help and assistance she might need. Thanks to her father's efforts and foresight, she'll have no less than that, Linda promised silently, looking over at Cathryn and seeing the sun shine on her cousin's delighted, smiling face.

Cathryn was truly fascinated. Her eyes were gleaming as she watched a woman her own age, swinging on a swing that hung from a huge tree branch. Swinging back and forth, her hair flowing out behind her, her cheeks rosy and her mouth smiling, looking like a young, carefree child. Under the tree, a staff member, a clean-cut and athletic young man, watched her with patience and care.

～

Linda and Nick helped Cathryn get settled into her own room in a cabin that she shared with one other person, and with sleeping spaces for two staff members. Rex never left Cathryn's side. The well-behaved little dog followed Cathryn carefully, looking up at Linda, his head tilted to the side, his brown eyes wide and round, as if he wanted to know if it were true that he and his mistress would now be allowed to live together in some semblance of peace and order.

With a feeling of satisfaction and tranquillity that they hadn't known in a long while, Nick and Linda drove home.

～

"It's very nice here, Linda," Cathryn said over the telephone some days later. "Even when I get *really* angry, no one else gets that way. I don't know why I feel so safe in a strange place, but I do.

"And the food! You wouldn't believe the food! I can get a salad or fruit anytime. Even in the middle of the night! There's *always* someone in the kitchen. Even a candy bar or cookies, if I want. Can you *believe* that?" she laughed.

Cathryn didn't give Linda a chance to answer before she added, "My knees don't bother me so much. The doctor told me he's cutting the medicine down a little bit every few days, if that's okay with me." She laughed again.

"I told him, *that's* for sure."

Linda listened to her, leaning back on the couch against Nick's shoulder, smiling.

"I'm glad, Cathryn. You've no idea how happy it makes me to hear you sound like this."

They made plans for Linda to visit again in a couple of weeks. Cathryn said, "I've got to get off the phone, Linda. My friend Joe wants to play Bridge, and I haven't done that in a long time."

༄

For a few days, Nick and Linda walked on the beach and ate late breakfasts in the little cafe. At night they watched movies together and ate popcorn in Linda's living room, sitting close to one another on the couch. Sometimes they sat out on the deck and watched the stars, wrapped in each other's arms.

And Nick called Scott and Jimmy every other day or so.

༄

Before the words were spoken, they both knew that it was time for Nick to leave, to go back home. Their mission was accomplished.

Eighteen

Parting, sorrow and strength…

NOTHING THAT SHE TOLD herself, nothing that she said to Nick, nothing that she did could have prepared her for the devastating feeling of emptiness that enveloped her early that morning as she and Nick gathered his belongings together, put them in the car and drove forty miles from her house to Lindbergh Field. Linda's face was pale, her eyes wide and sad, and she felt a sharp ache deep within her chest.

She took a deep breath and let it out slowly. Everything she saw through the windshield, as they drove south on the freeway along the ocean, had a vaporific, shimmering, illusory quality about it. It was like looking through the escaping gases over a bonfire. She felt an uncomfortable pressure in her abdomen and near her heart. She recognized the sensation of loss.

Nick had offered to drive, but Linda told him, "No, Nick, it's okay." She needed to be doing something. She changed the radio station every few songs, then finally put a CD in the player. Nick put his arm up across the seat behind her, once he touched his fingers to her hair. Then he looked over at her and put his hand softly against her cheek in a gentle, smoothing motion, but neither of them said anything.

There isn't anything left to say, Linda thought.

She turned into the entrance to the west terminal. Ironically, the pure sound of Mariah Carey singing "Never Forget You" came from the speakers as Linda pulled into a parking space. She hesitated for a second, listening.

"I won't... see your smile, And I won't hear you laugh anymore.... Every night, I won't see you walk through that door..."

Linda turned the car engine off.

ᢒ

Two nights ago, she had told him, "I'll tell you the truth, exactly how I feel. I love having you in my life. Nick, you helped me through a time that was so unbelievably ugly. I'll be grateful to you forever. You're an exceptional man, you really are. A special human being.

"But, I do understand about Chicago. Your parents are getting older and they'll probably live there the rest of their lives. I know you miss Scott and Jimmy all the time. And I *know* you care about me.

"And, I also know it's time for you to go back home, to your *real* life."

ᢒ

But, she hadn't expected to feel the change like this, though. Not such a severe, sharp, cutting feeling of loss.

What's the matter with me? she wondered. She had had affairs before. But, she had always felt that sharing life with someone else made more sense than going through it alone.

I love a beautiful sunset, she thought. *I appreciate a smiling child. I enjoy wind, rain, sunshine and snow. And I loved them even more with Nick at my side. But two people have to be aligned. They have to have the same purposes and goals. They have to want to go in a similar direction.*

We had our purpose, she thought. *And we accomplished it. Now it is okay to let go.*

Unconsciously Linda shrugged her shoulders a little, and then she shivered.

"What?" Nick asked gently.

"Nothing. Just life," she sighed, looked over at him quickly. Then she started to get out of the car. He put his hand on her shoulder and stopped her.

But, there was nothing else that he could say. He touched her hair lightly, watching her profile. He *was* going to miss her. Then he thought of the boys and he knew he had to go back. As special as the past months were, he wanted to see them, to be near them, near his parents.

California was a million miles away from his real life. And he had to go back to work, he told himself again, for the hundredth time.

His boss, Earl Townsend, had been unbelievably decent about what had turned out to be a *very* extensive leave of absence. But Nick couldn't push it much longer. He knew that if he did, ultimately he would simply be replaced.

He told himself that there were good and important reasons to go. But, that didn't stop the hurting.

ৼ

After Linda parked the car, they walked together into Delta's terminal. Nick checked his suitcase through, and slung the duffel bag over his shoulder. He was dressed in jeans and a tan shirt, open at the neck, but he looked different than that first day when he had arrived in San Diego. He was tan from their walks on the beach and the lines of fatigue were gone from his face. He looked stronger.

Linda gave him a shaky smile, but feeling on the verge of tears, she turned away.

She was determined not to start crying.

Nick didn't miss the struggle she was going through. He was experiencing his own.

He took her hand as they walked to the gate, but as soon as he did, she moved her arm away to adjust the strap of her purse, so that she could walk alone, not touched by him. It was easier for her that way.

They sat uneasily next to one another at the gate for almost ten minutes.

Finally, the attendant's voice came over the loud speaker announcing, "Ladies and gentlemen, we'll begin boarding Delta's flight 555 to Chicago O'Hare in just a few moments."

Nick turned to her. He began, "Linda, I'll call you when I get home. I'll…"

"Don't, Nick," she said firmly, putting her fingertips against his lips for an instant. "No promises, okay? Please, *don't* do that," she said. Then, she stood up, finally ready to let him go.

Really ready now. The ache was drifting away, dissipating.

She smiled a warm, genuine, caring smile.

Nick stood up, put his arms around her and pulled her to him one more time. He bent and kissed her mouth and she let him, feeling his warmth and strength, but something else, too. Gradually, as if it were seeping through her entire being, Linda felt *herself*. She felt whole and surprisingly strong. The sensation of loss, of crumbling, was gone. She was going to be okay.

She smiled up at Nick, her gaze going to his gentle eyes, his soft mouth, his strong chin.

"Take good care of yourself," she said. "You are the most special person I know." Then Linda leaned against him, pressed her lips against his warm, smooth cheek for a long moment and turned and walked away.

Nick watched her go. Somehow she looked taller. He waited and watched, but Linda didn't turn back. Then Nick got in line to board the plane, to go back home to Chicago — to his children, his parents, his work.

༄

Linda walked out of the airport into the clear air. A mild breeze rustled leaves on the trees in the parking lot. The sky was bright blue over her head. It was a lovely December morning, sunshine-filled with deep shadows and vibrant colors.

Linda took a deep breath. She could smell the ocean and feel the pleasant warmth of sunshine on her face. She put her sunglasses on and walked to her car feeling happy, very good, and very whole.

She and Nick had won the battle for Cathryn. Their friend was going to be okay. Maybe she would never be able to live on her own, but then again, maybe she would. At least she had her dignity back.

And Nick. She had never really believed that she would be able to love him and be loved by him. It was a dream from twenty years ago. And, she had no regrets.

ॐ

Linda simply wasn't the same person that she had been in the seventies and eighties. It wasn't really that she had changed in some dramatic way. She was just more Linda, more herself.

The experiences of the past two decades had managed to wash away what was superfluous, leaving in their wake what was really her.

Sometimes it was tricky to handle, but mostly it was becoming very comfortable. *I was always trying so hard, wanting so badly. Now … now, I'm just okay,* she thought, peacefully.

She smiled, and her brown eyes sparkled.

ॐ

Maybe it's time to finish my article about relationships, the struggle of men and women, she contemplated, as she got into her little BMW and headed for home. She looked out the car window as she drove along the Pacific Ocean.

Watching the water shimmering in the sunlight, she felt as if she owned it, as if it were all hers.

A favorite line came to mind from *Don Juan.* "Man's love is of man's life a thing apart, 'Tis woman's whole existence…"

"Is that true, though?" Linda questioned out loud. "Do men feel what women feel? Does a man want the things a woman does?"

God, she thought, *I'm talking to myself. Yeah, I'll write about relationships. Everyone else is,* she mused. *Now I've got some first-hand experience.*

I do truly love Nick, but I'm not made weak by that love. He was supportive, never debilitating. My viewpoint was every bit as important to consider as his own.

Whatever we do now, wherever we are, we do feel love for one another. And we don't have to be made weaker by that feeling. In fact, I think today we're both stronger than we were before our lives came together again.

As she drove north along the freeway, Narada playing sweetly, poignantly, on the radio, she felt high, the way she did after a good work-out, the way she did when the words of one of her articles clicked and perfectly conveyed her thoughts and her feelings.

It's like becoming stronger, like steel, from the inside out. As if I can more comfortably confront and handle whatever the world throws at me. I like that.

Linda was still smiling as she drove.

God, I love San Diego, she thought, breathing in more of the clean, salty air.

A Delta 747 passed overhead.

Epilogue

Justice...

SIX BUSY MONTHS PASSED quickly for Linda. It was spring again and very lovely.

During those months, a discovery was made concerning Dick Brauning. Criminal acts that he had committed while he was employed at Hardwick's office were finally uncovered. And, these revealed the reason for the abrupt end to his career with that not very noteworthy law firm. As it turned out, Dick had *not* been the victim of others, but the perpetrator in the real estate venture that Linda and Nick had read about in the lengthy microfilm file in the courthouse records.

It had all begun to unravel when Ronald Hardwick was innocently looking for paperwork that Dick was supposed to be handling for one of Ronald's clients. He had accidentally stumbled upon a file in Dick's desk containing papers that proved beyond any doubt that Dick was falsifying corporate documents, while ostensibly practicing law next door to Ronald's office.

Ronald had been outraged when he confronted Dick with the file proving that Dick was the impetus behind the production of false corporation documents and stocks for companies that did not exist. Dick Brauning, abusing his knowledge of the law, had specialized in evading the parts of it that he did not like. Especially the parts that limited his personal profit and power.

Ronald had told Dick, "You're a dishonest, walking keg of dynamite, and I want you to pack your belongings and get out here." And, at that point, Ronald Hardwick didn't give a damn if Karen liked it or not.

Pathetically, Dick Brauning wasn't any more clever as a thief than he had been as a salesman, a cop or a lawyer.

૱

Ronald Hardwick was not the only one who was uncovering truths about Richard Brauning. It would take the District Attorney's office quite a while, however, to investigate and document Dick's actual part in the scam. Dick Brauning's one skill was in shifting the responsibility for his crimes to others. This talent of his had been grossly underestimated by his former associates.

But, as it turned out, Mrs. Betty Tyson's nephew, Norman Lewison, an assistant district attorney, took a special interest in pursuing the Brauning matter. After all, he remembered Dick Brauning as the off-duty policeman who had falsely arrested his aunt some years ago. After that incident he had harbored suspicions about Richard Brauning. The fact that Dick was now a lawyer did nothing to mitigate his feelings.

For a while, Dick Brauning went merrily on his way, comfortable in the belief that others would be incarcerated for his fraudulent documents and criminal acts. Though these were crimes he had devised himself — despite the signatures that appeared on the papers incriminating former friends and business partners — Dick decided to surreptitiously sacrifice them to his own greed and safety.

But, he made three serious mistakes. The first was when he falsified the legal documents. Next, when he decided to send them across state lines by fax and first class mail, causing his offenses, to reach the federal level, and, eventually, federal retribution.

His third was in believing that his devoted wife would once again bail him out. That their marriage contract was a fealty behind which he could hide, even though he had implicated several people with whom Karen was still closely connected.

The lawyer would eventually be brought to trial. Unfortunately for Brauning, his case would be heard by a severe, gruff judge, a rather venerable and honorable older man, who was sick to death of infringements on the law by lawyers who then remained unscathed.

Having a slightly different viewpoint than that of his colleague Judge Humphrey, Judge Murray Thomas felt that these were the men and women who were supposed to protect and enforce the legal system, not methodically, greedily and arrogantly debase it for their own personal gain.

Eventually, Dick was found guilty of all charges against him and was sentenced to four years in prison.

After a failed appeal and several months in a holding cell in the San Diego jail, Dick was sent to the maximum security prison at Chino, where he was given ample opportunity to defend himself — this time from being the object of his fellow inmates' affections.

After all, Dick Brauning had been both a cop and a lawyer. His story was in all the papers and several disgruntled inmates eagerly awaited his arrival.

✧

Following Dick's incarceration, Karen Brauning resourcefully managed to pick up the pieces of her life. She and the judge carried on business as usual for a while, but, it seemed that they continuously argued and fought over one thing or another. Their upsets escalated, erupting so violently, that one night, with Karen screaming shrilly in the judge's ear — as Eleanor sat patiently at home waiting for her husband — neither one of them saw the drunk driver in a Ford truck crash his battered vehicle over the median. It came careening crazily onto their side of the freeway, and, ironically, Jerome Humphrey and Karen Brauning died in the same sin in which they had lived, in one another's arms. Only this time they were thrown into that position by the impact of crushing steel upon steel, rather than the force of selfish and irresponsible passions.

But…. *De mortius nil nisi bonum. Say nothing but good of the dead.*

✧

As for Sylvia and Barry Wilson and their board and care home, they pretty much caused their own punishment. Linda was preparing a scathing report to send to the Medical Board in Sacramento so that the home would be investigated, and, hopefully, shut down.

But, even before the letter was finished and in the mail, Barry had one drink or one sniff too many one night. While Sylvia sat in the kitchen reading a newspaper article about the horrible, accidental death of her former colleagues, Karen Brauning, private conservator, and the honorable Judge Jerome R. Humphrey, Barry collapsed on the floor next to his bed with a lighted cigarette in his hand.

The dry wood of the ceiling of the make-shift cabin went up in flames in a matter of moments, and sparks flew madly through the air, setting fire to the roof of the main house. Sylvia didn't notice anything until the smell of smoke began to fill the kitchen. By then it was too late. The antiquated sprinklers eventually came on, but they were not able to prevent the raging blaze from destroying the house.

Sylvia stumbled over the cane of one of the two brothers who sat startled and unmoving on the couch in the living room. As they watched, Sylvia fled for her own safety, leaving the two disabled men behind in their terror.

When the Fire Department arrived, the firemen were able to get one of the brothers out safely, but, the other died, cradled in his brother's arms. He had suffocated from inhalation of smoke.

All the other residents in the far wing of the house were rescued by the firemen. They were coughing and terrified, but eventually they would be all right. Nancy, heavily medicated, hardly knew what was happening as she was led safely through the sliding glass door of the room she had shared with Cathryn months earlier.

It was extremely difficult for Sylvia Wilson to explain why she was a half block away from the house when the fire trucks arrived on the scene, with the residents who were entrusted to her care screaming and crying from within the blazing, crumbling walls.

Barry lived through the fire, though his face and arms were badly scarred. He drunkenly slept through most of the screaming from the tragedy that he had caused.

⤳

The NME organization investigation disclosed rampant psychiatric abuses within the hospital chain and these led to criminal fraud charges being filed against it. Eventually NME was forced to pay three hundred seventy-five million dollars in civil and criminal fines.

This was not the end, however. The Federal government began investigating individuals involved in the scandal. A former executive of the psychiatric division admitted to paying kickbacks to more than fifty doctors and others. The Chairman of the US House of Representatives Subcommittee on Crime and Criminal Justice, reported that law enforcement officials told him that "a good many people will go to jail."

Following this, NME severed its ties to psychiatry and dumped its psychiatric division entirely.

⤳

Linda drove to Seguro often to visit Cathryn. She spoke to the friendly, efficient and caring people there, and she walked and talked with Cathryn. Every time she was there, the tranquillity of the place — abounding with wildlife and bordered by a sparkling, blue stream that ran along the rear acreage of the huge property — brought tears of joy to her eyes and gladdened her heart beyond belief. But, the memories of Cathryn's former homes would never entirely fade from her mind.

After only one month, Cathryn looked very different. She began losing weight and her cheeks glowed with color from her walks in the sunshine. Her muscles were becoming toned again from hiking into the woods, and her skin was looking healthier from the wholesome meals and the needed vitamins and minerals that she was getting.

At each visit, Linda thought that Cathryn's eyes looked more the way they used to, more focused, with a sparkle returning to them, in the absence of the strong, mind-altering medications that had been affecting her brain and nervous system.

Sometimes Linda took her notebook computer with her. She and Cathryn took long walks. They sat by the stream and ate the picnic lunches that the kitchen staff packed for them. Linda wrote while Cathryn read a book or watched the fish swim by in the clear water. At night, Linda stayed with Cathryn in her comfortable cabin, in an extra twin bed under the window. There always seemed to be the wonderful smell of wood burning in a fireplace close by, while Linda watched the stars shining brilliantly in the dark sky.

৵

One Monday in June, Linda drove home after a three day visit with Cathryn. It was a long trip, over three hundred miles, and it was dark when she pulled into her garage, feeling tired but content. It gave her so much peace of mind to see Cathryn in the environment of Seguro. She could tell that her cousin was doing better each time she visited.

It was nine o'clock and her answering machine was flashing. She pushed the button as she walked into the kitchen to get a glass of water.

"Linda, it's Kyle Williams. The editors loved the article. Give me a call tomorrow morning at the office. Good job, kid!" The machine beeped.

"Hi, Mom, it's me. Hope your visit was good. Give me a call when you get home. I love you." Julia checking up on her. Another beep.

"Hi, Mom, Julia told me you'd be back home tonight. I'm gonna be in L.A. tomorrow. I'll give you a call when I get home. Love you. Bye," her son's deep voice.

Another beep. Then, "Linda, it's me, Nick. I'm…I'm sorry I missed you. I want to talk to you. I'll try again in about an hour. It's a little after ten-thirty here."

He paused for a long moment. Then, he said, his voice soft,

quiet, "I want to talk to you *tonight*. Hope things are going well. Don's kept me informed about Cathryn. Looks like you pulled off a miracle for her, Linda. You're amazing. I'll call back."

As the message played, Linda walked dazedly over to her desk. She sat down and listened to Nick's familiar voice, her hand holding a glass of water somewhere in space in front of her.

In spite of herself, her pulse quickened and she felt the heat of the flush in her cheeks.

Linda called Julia back, trying to sound unruffled and calm. She could have gotten past Mike, but Julia asked intuitively, "What's going on? You sound funny, Mom."

"There was a message from Nick tonight. He said he'd call back. I haven't talked to him since he was here. It's almost six months. I don't know why he's calling," Linda answered, puzzled, dreamy.

"Well, you will, as soon as he calls back, Mom," Julia responded knowingly.

"Very often my daughter sounds like the mother," Linda laughed. "You're right, honey. I'm going to take a hot shower and get ready for bed. It was a long drive, but Cathryn looked great. I feel good."

"I'm glad. I love you, Mom. How 'bout having lunch with me tomorrow?"

"You're on. I've got to talk to Kyle in the morning. They liked my article. I'll pick you up at noon, okay?"

"Awesome!" Julia said. "We'll celebrate another message sent by you and received by your public. You're doing great, Mom."

"Thanks, sweetheart. I'll see you at noon. Sleep good."

"G'night."

꒰

Linda took her shower, put on a T-shirt and shorts and snuggled up on the couch. She was nervously flipping through the channels with the remote, trying to find a movie to distract her. Then the phone rang and it was Nick.

His words poured out over the long distance line to her, "Linda?

God, it's good to hear your voice. How are you?" He didn't wait for her to answer. "I'm coming back to San Diego. My firm has a subsidiary company in La Jolla, did I ever tell you about them?"

No, she thought, *you never did.*

"I requested a transfer there," he went on rapidly, "and it came through approved this morning. And, good old Steve has yet another connection," he paused now to laugh heartily, "who has a condo I'm leasing in Del Mar."

Linda didn't say anything. She was barely breathing, her lips parted slightly.

Nick went on quickly, "Scott can't wait to learn how to surf this summer and Jimmy wants tickets for the Padres and the Chargers games during Spring vacation and Thanksgiving. And my mom asked me the other day if I didn't think she's put up with enough snow in her lifetime! Can you believe that?"

His voice, so excited and so eager, paused, and then dropped almost to a whisper, "Linda, I can't wait to see you."

She couldn't see his eyes, except in her mind. But, she knew that like his voice, they were full of love and caring and truth.

Linda had tears in her eyes, and this time she didn't give a damn.

Finis

The following is an excerpt from

Until Proven Innocent

a new novel by

Diane Klein

Coming in 2001

Prologue

I'm just a writer. But, many years ago, when I became discouraged and gave up teaching in the Chicago Public Schools, I thought maybe I could be a doctor or a cop and do someone some good. I hadn't been able to do much of that as a teacher, despite how much I had liked working with the kids.

But, after I started a microbiology class at a junior college, a professor who was not too much older than I was, told me when I could go to the bathroom. I promptly decided that I wasn't going to make it through all that additional schooling after all, and I dropped the class and applied to the Chicago Police Department.

I was called in for an initial exam and I passed it. But, by the time they got around to notifying me that they wanted me to come in for the next step, I had already left Chicago for my next adventures, and the idea of becoming a cop disappeared from my plans.

Good thing, too, I thought that afternoon, when I found myself standing in a morgue next to a table bearing a forty-three year old homicide victim. I found myself looking into the blank, staring eyes of a body that was void of any life force. The body was caked with dried streams of blood from a multitude of stab wounds to the chest, but that was the easy part.

The man's face still bore the kitchen knife that his enraged lover had plunged into him just above his cheekbone. They were not going to remove it or wash the blood until the autopsy. And, this was being delayed while it was determined if the victim, whose body parts they had to remove, examine and weigh, was HIV positive or not. It turned out that he was HIV positive. There was no autopsy done on that body.

Then I was shown a refrigerated room for preserving these inanimate pieces of meat on metal rolling tables, in body bags or under white sheets, sometimes for days or even as long as months. The smell wasn't too bad, mostly chemical rather than the stench of gases that I learned is released by opening up decaying flesh. It was a holiday, Memorial Day, and no autopsies were being performed until the next day.

We were there for over an hour, and I was surprised that I didn't have more of a reaction to the sights I had just seen. But they were so completely out of the realm of my usual observations, and they were so violent and final, that I felt almost numb to alarm or discomfort.

That is, until about a half an hour later, when Detective Morris dropped me off at my hotel. As I walked down the hallway to my room, I was shaking somewhere deep inside my own body. *Jangled*, I told Nick later. I felt so damn jangled. My insides were trembling while my outside appeared still and calm.

In my mind, I can still see the blood encrusted face of that man, his eyes open, but, unseeing, with the white plastic handle of a large kitchen knife jutting out from just under his right eye. There were streaks of blackened dried blood, like streams of dark tears down his cheeks. And, his face seemed to be turned towards me in a frozen mask of death.

No, I would definitely not have made it as a Chicago cop, and, though I have known that for some time, it hit me then as hard as if a heavy metal wall had fallen, and it made me marvel even more at Gerry's chosen profession.

జ

I had never flown first-class before and I've always been somewhat fascinated with the whole scenario surrounding boarding and getting seated on an airplane. There seems to be such a mix of emotion, tradition and superstition amongst the travelers who ascend into these airbuses for business or pleasure, each day, every day at all hours. I've always wanted to better understand the anxieties of securing overhead luggage and the preferences for that certain seat in that certain row.

God knows I've got mine. Put me somewhere on the aisle with easiest access to the restroom and I'm pretty happy. But, given my druthers, I prefer an exit row with some foot room, even on the little jumps from the Bay area to San Diego, and even though I'm only 5'5" and pretty average all the way around.

First class has always held it's own mystique. I've never gotten very close before, other than to travel through that different world on my way to coach, or else surreptitiously peering through those privacy-demanding curtains as I've stood waiting my turn for a rest room.

But, now, my own first-class adventure was taking place. Thanks to Nick and his many frequent flyer miles, who only said to me, "You should have the experience." I hug him from afar for that strange and wonderful beginning to a pretty ghastly trip.

⌐ꝏ

I'm forty-four and I'm a writer. That is, according to the definition that is the best description of such a profession that I've ever heard: "Writers write."

They are those people who feel that they have to play with words, who long to communicate to others their impressions and deepest thoughts, their imagined scenes and stories, or their most hidden dreams and most radical and blatant viewpoints.

In other words, those people who just cannot shut-up. People who want to paint a picture, or play music, or create a poem, or reveal the world, or expose the bad guys, or create the future. Those people are the writers. Some are more motivated than others. Some are most certainly less realistic than many. I am one of those guys.

When I first heard about this story of evil, the blood, the abuses, the danger — my nerves came more alive. *What a story to tell*, I thought.

Could I get close enough to the principles to feel their tremors, to experience their consternation, to know what emotions were behind their blank expressions or their trembling fingers or slightly twitching eyebrows? Could it somehow do some good for others to know?

I would never know unless I gave it a good try. I flew into Columbus, Ohio so that I could tell it from the very beginning.

॰ॐ

Last November, Lt. Montgomery had called Gerry into his office. Her partner, Henry, was off investigating a fellow cop on a physical abuse charge that his wife had filed. After the lieutenant told Detective Hunter to sit down on one of the well-worn chairs in front of his gray metal desk, he began to compliment her on recent achievements. This alerted Gerry immediately. *What gives with the praise?* she thought just a bit nervously.

Then, he finally got around to telling her that he wanted her to take a very high profile case, along with a detective from Grandview Heights, investigating a cop from Columbus. The alleged perpetrator of several sexual crimes was a forty-eight year old sergeant, who lived in Grandview Heights, an upper middle class suburban area just outside of Columbus.

Eli Wilson had lived in Columbus before, and that's where the alleged abuses had started. But, it appeared they had continued into Grandview Heights, and therefore both police departments were involved in the investigation.

Gerry explained to me how this scenario seldom worked well. We were on our way to interview Kathleen, the sister-in-law of the supposedly very bad cop. First, we met with Chuck Verdacci, a young looking, clean cut guy in neat clothes, fresh short haircut and dark rimmed glasses. He climbed into Gerry's unmarked detective car with us.

"Cops are not generally very trusting of one another at first," Gerry told me, after we started our journey. "It takes a while to get to know another cop and feel good about working with them."

"It's even worse when it's two cops from different departments," she said, gesturing towards Chuck. "And, we're all pretty territorial. We don't easily give our confidence to a cop from another PD. So, when I first met Chuck, I thought, 'Oh, great. Some inexperienced young kid that they put on this so he won't get anywhere in a case where a police supervisor is being charged.'"

I looked at Chuck's profile in the front passenger seat then, and he was smiling at this. Chuck had eleven years of experience as a law enforcement officer on the streets, with four years as a detective. He was no kid.

"Yeah, we're definitely territorial and cautious," he concurred. "Takes a while to feel one another out. You know, cops are pretty realistic generally, and they know there are the good guys, and they know there are the bad guys," he said, turning back towards me. "And, once they've been burned, they're pretty careful."

Fortunately, he and Gerry had hit it off well, unlikely as that was at the beginning.

"Defense attorneys for cops will do their damnedest to make the *investigators* look like bad cops," Gerry told me, as the three of us drove to see Kathleen at work. "They'll go after any little bit of dirt they can dig up, if you're trying to go after a fellow cop.

"When Chuck and I first met, I looked him over, and then I said, 'I sure hope you're squeaky clean, kid.'" She smiled over at the young-looking detective in her passenger seat.

"'Yeah, *I* am,' he told me without a second's hesitation. 'Are *you*?'" Gerry laughed heartily and Chuck turned towards her, nodding his head and smiling more broadly now.

As we drove, they explained the circumstances of the case to me and how it happened that they were two cops involved in investigating a very powerful and influential cop. A powerful and influential cop who, it was thought, just happened to have been sexually molesting his step-daughter, his niece and his own daughter for many years.

One

The elevator moved down the shaft slowly. The only passenger, an attractive woman in her early forties, pressed her body against the antique mirrored corner of the small space. Her body was trembling and a light film of perspiration shone across her forehead making her smooth skin glisten in the muted lighting of the small mirrored and dark paneled space.

Her dark brown eyes were round with shock and fear and she stared straight into the space directly in front of her as though something or someone was there. But she was alone, entirely alone.

She was a trim woman, well manicured and dressed in a beige wool business jacket and skirt. Her lips were parted slightly, she was breathing rapidly and the fingers of her left hand gripped the heavy metal rail at the side of the car. Spattered erratically across her left sleeve and hand were heavy dark red drops of drying blood that dulled her thin gold wedding band and streaked her skin and clothes....

About the Author

D iane Klein was born in Chicago, Illinois, and attended Northwestern University on an Illinois State Scholarship where she received a B.S. with an English major and French minor. She lives with her husband in Southern California. Diane welcomes communication from her readers:

diane@dianeklein.com
www.dianeklein.com

If you liked this novel, and would like to pass one on to someone else, please check with your local bookstore, online bookseller, or use this form:

Name _____

Address _____

City _____State _____ Zip _____

Payment by: ☐ Check   ☐ Money Order   ☐ Credit Card

Credit Card Number: _____

Expiration Date: _____

Check which: ☐ MasterCard   ☐ Visa   ☐ American Express

In the Name of Help _____ copies @ $13.00 each $ _____

California residents, please add 7.75% sales tax $ _____

Shipping: $3.20/first copy; $1.60 each additional copy $ _____

Total enclosed, or charge my credit card (above) $ _____

_____
Signature for Credit Card Purchase

For more than 5 copies, please contact the publisher for quantity rates. Send completed order form and your check or money order to:

Laguna Coast Books
Post Office Box 2086
Laguna Hills, California 92654-2086
Toll Free: 1-877-717-BOOK (2665)

or order via our Web Site at **www.lagunacoast.com**
Major Credit Cards accepted.

International shipping is extra. Please contact us for the shipping rates to your location, if outside the United States.